Meet Me at
the Pier Head

Meet Me at the Pier Head

Ruth Hamilton

MACMILLAN

First published 2015 by Macmillan
an imprint of Pan Macmillan, a division of Macmillan Publishers Limited
Pan Macmillan, 20 New Wharf Road, London N1 9RR
Basingstoke and Oxford
Associated companies throughout the world
www.panmacmillan.com

ISBN 978-0-230-76906-9

1 3 5 7 9 8 6 4 2

A CIP catalogue record for this book is available from the British Library.

Typeset by Ellipsis Digital Limited, Glasgow
Printed and bound by CPI Group (UK) Ltd, Croydon, CR0 4YY

*I dedicate this work to all survivors of abuse
in childhood and to organizations whose members
and supporters give help to the young of today.*

Acknowledgements

The usual suspects – my family and friends, my care-givers and my animals.

PC Greenwood, probably no longer with us, thank you for ending the nightmare.

1958

One

Theodore Quinn's office currently held three points of view. He could look at Myrtle Street through one window, or turn his chair and study the playground through a second window, or he could carry on trying to be stern while telling off one Colin Duckworth. It wasn't easy, yet he needed to keep his eyes pinned to this likeable nuisance of a child. A born comedian, Colin pretended to be stupid when he was, in effect, brighter than some of the teachers.

I must not laugh, must not, will not – I'll explode shortly. Look at the state of him. He puts me in mind of a bundle of soiled clothing ready for what people hereabouts call the bag-wash, but he's a great kid and I like him. He knows I like him. Dear God, he's doing that ploughed field thing with his forehead again.

Theodore Quinn had dignity up to a point, two passports, a degree, a doctorate, a teaching qualification, headship of a school, and a sense of humour that threatened to be his downfall. He had taught for over eight years in the city of Liverpool, where the children had a terrible attachment to and affection for the ridiculous, and they made him laugh. For them, rules were rough guidelines at best, a call to arms at worst. He tried to pin a professional glare to his face. 'Why, Colin? It's almost time to go home, but you and I will stay here till we get to the bottom of this. I suppose you're expecting to play football tonight. Am I right? You and the other lads down at the park having a kick-about?' This place reminded him of the Bronx, his last home in America; the only difference lay in the accents.

Colin Duckworth, reddish hair standing on end as usual, shifted awkwardly from foot to foot. 'I never done nothing,' he mumbled, his eyelids fluttering wildly. Blinking was Colin's 'tell', the signal that accompanied his lies. Some kids wept or tugged at an earlobe, while others played with their hair or rearranged clothing, but this young chap was a blinker. At this moment, he was probably looking at life through the equivalent of very fast windscreen wipers, while his deepening blush clashed loudly with his disordered mop. 'Colin?'

'Sir?'

'Never did anything,' Theo said in a vain attempt to correct the boy's English. 'You never did anything, not nothing.'

'That's what I said.'

'Not quite.' The head of Myrtle Street School knew better than to embark on a lecture relating to verbs, participles and double negatives at this particular juncture. Colin Duckworth didn't care about grammar, as he intended to be an Olympic swimmer (speciality the butterfly stroke), the first man on the moon, and a player for Liverpool Football Club. In his spare time, the gutsy eight-year-old would work on the docks with his dad. 'Well?' Theo asked, arching an eyebrow.

'Well, what, Sir?'

'The roof, Colin. You were seen on the roof. You crossed the roof, picked up a ball, threw it down, then slid down a drainpipe which is now loose.'

The child sighed heavily. 'I must have slept-walked, cos I don't remember nothing, Mr Quinn.'

'Sleep-walked.'

'That's what I said. It was scary, waking up on a roof. I could have fell off, Sir, and broke me neck or me back and ended up down the ozzie for operations and all that if I had fell off.' His voice faded during the delivery of this longer sentence. He was losing the battle, and both occupants of the head teacher's office knew it. No one ever won when it came to a battle with Blackbird.

'Fallen off,' the headmaster said.

'Yeah, that as well. Me whole life flashed in front of me eyes. Dad says that's what happens just before you die. Sir?'

'Yes, Colin?'

'How does me dad know that? He's never died, has he? I mean, if you've never died, how can you be sure . . .?' The boy's voice faded due to a complete lack of conviction. He'd tripped over his own tongue, hadn't he? He'd dug his own grave again. Mam often fired such accusations when he wasn't telling the truth. Oh no, Blackbird's brain was clicking; Colin could almost hear it shifting up a gear.

Theo stirred himself. 'You didn't die, but your life flashed in front of your eyes. Or are you making this up, I wonder?' This terrible boy was very bright, advanced enough to have skipped a year. *I must get Miss Cosgrove to send me his work. Looking at his work will be a darned sight easier than looking at him. And he has wonderful parents . . .*

'Me, Sir? Erm . . . it must happen when you nearly die or think you're going to die. Or something.'

The head of Myrtle Street School stood up and walked to the playground window. For some reason, he could no longer manage to look at Colin Duckworth. He stared at the flat-roofed buildings that were supposed to be temporary measures. Thirteen years had passed since the end of

5

hostilities, and the makeshift replacements for classrooms had begun to look old, shabby and permanent.

'The school got bombed before I was borned,' Colin informed him as if reading his head teacher's mind. 'So I never seen it, Sir.'

'I know.'

'Caretaker was killed stone dead. He was an 'ero.'

'Yes.'

'That's why we have the prefab classrooms, Sir.'

Sir grinned and shook his head almost imperceptibly.

'Them flat roofs is no good, Sir. Me dad said so, Sir.'

'Quite. And you could have put your foot through the felt. We need a new roof, because the rain gets in. You might have stood on a weak spot and ended up inside the building with two broken legs and some broken furniture.'

Colin bridled and folded his arms. 'I'm not soft enough for that, Mr Quinn. I was dead careful.'

'In your sleep?' Theo spun on the spot and scowled at his companion. Keeping a straight face in the company of Colin and his ilk was never going to be easy. 'You were careful in your sleep? Well, isn't that a novelty?' He mustn't laugh. *Don't laugh, Theo* continued to be his mantra as he glared at the boy.

Colin swallowed hard. The thing about Blackbird was that he had his limits, and punishments were harsh. Not the cane, not a slipper, not even a ruler – oh, no, because that kind of stuff would have been too easy, too quick. Blackbird did detention. Detention meant pages of sums or something really horrible like geography or history or French. This headmaster felt that children should begin to learn a second language in junior school. 'I was a bit awake. Not proper, just a bit not asleep. Like a dream, Sir.'

'I wonder. You're something of a miracle, then?' *Keep a straight face, Theo. You can laugh when he's gone.*

6

'Eh?'

'You can see in your sleep.' He flapped his 'wings'.

The wings were part of the black cloak he wore so that people knew he was coming. Sir had a degree in something that sounded like cycle-ology, and he wore a gown. It flapped, so his nickname was Blackbird. 'Sorry, Sir.'

'There was a ball on the roof, Colin. Where is it now?'

The child squirmed, and his eyelids shifted into neutral.

'Where?'

'Our back kitchen, Sir. Under the sink with Mam's cleaning stuff, like.'

'And whose property is that football?'

'The school's, Mr Quinn.'

Theo sat at his desk once more. 'Bring it back Monday morning. Tell your father I want to see him when he can spare the time.'

Colin's face blanched. 'Can I not just get detention, Sir? Me dad'll go mad at me for pinching a ball.' Even geography would be preferable to his father's disappointment. Roy Duckworth didn't beat his kids, but he was very good at doing disappointed. His mother, too, was great at looking hurt.

'No, he won't go mad, because I won't tell him about the ball. I need to speak to him regarding another matter.'

'Oh.'

'You may go now.'

The child blinked warily. Was Sir going soft in the head? The ball was a real casey, leather, with a lace that tied it up. 'So no punishment?'

'We'll store this up for next time, Colin. One more infringement, and you'll get two detentions.' He smiled at the bewildered child. 'Go before I have a change of heart, son.' *And before I fall apart, because you look ridiculous. Gaps in your teeth, that silly hair – no, I mustn't look at you.*

7

Alone in comparative silence, Theo sat chuckling quietly while listening to the low, almost inaudible hum of a working school. It was balm for his soul, because he loved children, especially the naughty ones. In his experience, the imaginative and difficult pupils often grew up to be the better achievers, the workers, the providers of the future.

Theodore Quinn had made his own future, and he had been an angry, recalcitrant child. No, he didn't want to think about all that mess just now. The summer break was about to begin, and he was one teacher short for the coming school year. There was a general shortage of teachers, and just one applicant had emerged for September's reception class. She was from the south. Theo sighed. Would she need an interpreter? He remembered his own difficulties when, at the age of twenty-nine, he had arrived with a bundle of qualifications and a teaching certificate. Liverpool's accent and vernacular had confused him, while the children had been in awe of him, because he was a Yank.

He still had his little blue book, a hard-backed item containing a list of words like tom*ah*to and T*yous*day instead of Toosday. Then there were the Germanic-type elements like either and neither. The English clung to the original rule that the second vowel took charge . . . Then sidewalk was pavement, faucet was tap, a car hood a bonnet, a car trunk a boot. That same car rolled along on tyres rather than tires, while vehicles in the sky were aeroplanes, never airplanes. English English was more elegant than American English, though this tiny island owned dozens of accents, and each ruined the language in its own special way. It was all good, clean fun.

Theo grinned as he remembered his early experiences as a teacher. 'Are you a cowboy, Sir?' they had asked on his first day in a classroom. 'Or a film star? Can you ride a horse? Did you have a gun?' Yes, he had been an object of interest for a short time. But, like anybody else from overseas, he had been absorbed by Liverpool, accepted, even loved. Of one thing he was certain: he was an excellent teacher. His father, an Irish Liverpudlian who had emigrated to America decades ago, had a saying. 'Do it right or stay in bed. No half-measures, lad.' That had been good advice from a hard drinker.

Dad had remarried after Mom's death, and Theo had met his now adult half-siblings on several occasions, but he had no intention of returning permanently to America. This was home.

Somebody tapped at the door.

'Come,' he called.

It was Colin Duckworth again. With his gap-toothed smile, unruly hair and bright pink blush, he looked like something from a circus. 'Sir?'

'Yes, Colin?'

The boy hovered in the doorway. 'Was you in the war, Sir?'

'I was.'

'Was you in it before the rest of the Yanks, Sir?'

'I was.' Theo repeated. 'It's were you, by the way.'

'Me, Sir? No, Sir, I weren't in it, cos I weren't borned. Was you with the RAF?'

'Rear gunner, yes.' Once again, he had lost the battle with Colin's English.

'Did you shoot Germans down, Mr Quinn?'

'I did. It was my job, you see.'

Colin punched the air with both fists. 'Yesssss. I've won a go on Bernie Allinson's new bike. Thank you, Sir.' The boy withdrew and closed the door.

Theo found himself doubled over his desk laughing. 'Seek and ye shall find' had always been his maxim as a teacher. Children should never be afraid to ask questions, but some of their queries required delicacy. 'Do babies come out of the woman's belly button?' and 'What does bugger mean, Sir?' were not unusual. He'd been forced to explain why fish didn't drown, why America didn't have a king or a queen, how aeroplanes managed not to fall out of the sky, and why the Nazis had murdered Jews.

He dried his weeping eyes. 'They'll be the death of me,' he mumbled. 'And what about Miss Bellamy? How will she cope?' He picked up her application. She had taught for five years in a private college for girls in Kent. Her address was Bartle Hall, Chaddington Green, and she was unlikely to have encountered the colourful language known as Scouse. The letter was interesting.

During teacher training, I practised for four weeks in an East End of London school. The experience enlivened me and I wish to work in the state sector for that reason. My main subject is English; my supporting subjects are drama and mathematics. My notice at the college has been served and I shall be available from September.

Availability would have to suffice, but would she stay? The current reception class teacher had spent her whole working life at Myrtle Street and was due to retire. Miss Ellis was part of the building, and she would certainly be missed. But a new eye might be a good thing, so he would keep his mind open until the interview. He shook his head. One applicant. Oh, well. God was good, according to Dad. There again, Dad was an alcoholic, though he refused to acknowledge the fact. 'I'm a drunk,' he always said. 'Only the rich can afford big words like alcoholic.'

Theo rose to his feet and walked across the room, reaching to push a button above a filing cabinet. The end-of-school bell rang throughout the building, prefabs included. It was Friday, and two empty days lay ahead. Soon, there would be six lifeless weeks, but he would cope, no doubt, by concentrating on his main source of income, one that paid so much better than teaching.

He removed his Blackbird wings and hung the gown on the door. There were relatives in Liverpool, decent people from his dad's family, but he didn't like to impose on them too frequently, so a different occupation would keep him busy for yet another weekend – and for the summer break. Perhaps he might have a few days in London or Paris, but travelling alone was seldom fun.

Standing at the outer double doors of the main school, he watched the children as they jumped and whooped their way towards two days of freedom, a freedom he had never experienced at their age. *Don't go there, Theo. You know it only drives you wild; you can do nothing to change it, and little to improve the future. Except here, of course. You might make a difference for the pupils at Myrtle Street School, but . . .*

'Mr Quinn?'

He turned to his left and looked into a pair of impossibly violet eyes in a face that was truly lovely. 'Yes?'

'I'm Tia Bellamy. I chopped the P, the O and the R off my name, but I applied under the full terrible title.'

'Miss Portia Bellamy?' he asked, feeling rather stupid. She was tall, elegant and striking. Her hair was either dark blonde or light brown, and she was beautifully dressed in garments far too precious for Myrtle Street. 'Your interview's next week,' he reminded her. 'You've arrived a little early.'

Undaunted, she smiled broadly and displayed perfect teeth. 'I don't do late. I'm here to explore Liverpool,' she said. 'After all, should I be fortunate enough to be offered the position, this city would become my new home, so I need to look at it.'

He closed his slightly gaping mouth. The woman spoke in perfect, BBC-here-is-the-news-style English. 'Would you like to look round inside the school?' he asked after a sizeable pause. She wore the air of a woman in charge, and he felt somewhat daunted by her obvious self-certainty.

'Thank you, yes.' She continued to smile. 'You're American,' she added.

He nodded. Miss Tia Bellamy seemed to be a forthright, outspoken and relatively fearless person, so perhaps she was fit for Liverpool after all.

'Am I right?' she asked.

'You are indeed, though I'm also a British citizen, so it's a two-passport job. I guess I'm a hybrid. When I'm in the US, they think I'm English, so I'm a foreigner both sides of the Atlantic. You'll be something of a stranger here, too. The children may well understand you, though you might need someone to translate when they start chattering. They talk almost incessantly and very rapidly. We have a strong accent in these parts.'

She cocked her head to one side. 'Yer what? I done dialect and all that kinda stuff at college, like, Mr Quinn.' The K in the word *like* emerged guttural, right from the back of her mouth. Pleased with herself, she nodded at him. 'See? I can manage, Sir.'

Stunned, he gasped again. This time, instead of closing his mouth, he laughed. 'Drama?'

She nodded and giggled simultaneously. 'I do two kinds of Irish, Glasgow, Edinburgh, Liverpool, inner Lancashire, Cockney, Somerset and Birmingham. The North-East defeated me completely, I'm afraid.'

She reminded him of someone . . . someone famous. It was the eyes, he decided. 'Are you by any chance related to Isadora Bellamy?' he asked.

Tia grimaced. 'I am, but I'd rather people didn't know

just yet. Yes, I'm the product of Isadora and Richard Bellamy. The dynasties probably date all the way back to Shakespeare's days. I have a feeling that some scruffy little ancestor of ours made tea and ran the box office at the Globe or some such dreadful hole. These days, we train for different occupations as fallbacks during resting times, but we were all expected to join our parents as actors.'

'All?'

'There are three of us, mere females, named after Shakespearean heroines. We are one nurse, one teacher and one wild child. The wild child plays drums and other percussive items in a skiffle band, and none of us wants to act. Pa is distressed, but we're sticking to our guns. Cordelia – we call her Delia – is lost in the bowels of London with some disgraceful boys, strangers to soap and water, who wield laundry washboards and guitars. Juliet's a qualified nurse, currently training as a midwife, and I've just avoided the immediate wrath of my father by disappearing while he was away being Mark Antony. My mother's been sulking in the bath for several days. She'll shrink if she doesn't pull herself together.'

'Whoops.' Theo found himself grinning. She had humour, and she seemed not to mind laughing at herself and her family. 'So will you disappear again during term time to play Ophelia?'

She snorted in a way that fell well short of ladylike. 'No. I'm a teacher to the marrow, Mr Quinn. But if I get the post, I shall do your pantomime, your nativity play – whatever you wish. I like writing for children. As for the community, it can take me as I am, warts and all.'

'Good.' In Theo's opinion, warts would do best to steer clear of so decided and confident a young woman. He opened one of the twin doors and followed her inside. She stopped to study Work of the Week, a wall covered by children's efforts in most subjects. 'You wear your gown, then,' she remarked while looking at a painting entitled *Blackbird*.

'Yes. The little ones think it's magic. Older pupils know better, of course, but this artist is only six. Note that I am depicted in flight. She probably believes I emerged from an egg the size of a house in a nest as big as Texas. It's fun.'

The sole applicant nodded. 'We appear to share a philosophy, then, Mr Quinn. My number one rule involves making children happy. I find they learn and remember more in a relaxed atmosphere.'

'Did you apply that theory at the college, Miss Bellamy?'

She awarded him an are-you-crazy look. 'Not at all. A worker in a sausage factory makes sausages. I followed the curriculum before following my instincts and getting out of there.'

'To Liverpool?'

'I have three interviews; Southport, St Helens and here.'

Theo frowned; he had competition, then. 'Southport's rather elegant. If you're looking to make a difference, here would be better.'

'Or St Helens,' she murmured.

He agreed, but with reluctance. 'The land's owned by an earl, and many of the townsfolk belong to a glass magnate. It's a bit grim, but so is my catchment area.'

'I noticed.' Boldly, she faced him. 'Are you prepared to fight over me, Mr Quinn?'

Without flinching, he met her gaze full on. 'No, but I'm almost ready to make an offer for you.' Chortling internally, he watched her blush. 'There will be an interview with a board, but if I want you, I'll get my way.'

She walked into a classroom, angry with herself. Why

had she blushed? Yes, he was attractive; yes, his words could be interpreted on more than one level. But surely he was married? He wasn't old, wasn't young, took his job seriously, and—

'This is Junior Standard One,' he said from the doorway.

'Yes, I read that on the wall in the corridor,' she replied smartly.

'Good. I like my teachers to be literate.'

She tapped a foot. This was a confrontational man, and she liked a challenge. He was laughing at her. What would Ma have done? She ran through a list of Ma's films. Ah, yes; *To the Ends of Earth* sprang to mind. Tia turned and gave him her haughty look. 'I've been reading for twenty-three years, Mr Quinn. My date of birth is on my application form and, if you are numerate, you'll work out by simple subtraction the age at which I began to read.'

He grinned again. 'Touché, Miss Bellamy. Shall we proceed to the infant department? At this point, I'll inform you that my children come, for the most part, from poor but ambitious families. Many arrive able to read a little and to write their names. They can dress and undress themselves, count, draw and sing nursery rhymes. Rhythm is important. Poetry is a good tool.' He led her to the infant classrooms and left her there. 'I'll be in my office,' he told her.

He marched off. No. It mustn't happen again, because it shouldn't happen again. Perhaps it would be better if she took up the post in St Helens or Southport, because she was too . . . too interesting. He didn't want to be interested. Interested meant complicated, and he was no longer fit for complicated.

After switching on his Dansette to play Humphrey Lyttelton's *Bad Penny Blues*, Theo sat at his desk and listened. He liked Lyttelton, especially this piece, which was jazz with humour. Yes, humor had a U in it these days. *Am I losing my sense of humo(u)r? What's the matter with me? How many times must I go through these stupid hormone alerts? She's lovely; live with it, Theodore. And she's knocking on your door in more than one sense. Pull yourself together and deal with the immediate.*

He lowered the Dansette's volume. 'Come in.'

In she came. She had pearl earrings and a big smile; she had leather shoes, a grey suit, and a charm bracelet that tinkled when she moved her right arm; she also had a large diamond solitaire on the third finger of the left hand. 'You're engaged to marry?' The words emerged of their own accord from his dry throat.

'Ah.' Without waiting to be invited, she sat on the chair facing him across the desk. 'No. It was my grandmother's. She was Dame Eliza Duncan. The ring is very useful for warding off predatory males. Sometimes, I wear her wedding band with it.'

Theo's disobedient right eyebrow arched itself. 'Drastic measures, then?'

She shrugged. 'Men in Kent guess who I am, smell money and become nuisances. I look like my mother and my maternal grandmother, so I attract unwanted attention.' She shrugged. 'I deal with it my way.'

He decided to change the subject. 'What do you think of my school?'

Tia met his steady, dark brown gaze. 'It's old,' she replied.

'And?

'I like old. It's as if all the teaching has soaked into the walls – the learning, too. A school in London where I practised was similar. I missed three days due to head lice and fleas, but I went back once I'd deloused myself. The children were needful and great fun.' A frown visited her face. 'Pa got me the post at the Abbey College. Friends in low places, you see.'

He nodded. 'The money may be less, and you'll have to serve probation if you move into the state system.'

'I'm aware of all that, thank you.' Her smile returned. 'I want to live in Liverpool.'

'So you'd rather work in my school?'

'Probably. Though I do have a car, and the other towns are near enough.'

'When are your interviews?'

'Southport Monday afternoon, St Helens Tuesday, here Wednesday.'

Theo rose to his feet and held out his right hand. 'Time to go home, Miss Bellamy. Delighted to have met you.' And that was the truth.

She stood up and took his hand. 'I have no home yet, Mr Quinn. I'm staying in a small hotel overlooking the river, but I'll be searching for somewhere more permanent. Liverpool appeals to me. They're friendly here.'

He smiled and retrieved his hand. 'They are. But, as in every city, you must keep an eye on your belongings. Oh, if you're looking for a place to live, buy the evening newspaper.'

'I've applied already through lettings agencies.' She turned to leave.

'Miss Bellamy?'

'Mr Quinn?'

'How would you deal with a child suffering physical and psychological abuse at home?'

Tia turned and froze. 'Tell the welfare people? Get the National Society on to them?'

'And if you feared that such actions might lead to the further injury or even the death of that child?'

'Couldn't he or she be removed immediately?'

'Not always,' he replied.

She frowned. 'I'm a member of a gun club. Sorry, I didn't mean to make light of it. I'd move him or her.'

'She'll be in your class if you take the post. We've had the new intake here on visits, just four or five of them at a time. Rosie Tunstall's her name. You'd move her to where?'

'Any bloody where I could find, Mr Quinn.' She shook her head slowly, sadly. 'Why do people hurt small children?'

Don't think about it, Theo. Forget it; it's ancient history. 'Moving her might be illegal,' he said quietly. 'It would be kidnap.'

'Better than a funeral,' she almost snapped. 'Why are you smiling?'

'You echo my thoughts, Miss Bellamy. Let's see what September brings, shall we? I'm doing research on the family. We may have a clearer idea by the beginning of the next school year.'

Once again, she tapped a foot. 'So the job's mine?'

'Probably. I'll see you on Wednesday unless you accept another offer. Will you let me know if you do?'

'Of course.'

'Until then, Miss Bellamy.'

'Until then, Mr Quinn.' She left.

Breathing was suddenly easier. He removed Humphrey Lyttelton and listened for a while to Debussy's *Clair de Lune.* Resting his head on folded arms, he tried to relax. Miss Cosgrove of Junior Standard Three fame had set her cap at him months ago. Not that she ever hid her corrugated ginger hair under a cap, though she did bat invisible eyelashes at him.

But like a rogue elephant, Theo kept his own company. He wasn't available. The decision had been made at the end of the war, and he didn't need to flick through

18

his paragraphs of reasons. He was off the market. It wasn't easy. A reasonably good-looking bachelor of thirty-eight with his own property and car was a desirable item on a woman's shopping list, but he was not for sale.

He raised his head and stood up as Claude Debussy's wistful piece reached its final notes. From the side window, he watched Miss Portia Bellamy as she talked to some of the children. Her car, parked behind his, was the twin to his pre-war MG, though his was racing green while hers was red. Similar tastes, similar attitude to classroom work, similar humour with a U in it. 'God,' he whispered. 'Into the valley of death rode the six hundred and one. Sorry, Alfred Lord Tennyson.' He would manage; he had to manage . . .

When she had finally left, Theo went for a word with Jack Peake, school caretaker. 'Don't tell anyone about Colin and the football, Jack. I made a promise. See if you can fix the downspout. If you can't, we open fire on the Education Department on Monday morning.'

'Got your gun loaded, Mr Quinn?'

'I sure have, Mr Peake. Organize a posse and bring my lasso.'

He left the building and drove home, picking up the mail as he walked through the hall of his rather imposing house in Allerton. After throwing assorted envelopes on the kitchen table, he set the kettle to boil. Oh yes, he was becoming thoroughly English, though he seldom poured milk into his cup. Tea in America was usually iced and taken only on stifling hot days. Britain didn't do many hot days; had Noah lived here, he would have built an ark every summer.

This evening's meal would be quick – jambalaya. So he rolled up his sleeves, picked up his mug of tea and went to fetch the lawnmower. If the front lawn suffered any more neglect, it might become habitat for a tribe of pygmies. In fact, they'd be able to erect two-storey edifices and still be invisible.

It would be necessary to begin with a scythe, and that meant hard work and sweat on an evening as untypically balmy as this one, so he finished his tea and went inside to divest himself of decent clothes. He pulled on a pair of khaki shorts and a short-sleeved shirt which he left unbuttoned, and emerged almost naked from the waist up. Bringing down the tone? No, he was bringing down the grass.

Damp and hot after all the scything, he began to mow. Feeling proud of his one-year-old Victa, he made fast work of the front lawn before resting on a flat stone at the edge of his rockery. The slugs were back, so bang went another hosta. Gardening was a fight for survival, and slugs were damned tough.

After so much physical effort, Theo felt too warm for jambalaya. He didn't relish the idea of dealing with heat, so the chorizo, chicken, rice and tomatoes would wait their turn. A sandwich should suffice, surely? He had ham, salad and beer in the fridge, and a young woman gazing down at him. 'Miss Bellamy?' Acutely aware of his state of undress, he leapt to his feet. 'Are you following me?' he asked, humour trimming his tone.

'No,' she answered smartly. 'I've been sent.'

'I see.' He rubbed dirty palms down his shorts. 'By whom?' he enquired.

She pulled a handful of papers from her bag. 'Hang on a mo,' she said. 'I'm a little flustered. Let me find the whom.'

He managed not to grin. Seeing her flustered was extremely amusing.

'Here's the whom,' she murmured, a slight smile visiting her lips. 'There are two of them, a Maitland and a

Collier. They've written to you – it says so in their letter to me. I registered with several letting agents before I came up to Liverpool.'

'Ah.' He remembered the unopened mail on his kitchen table. 'The flat was completed just recently; in fact, the paint may still be wet.'

'Shall I go away, then?'

His mind was breaking all speed limits. This was awkward. 'Well, I may already have a tenant, but I'm unsure. He's thinking about it.' *She's beautiful. Seeing her at school will be enough . . .*

Tia turned away from him and looked at the house. The man was distracting, dark hair, eyes the colour of plain Swiss chocolate, good musculature, tanned skin. 'You own the whole house?'

'Yes.'

'How many rooms?'

'Eighteen in all; nine up and nine down. The upper flat is self contained, with the entry door up the side of the house.'

'You live on the ground floor?'

'I do.'

'Alone?' she asked.

He arched an eyebrow. 'Yes.'

'Oh. Er . . . may I look at the accommodation?'

She's so damned pushy. 'Of course. I'll follow you up. The keys are on my hall table – do go in and get them. There's a metal Liver Bird attached to the key ring. The door's black and halfway down the right hand side of the building. I'll just . . . er . . . yes.'

It was her turn to raise an eyebrow. 'See you later, then, after you've just yessed.' She got the keys, came out of the house and stood for a moment looking at him. He was an oddity, friendly one minute, guarded the next.

Did she want to live above the boss? More to the point, would he like living below her? 'Would my being tenant here bother you?' she asked.

Forthright, isn't she? 'I have no idea,' he answered truthfully. 'I must go and yes myself into a shirt and trousers.' He needed a shower, but there wasn't time. This forward young woman made him feel slightly inadequate, as if she had his measure, as if those violet eyes could penetrate through to his innermost secrets.

Tia entered the small ground-floor hallway of the upper flat. She climbed the stairs feeling like a seven-year-old on Christmas Day. It was stunning. Victorian mouldings remained throughout; he had been faithful to the age of the house. The place upstairs was spacious, with three bedrooms, a dressing room lined with wardrobes, bathroom, kitchen, living and dining rooms, and even a sunroom-cum-office at the back. She loved it immediately.

Theo, on the stairs, listened while she scuttled about, heard her exclaiming to herself as she discovered fireplaces, chandeliers hanging from original ceiling roses, picture rails, old cupboards preserved in recesses. What should he do? Lie to her about a friend moving in? Tell her that the board of governors might object to a single woman living under the same roof as a single man? And would the talcum he'd applied conceal the smell of sweat? He should have opened his mail . . .

'I want it,' she said as soon as he entered the living room. 'Did you do all this?'

'More or less,' he replied. 'People these days are quick to pull out old fireplaces and built-in cupboards and cornices. They board over panelled doors, too.'

'Silly.'

'Absolutely.'

Tia sighed. 'You're not going to let me have the flat,

are you? I'm quiet most of the time, and I'll wear Gran's engagement ring. Simon's following me up here from Kent, so he can be my intended.' She frowned. 'Actually, he intends to be my intended, though my unbearable father doesn't approve because Simon's half Jewish.'

'And what are your intentions?'

'He's not on the shortlist. In fact, he's not even on the long list, and I've told him that.'

Theo shook his head. 'There's a long list?'

'Of course there's a queue. I'm Roedean and Oxford educated, I'm easy on the eye, I know how to use cutlery and have all my own teeth, and I'll be a very wealthy orphan when Ma and Pa shuffle off.' She winked at him. 'Please, Mr Quinn. You're my mentor if I get the post, so why not look after me, make sure I'm safe in and out of school?'

He raised his hands in a gesture of defeat. Portia Bellamy promised to be entertaining, at least. She'd even winked at him. 'Right. Pass the interview, accept the job, and I'll think about it. But I'll have to advise the governors about your wish to live here. Some people remain as Victorian as my house.'

She squealed like a delighted child. 'Can I see your flat? I just love this house. It's so much more homely than Bartle Hall.' She felt a small stabbing pain in her chest – she shouldn't be unfaithful to her now decrepit childhood home.

They entered his domain. 'Make yourself comfortable,' he urged her. 'I'm going to have a quick shower – that garden was hard work.' He left her to it and dashed off to clean up his act. Roedean and Oxford? He stank as if he'd arrived via a farmyard and a boxing ring. Jeez, women didn't half complicate life.

When he returned ten minutes later, Miss Bellamy, no longer elegant, was on hands and knees beneath his dining table. Strands of her abundant hair had slipped their moorings, and she was trying to coax Tyger out of retirement. 'He's difficult,' he advised her. 'A one-person cat.'

She raised her head and banged it on the underside of Theo's solid furniture. 'Bugger,' she exclaimed softly.

'Did you learn that at Roedean?'

Tia emerged, a grimace attempting to conceal her beauty. 'You'd be surprised, Mr Quinn. We had our own curriculum to follow.' She clambered to her feet, one hand rubbing her head, the other releasing the rest of her hair, which tumbled over her shoulders. 'Bugger,' she repeated. 'A Roedean girl's education takes place outside the classroom.'

'Midnight feasts?'

'And the rest. The trouble is, it's difficult to get past the guards. They have machine guns, tanks and landmines. Limbs and lives have been lost; the four tunnels we were digging collapsed and buried ten of us. It's like a concentration camp but with stiffer rules. Well, at least I've made you laugh.'

She flopped onto the sofa. 'Water,' she begged. 'Oh, wait a minute. Why is one door locked?' She pointed towards the hall.

'Body parts,' was his cool response.

'Human?' she asked.

'Of course.' He strode off to the kitchen. It was almost as if she was in charge of every situation; yes, she was a true product of a top public school, composed, alert, well groomed and horribly competent. She was going to get on his nerves, wasn't she?

Tia accepted the glass of water and ice. 'Thank you.'

He tried not to look at her. With her loosened hair, she looked wild, wanton and truly beautiful. 'I'm going to have a sandwich,' he told her. 'Will you join me?'

She glanced at her watch. 'No, thanks. I have another place to see in case you turn me down. Perhaps I'll be safer if you do refuse to house me.'

'Oh?'

She shrugged. 'Body parts. I might go to pieces if I move in here. I'd hate you to see me in pieces.'

Theo found himself grinning; she was almost as much trouble as Colin Duckworth. 'I'll see you Wednesday afternoon, then, Miss Bellamy.' He stood up and held out his hand, but she was busy tying back her hair.

'I look a mess,' she declared as she studied her reflection in the over-mantel mirror.

'You look fine. Go and mither someone else, please.'

'Mither? Your English is good for a foreigner.'

'Thanks.'

She completed her struggle with the abundant and disobedient mane of hair. 'If I live upstairs, might my sisters be allowed to visit me?'

He shrugged. 'It will be your home, so treat it as such. It's big enough for a family.'

She shook his hand firmly. 'I have as much to learn from your children as they have from me. After all, once I've done napkin folding and a ten-course place setting, I shall be out of ammunition.'

'You don't fool me, Miss Bellamy.'

'Hmm. We shall see about that.'

He walked her to the door and watched as she folded herself into the sports car. She pointed to his green version. 'Snap,' she called before roaring off towards some other innocent landlord. The legs were as good as the rest of her. Oh well, sandwich and a drink, then off to speak to the Chair of Governors, a local councillor with sense and backbone. 'Do I need a no or a yes?' he asked Tyger. 'Do we want her here, wise one?'

The cat, aged and almost toothless, chewed languidly

on a tasty morsel of ham. Inherited with the house, Tyger had decided of late that his hunting and running days were over. He swallowed the ham, yawned and fell asleep on his owner's knee. 'I'm gonna miss you,' Theo said. The cat didn't mind if his master spoke Americanese. It would soon be time to say goodbye to this picky-choosy-with-food feline who had adopted the new resident of Crompton Villa six years ago. 'I remember you when you killed birds and frightened small dogs. You were my boss, Tyger.'

The cat's engine began to run, a loud purring that reminded Theo that there was no pain just yet. 'Hang in, boy. I have an errand to run.'

Two

Delia Bellamy ducked into the tiny entrance to the priest hole and slid home the panel. The place stank like old books, though nothing was stored in any of Bartle Hall's secret hides. She banged her head, an elbow and a hip. 'The bloody priests must have been dwarves,' she muttered. 'Jules? Are you in here?'

'Shush. Come and listen. Pa's gone super-Shakespearean, the tragic, wounded hero with a knife in his back, all *et tu Brute.* Is Tia here yet?'

'No, she's still on her way back from the frozen, pagan north. He's smashed my drums. If he's gone tragic, he's definitely Lear, the mad old monarch. I should sue him, and I might just do that. I'm twenty-three, not twelve, and I might change my name to Goneril or Regan.'

Juliet waved her small torch. 'Come here and listen to him,' she whispered. 'He is completely delusional. I'm very worried about him, and about Ma, too.'

Delia edged her way into the cramped space next to her younger sister. Their father was just feet away in his study, and he was beyond angry.

'Notice?' he roared. 'Notice? Why wasn't I told she'd handed in her notice? What? Yes, I know she's twenty-six – she's my daughter, damn it. Why wasn't I informed? I'm aware that she's an adult, for God's sake. Where is she? Where is Portia? I demand an answer.'

Delia blew a very damp raspberry.

'Stop it,' Juliet breathed. 'He'll hear you.'

'I don't care; he broke my drums.'

'I'll break your neck if you don't shut up.'

'You'd need a ladder to reach my neck, short person. Now, hush.'

Richard Bellamy continued to berate the headmistress of the Abbey College. 'Do you know who I am?' he bellowed. 'My girls are special. They're precious; Portia in particular is singularly gifted. I asked you to employ her in your school, close to home, so that I might keep an eye on her. She could well have appeared in the West End, or even Stratford, and you've let her slip through your fingers.'

Delia shook her head to rid herself of dark thoughts on the benefits of euthanasia. If Pa were a horse . . .

'Where's she gone?' he roared. 'You have no idea? Has anyone applied to you for a reference? Confidential? You are not obliged to disclose? Not obliged . . .? You are an idiot, madam. If anyone in my sphere asks about a good school for girls, I shall tell him or her to steer no daughters in your direction. You clearly have no sense of duty.'

Delia and Juliet jumped when he slammed down the receiver and strode out of the study, its weighty door crashing in his wake. The trouble with Pa was that he never knew when to give up. Ma, on the other hand, appeared not to be sure when to start, but that was just one of the side-effects of her increasingly close relationship with gin. Living with Pa had driven a beautiful and talented woman to drink.

Richard Bellamy's career continued to stagger on. He blustered about on stage and screen under the direction of the few who remained impressed by his family name. The Dynasty was all that mattered; his daughters should follow in the footsteps of their predecessors, should fly the Bellamy/Duncan flag with pride.

'I think he's finally flipped,' Delia mumbled. 'I'm worried about Tia.'

'Why?' Juliet asked.

'Well, he wrecked my drums, so what will he do to her, his star, his favourite? I'm afraid he might lock her up or have her followed. She shouldn't come home. When is she supposed to be back? Didn't she say something about getting here in time for dinner? We have to help her, Jules. She really wants to go back to Liverpool, because she got the job she wanted.'

'How can we be of use?'

'Er . . . we can dash through the gardens to the gate and stop her before she reaches the home stretch. After that, we'll just have to make it up as we go.'

'We can't book her in to stay at the Punch Bowl. Word would get out in minutes.'

'She'll have to sleep in the stables. If it was good enough for Jesus, it'll have to be good enough for her. Oh, Jules, why couldn't we have a normal family with an ordinary life?'

Juliet giggled. 'Tia and I are trying to break free by getting a career, but you're playing right into his hands with your skiffling. Mind, Tia inherited his quick temper, so heaven knows how she'll react when we tell her Pa's on the warpath.'

Delia wasn't listening properly. 'I can't skiffle; he's wrecked my drums.'

'Buy more.'

'I shall.'

They crawled out of the hole into one of the many corridors that wound their way round Bartle Hall. It was a warren of a house, its older parts erected in the fifteenth century, the rest added on randomly for a further three or four hundred years. Pa had inherited the place, and his three daughters had enjoyed a wonderful childhood within its walls. Hide and seek had been brilliant, as had dressing up in Ma's clothes, shoes and makeup.

But the girls were grown now. Fiercely close to and protective of each other, they were almost a secret society. Portia, the eldest, had nominated them the Blyton Three in deference to the author whose works they had devoured hungrily in their formative years. Portia was on her way home, and her younger siblings fled the house and raced through the shrubbery until they reached the gates. They sat on the stump of an oak felled by lightning, each fighting for breath, each determined to save the firstborn sister. Almost automatically, they held hands.

Inside the house, an angry Richard stood over his wife. She was spread out on a chaise longue, an empty glass lying on her chest. Isadora Duncan, she had been, sharing her name with a dancer who had died tragically in a freak accident. 'God took the wrong one,' he murmured. 'I should buy you a long silk scarf and send you out in Portia's sports car, see if we can recreate the other Isadora's final performance.'

He sat on a wicker chair, staring at the woman he had married, the wife who had failed to produce a son. She was snoring again, mouth slackened, hair like a rats' nest, clothing stained and creased. No wonder his girls were wild; they'd had no female parent to guide and advise them. In the early days, she'd often been away at work, but now she was planning to drink herself to death. She was doing this with malice aforethought, knowing that her husband would be blamed for her long act of suicide.

Filled with righteous indignation, he walked into his own dressing room. He usually slept here, as her snoring kept him awake. It occurred to him that he might move further away, perhaps to the other side of the house where Isadora could no longer disturb him. But with many rooms closed off due to the lack of servants, Bartle Hall was fast becoming a shell.

'My father would have hated to see the decline of this place,' he grumbled.

Cursing quietly under his breath, he dressed for dinner.

Meanwhile, Delia and Juliet waited for their sister. Juliet, smallest and youngest of the three, was blonde, pretty and, although quieter, almost as confident as Tia. Delia was different. Thin and quite ordinary, she shone when excited and had quite a few fans in the music business. Music was the love of her life, because it allowed her to be her own individual self. She considered herself unattractive, and had decided to do something unusual with her existence, so she had taken lessons and learned to drum. 'I think we all have to get out permanently, Jules. Nanny will look after Ma, and Pa will carry on acting till he drops dead or stops getting work.'

Juliet agreed. 'I'll nurse in Canterbury. Will you return to London?'

'Yes. But first we have to save Tia. I've still got the group's van, so I'll follow her up to Liverpool with her stuff – that car of hers barely takes two suitcases. First of all, we must hide her. What about Rose Cottage? I know it's been empty for a while and the roof leaks a bit, but she can manage in there for a couple of days. We'll smuggle out the camp bed and some linen, take food for her, and pack all her clothes and so forth in the van. Oh, and we'll need to hide the MG.'

They chattered on about the planned adventure, each making a mental list of Tia's belongings. Juliet, the quiet one, allowed Delia to gabble on. When push came to shove, Delia made all the noise while Juliet became the organizer. But Tia was their rock, and both would miss her. She was beautiful, kind, clever, witty and here. The open-topped bright red MG slewed to a halt, and both Tia's sisters and best friends jumped up to greet her.

Juliet reached the car first. 'Tia! Tia, go along the back lane to Rose Cottage. I'll sit on the rear shelf of your mad car and Delia can go in the passenger seat.' She climbed in. 'Come on, Delia. If we're late for dinner, he'll throw another fit.'

Tia closed her gaping mouth. 'What's going on? What have I missed?'

'Father's flipped,' Juliet replied. 'He phoned the college and told Miss Monk that he should have been kept informed of your escape plan.'

'God, it's like bloody Roedean all over again. Does he know about Liverpool?'

'No,' the younger sisters answered in unison. Delia carried on. 'I got back from London yesterday. I forgot to lock the back door of the van, and he pulled out my drums and smashed them with an axe. Then Jules got quizzed about midwifery and why did she want to do it. The point is, you're his only hope. He's always doted on you. Tia, he's lost his grip on reality. Ma's in a bad way, too, and that's his fault, I'm sure.'

Juliet intervened. 'Never mind all that for now. Rose Cottage. Hide the car up the side. We'll get what you need, and Delia will follow you to Liverpool with your things. If I can get time off, I may come, too. The Blyton Three go to Liverpool, eh? Good title.' She tried to get comfortable in the not-really-a-seat behind Tia.

Delia sat in the front next to the driver. 'This is going to be a bumpy ride in more ways than one. Put your foot down, Tia. Jules and I will run back home in time for dinner, and we'll see you later.'

Little more was said. As soon as she reached the cottage, Tia was suddenly alone, because her siblings fled immediately to report for duty to the despot who was their father. She stood in a garden that had once been pretty; it was now wild and covered in rose bushes gone crazy, suckers everywhere, more thorns than blooms. This little house had been Ma's retreat whenever she'd needed to get away from Pa. Nanny Reynolds had always accompanied her, but Ma's newer escape came in a bottle, and both women remained at the Hall because Isadora's main occupation was sleeping.

Inside, Tia sat among neglected remains of her mother's past – books on the shelves, shawls draped artistically across seats and tables, photographs of a young Isadora Bellamy playing Portia, Cordelia and Juliet. Across the chimney breast were oil paintings of her children, each named after one of the heroines hung over the dresser. Her crochet work sat on a low trolley whose bottom shelf supported a sketch pad and pots of water-colour paint.

This was the last of Ma. This was a eulogy, a grave-stone, a heartbreaking memorial for a destroyed, lonely and desperately unhappy woman. Tia's anger bubbled to the surface. 'He has to be stopped,' she said aloud.

She sat in a wooden rocker and began to weep. Richard Bellamy had crushed his wife slowly, mercilessly, and his oldest daughter lingered now among Ma's remains. 'I can't stay, Ma,' she sobbed. 'And I can't take you with me, because you're too ill.' It was like abandoning a child, a helpless foundling dumped on a cold and unforgiving doorstep.

Tia dried her eyes. 'The quality of mercy . . . droppeth like the gentle rain from heaven,' she said, misquoting her namesake. Portia would not have sat here weeping; Portia would have made a fabulous speech on behalf of the threatened or afflicted. 'Pa's had his pound of flesh many times over,' she muttered grimly. 'I'm going in. Let's hope there's no carving knife on the table.'

She dried her eyes and dabbed at her nose. A few minutes were needed while she composed herself, as she was about to face Julius Caesar, Henry V, Richard III, Hamlet and the fool who lived in Bartle Hall together. 'Your line of the dynasty is about to fade away, you bumbling, smug, self-satisfied braggart. My mother was beautiful and talented.' Tia would take the photographs, the portraits and Ma's framed watercolours to Liverpool – as long as Delia and Juliet agreed, of course.

Anger sustained her while she reversed onto Rose Cottage's dry, rutted approach road. Quickly, she drove up the main driveway to the Tudor frontage of her childhood home. Let him try. *Just try to keep me here, you washed-up wreck of a man. I may even involve the police. I am my own self and I belong only to me. I cannot and will not be bullied by you, Bellamy. You will not trap me no matter how hard you try. You have no real power. Without my mother's financial support, you would be deader than the dodo.*

She marched into the dining room like a guard changing duty at Buckingham Palace, spine straight, head held high, chest out, arms swinging. For a few beats of time, she reacted internally to the unexpected presence at table of her mother, but she did not pause, as she refused to allow her anger to dissipate.

Richard rose to his feet. 'Portia, darling! Where on earth have you been?'

She stopped well within his reach. 'Father,' she snapped.

He frowned. The word 'father' meant business. Even so, he bent forward to accept a kiss from her, but she stepped aside. 'What's the problem?' he asked.

'You are,' she replied smartly. 'You destroyed Ma's life,

and your daughters have all suffered because of your periodic attempts at rigid control. It stops now. None of us wants to act. Delia is a good drummer and Juliet's going to remain a nurse. As for me – well, the further away from you, the better.' She looked at her mother. 'None of this is your fault, Ma.'

Isadora blinked and raised her glass. 'To my happy marriage,' she slurred. 'Which lasted for two years at the most.' Staring directly at her husband, she nodded. 'You, sir, are a bloody awful actor, the butt of so many jokes in the business, a terrible husband, a bad father and a total ass.'

'How dare you?' he roared.

She giggled. 'Because I'm nearly dead, thanks to you.' She grinned and winked at her eldest daughter. 'Girls, you have many, many half-brothers and sisters all over the place.' She waved a hand, spilling most of her wine on the tablecloth. 'He rutted. He was a total rutter.' After taking a few seconds to alter her focus, she spoke to her two seated offspring. 'Get away as fast as you can, girls. Nanny Reynolds will look after me.' A loud hiccup interrupted the flow. 'I have more money than he does, so—'

'You're a drunken hag,' he proclaimed, his tone ominously quiet.

'A rich drunken hag,' she replied. 'And not a penny piece will come your way. It will all go to my daughters.' She beamed at the rest of the company. 'Do eat, children. I know it's difficult with a tyrant in the room, but be comforted. You never had to share a room with him. His feet stink, and he farts frequently.' She belched loudly, and everyone but the master smiled or giggled.

'You are a disgrace,' yelled the master of the house. 'You have no control over your drinking, and you have turned our daughters against me.' He glared at his wife before storming out of the room. He would deal with his family later.

Tia sat and dug into the food; having driven almost non-stop for most of the day, she was starving.

Isadora grinned broadly. 'It hasn't been terribly easy, girls. But it seems to be working quite well, wouldn't you say?'

All three froze in their seats. 'Ma?' they chorused.

Her grin rearranged itself into a sweet smile. 'Try to be quiet. I know I've gone rather a long way with the act, but it was the simplest way.'

Delia closed her mouth so suddenly that she bit her tongue.

'You see,' Isadora continued, 'it was a case of whither thou goest. We got the parts because we were a pair, and I could carry him. So I retired drunk. And I admit that I was a drinker for a while. Yes, I almost succumbed. He's easily fooled, and he now believes me to be an alcoholic.'

'But . . . but you're not drunk,' Juliet whispered.

'No, I'm serfectly pober.'

Tia shook her head and smiled. 'Ma, you're one hell of an actress.' She jumped up, ran round the table and hugged her mother.

'Yes, I am good, what? I snore and belch beautifully. Oh, and my divorce is being arranged. I am only fiftyish, and I shall rise anew, a phoenix from the ashes. Nanny Reynolds and I will ride again, possibly to Hollywood. My agent knows the facts of the matter, and good use will be made of my true story, the sooner the better. I am sick of the smell of gin, can't wait to get back to Chanel No. Five. He won't know what's hit him, because I have evidence by the ton.'

'So you're not an alcoholic?' Delia's face remained a picture of disbelief.

'I was on my way, Cordelia, no doubt about that. Then I had a word or two with myself and with Nanny Reynolds – Joan. I managed to overcome the demon with

Joan's help, and we hatched our plot. With the three of you away so frequently, I managed not to upset you by forcing you to watch me playing the dipsomaniac, so I kept on snoring and looking like an unmade bed. It drove him mad. Work is drying up for him. I'm the one they want, and I refuse absolutely to play alongside him again. Joan and I are going into hiding, so leave me your addresses.' She looked at their blank faces. 'Come on, eat up. Son of Satan may be back shortly.' Smiling sweetly, she blew them a kiss and left the room.

'Hell's bells,' Tia exclaimed. 'That is one strong lady, sisters.'

Juliet frowned. 'What'll happen to Pa?'

'She'll look after him up to a point,' was Delia's answer. 'Ma is no monster. And she's right – he is a terrible actor, still stuck in the 1930s, a stuffed shirt with big ideas and no discernible talent. The landlord at the Punch Bowl does a terrific imitation of him. Everyone mocks him behind his back while being polite to his face.'

'Sad,' said Tia, 'but Ma needs her freedom. Let her achieve it her way.'

They ate what they could manage before carrying dishes into the kitchen where Mrs Melia, cook and house-keeper, greeted them happily. 'Girls, don't you all look lovely? Tia, you should wear a headscarf if you're going to drive with no lid on the car. Delia, I swear you're still growing, while Juliet seems to have shrunk.'

Juliet giggled. 'I must remember not to have such hot baths – I can ill afford to lose height due to shrinkage.'

'I was listening,' Mrs Melia mouthed silently. 'Your mother's a star.'

The Blyton Three left the kitchen and repaired to Delia's old room. Delia had a huge four-poster with drapes too ancient to be touched, so they remained tied open. During the years of childhood, the girls had all slept here in the large bed, although each had her own room. There was safety in numbers, especially when Pa was on a rant.

'We could have sent your stuff by rail, Tia,' Juliet said.

The senior sister shook her head. 'You don't know what I want, because I don't know what I want. Yes, I do. I want Ma up and about and doing what she does best.' She pondered for a moment. 'I wonder if he'd let Ma and Nanny stay with me for a few weeks while the divorce gets sorted?'

'Pa?' Delia raised her eyebrows.

'No. My landlord. He's also my boss. I've a three-bedroom flat, and he said I should use it as my home. He lives downstairs.'

A knowing look passed between the younger girls. 'Is he nice?' Juliet asked, her tone nonchalant.

'Yes,' Tia replied. 'Though he does have a locked room with body parts in it. And a very antisocial, geriatric cat.'

'Handsome?' was Delia's question.

Tia shrugged. 'He was probably a pretty kitten, but these days he—'

'The man,' Delia snapped.

'Oh, yes. Especially when naked.'

Juliet blinked rapidly. 'And he has body parts in a locked room?'

'Joke.' Tia poked out her tongue.

'You've seen him naked?' Delia wore her imitation stern face.

'In shorts and an unbuttoned shirt, yes. He was mowing the lawn. Tanned, toned and terrific.'

'Danger zone,' chorused Juliet and Delia.

Tia awarded them a withering look. 'Don't start Blytoning on me.' The words danger and zone had been used whenever Pa came home. 'We won't be the Blyton Three for much longer.' She sounded sad. 'I miss this house. It's impractical, cold, damp and adorable. Remember Christmases in the grand ballroom? Two log fires, two huge trees, all that glitter. Ma at the piano, choirboys at the door, Pa trying and failing to be human.'

'We're separated now,' Juliet complained. 'I get lonely.'

'It's the way of the world, Jules.' Delia yawned. 'And now, divorce. Ma is one brilliant actress, though. He thinks she needs drying out, but he'll be the one hung out to dry. She's a real trooper.'

Juliet felt a bit sorry for him, and said so, but the others shouted her down. He was selfish, unpredictable, narcissistic, dictatorial, churlish, presumptuous and utterly without talent.

'Heartless,' Juliet mused.

'Yes, he's that as well,' Delia almost barked.

'No, we're being heartless. He's in his late fifties and—'

'And he's old enough to know better,' Tia insisted. 'Jules, I know you're a good Christian, but stick to the facts. He wrecked Ma's life, and he'll try the same with us. He has a fear and a hatred of women. I blame his mother – she treated him like a prince one minute, a reprobate the next. Women confuse him. Stop worrying.'

Juliet didn't stop worrying, though she said no more.

They chatted until sleep overcame them, all on top of the eiderdown, all fully clothed. When morning came, they giggled like five-year-olds, had a pillow fight and exchanged jokes. After attempting and failing to use a very old, creaking bed as a trampoline, they sat and regained breath. They all needed fumigating, so they separated and went to three bathrooms, each girl hoping against hope that the weary boiler would cough up a few gallons of hot water.

After breakfast, Tia, in search of some privacy, drove to Chaddington Green's sole telephone box and made an essential call. Suddenly nervous, she began to shake slightly. 'Pull yourself together, Bellamy,' she said, balancing a pile of pennies on the press-button-A-or-B box.

He answered. 'Theo Quinn, Myrtle Street School.'

'Mr Quinn.' She cleared her throat. 'It's Tia Bellamy.'

'Ah, Miss Bellamy, of course. I recognized your voice immediately. I trust you are well?'

'Yes, thank you. I need to ask a favour, and it's a big one.'

'Fire away.'

Words tumbled out of her throat at high speed. She explained about Ma and Nanny Reynolds, about divorce and Ma needing to get away while it all happened. 'She probably has photographic and witness evidence, so it might become nasty. Nanny looked after us when we were small; now she cares for Ma, so she'll be with her.'

The pips sounded, and she fed more copper into the greedy box. 'Just for a week or two. Liverpool's quite a distance from Kent, and he won't look for her there.' There was a pause. 'Mr Quinn?'

'I'd be proud and delighted to have Isadora Bellamy in my house,' he said.

Tia swallowed. 'Don't be delighted, please,' she begged. 'It has to be a secret.'

He laughed. 'I'm good at secrets, Miss Bellamy.'

'I expect you have much to hide, Mr Quinn, with all those body parts. Just two more bodies, intact and probably disguised.'

'OK. Don't waste any more money. I shall see you soon.'

'Thank you,' she breathed before replacing the receiver. She gathered up her remaining pennies and returned to the car. His voice was so pleasant, and he seemed to have humour, which was an absolute necessity in teaching. Body parts, indeed. She giggled as she started Evangeline, her precious MG, wondering whether

Mr Quinn had named his car. Did Americans christen cars? Rumour had it that Mr Ford's company was about to launch a vehicle named after his son, Edsel.

Why wasn't Mr Quinn married, she wondered. He was handsome, capable – look how he'd made one house into two flats. He had a decent job, dressed well unless gardening, owned a pleasant personality ... Perhaps he preferred men, though she suspected not. Why did she suspect not? 'No idea,' she said aloud as she drove homeward.

When she reached Bartle Hall, she ran straight up to Ma's room. Ma was on the chaise, being 'drunk'. 'Hello, Tia,' she slurred. 'If you want your father, he's in his dressing room.' She waved a hand towards the other door.

Unfazed, Tia sat on a stool and whispered to her mother, 'I'll leave my address with Nanny. My landlord says you can come and stay, both of you. Get out of here before the nasty stuff starts flying about.'

Richard made an entrance. He glared at his wife, sniffed at his daughter, then stalked out like a disgusted pantomime dame. In his silky smoking jacket, he looked every inch the ageing, never-quite-made-it thespian.

Isadora sat up. 'He didn't finish what you started at dinner last night, then? Didn't we all think he was going to argue with you?'

Tia shrugged.

Joan Reynolds came in, closing the door quietly. Tia hugged the woman who had cared for her, Delia and Juliet. 'He's up to something,' Joan said. 'Keep an eye on the car and the van, because he knows about batteries and the rotor something or other, so he may disable them. He's been staring at both.'

'He wouldn't,' Tia gasped.

Isadora disagreed. 'I think he's ready to give up on Juliet, but you and Cordelia remain in his sights. Look,

41

he'll be back to dress shortly, because he's going up to London to see his agent. Find Cordelia and take both vehicles to the village. He'll be on the one o'clock train, and he won't be back until this evening. He believes you and Cordelia are home until the weekend is over, but you must leave this afternoon. Go on, shoo. Joan will help you pack when the coast is clear. By the way, don't worry about Rose Cottage. Joan and I will take care of all that.'

Tia ran to get her sisters, explaining to them in a whisper that they had to save their engines from sabotage. They spilled out of the house and found that both vehicles remained in working order. 'Why is he like this?' Juliet asked. 'Why can't he just let us get on with the lives we've chosen? So you have to leave today, both of you?'

'Get in the van and shut up,' Delia hissed quietly. 'We return at one, pack the van, then yes, Tia and I must go.'

'I can't get time off,' Juliet moaned. 'I'm on a split duty tomorrow.' She climbed into the van, and both vehicles moved slowly down the drive, turning left at the gates and heading sedately towards Chaddington Green. Undue haste within Pa's sight might make him suspicious, so they travelled at a leisurely pace, parked, and went for coffee in a small and comfortable cafe.

'I like this village,' Juliet said. 'I love Kent. That's why I chose to train in Canterbury. But with Ma gone, will we still have Bartle Hall? Pa can't afford to save it, can he?'

They all stared through the window at the square of common land that had given Chaddington Green its name. It was the stuff of picture postcards, with a duck pond, clusters of cottages, some of them thatched, a short stretch of pretty little shops, a church, just one inn, and friendly inhabitants.

Tia spoke. 'Ma won't let our home go. She'll buy it from him, I think.'

'He won't part with it,' was Juliet's opinion. 'It's proof of his identity, property of the Bellamy dynasty.'

'The place is falling to bits, and everybody has a price,' Tia said. 'He's spent his money in his London clubs and on women. Ma will shift him.'

Delia nodded sagely. 'She saved; he didn't.'

'And the Duncans were always richer than the Bellamys,' Tia mused aloud. 'When she stops pretending to be blotto, our mother will be a force to be reckoned with. But while it's all going on – the divorce, I mean – she may need us. I know she can afford hotels, but she may become anxious about being noticed. We back her up, girls.' The Blyton Three balled their right hands, elbows on the table, three fists meeting in the centre above a sugar bowl. 'Victory,' they said in unison.

The owner of the cafe laughed, while other customers grinned. They all remembered the Bellamy sisters riding through the village on bicycles or ponies, always up to mischief, always loved.

With an hour to spare, Tia rang Theo again to warn him of the change of plan, and then the three girls repaired to the green, spending twenty minutes or more in the children's cordoned-off section where they played on swings, a seesaw and a metal slide. While each sister feared that this might be goodbye to the village, each one hoped and prayed that she was wrong. But the trio were certain of one thing: it was adieu to childhood.

With that in mind, they did racing round the duck pond, leapfrog, and the four-legged jog. Based loosely on the three-legged race, it meant that the girl in the centre had minimal control, as each of her legs was fastened to a limb of one of her sisters. Juliet, who had learned long ago that being the youngest, the shortest and the lightest meant pain and distress, was tied to her siblings with two scarves, and the fun began. Supporting their baby sister with arms across her back, Tia and Delia dragged her across the green.

Old people seated on benches began to chuckle. Even the ducks stopped begging for crusts when the strange, three-headed, four-legged creature passed by. Juliet, churchgoer and angel to the sick, allowed a few choice words to emerge from her pretty lips.

'I'm gonna tell the vicar you swore,' Delia said.

'Shut up,' snapped the victim. 'And stop. I shall be of little use to patients when you've managed to break both my legs.'

They stopped, released her from captivity and sank to the grass.

'Do you think we'll ever grow up completely?' Tia asked.

'I hope not,' was Delia's answer. 'If I grow any upper, I'll be too tall.'

'Too tall for a man?' Juliet asked mischievously.

Delia shrugged. 'Too tall for me,' she answered.

Tia held her tongue. For some years, she had suspected that Delia was different. Unlike the other two Bellamy girls, she kept herself plain, unadorned and in clothes that might be termed neither feminine nor completely masculine. She wore jeans, shirts, socks and flat shoes, no makeup and no perfume. Boyfriends had never appeared on the scene, though she was very close to the lads in the skiffle group.

'You're pretty if you'd just clean up your act,' said the innocent Juliet.

'I am what I am.' There was an edge to Delia's tone.

Tia jumped up. 'Time for my escape, girls. The London train should have left by now, so we'd better make hay before sundown.'

Juliet sat with Tia for the ride back to Bartle Hall. 'What's the matter with Delia? Why does she get so . . . so surly?'

Tia kept her eyes on the road. Surely Juliet, a nurse, must have read about people's differences? 'It's just the way she's made, Jules. I want you to find Kingsley the bear and Charlie, my blue rabbit. They'll be in the nursery.'

'Taking them with you?'

'Yes.'

'What about books?'

'I'll get them.' There. That was the subject changed, thank goodness.

The afternoon became a blur of activity. Two ancient trunks were retrieved from the attic and placed empty in the van, as they were heavy enough without Tia's extensive collection of clothes. She dealt with her own books and clothing, while Delia and Juliet concentrated on memories, which included a rocking horse bought for Tia's third birthday and a large dolls' house, including furniture and battery-powered lighting.

Joan Reynolds supervised proceedings and collected Tia's jewellery, handbags and large assortment of hats and shoes. The cook, Daphne Melia, packed sandwiches and drinks for both drivers before bidding them a teary farewell.

Isadora was remarkably calm. Seated on her chaise with each arm round one of her precious girls, she advised both to take their time while driving north. 'Be happy,' she ordered. 'Skiffle all you like, Cordelia, and I know that you, Portia, will be a wonderful teacher. There is little point in trying to reason with your father, so make no attempt. Help your sister to settle in,' she begged of her middle child.

'I will, Ma. I can keep the van for another few days, because the lads have hopped off to France for a fortnight.' She blushed. 'We're so proud of you, Ma, and so glad you're not alcoholic.'

The mother studied this daughter. 'Are you lesbian, dear?' she asked.

'Yes. Yes, I am.'

Tia sighed with relief. Delia had needed to offload that information for years.

Isadora smiled. 'I do hope you meet someone as good and as kind as you are, sweetheart. Be aware that some people will castigate you, but, unlike men, you can't be jailed. Poor Oscar served time, but Queen Victoria decided that lesbianism didn't exist, since she couldn't imagine what women might do together.' She took hold of Delia's face and kissed her on the forehead. 'Be yourself, and to hell with prejudice.'

She turned to Tia. 'Enjoy your work, dear child.'

'You will come to stay, Ma? Mr Quinn says it's fine with him, and he won't tell anyone who or where you are. Nanny has the address.'

'When my lawyer has organized the papers and other evidence, Joan and I will be with you. Thank Mr Quinn before we get there. Now, you must go while enough daylight remains. I'll be in touch.' She turned to Delia. 'When you leave Portia in Liverpool, go back to your place in London. If reporters find you, tell them nothing. Your father's predilection for young women will be big news.'

'Yes, Ma.'

The girls rose and stepped back, still facing their mother.

Isadora beamed at the pair. 'Remember when the Blyton Three tried to prove that Mr Jenkins at the Punch Bowl was selling drink brought in by smugglers through tunnels under the village green?'

Tia and Delia smiled.

'And when you decided that Miss Evans-Jones was stealing books from the library?'

Tia tried and failed to look contrite.

'Then you wanted the vet prosecuted for murdering your pony, Portia.'

'Oh, yes,' Tia replied. 'Those were the days.'

'It was playacting,' Isadora said. 'You turned your lives into an epic adventure, and you were all offered places at good drama schools. It's in you. If you ever change your minds and decide to follow me into film or theatre, tell me. If you don't want that, it really doesn't matter. Chase your own dreams, not mine, not your father's. Now, go.'

They kissed their mother and left her room. 'Ma says she'll look after the stuff in Rose Cottage,' Tia said. 'Her watercolour paintings, the photographs and the portraits of us.'

'Just as well – the van's so full, it might expire.'

'My car's stuffed as well, Delia.'

They found Juliet ironing her uniform. 'When shall we three meet again?' she asked, her tone clouded by unshed tears.

'Soon,' Tia promised. 'Please don't blub, Jules, or we'll all be weeping. Remember, it ain't over till the fat lady sings.'

'And who's the fat lady?' Delia asked.

All three answered together, 'Mrs Melia, Delia.'

Juliet giggled. 'We are cruel.'

'Power to the Blyton Three,' called Tia.

They pressed three fists together and shouted, 'Victory,' before the two older girls left their baby sister to her ironing. She didn't follow, as she was too upset to stand and watch them leaving Bartle Hall.

'Why do I feel as if this is goodbye?' Delia asked.

'Because we're leaving.'

'I mean goodbye forever.'

Tia snorted. 'Just let Ma do her worst and her best, sis. Never give up. The Blyton Three always had hope. Remember that.'

'Pandora's box,' Delia murmured. 'Nil desperandum.'

'Yes, that as well. Come on, I'll lead the way.'

It was a long drive. They stopped on a B road north of Birmingham, pulling into a dirt lay-by to eat and drink the offerings of Mrs Melia. Tia was stiff and complaining loudly of old age catching up on her. 'My calves have petrified,' she moaned.

'It's that daft car,' Delia told her. 'You have to drive almost lying down. Anyway, the van loaded with all your junk is hard on the arms, so shut up.'

'It's not junk.'

'Matter of opinion.' Delia bit into a crusty cob filled with salad and ham, while Tia gulped down some welcome lemonade.

'Juliet doesn't know,' she said, wiping her mouth on a handkerchief. 'About you, I mean.'

'I'll tell her when she's ready,' Delia spluttered, her mouth full.

'Younger than her years in some ways,' Tia pondered aloud. 'Very organized, yet frail. I'm sure she won't be judgemental, though.'

Delia swallowed. 'It doesn't matter how she reacts, because I am what I am. Of course, I don't want to lose one of my sisters; I love both of you, but I really think I was born like this. I don't wish to be a man, by the way, but I'm never going to be a frilly girl with lipstick, high heels and bangles. You and she are so feminine and beautiful, and I'm . . . I'm me.'

'I'm glad you're you. Have you met anyone?'

'Yes, I think so. She follows the group all over London, but she prefers my company to the boys'. Time will tell. The signals aren't always clear.'

Tia laughed. 'They can get a bit confusing on my side

48

of the fence, too. Simon is moving to Liverpool. I've told him he's more of a brother, but I think he suffers from selective deafness. He thinks Pa put me off because of the Jewish thing, but that's not the case at all.'

'He's just not right for you, Tia. We can all see that.'

'Pity he can't. Let's eat up and get back on the road; it'll be dusk in a couple of hours. I suppose we could have slept in the van had it not been full.'

'Your fault.'

'Oh, eat up. We're more than halfway there.'

They finished their al fresco meal in silence, went for petrol and used facilities that were primitive but necessary, since neither girl relished the idea of driving a further hundred miles with a full bladder. 'I've never seen Liverpool,' Delia said.

'Think London, but smaller. Oh, and the accent's interesting.'

'Let's be off, Tia. And I'm not emptying the van tonight. Perhaps your man might do it for us.'

'My man? Why do you say he's my man?'

Delia shrugged. 'It's just the way your eyes have lit up the two or three times you've mentioned his name.'

'What?'

'All right, don't get your knickers in a knot. Drive, Tia. After all, you're in charge, aren't you?'

Three

While Tia Bellamy made her way upcountry, her soon-to-be boss was chairing an informal meeting in his office at Myrtle Street School. The subject under discussion was a frail five-year-old girl who was due to start school in September. Undernourished, ill-clad and often bruised, she was almost certainly the victim of domestic abuse and wilful neglect. Her situation had been noticed by neighbours some weeks earlier, and action was about to be attempted.

Roy Duckworth, father of repeat offender and lovable rogue Colin, had brought with him Tom and Nancy Atherton, a married couple nearing pensionable age who lived next door to Rosie Tunstall, her mother and her soon-to-be adoptive stepfather. The fourth person attending on this day was Jack Peake, caretaker of the school. All were worried about little Rosie, all lived in Isabel Street, and all were trusted implicitly by Theo Quinn.

'It's a brothel. No use tarting it up and colouring it in with posh words,' said Tom Atherton. 'Let's speak plain. You can hear them at it in both front rooms, downstairs and upstairs, especially at weekends. It's a bloody nightmare. Am I right, Nancy?'

'You're right, love, but don't swear in front of the headmaster or you'll end up in detention doing the American War of Independence or Custard's Last Stand.'

She carried on with her knitting; she was making a green cardigan for Rosie.

'Custer,' her husband told her.

'Is Maggie coming?' Roy Duckworth asked, referring to Rosie's maternal grandmother. 'Not like her to be late for something as important as this.'

'She's been working this afternoon.' Theo stood up and glanced through the Myrtle Street window. 'She's just walked through the gate. Now, remember, we don't want to upset her any more than necessary, so we keep this short. But we need the police to raid the place while Rosie's mother and friend are entertaining clients, so Maggie's daughter will be taken into custody as a result.'

Roy nodded. 'OK. But we have to be cruel to be kind.'

The group became quiet; the only sound available to human ears was the strangely soothing click of Nancy Atherton's knitting needles.

Theo stood up and smiled encouragingly when Maggie Stone entered the room. 'Maggie, you know everyone here.' He waited until the greetings had died down. 'I was just about to say that you need to be in Mr and Mrs Atherton's house when the raid happens. With luck, Rosie will be handed into your care.'

The new arrival put a hand to her mouth. 'Oh, this is terrible. Sadie's my daughter, and here I am, planning to put her in jail. It doesn't feel right.'

Tom Atherton took Maggie's hand. 'Listen, love, it's the only way. Your Sadie's an adult. She should think enough of that kiddy to get her out of there and down to your house, so that they could both—'

'He said if Sadie runs to mine, he'll burn our house down with us inside it. Rosie's not allowed to visit me in case she says something out of turn. How will he react when Rosie's at school with loads of people to talk to?'

'That's why we do it before she starts school, Maggie.'

Tom squeezed her hand. 'Come on, queen, we can't have arson on top of everything else, can we? Miles Tunstall has to go to jail before he starts playing with paraffin and matches. It makes sense, love.'

'He's right,' Nancy said.

Theo shivered internally, but said nothing. Employing familiar tactics, he swallowed memories and nightmares, flame and smoke, imprisoning them deep inside his core. Nothing could touch him now as long as he kept himself calm and controlled. He was adult, he was in England, the past was the past, and he had responsibilities.

Maggie continued. 'I know he's adopting our Rosie, but he doesn't give a damn about her. What about when he puts her on the game in a few years? Oh yes, if they ran to me, he'd burn my house down with my little granddaughter in it, and he'd walk away whistling.'

'She's right, love. I've heard him a few times threatening to set fire to Maggie's house.' Nancy Atherton changed needles.

Maggie nodded and dried her eyes. 'He's not normal, that one. In trouble for years.'

'Dangerous,' was Jack Peake's spoken contribution. 'Even at school, he was thieving, beating other kids, starting trouble everywhere he went. One of the places he went was borstal, and that's where he learned to be a real criminal. Then in jail when he was older, he met the experts and the result is the upstanding pimp and dealer in stolen goods we see today.'

'That's why arrest's the only way,' Theo said. 'He won't get bail, not from what I heard – in confidence, of course, from a source I mustn't name. But your daughter will. Then you can take care of both your girls.'

'Yes,' Maggie replied, tears pooling in her eyes. 'Oh, yes. I can take care of them, all the while looking over my shoulder in case the rat gets out of custody. Where can we run when he gets out? And my Sadie might go back on the game whether he's locked up or free.'

'That's another bridge,' Roy Duckworth said. 'Truth is, it's us, his neighbours, who'll be putting an end to his little empire. He won't know that you were in on it. He's dragging our street down. I've lived on Isabel Street since I married Trish, and how long have you been there, Tom?'

'Thirty-two years,' Tom Atherton replied.

'That's right, love,' his wife agreed. 'Knew them all, we did. The Poveys, the Kennedys – they had a lad with a club foot – Dora Entwistle with the dark moustache, the O'Hallorans, the Flynns, the Morrisons, the—'

'Shut up, petal,' her husband begged. 'You're only half-way down one side of the bloody street.'

'You're right, love, but don't swear till we get home.' She continued to knit the cardigan for little Rosie.

Theo squashed a wry smile. Tom and Nancy Atherton were a comedy duo; most statements they made began with 'You're right' or 'She/He's right', and it was clear that Tom cherished her. This was the way it was supposed to be, he told himself. This was happily ever after, something he could never experience.

Tom continued to hold Maggie's hand. 'I'll get the cops, love. I'll fetch them to our house and they can pin their lugs to the wall and listen. It will be nothing to do with you. You can stop upstairs in our house while it's all happening, then you can take Rosie home. He'll not be locking her in the coal shed no more after that.'

'Thanks for keeping an eye on her,' Maggie managed. 'And feeding her, too. I'm that ashamed of our Sadie . . .'

Theo glanced at his watch and jumped up. 'Sorry, folks, it's not that I don't care about Rosie, but Jack and I have to go – he's giving me a hand with something at home. Mrs Stone – Maggie – try to hold yourself together while this terrible business is going on. The rest of you, look after this lady.'

He awarded his full attention to Maggie Stone, bending over to look into her eyes while he spoke. 'There's no other way of handling it, believe me. Any time you feel despair, fear or panic, remember Rosie. She hasn't yet reached the age where she can make her own decisions; all she can do is learn from the pattern of family and school. You know we'll do our best here, but I'm hoping we'll find a way for you to be her family.'

'He's right,' Nancy said, hurriedly finishing her row of stocking stitch.

'We'll meet again on Friday.' Theo grabbed his briefcase. 'And on the following Friday, we carry out the plan. Maggie, I'll be upstairs with you in Tom and Nancy's house on that evening. You aren't alone – just remember that.'

'But—'

'But nothing. I'm not having you listen to all that nasty business by yourself. Friday is the Tunstalls' busy night, so Rosie will be in the shed. You'll need support, Maggie.'

'Thanks, Mr Quinn.'

'Theo. Outside school hours, I'm Theo or Ted. OK?' He gave her a big smile and followed it with a hug. For an unguarded moment, he thought about his own mother, the way she had hugged and treasured her boy until— No, he wouldn't go there.

'Thanks,' Maggie said, the word distorted by tears.

When the Athertons, Maggie and Roy had left, Theo and Jack checked school security. As they walked through the gate, Jack glanced sideways at Theo. 'Are you sure you know what you're doing? She's a beautiful woman, that Miss Bellamy.'

'Not my type.'

The caretaker laughed. 'She's everybody's type. Good-looking, great clothes, posh voice, money, interesting car—'

'A teacher, Jack.'

'So? That shouldn't stop you.'

'Get in the car and shut up. If you're going to carry on like this, I'll help her to move in and you can go home. No suggestive remarks, right? Her sister's coming, too. No personal questions. We just carry her stuff in and leave them to it. Don't let me down, Jack.'

'Would I ever? Have I ever?'

'There's a first time for everything.'

Jack, after muttering darkly about some people not knowing which side their bread was buttered, climbed into the passenger seat and folded his arms like a teenager who'd been told off unfairly.

Theo sat next to him. 'Don't sulk. I get enough of that from the children.'

'You're right,' Jack said, the pitch of his voice lifting in an attempt to imitate Nancy Atherton.

'Shut up and get on with your knitting.'

They arrived back to find furniture vans blocking the driveway. Theo opened the door to the upper flat, allowing men in brown overalls to carry up sofas, armchairs, beds, dining furniture, dressing tables, chests of drawers and boxes of smaller items judged by sales people to be necessary in the setting up of a home.

'You're letting it fully furnished, then?' Jack asked, wondering how on earth a headmaster could afford such an enormous house.

'It seems so. Though it was almost unfurnished, because this lot is three days late.'

'And she's due any minute?'

'They're due. Miss Tia Bellamy and her sister, Miss Delia Bellamy.'

'Two for the price of one?'

'She isn't subletting, Jack. I told her to use it as her home, so if she wants guests, she has guests. You stay here and wait for them – sit on the wooden bench. I'll feed Tyger.'

The cat was weary, as usual. Theo tempted him with tinned salmon, feeling very guilty because of the poverty he had witnessed during childhood, though love for his feline companion overcame the distress. Tyger had been his sole companion for six years, and it looked as if this one close domestic relationship was drawing to a close.

Tyger sniffed the offering and drew back, baring his few teeth as if intending to hiss and spit. This was it, then. This was the end. Mom had always said about cats, 'If they don't drink and don't eat, and if they're old and tired, the kindest thing is a goodbye shot.' Had she meant a bullet or an injection? He stroked the striped fur on his old friend's head, picked him up, looked at the clock and walked outside. 'Jack?'

'Yes?'

'I have to go out.'

'Oh?'

'I'm taking Tyger to the vet. It's just round the corner. If anything can be done for him, I'll get it done. Otherwise, well . . .' He sighed deeply.

'Shall I come with you?'

'No. Wait here for Miss Bellamy. I shouldn't be long.'

Jack waited as instructed. He smoked a couple of cigarettes, plucked a few weeds out of a border, said cheerio to the deliverers of furniture, decided he was bored and went inside. The boss had left the door to his flat unlocked, so Jack made his way to the kitchen and set the kettle to boil. If Mr Quinn's cat was going to die this evening, the poor man would be in need of a cup of tea.

*

'Jack?'

He turned. 'Mr Quinn? You all right, Sir?'

'It's Theo unless we're in harness, Jack. Or Ted, if you prefer.'

'I thought I'd just put the kettle on, Sir – I mean Theo. What happened?'

Theo swallowed. 'I traded Tyger in for a newer model.' Two tears made their way down his cheeks while he held up a tiny box with holes punched in the top. 'This is Tyger-Two. Another stripy one.' He sniffed. 'I kept my hand on Tyger till I was sure he'd gone. Then the vet gave me this little article.' He opened the box. 'He was fished out of the brook with his brothers and sisters. Every one of them was saved. We have a terrific vet. So I seem to have won a bundle of trouble in a cardboard carton.'

Jack peered in. 'It's all mouth,' he said.

Theo gave the kitten the bit of salmon Tyger had refused. 'A lot of growing to do, Tyger. Now I have to train him,' he told the caretaker.

'No, you don't. Dump him where the old cat used to pee, and he'll make his own arrangements. For nights, find an old tray and put sand in it. You just watch – he'll behave exactly the same as the old cat did. He'll sleep where he slept, walk where he walked and eat you out of house and home.'

Theo sat and lifted the kitten out of his box.

'He's handsome,' Jack said.

'A tiger in miniature,' sighed the kitten's new owner.

Jack heard vehicles arriving and, as Theo appeared not to notice, he dashed outside alone. He spoke to Tia when she alighted from her MG. 'Theo – I mean Mr Quinn – is a bit upset because his old cat just died, so he's inside, Miss.'

She brushed past him and walked into her landlord's

living room. 'I am so sorry,' she said. He was using a shirt cuff to mop up the tears. 'I know,' she continued. 'When my pony had to be destroyed, I wanted to sue the vet. This happened just now, did it?'

'Yes, and the vet gave me this ravenous little beastie instead.'

She smiled. 'Dry your eyes on him, Mr Quinn. Let the tears for the old cat be wiped away by the new. Incidentally, that's one gorgeous kitten. There's a man outside, by the way.'

'School caretaker, Jack Peake. He's here to help you get your stuff upstairs, as am I.' He placed the kitten in a basket, followed Tia out and closed the door. No matter what, life moved. Poor old Tyger . . .

Jack was standing at the side of the house, and he was covered in clothes of many colours. 'The trunks are heavy,' he explained to Theo. 'She's brought more frocks than bloody Lewis's, plus about forty pairs of shoes—'

'Shut up,' Delia snapped. 'You've still got the toy department to deal with.' She walked upstairs with a pile of suits and blouses.

'Toy department?' Jack asked.

'Rocking horse, dolls' house, a bear and a rabbit.' Tia's face was serious.

'Ar, ey,' Jack moaned as only a Scouser can. 'Me ma says I haven't to carry nothing heavy on account of me trouble, like.'

Tia folded her arms and tapped a foot. In her best Liverpoolese, she answered him. 'Listen, la'. My ma's bigger'n your ma and she'll give you the rounds of the kitchen if you don't shape. If you want trouble, she'll 'ave you down that back alley with your arse on fire quicker than you can shout for 'elp.'

In spite of his heartbreaking loss, Theo had to turn away in order to prevent his smile becoming laughter. Delia, by no means as pretty as her sister, reappeared and delivered a very damp raspberry in Tia's direction. 'You must have an outfit for every day of the year.'

'Not Good Friday. I stay in bed on Good Friday and wear only black.' She turned to Theo. 'The furniture's lovely, Mr Quinn. Amazingly good taste for an American.'

He smiled at her. 'Me owld feller's an Irish Scouser, Miss.'

'Ah yes, I forgot. You're half and half, aren't you?'

'I am indeed, and I've no idea which half is the more dangerous.'

The banter continued until the van was unloaded. Theo carried the dolls' house while Jack dealt with the antique rocking horse.

'Come into my place,' Theo said to the girls when Jack had left to catch a bus. 'I made a chicken salad and an apple pie. My guess is that you've lived on snacks all day.'

'We have.' Delia eyed her companions as they entered Theo's domain. As well as three adults and one kitten, there was another presence in the room; she could almost taste it. Theo and Tia scarcely looked at each other. Ah. Cupid was here.

They sat at the dining table eating a delicious meal, welcome after many hours on the road. Delia, while appearing to concentrate on filling her stomach, watched her sister closely. Tia glowed. She had a habit of glowing, but on this occasion she was radiant, animated and talkative. Her voice was slightly high-pitched, while the subject matter was deliberately cheerful, designed to deflect attention almost totally from herself, because she was in hiding. She spoke about their journey, the appalling condition of public conveniences, her lovely flat and the dressing room big enough to accommodate her vast collection of garments and accessories. 'I'm a magpie,' she explained. 'I collect things.'

Delia took a chunk of crusty bread and tore into it, smearing a little butter on its soft interior. There were two Tias – or were there three? There was the carefree, runabout child who had dashed about just this morning on the green – was that only this morning? It felt like days ago. The Tia here and now was reacting to a very attractive man, her landlord and her boss. Messy. Elegant Tia emerged when required. Elegant Tia was another coat of armour. So was the child the only real Tia? Was the child going to become mother to Tia? What was the quote? Oh yes, *the child is father of the man.* So was this big sister still adolescent at the age of twenty-six? Or was there yet another side to this clever, complex female?

Then the penny dropped; Tia, like Ma, was a consummate actress. 'Thanks for the lovely meal,' Delia mumbled. 'I'll go and do a bit of tidying. Bring my apple pie up, please, Tia.' She left in a hurry.

Tia found herself relaxing. Delia was an astute, intelligent woman with good instincts, and her presence had inhibited her older sister. Now, Tia could be herself, couldn't she? Looking up, she saw that he was gazing at his new kitten. 'Are you all right?' she asked.

Theo shrugged. 'It's not the worst day in my life, though it comes in at about number four. Tyger was here when I moved in; he refused to leave with his owners when they went. I inherited him. Once again, I seem to have won a cat. That poor scrap was left to drown, so what could I do?'

'He's pretty.'

'They're all pretty till they start eating furniture.'

She laughed.

'My mom usually kept a cat,' he mused, almost to himself.

'Is she still in America?'

He nodded. 'She's buried there, yes. In Georgia.'

'Oh, I'm sorry. I thought you came from New York City.'

'I did.'

'And your father?'

'Remarried. Living in Plainfield, New Jersey, and working in Perth Amboy. When I was old enough, I moved back to New York before coming to England.'

'Ah.' She paused. 'May I help myself to apple pie? I didn't realize how hungry I was till I started to eat.'

'Of course. Cut a slice for your sister.'

Taking this as dismissal, she excavated two portions of pie and placed a blob of whipped cream on top of each. 'May I borrow spoons until I find my own?'

'Please do. Oh.' He gave her his full attention. 'You're going?'

Tia felt heat arriving in her cheeks. 'Er . . . I thought that was what you meant.'

He stood up. 'I imagine you need sleep, Miss Bellamy. It was a long drive. But before you leave, may I ask a small favour?'

She nodded.

'If I give you a key, will you look in on this little chap while I'm at school? He's young, and he'll miss his family.'

She was suddenly sad. 'I'll do that with pleasure, Mr Quinn.'

'Theo out of school.'

'Very well, Theo-out-of-school.'

At last, they looked at each other. She was very pretty, he thought. She was also clever, interesting, witty, funny and kind. And her laugh was cute, like bells tinkling – *oh, stop it, Theo. You know the rules, and you should have waited for a male tenant.*

Tia wasn't aware of having reached any sensible conclusion about Theo Quinn; he confused her, and that fact might prove ... where were her words? Diverting? Alarming? Apple pie. She put his spare key in a pocket, picked up the dishes and waited till he opened the door.

'Good night, Tia,' he said.

She walked up the side of the villa to her own door, which Delia had left on the latch. A great deal of tidying had been achieved. 'Delia?' she called. 'Apple pie for two. Thanks for all you've done.'

'Coming.'

They ate cross-legged on a rug in front of the fireplace.

Delia, always hungry yet permanently thin, finished first. 'That was some dance you two were performing down below,' she said.

Tia swallowed a mouthful of pie. 'Dance? What dance?'

'The Avoidance Tango. So busy not looking at each other, you chattering like a young gibbon, he concentrating on the kitten—'

'He had his cat put down today, Delia. He was crying when we arrived.'

'Oh.' Delia held up her hands in a gesture of defeat. 'OK, don't shoot. He's very attractive, nearly handsome enough to make me change sides. He looks like a gorgeous, sun-kissed Italian or Spaniard. And a man who cries is a man with soul.'

'That's a line from one of Ma's films. Pa was in it, too.' Tia went for a change of subject. 'Do you think the divorce will happen?'

'Abso-bloody-lutely. I've seen the preparatory paperwork, rooted it out of Ma's bureau when she was in the garden with Nanny Reynolds. Pa is photographed with an assortment of young females, and Ma's lawyer has collected signed statements. Oh yes, just you wait for a couple of weeks and it will be in all the gossip columns.'

'I'd better get this place ready if they're coming to stay. Will you help?'

The younger sister yawned. 'Tomorrow. Let's get some sleep.'

Tia climbed over boxes and bags until she managed to reach her bed. Delia, bless her, had made it up with fresh, new sheets, blankets and eiderdown. Nightdress? *Oh, bugger that; I'll sleep in my underwear and clean up my act tomorrow. I should really have a bath, but I'm too . . .*

Her head hit the pillow and she was out like a light within minutes. She dreamed of cats, kittens and Dresden, her long-dead pony.

The luminous hands of her wristwatch announced two o'clock when she woke in an unfamiliar room whose shadows were eliminated by a bright, full and low-hanging moon. Stepping carefully over her possessions, she went to close the curtains, and saw that she had probably been disturbed by more than moonlight. He was digging. A small suitcase lay on the grass behind him; he was burying his beloved cat.

Tears welled in her eyes and spilled slowly down her face. Theo Quinn was a good, kind man. About six feet in height, strong and tanned, he was also decorative, sensitive and capable. Although she couldn't see his face, she knew from the occasional movement of an arm that he was dashing saline from his cheeks, and she wept with him. A coat hung on the back of her door, and she longed to don it, run downstairs and hold his hand, but she wouldn't. This was a private funeral and a private man, and Tia should avoid intrusion.

As she drew her curtains towards the closed position, he turned to pick up the case containing Tyger. Movement in his peripheral vision made him look up, and he froze. Their eyes locked as if drawn together by some weird kind of magnetism. Madam was wiping her face on new curtains, ten shillings a yard plus lining and weights, plus maker's fee. She was dressed in some sort of under-slip with thin straps over her shoulders. And now, she stood as still as stone, watching him watching her.

Come on, Theodore Quinn, pull yourself together. Come on, Tia Bellamy, pull your curtains together. It can't happen, not now, not ever. Romance is for other people, not for you, Theo, because . . . Oh, to hell with the because. He picked up the case and placed Tyger in the grave.

Tia returned to her bed. Delia might be right; perhaps the band was playing, and he and she were blocking out the rhythm. Simon would be here soon, Simon who loved her. Simon, who refused to take no for an answer, was relocating to Liverpool in order to wear her down. She would not be worn down, but he was persistent. His father was Jewish, his mother Christian, and Pa had hit the roof when he'd heard Simon's surname. Pa might have been a great help to Hitler or Mosley, since his atti-tude towards minorities was appalling.

She fell asleep eventually, this time dreaming about a tall, beautiful man standing over her as she reached for an old cat under a table, a striped animal that refused to come to her. The brown-eyed man smiled down at her while she crawled across a rug. 'He's a one-person cat,' he said, his accent slightly American.

'You're a no-person man,' she accused him. 'Why?'

He stared at her. Near-black wavy hair had tumbled onto his forehead. His eyes, usually so warm and friendly, were suddenly free of expression. 'I must give you a copy of the curriculum,' he said. 'And a statement book for each child. That way, we can account for the progress and development of every individual.'

Simon was pulling at her arm. 'Go away,' she ordered.

'Come on, Tia.'

'Go away.'

'Wake up now, or I'll get a cloth and cold water.'

The victim opened one eye. 'Ah, it's you, Delia.'

'Who did you think it was? The Boys' Brigade?'

Tia sat up. 'I was dreaming.'

'Were you, now? About your beautiful landlord?'

'Cats, if you really must know. I have to look after the new Tyger while Theo's out. And I really wanted to observe at the school.'

'Go, then. I'm sure I can kitty-sit.'

Tia yawned. 'What time is it?'

'Almost ten.'

'What? Why didn't you wake me?'

Delia shook a finger under her sister's nose. 'Your royal highness, I am deeply sorry. But one's bath has been run, and if one would kindly amble unaided towards the facilities, one might soak oneself and find clean clothes before one begins to pong.'

'Oh, pong off, Delia. Take the key from my dressing table, go down and make sure the kitten's OK.'

'Yes, ma'am.'

When Delia had left, Tia scraped her abundant hair into an untidy bun on top of her head. After crumbling sweet-smelling bath cubes into the water, she stepped in and allowed her aching body to relax. Delia was right; driving hundreds of miles in an MG was an uncomfortable experience. Should she sell Evangeline and buy something sensible? No. Twenty-six was surely rather young for sensible?

Strangely, Juliet seemed to be the most robust and

pragmatic of the Shakespeare trio. She loved her job, worked hard at it and stayed resolutely in Kent in case Pa needed help once the divorce was over. Perhaps Juliet was a saint in training? Or maybe she was just the one with the most common sense.

Delia talked rationally, yet her commitment to modern music came high on the agenda. She was going to try to buy new drums here, in Liverpool, a city famous for its brilliant music shops. If Scotland Road's instrument emporium was good enough for Americans, it was worth a visit by Delia Bellamy. 'They cross the Atlantic to buy in Liverpool,' she had said. 'So I'll take a look.'

As for herself – Tia knew she was a born actress with absolutely no interest in pursuing that avenue. She liked children, wanted to work with them and to use drama as a tool, a vehicle that could carry pupils through reading, through self-expression and, thereafter, through life. It built character and confidence, attributes so important in areas where poverty and deprivation were apparent. 'I am the light,' she told herself aloud, wondering if that might be blasphemy. Wasn't it from the Bible . . .?

Delia entered the bathroom with a very small cat in her hands. 'This is a good boy. I took him out and he delivered as ordered. Now, are you going to school or not?'

'Not today. I'll organize the dressing room, sort through my books and put up some pictures. Will you buy groceries when you've looked at drums?'

'Of course.' Delia paused. 'Are we feeding the one below?'

'No.'

'Right. I just thought he might like us to return the favour.'

'He isn't driving all the way from Kent. And remember, he's my boss, too. Some distance must be maintained.' As the words fell from her lips, she knew she was lying. She wanted to know him.

'As you wish, ma'am. I'll make a pot of coffee. You get dressed and take over kitty-sitting.'

When Delia had left in the rattling old van, Tia carried Tyger downstairs, fed him and took him outside where once again he performed his duties perfectly. This was a promising kitty. The garden was beautiful; it was apparent that Theodore Quinn took pride in his place of residence. There was a tiny summerhouse, a shed and a greenhouse. This was clearly a tidy, organized man.

She carried Tyger over every inch of his immediate territory, talking all the while about the apple trees, the hedges, the thorns on the rose bushes and how to avoid drowning in the pond. 'This is a magnolia,' she told him. 'Your master does well to establish one of these so far north. It may not flower every year, but you must respect it. You are one fortunate feline to be taken in by someone like Theo.'

Clearly unimpressed, the kitten yawned.

In the front garden, she stood by the new grave. 'The other Tyger,' she said. 'We don't even know how old he was, because he belonged to the house, you see. Now, you've been chosen by a very special man, so look after him. I think he gets a bit sad.'

'Do I?'

She swallowed hard. *He's behind me. This is like bloody pantomime, but without the audience to warn me. I never heard his car arriving because I was at the back of the house. I'm blushing again. This is beyond embarrassing.*

Tia turned and there he stood. He had been listening; how much had he heard? 'Sorry,' was all she managed at first. She drew herself up to her full five feet and nine inches. 'I was showing him his territory.'

He nodded. 'Yes, I watched you from my kitchen window.'

She thrust the kitten at him. 'He did his duties for Delia, then for me. He's had two tiny meals, and he likes Charlie, my blue rabbit. Perhaps I'll buy him a soft toy.'

'That would be appreciated, Tia.'

Was he laughing at her? 'Are you laughing at me?'

He nodded. 'You remind me of me. I've talked to animals all my life, and it's good to know I'm not the only idiot on the planet. Will you come in for a sandwich? I seldom make it home for lunch, but I wanted to see Tyger-Two. Thanks for taking care of him.'

This is not going to be as easy as it might have been, Portia Bellamy. He's stunning; you'd better start looking for somewhere else to live. What's the point, though? You'll be working with him. Stop staring, for goodness' sake!

'Tia? A sandwich?'

'Er . . . no, thank you. Delia will be back shortly with her drums.'

Theo raised an eyebrow. 'Drums?'

'She won't practise here. I shall make sure of that.'

'Pity. I play a few chords on the guitar, so she might like to try the drums out in my flat. This evening, perhaps? The house is detached, so we'll disturb nobody.'

'I'll ask her.'

'Do that. Come with her if you think you can tolerate the noise.'

She hesitated, opened her mouth, closed it again.

'Well, Miss Bellamy?'

'I have a great deal to do,' she said after the long pause. But might Delia speak out of turn to him? 'I'll come down tonight if she gets some drums. She's very particular. Oh, and skiffle is somewhat noisy.'

Theo nodded. 'Right. I'll raid the wine cellar.'

'You have a wine cellar?'

'Of course, and it's well stocked. It's called Warburton's. It's on the main road, wedged between fish and chips on one side, haberdashery on the other.'

If he pulls my leg any harder, it will drop off. You like a man with a sense of fun, Tia Bellamy. You like a man with good musculature, generous lips, square jaw, dark hair, warm chocolate eyes . . . Stop this now, you damned foolish woman.

Delia broke the strange and uncomfortable spell by rattling onto the driveway and up the side of the house with her group's disreputable and noisy vehicle. She alighted and ran round to the front garden. 'Got some,' she said triumphantly. 'Scotland Road was brilliant once I broke through the language barrier. Hi, Theo.'

He grinned at Delia. With her face illuminated by excitement, she was almost pretty. 'Bring them into my place,' he said. 'You don't want them stolen from the van.' He turned to Tia. *God, why do you have to be so bloody perfect?* 'I'll see you both at about seven this evening. Delia, I play the guitar, so we'll have a session.'

'Great. Give me a hand, please.'

Once more, Tia was in charge of Tyger while the drums were carried into the ground-floor flat. *We are the three Ts. Theo, Tia and Tyger. I should have taken the post in St Helens. I should have found a different flat. No, I like this one. And he fascinates me, but I'll get used to it because I must. Simon will be my shield – is that cruel?*

Theo reclaimed his kitten. 'Thanks, Tia. Miss Ellis says if you want to come in for a couple of hours tomorrow, she'll show you the ropes. Not that we make a habit of hanging our kids, but punishment is sometimes necessary, and you need to learn how to tie the knots.'

Tia found herself grinning. 'So that's where you get your body parts?'

'Young meat is tender. And I also use hospital morgues, because sometimes I need bigger bits. They require simmering for several hours.'

She nodded thoughtfully. 'That chicken salad you gave us – was it really chicken?'

'Oh, Miss Bellamy, I never answer such questions. You enjoyed the food, yes?'

'Yes.'

'I made the pie with apples from my own trees.'

'It was good.'

'Thank you. See you later, then.' He took Tyger from her and walked away.

Determinedly, Tia climbed the stairs, found nails and hammer and began arranging pictures on her walls. Life wasn't all about pretty kitties and handsome landlords. She sorted through books, dusted their covers and arranged them on shelves at each side of the fireplace in her sitting room before repositioning furniture to suit her own idea of comfort and order. The dining room was easy – one table, four dining chairs, two carvers and a sideboard. She sorted out the kitchen and found that Theo had thought of everything from a fish kettle to cruets. He was rich, far too wealthy for a headmaster of an infant and junior school. She found decent cutlery, moderately expensive dinner and tea sets, good table linen, substantial pots and pans.

Delia dashed in. 'He's going to phone people from his office – trying to get messages to skifflers.'

'Is he, now?'

'Two Johns, a Benny and a Steve. And a few more, including a chap called Corkscrew. He can bite the tops off beer and wine bottles, apparently, though he has lost teeth when opening champagne.' She sidled up to her older sister. 'I told Theo you can sing.'

Tia was unpacking a heavy-bottomed frying pan while Delia delivered that sentence. 'And?'

'And that you know Lonnie Donegan's work.'

'No, you didn't.'

'Yes, I did.'

Tia raised the weighty pan. *This is like pantomime again, no you didn't, yes I did* . . . 'Have you any idea of the damage I might inflict on you with this cast-iron pan?'

Delia shrugged. 'Do your worst, then. I'm prepared to die for my art.'

'Art? Two washboards, a tea chest, a set of false teeth and a whistle?'

'Listen, your royal bloody highness, we take everyday things and make them musical. We even twang one of Ma's garters – we call it the B-E-S-O – the Bellamy Elasto-phonic String Orchestra. We had it fine-tuned especially. With the right tension in a cool room, we can hit top C.'

Tia sank onto a stool and began to laugh. Having a mad sister could be trying, but it was also fun. 'OK, OK, I give up.' She was going to be embarrassed; singing in the presence of her boss with a skiffle band whose members she had never met wouldn't be easy. She knew Delia, of course. And him. Him. *He won't mind if I mess it up; he likes me, I know he likes me.*

After all her labours, Tia took a second bath. She washed her sun-streaked hair, dried it, brushed it and left it hanging like a shining waterfall almost to her waist. Right – clothes. She found three-quarter-length blue jeans with striped turn-ups that hugged her shins, some white socks, blue canvas shoes and a crisp, sleeveless, blue-and-white striped blouse. Skiffle was casual, so she would be casual.

*

At seven o'clock, she was applying makeup so skilfully that it appeared not to be there at all. Delia had already gone downstairs after washing dishes used during their evening meal. People were arriving; Tia heard them talking and laughing as they carried their instruments into the ground-floor flat.

She descended the stairs, locked her outer door and walked down the side of the house. Nervousness was new to her. She knew about stage fright; it was an essential part of theatre. Anyone who felt nothing before stepping onto a lighted stage was not an actor, but this was different. A practice with Delia's band was fun, no more and no less, so why did she feel so edgy? *Because, Portia, you've been window-shopping, and he may not be for sale. Yes, he's easy on the eye, but you don't know him, and he's too old for you. Go inside and get this over with.*

Furniture had been pushed against the walls. Delia was keeping company with her new drums, while Theo tuned his guitar. He stopped to introduce Tia to the rest. There were the two Johns, one with washboard and metal thimbles, the other carrying a banjo. Corkscrew sat with an autoharp on his knee; he was clearly going to hold it like a zither, as this position probably made it easier for him to disable strings he wasn't using. A Pete had a twelve-string guitar, while a Steve with severe acne held a kazoo in his right hand. Everyone seemed friendly.

'Here's our singer,' Theo announced. 'It seems I've been demoted.'

'You sing if you want to,' she said. 'I'm quite happy to listen.'

Banjo John thrust a microphone at Tia. 'Stand near him,' he said, pointing to Theo. 'Then you can both sing.'

Washboard John joined Delia and discussed rhythm, then all the musicians played through 'Puttin' on the Style'. They worked at it until some semblance of cohesion was achieved, after which miracle Tia began to sing. She had a voice that covered two octaves, and while the upper eight were delivered clear, the lower end of her range was husky. After the first verse, her companion sang with her, and she descanted over him in parts. She began to suspect that she was actually enjoying herself.

A Benny arrived with his tea chest bass. He complained loudly about having been refused access to two buses because of his instrument. The Lonnie Donegan song died while Benny waxed Scouse-lyrical about the state of the bloody country and bloody bus conductors who thought they had God-given power over travellers. 'It's only a sodding box,' was his final stab at Liverpool's transport personnel. 'You'd have thought it was a bomb.'

Theo turned down the amp. 'Hi, Benny. This is Tia, and her sister on drums is Delia. They've escaped from Kent.'

Tia giggled. Theo was joking, yet he had hit the nail so hard on its head that it was buried in a wall.

'Well done,' Benny grumbled. 'Just don't take anything bigger than a matchbox on a Liverpool Corporation bus.' After delivering this piece of advice, he surveyed the company. 'What a motley crew,' he pronounced. 'We've got a third of the Travelling Turnarounds, half of the Skiffling Skittlers, Quintessential Quinn, two birds from Kent and a Quarryman. Who let you in, Lennon?'

'Nobody,' answered Banjo John. 'I just materialized.'

When Benny had settled down next to Delia, the band made its less-than-perfect way through 'Rock Island Line', 'Lost John', 'Diggin' My Potatoes' and 'Gamblin' Man'. By the end of the set, they were beginning to sound something like a band.

They had a beer-and-crisp break during which Theo had the opportunity to study covertly his tenant/probationary teacher. He wondered whether her hair felt as silken as it looked, noticed that her eyes were less violet and nearer to blue, as if they reflected the colour she had chosen to wear. She was stunning, perfect figure, beautiful face – and she could sing. *Theo, you have dug a hole where your heart used to be, but are the sutures refusing to hold?*

Just once, she turned away from Banjo John and looked at Theo, their gazes locking across the room. He smiled at her; she raised her beer bottle at him. Corkscrew, now trained not to bite through bottles when ladies were present, also had his eyes pinned to her. She was used to this, was becoming inured to it, though Theo was . . . different, noticeable, sad even now. *Be brave, Tia. Go and talk to him.*

She followed her own orders. 'This is fun,' she told him. 'He plays the banjo and the guitar.' She waved her free hand at Banjo John. 'Such a talented man.'

'And you're a good singer.'

She smiled. 'We sing well together, don't we?'

'We certainly do.'

Tia studied a map of old Liverpool on the wall behind his head.

'Yes,' she murmured, feeling that they were talking about something else altogether. Changing the subject, she asked about the various bands represented here.

'Liverpool's full of them,' he told her. 'We move about sometimes to practise or just for fun, but a couple of the groups are established and doing well. I play and sing for charities, but it's not my life.'

'Teaching's your life, then?'

'For the most part, though I do have an extra string to my guitar.'

Tia grinned. 'Body parts? The locked room?'

'Precisely.' He clapped his hands. 'Right, boys and girls. Let's have another go at murdering "Rock Island Line".'

Four

He was Uncle Miles. Uncle Miles was always nice to me till he stopped being Uncle Miles and started being Daddy. If I forget to call him Daddy, he gets mad. I am getting adopted by him, so he's my pretend daddy. I never had a real one.

We used to live somewhere called Everton, not far from here, and we moved to the Lady Streets when Mammy married him. The rent's cheaper here. I have learned the Lady Streets cos I am clever. Nana told me I am a clever girl, cos I could read before I was three and I am five now, nearly ready for school.

The Lady Streets are Elizabeth (like the queen), Muriel, Myrtle, Barbara, Isabel, Clementine, Annabel and Jessica. I live on Isabel Street; we came here a few weeks ago when I started being five. Mammy made me a big birthday cake, chocolate with five candles. He got me a scooter, but I can't play out on it yet till the heat dies down. Even after teatime when the sun isn't hot, I have to wait till the heat dies down.

We live in the end house. Mr and Mrs Atherton live next door to us. They are kind and nice and old and Mrs Atherton is making me a green cardigan for when I start school in September. She says bottle green is a bugger on her eyes, but she never shouts. Sometimes, they give me food. Mammy forgets to make dinners because of gin. He hits her. He hits me. I know somebody hits him, cos he comes home battered and bleeding and drunk. I try hard not to be frightened, but I am by my own self in the coal shed so much, and it's scary and dark. The coal is in there. Some of the coal is sharp and it cuts me and the black dust goes in the cuts. He just tells me to be more careful, but he hurts me worser than what the coal does.

The jumping up and down started after we came to this house. Auntie Flo, who's not my real auntie, is upstairs and Mammy is in the front room downstairs. They lie down and men jump up and down on top of them. That's when I go in the coal shed. The coal shed gets black in the night. It has no windows. Sometimes, things run about in there, mice or rats.

Nana lives in Clementine Street and I have to stay away from her. Nana is Margaret Rose, shortened to Maggie. She leaves secret Nana parcels with Mr and Mrs Atherton. The parcels have pasties in them or pies and cakes and biscuits. Mrs Atherton makes me fried egg butties or toast and jam. Once she made me a smiley bun with a happy face on top. She did the happy face with icing. Mr Atherton leaves the food tin under a piece of black cloth in the coal shed.

My name is Rosemary Tunstall. It was changed from Rosemary Stone.

He hits me mostly where it doesn't show like the tops of my legs. When he's drunk some beer, he misses and it does show. My writing arm is nearly better now, but my chest is still sore from kicking. He has big feet and I am a small person. If Mammy isn't drinking gin, she tries to stop him and he hits her. She can't have the jumping up and down men when he hits her, so Miles gets very mad cos the jumping up and down men give him money.

I have been to school for a visiting day. The headmaster is Mr Quinn and he wears a black cloak like a witch, but he is nice. Miss Ellis is nice, too. She is retiring. Retiring means going home and staying at home, so there will be a new teacher. Mr Quinn looked at my bruises and cuts and he made Miss Ellis look as well. She blinked a lot, like me when I am trying not to cry. I told them I fell downstairs. That's what I have to say when I get asked.

The Lady Streets are near town. I like town. There is a library and a museum and a place with paintings in it. Looking at the paintings makes me happy or sad or just peaceful. Town has shops. There is a lovely kind man with no legs who is my friend. He sits on a low trolley with wheels on and moves about by using his hands on the floor. On his hands he wears thick gloves. He has to do that or else his knuckles would bleed. People call him Harry the Scoot and they like him.

I asked what happened to his legs and he said the Krauts got them. I looked under my bed for Krauts who steal legs, but Harry meant Germans.

One day, Harry asked me to sing. I am a good singer. I did 'White Cliffs of Dover' and 'Long Way to Tipperary' while Harry played his mouth organ. We got loads of pennies and even some threepenny bits and a sixpence. He made me divide the money into two parts, both the same, and he called me a special girl. We had chips and one fish between us, no peas cos we ate with our fingers. He takes his gloves off to eat. Harry keeps my money in a Rosie box at his home. I am saving up. Harry is my best friend in all the world.

We have fun. He sits me on his legs; his legs go nearly to his knees, then they stop. He showed me how to cross roads, look right, look left, look right again and never stop listening. I am as light as a feather, so he can give me rides. We went to the Pier Head where Liverpool ends and the water begins. We went to his house which is all downstairs. Martha is his sister, and she looks after him. She has ordinary legs. She showed me the Rosie box with my money in it and she made me jam butties and a cup of tea. Martha *is my second best friend in the whole world. She is teaching me money sums. Twenty pence is one and eight, thirty pence is two and six, forty pence is three and four, fifty pence is four and two, sixty pence is five shillings.*

Harry is teaching me tables. Not tables with chairs; these are times tables. He says I have to have a head start and stay in front of everybody else cos I am disadvantaged. That's a big word. He must have learned it in the first war before the Germans blew his legs to kingdom come. I asked where kingdom come was and he said only God knows, because Germans know nothing about anything, and the armed forces is full of stuffed shirts. Harry says some funny things, but he is kind.

I am sitting on the lav at the bottom of the yard thinking. This is where I come when they wake up. It is nearly dinner time when they wake up. I have to be at school before nine o'clock, so I will have to get myself out of bed. Sometimes, I sleep late cos of being in the coal shed till nearly morning. I will be late for school. Colin Duckworth says you get . . . it sounds like attention if you are late more than once—

'Where the bleeding hell are you?'

She froze. Although the day was warm, her bones were suddenly chilled, and she began to shiver on the inside. There was no escape. The only door led into the yard, where he was waiting. Did he have the strap? Was he wearing his big, heavy boots? 'I'm on the lav,' she managed to shout in a shaky voice.

'You're wanted. Your mam needs cigs, and I want baccy and papers.'

'Coming,' she replied, her voice steadying. She didn't mind shopping. Shopping got her away from him for a while.

When she emerged the yard was empty. The scullery was empty, too. After washing her hands at the slopstone and drying them on her skirt, which was cleaner than the stiff, grey towel hanging on the back door, Rosie entered the kitchen. Nothing in the house was clean; it was all brown and messy and it smelled bad like rotted food and dirty rugs.

He was in the kitchen. He was spitting into the grate again.

'Money's on the table,' he snapped. 'You want twenty ciggies, my Virginia and a packet of papers. Get yourself some chips with the change. If there's a queue at the chippy, come back here first.'

'Thank you, Unc— Daddy.' She snatched up the coins and ran.

Outside, Mrs Atherton was wiping her window ledge. 'All right, Rosie?'

'I have to be quick, Mrs Atherton.'

'I see. Run out of smokes, have they?'

Rosie nodded, turned the corner, and ran full tilt into her grandmother. 'Nana,' she breathed. They were standing next to Rosie's back yard, and he could well be listening. Maggie changed direction and followed in Rosie's footsteps. When they were on safer territory, Maggie spoke. 'I've got you socks, shoes, knickers, two blouses and a gymslip. Nancy's making you two cardies, one green, one navy. Dash round to mine every morning and I'll get you ready. After school, come to my house again and change back into your rubbish. If I'm at work, I'll leave the key in the usual place.'

'Thanks, Nana. I have to be quick.' She ran to the corner shop, her steps hastened by fear.

Maggie Stone stood and watched the child who had to be quick, quick with the shopping, quick to get out of the way of visiting men, quick to avoid a kick from her mother's pimp. Poor little thing. No one was sure who her real father was. There was a possibility that even Sadie

79

didn't know who had fathered her daughter, because Sadie had been wild since leaving school. Maggie had a vague idea, but she kept speculation to herself.

Rosie dashed out of the shop, not stopping to look whether there was a queue in the chippy. If Miles had no ciggies, the whole world might hear the fallout. She waved quickly at Nana before dashing homeward; the faster she was, the better his mood would be.

But as she walked through the back yard, she heard an unfamiliar voice through the opened sash window. It was a bit posh, and it was female. Oh, no; he didn't like visitors unless they were jumping up and down men. With her heart in her mouth, she entered the scullery.

The woman was talking. 'So we from the welfare department are visiting the families of all reception class children due to start school in September.'

'Oh yeah?' Miles drawled. 'Are you visiting all them up Woolton, then?'

The woman cleared her throat. 'That's someone else's concern, not mine. We are concentrating on families living in poorer areas. Rosie may qualify for a free school meal or a clothing allowance.'

'We don't want nothing off you. We don't want your bloody charity.'

Rosie crept into the kitchen and placed on the table a brown paper bag containing Mammy's cigarettes and her stepfather's requirements.

'Thanks, love,' he said. 'Any change?'

Rosie nodded.

'Keep it. Go and buy yourself something, eh?' He smiled, displaying teeth of a muddy grey colour with several gaps. His lower jaw resembled unsteady gravestones in a long-neglected cemetery. He was getting fatter and uglier by the day, it seemed.

'Hello, Rosie. I'm Miss Garner. You'll be starting at Myrtle Street, then?'

The child nodded again.

'You're a quiet little girl.'

Rosie shifted her weight from foot to foot.

'Are you looking forward to school?' Miss Garner asked.

Miles Tunstall emitted a grim-sounding laugh. 'She's as old as the hills, aren't you, babe? She can read the *Echo*, count money, write her name, sing, paint pictures and do a bit of tap dancing. Not all at the same time, like.'

'Very clever, then? I'm sure you are, by the way.'

Miles waded in again. 'Thirty pence, Rosie?'

'Two and six.'

'Forty pence?'

'Three and four.'

'See?' he said. 'School's about education, not fancy frocks and free dinners. She's a good head on her shoulders. Off you go, Rosie, while the weather's nice.'

When the child had fled, Emily Garner studied the man of the house. He was unkempt, possibly hung over, probably out of work. The report she had received from an anonymous source via a clergyman was shut away in her office. Theo Quinn, headmaster of Myrtle Street, had begged Emily not to interfere at this point, but she had failed to understand why.

'We've had a report, Mr Tunstall. It implies that this house is sometimes rowdy at night. If the house is rowdy, Rosie will not get enough sleep for a youngster of her age.'

'She could sleep through a world war,' he replied smartly. 'Yes, we have parties, play cards and dominoes, drink some beer.'

There was something completely unsavoury about this man. Emily Garner gathered thoughts and briefcase,

81

picking herself up off the chair, to which her skirt had stuck in parts. The house seemed to wear a layer of grease on all surfaces. A further covering of dust decorated the base coat, and the room stank of historically aged dirty washing, rancid fat and tobacco. No child should be forced to live in such conditions, though she knew of happy children who came from homes similar to this one. Cleanliness was not next to godliness; a child needed love more than he or she needed a palace to live in.

So the extra factor here was likely to be a neglectful mother, plus a stepfather who thought giving change to a little girl while a welfare worker was present might be enough to provide him with a halo. 'Where's Mrs Tunstall?' she asked as she reached the doorway.

'In bed. A bit of a stomach upset,' he answered.

'I'll come back next week,' was her parting shot before she stepped outside to breathe in sweeter, cleaner air. Things in Rosie Tunstall's house were not right.

As she strode past the rest of the Lady Streets, she noticed a tall, bearded man standing at the bottom of Myrtle. He leaned casually against a wall, reading a newspaper. Emily Garner turned and walked towards the school while the man made his way down Ivy Lane, the road onto which all local terraces led. He walked past the end of Isabel Street just as Emily went through the school gate on Myrtle Street. She marched up to the head teacher's office and rapped on the door.

Theo welcomed his visitor. 'Hello, Emily.'

She sat down opposite him. 'It's a pigsty,' she informed him. 'Now, I know children who live in similar circumstances, but there's something else there. The stepfather reminded me of a snake, though I'm sure that's an insult to the reptile population. Mother was absent, supposedly in bed with a stomach problem. There's fear in Rosie's eyes, in her stance. She has bruised arms—'

82

'I know. May I ask who told you about Rosie?'

'A vicar. He can't disclose his source, but it must be someone who lives near enough to hear and see things.'

He studied her closely. 'Can you leave it alone for a few days? There's a plot on. We have neighbours onside, and Tunstall won't be granted bail.'

'You're getting him arrested?'

He nodded just once.

'For what?'

He tapped the side of his nose. 'If I told you, you'd mess it up. We want him red-handed, you see. Please, please trust me, and trust the good people of Isabel Street. He's a repeat offender, and we're praying that he'll be passed on to Crown Court this time. I'm begging you, Emily.' He delivered one of his most delicious smiles, broadening it when she shifted in the chair. Some women were easily distracted, and he was more than willing to take advantage of weaknesses when necessary.

'All right,' she said. 'How long do you need?'

'Until Friday night next week. Oh, you must come to our staff end-of-year party in a couple of weeks. We're having a quiz and a buffet.'

'How can I possibly resist?' she asked sweetly.

'And I promise we'll deal with Tunstall. Well, the police will.'

She stared hard at him. 'Is the mother fit to look after Rosie?'

'I don't know.' Sometimes, truth was best. 'But the maternal grandmother's nearby, and she's an excellent woman.'

Emily stood up. 'I'll hold back my report until you've had your pound of flesh, Shylock.' She glanced at her watch. 'Must dash and check in at the office, or they'll think I've emigrated.' She rose to her feet. 'Oh, and good luck.'

He stood and shook her hand. 'See you soon, Emily.'

When she had left, he sank back into his chair. 'The battle of Little Big Horn had to be easy compared to my job. I'll go and see Tia.'

He was thrilled with her. Miss Ellis was thrilled, too. Tia Bellamy wore bright, colourful clothes at school. It was all part of her plan to stimulate children. She was unconventional, imaginative and completely unafraid. Three times, she had come in; three times, the class of five- and six-year-olds had learned through drama, poetry, well-chosen prose and fun.

For a couple of minutes, he watched through a glass panel in the door.

The children pretended to be asleep while she sang to them.

Theo entered quietly and sat at the back. Part of his brief was to observe and comment on probationers, and he felt he might have been happy watching this one five days a week, full time. She reached the end of a song about Christopher Robin saying his prayers.

'The older boy,' she pretended to chide. 'We are asleep. You, too, must sleep.'

He folded his arms and leaned back, his head against the wall. The children started to giggle when he began to make exaggerated snoring and whistling sounds.

Tia tutted. 'You – yes, the big boy at the back – go at once to the headmaster's office. Go now, immediately, no dallying. He will deal with you sternly, because he's not a man we want to cross.'

He slunk out of the room with his head hanging low.

The children erupted.

Tia put a finger to her lips and the class quietened almost immediately. 'Shall we follow him?' she whispered.

'We can see whether he did as he was told. If he didn't, we must keep him in detention.'

She crept along the corridor with just under forty of Miss Ellis's children following behind her. Quietly, she opened his door to find him sitting quietly at his desk. 'Good boy,' she said before closing the door. She knew that he would be in no way diminished by the prank. He loved his children, and they loved him.

'Creep back,' she told the children. 'He's in detention.'
A little boy put up his hand. 'Miss?' he whispered.
'Yes?'
'Who's in charge of him?'
'He is. Silly, isn't it?'
She led Miss Ellis's class back to their room. He thought he was in charge. But was he? Since the skiffle night, a thaw had set in; they had even shared a fish supper last evening. Smiling a secret smile, she settled the reception class at their base where, in a near-perfect West Country accent, she delivered the words of Worzel Gummidge and Earthy Mangold. Thank goodness for Barbara Euphan Todd. Humorous books for children were few and far between. Perhaps she might write some.

Sir, in solitary detention, knew that Tia Bellamy would rise to the top of the tree within a very few years. She had instinct, performing skills, organization and dedication to her work. Maybe the latter characteristic would keep her at the coal face, but he knew that she was already capable of running a school. 'Our Roedean girl,' he whispered, a smile broadening his lips. 'Precious metal.'

Delia had left for London, where she and the band did the rounds of pubs and clubs. He missed her. Delia was one of the boys, a good drummer, an excellent woman who probably preferred partners of her own gender. 'Wish I did,' he mumbled. These days, he lived half in heaven, half in a warmer place where Lucifer ruled. 'Oh, Mom,' he groaned. No, he wouldn't think about . . .

Heaven was wherever Tia was. This had never happened to him before. Yes, there had been a few women, but none like this one. Thus far, relationships had been careful, had involved ruinous, clumsy contraception and fear. 'I am stupid,' he whispered. She wasn't even a probationary teacher yet – she was a mere volunteer, yet he was drawn to her like a suicidal moth to a lighted candle. It had been too quick, too fierce, and he knew that she was attracted to him, too. Delia had made a few remarks when her pretty sister had been out of earshot . . .

'Oh hell,' he said to the empty room. 'Why did she have to be so—'

Without knocking, she opened his door and insinuated her beautiful face. 'Am I in trouble, Sir?'

'Aren't you always?'

She came in. 'Sometimes I'm "when she was bad, she was horrid".'

'Close the door and sit here where I can keep an eye on you.'

She sat, wishing that he would keep more than an eye on her . . . No, no, she was becoming vulgar. 'Sir?'

'Teddy will do.' She had changed from Theo to Teddy after making a gift to Tyger of a little brown bear. 'You are brilliant with the children,' he told her. 'Miss Ellis says you have the gift of tongues, though not in the biblical sense.'

She shrugged. 'Nobody's perfect.'

'The . . . er . . . the young man who calls on you at the flat – he's Simon, I take it?'

She puffed up her cheeks and blew out the air. 'I told him again and again not to come to Liverpool, but he seems not to understand negatives like "No, I don't want to marry you". He thinks it's because Pa's prejudiced against Jews, yet he knows I ceased to obey my father years ago. The best way to get me to do something is to tell me that Pa wouldn't like it.'

Your father certainly wouldn't like me if he looked into my provenance, then. 'You're the best teacher I've had here.' *And the best woman I never had, can't have, mustn't have.* 'Will you be coming to the end-of-year party?'

'I'd love to.'

'Adults only.'

Tia frowned. 'So you won't let me in?'

He shrugged. 'I'm open to bribery.'

'OK, I'll raid my bank account.'

He made a conscious effort to sound disinterested. 'Will you bring Simon? We're all allowed a friend or a partner.'

'No. Are you coming with someone?'

Once again, he raised his shoulders for a moment. 'Let's bring each other, shall we? That will stop us ruining the evening for two innocent people.'

Her smile arrived immediately. 'So I'm dating my boss and my landlord?'

'Just a school function, Tia. And will you sing with me if I bring my guitar?'

She inhaled sharply. The school function bit had withered her hopes slightly, but the request, arriving on the back of his earlier words, moved her towards positive thought.

'Well?' he asked. 'Sing with me, please.'

She had the distinct feeling that he was alluding to much more than a vocal duet. He was nervous. 'Of course I will. Skiffle?'

'Skiffle.'

At last, he dragged his eyes away from her, opened a drawer and pulled out a large, buff-coloured, cardboard envelope. 'I like your breakdown of the maths system.

These cards you made are great for beginners, less threatening, one task only. You will upgrade them for brighter kids as and when necessary?'

'Of course. Coming to school for the first time can be painful, almost like being born again. Nine months in permanent darkness, then pain and light and Mother. We love our mothers unconditionally, relax, settle into a routine, have fun, receive and give love for five years. Then society drags us away and shepherds us like a flock into a place with more than thirty other lost lambs.'

'And the answer is?'

'Fun and tasks we stand a chance of mastering. Praise, patience, positivity.'

'Three Ps?'

'Another thing about pee. I won't waste my time or theirs on requests for lavatory time. They just go. We'll have two days with an empty classroom and all the kids will be in the toilets, as they term those places. But they'll get bored and come back, because my classroom will be an interesting place.' She pondered for a moment. 'Miss Ellis is a remarkable woman; it's a pity that she has to retire.'

Theo nodded. 'Another birth pain, then?'

'Indeed. More hurt. Will she be lonely?'

'No. She took in a widowed sister and her two daughters, so she has grown-up nieces who have children. She also shares her home with several cats and a parrot that has to be covered when the vicar calls. Miss Ellis's fiancé was killed in World War One. The cussing parrot was his.'

'Shame,' Tia said. 'She would have made a lovely wife and mother.'

So will you, Portia. God, this is so difficult. I want to see you all the time, wake with you, spend my life with you; I also want to send you away because . . . No dark thoughts, Theo. 'Are you going home now?'

'Shortly,' she replied. 'I'll look in on Tyger.'

'Thank you.'

He was wearing his *Closed For Business* expression again. Not for the first time, she sensed his powerful inner conflict. Teddy Quinn had a past, but he refused to discuss it. Perhaps if she were to tell him about her own trials and triumphs he might open up? 'Are you still in detention?' she asked.

'Definitely,' he answered. 'I'm doing one hundred lines – I must not snore in class.' He stared hard at her. 'I believe you've travelled all the way from Kent to alter all of us, Miss Bellamy.'

'I shall leave my mark on the children, yes, but you'll get no body parts out of me, Mr Cannibal.'

'Spoilsport.'

'Oh, I'm going home. I'll water the garden, the bits with no sun on them.'

'Again, thank you.'

And at this point, all hell broke loose.

Jack Peake crashed into the room, a hand pressed against his chest. 'I went . . . I was just going to see . . . oh, God.'

Tia jumped up. 'Sit here. Please don't do anything untidy like having a heart attack. Sit, Jack.'

He sat. Tia took a bottle from the caretaker's overall pocket. 'Two drops?'

Jack nodded.

'Tongue up,' she ordered before administering his medication.

Theo's jaw dropped. 'I wouldn't have had you heaving all that heavy stuff upstairs to the flat if I'd known you were ill.'

Tia glared at her boss. 'It's a bit of angina, and he's fine. This is his way, Teddy, his life. Don't penalize him

89

because he's made a choice. We know nothing about any of this, so we say nothing. Please!'

Jack's breathing steadied. 'Let me die my way, Theo. If I lose the job, I'll be dead in a week, anyway.'

'And don't blame him for telling me,' Tia snapped. 'I found out when he was helping me move in, and I promised to say nothing.'

Theo shook his head. 'I have a duty, Tia.'

'This man is loved here, and he loves the school. Let's find out what's happened, anyway.' She gave her attention to her patient. 'Two drops enough, Jack?'

He nodded. 'I'll be right in a minute, queen.'

'Good. When you're ready, tell Mr Quinn what's going on. Would you like me to leave?'

'No.' Jack grabbed her hand. 'Tia, Theo, they've just found Miles Tunstall's body on Ropers Park off Ivy Lane. Looks like he's been strangled. Neck's broke, and he has bleeding in his eyes or something.'

'Petechial bleeds,' Tia murmured. 'Capillaries in the eye burst during strangulation or suffocation. My sister Juliet had to learn that stuff.'

'Who the hell did it?' Theo asked. 'And where's the child?'

Jack shrugged before emitting a shuddering breath. 'Tom Atherton took her to her grandma's. He called here on his way back and told me. Tunstall was seen walking along the lane with a very tall, well-built man with a black beard and a rolled newspaper under his arm. They were chatting.'

'And Mrs Tunstall?' Theo asked.

'In bed, drunk as a rabid skunk, never heard a thing.'

Theo picked up the phone and got through to Welfare. 'Emily Garner, please.' He waited, fingers tapping on the surface of his desk. 'Emily? Theo Quinn here. You visited the Tunstalls today. Yes, yes. No, it's not about that. No, it won't be happening, because Miles Tunstall's dead. Dead, that *is* what I said!' He paused and put his spare hand over the mouthpiece. 'Tia, make Jack some hot tea, milk and sugar the way you heathen English take it.'

Tia left the two men and went to the staffroom. Life in Liverpool was certainly exciting and not always in a good way.

'Have you calmed down?' Theo said into the phone. 'Just listen, please, Emily. Did you notice a tall man, black beard, with a newspaper under his arm?' He paused. 'I see. He was reading the paper. Was he on Ivy Lane? Right. Would you know him again? OK. Get to the police station and tell them what you saw. Thank you.' He replaced the receiver. 'Who witnessed the two men together, Jack?'

'Nancy or Tom Atherton, not sure which. We don't need to get the house raided now, do we?'

'Small consolation. Who the hell killed him, Jack?'

'Not me. My legs are hardly strong enough for dominoes today, never mind murder.'

'You know we should tell the authority about your angina, don't you?'

'Yes. Oh, do what you have to do. I'll get an allotment and die in the potting shed like all the other owld codgers.'

Theo shook his head. 'We'll think about that later. Right now, we have a dead man whose house was going to be raided by cops in a few days. I've already told the police of the plan, and they were happy to cooperate. Did he have enemies?'

Jack snorted. 'He got battered regular in the Scotland Road pubs. There was Flo's brother for a start.'

'Flo?'

'Sadie had her meetings downstairs, and Flo had hers in the room above. Tunstall paid them both pennies and pocketed most of their earnings himself. And he battered that kiddy. So it could have been Flo's brother or his mates, or it might have been somebody sticking up for Rosie. Nobody liked Miles Tunstall.' He shook his head slowly. 'But I don't know any big men with beards round here. There's a few with moustaches, and most of them are men, but beards? No. The only beards I remember were white and on the chins of old merchant seamen. I'm at a loss here, Theo.'

Tia entered with a tray bearing three mugs of tea and a plate of biscuits.

'Thank you,' Theo said.

'Are you feeling better, Jack?' she asked.

'It's slight angina,' he replied, emphasizing the middle word.

'I'm getting you another cleaner,' Theo said.

'They won't pay another . . .' Jack's voice died when the boss raised a hand and ordered him to be quiet.

'The cleaner will be paid.' Theo picked up his cup. 'You're a quick learner, Miss Bellamy. Tea the American way, no milk.'

Tia looked at him sternly. 'Bloody colonials,' she said. 'Jack, have a semi-sweet biscuit. A few days ago, I spoke on the telephone to Juliet, my baby sister, who's a nurse. Cut down sugars and fats and take gentle exercise. You need more help here at work. And no smoking.'

'Might as well cut me bloody throat,' the caretaker moaned.

'Do as she says, or I'll cut it for you.' Theo's tone was serious, though he raised an eyebrow as he spoke. 'We don't wanna lose you.'

'Colonials,' Tia repeated. 'Then we wonder why our children can't spell. If they deliver aloominum instead of aluminium, it will be your fault.'

Theo ignored her. 'Go home, Jack. This place has remained standing for decades – well, apart from when your predecessor was killed. It won't collapse if you take a couple of days off. I'll lock up.'

He looked at Tia. 'I might employ Maggie Stone. Rosie must be made to feel secure. She can stay with her grandmother while the cleaning's done after school, because that child needs to develop a close relationship with an adult. I'm afraid Sadie Tunstall's drowning in drink, so she's hardly going to fill that role.'

Jack stood up. 'Sadie's still the little girl's mother, Theo.'

'I'm aware of that. But I'm hoping to get our welfare officer to assist in taking Rosie away from that house and into Maggie's care. An alcoholic mother can mean an alcoholic daughter in the fullness of time.' He drummed his fingers on the table again. 'They're sure he's dead, Jack?'

'Just a bit dead, yes. His neck's broke. Put it this way, he'd be no good in a football match unless they propped him up and used him as a goalpost. I think I'll go home.' After placing his mug on the tray, he said, 'Ta-ra, kids,' and left.

Tia spilled a word into the uncomfortable silence that divided the remaining two of them. 'Murder,' she whispered.

'Yes.' He walked towards the door and pressed the bell to mark the end of today's school. 'He was hated. The police know that the Athertons, Roy Duckworth, Jack and I wanted the place raided on Friday. We left Maggie's name out of it, since she's Rosie's grandmother. I have an alibi, as do Jack and Roy – he will have been at work. As for Tom and Nancy, they barely have the energy to scrape the skin off custard. They won't be suspects.'

She returned to her seat. 'It might have been a false beard on the tall man. They're used all the time on stage, and there'll be a theatrical costumier somewhere in the city.'

'You think of everything, don't you, Tia?'

I think of you often. Sometimes, I want to run away from the torment, because this can't be love, not in so short a time. It's lust, that's all. 'No, I don't think of everything. I say what I know, Mr Quinn.'

He nodded thoughtfully. Mr Quinn, his full and formal title, meant he was in trouble. This was role reversal, because Myrtle Street was his school, not hers. She was an arrogant broad, and yet . . . 'I must go to the police station after I lock the school,' he said. 'And I have to make sure that Rosie's settled with her grandmother. I may see you later.' He stalked out of the room, sent the cleaners home and sat on a bench in the hall, elbows on knees, head in hands.

'Teddy?'

Shit, she's followed me. He raised his head. 'What?'

'Will you come up later for a meal?'

'I doubt I'll be able to eat.'

'Bring some body parts, and I'll cook them.'

'Spleen and chips? No thanks.'

'Have you nothing else?'

He almost smiled. 'Two big toes, about a pound of tripe and a kidney.'

'Tripe?' She raised an eyebrow.

'It's stomach. You cook it real slow with onion and white sauce.'

'You are disgusting.' She took his hands and pulled him to his feet. Her breathing altered slightly. Had he felt the bolt of lightning that had travelled along her arms? 'I'll go now,' she said. 'See you later.'

He watched as she walked away. Wearing high heels today, she almost matched him in height. She probably wore them deliberately; it would be a power thing. The damned woman was burning through his resolve, his curriculum, his rules and, he had to admit, through his hitherto chilled and deliberately desensitized heart. She was causing him to suffer sleepless nights, disturbing dreams if or when he did drop off, and a great deal of soul-searching.

He checked the boiler room, classrooms, staffroom, cloakrooms and lavatories before securing the building. After locking up the prefabricated classrooms, he climbed into his car and drove away. On Clementine Street, he parked his car and knocked on Maggie's door. Rosie opened it.

'Hi,' he said. 'And how are you today, little lady?'

'Is my mammy all right, Mr Quinn?'

'I believe so.'

Maggie appeared, a tea towel in one hand, a plate in the other. 'Rosie, you go and set the kitchen table.' She waited till the child had gone through to the rear of the house. 'Sadie's coming to stay here,' she mouthed. 'I'll try my best, but she won't stop drinking, I'm sure. Come in.'

The house was shabby, poorly decorated and scrupulously clean. He got straight to the point. 'I want you to work for me, Maggie. Give up your other job and clean my school. You may also want to look after my flat and Miss Bellamy's – we live in the same building.'

She sank into a chair. 'But you've got two school cleaners; Jack told me.'

He nodded. 'Yes, we have two at Myrtle Street, that's correct.'

'The corporation won't pay any more. I know, because I've applied.'

'I'll be paying you myself.' He raised a hand when she opened her mouth to speak. 'Maggie, I have two jobs. I have the school and another source of income. Miss Bellamy and I can pay you for keeping the flats clean, and I shall pay you for working at the school. Just don't tell the other cleaners.'

She swallowed. 'What's your other job?'

'One I do from home; that's all you need to know.'

'Oh.' Maggie smiled for what felt like the first time in hours. 'How much?'

'We'll work that out. You'll be well paid. Three after-school sessions, and a full day at the flats. Rosie will want for nothing.'

Her face changed, and she covered it with the tea towel. Unused to generosity, she wept behind the barrier of cloth.

'Don't cry, Maggie. I'll look after you and Rosie, and I'm sure Miss Bellamy will help. She's still only voluntary, but she's got her fingers in more pies than Simple Simon.' He bent over her. 'Sometimes, she makes me feel that she's the boss. She put me in detention today for misbehaving in Miss Ellis's class.'

The cloth was removed in a second. 'No!'

He nodded. 'Gentry, you see. She's a product of the best girls' school in England and damned cheeky with it.'

'You like her.'

He nodded. 'She's brilliant, and Rosie will be in her class.'

'Good.'

Theo made for the door. 'Bye, Rosie,' he called.

The child arrived at the doorway to the kitchen. 'Is he really dead?' she asked.

'Yes, Rosie.'

She turned to her grandmother. 'Nana, are we having the yellow cups and saucers or the flowery ones?'

'Yellow, sweetheart. The flowered ones are for posh. Your granddad bought them for me years back.'

'He's dead, too,' the child informed her soon-to-be head teacher.

As he left the house, Theo thought about Rosie's almost non-reaction. This was how children became hardened; this was how delinquents were created. He allowed himself a moment to consider his own past, his rebellion, the pain he had internalized until it had broken out like a rash on his soul, his shattered heart, his psyche. *Stop this, Theo. You lashed out, but you pulled yourself together and got out of the hellhole. What you saw, what you heard . . . No. It's over. The smoke has cleared and the screams have stopped. And you are on your way to an English police station, so pull yourself together.*

Five

Ropers Park had become Roped-Off Park, a crime scene, a no-go area guarded by over-sized constables with un-smiling faces and shiny shoes. The Lady Streets had been invaded by a plague of policemen who hovered like mas-sive bluebottles as they questioned people for the second or third time. Did they know a tall man with a black beard and a newspaper? Who had a grudge against Tun-stall? Did they know Tunstall? Where had they been at the time of the murder?

The force had even arrived at the school, and its headmaster was not best pleased. A school needed to have a rhythm, and children should be warned if their day was about to be disturbed, but this was murder, and murder was a serious business. 'Just don't frighten them,' he told the sergeant in charge. 'After all, they're very young and impressionable.' He was glad to go home when the working day ended.

Tia looked through her kitchen window. Theo was sitting in the rear garden with his body language giving out the *Do Not Disturb* message, arms folded across his chest, head leaning back against the deckchair, eyelids lowered, knees together, feet keeping close company with each other. He looked about as relaxed as a man positioned at the business end of a loaded gun, so Tia wasn't fooled. Within days of seeing Theodore Quinn at work and living above him, she had come to know him well. Why? Because she liked him. *Keep it at liking, Tia. For God's sake, don't let it happen.*

He opened his eyes, and she stepped away from the window immediately. *Did he see me? Does it matter? Because stuff like this doesn't move in one direction only. Like two weather fronts, we have collided and caused a maelstrom. He likes me, too, but there's something; a part of him isn't always open for business, which is why I must slow down. Yet he's so good with the children and the staff, though his moods seem to change so suddenly. Is there a chance he might be crackers?*

She tackled her shepherd's pie; if she had to force-feed him, she would do just that. The man was in shock, so food was probably off his list tonight. Having gone innovative again, she wondered whether he would like her dash of nutmeg, her teaspoon of soured cream and the bouquet garni she *must* remember to remove before serving. Salad dressing, toss the salad around a bit, smooth the potato over the pie, plough the surface with a fork and shove the lot under the grill. Except for the salad . . . phew. It was a warm evening.

After a quick, cold-water wash in the bathroom, she descended the stairs and turned left for the back garden. Placing a little finger at each corner of her mouth, she produced a whistle that had confused many hockey teams, a netball coach and, on one occasion, even a policeman, who had whistled back before searching for a non-existent colleague.

Theo opened an eye. 'What?' He was not impressed by the whistle; he'd heard it before when she'd been practising playtime supervision. 'What?' he repeated.

'I've cooked a meal.' She awarded him a winsome smile, one she reserved for special people.

'Oh. You expecting the Congressional Medal of Honor? Purple Heart? Round of applause?'

'An OBE and an appetite will suffice. Come on, Teddy. You must eat.'

He stood, folded his deckchair and put it in the shed before following her upstairs. She was a determined type and, yes, she was getting on his nerves. *You knew she'd get on your nerves, Theo. She's beautiful, elegant, common as muck in her own endearing way and, above all, a fusspot, as the English say.* 'I'm not hungry,' he told her as he stood at her table, pouring iced water into one of the tall glasses. 'Murder seems to suppress the appetite.'

'Did you have lunch?' she asked.

'Yes.' How the hell did she manage to make the most ordinary questions sound provocative?

'And since then, a nasty, child-beating, wife-pimping toad has been killed within a few hundred yards of your school.' She dished salad onto his side plate. 'I'm not God,' she continued, 'so I can't judge, yet Mr Tunstall's character sounds rather less than charming. No one has a good word to say about him. The world is probably clea-ner without him.'

'I don't like murder,' he muttered, his voice almost a whisper.

'It happens,' she advised him. 'You need only read a daily newspaper to find that someone or other has been removed.'

He fixed his gaze on her for several seconds while deciding what to say, how much to tell her. 'I know.' He paused for thought. 'My mother was murdered,' he said, his voice still soft.

Tia sat down suddenly. *His mother? Oh God, no wonder*

he looks sad occasionally. If anything of that kind happened to Ma, I'd be permanently crazy. 'I am so sorry,' she told him. 'When? How old were you when it happened?'

'I was ten – young enough to need a mom, old enough to want vengeance. My teenage years were difficult.'

She managed to close her gaping mouth. 'I'm not surprised. Hell's bells, Teddy, how did you hold yourself together?'

'I didn't. That's one of the reasons why I like to see schoolchildren happy. A miserable child might never reach his full potential.'

For Tia, this explained so much. He went from happy to sad within an hour, from gregarious to isolated, from humorous to pensive – no bloody wonder. She swallowed, though the lump in her throat was in no way connected to food. 'Who killed her?' she asked in a whisper.

'Cowards. They wore masks; they were never caught, although two were shot dead at the scene.'

'When? Where?' The fact that he looked tired and hurt and troubled was no longer surprising. She placed a hand over his. 'Sorry. I don't need to know the details.'

He nodded, retrieved his hand and began to eat. 'Tastes good,' he said. 'Different, but good.'

He had changed the subject, and he had to be allowed that prerogative. 'I can't seem to obey recipes,' she said, determined to concentrate on mundane matters. 'Unless I get my hands on a grater or a garlic press and put my own touch to the mix, I feel I haven't been creative. Not all my cooking is well received, so don't feel obliged to clear your plate just to be polite.' She paused. 'Teddy?'

He looked at her again. 'Yes?'

'It's not your fault. The neighbours turned on him, and you saw the little girl for yourself and became distressed, or so I was told. Did you hire someone to kill him?

101

No. Did you want him dead? No, you wanted him locked up.'

He put down his knife and fork. 'I'm not sure that Rosie and her grandmother will be safe. It's possible that Tunstall had cohorts and family who may seek revenge.'

'Then they're looking for a tall man with a dark beard.'

'And if they think that Sadie or Maggie hired that man?'

'Stop it, Teddy.'

He glared at her, though he was smiling internally. 'You can't follow recipes, don't obey rules – God alone knows what you'll do with my curriculum. What is it with you, Portia? Are you naturally non-conformist and argumentative, or have you worked at it?'

For several seconds, she pretended to process his question. 'Got a distinction in both subjects. Eat your dinner.'

For a reason he couldn't be bothered to question, he did as he'd been told. Was this cook a woman who must never be gainsaid?

'How's Tyger?' she asked.

Theo swallowed. 'Terrible. I'm thinking of changing his name to Ivan. He eats socks and waste-paper baskets. Oh, and he tries to climb drapes. I found him hanging by a thread and screaming like a human baby in the dining room. I'm going to replace the drapes – I mean curtains – with shutters.'

'Like the ones you wear?' As soon as the words were out, she wished she could bite them back. 'Sorry,' she said.

He gave her a forgiving smile. 'No, you're not. You speak your mind instead of pussyfooting around like so many people and my darned cat. Though he's lovely when asleep with the bear you gave him.' He paused. 'Now you know why I am as I am, but you must tell nobody. At school, I manage to remain on an even keel, but that's my role, you see.'

Tia agreed about non-disclosure. 'Both our mothers have to remain out of the public domain. As for your role, I understand. Teachers are actors.'

'True. When do you expect your mother?' he asked. 'I can't wait to meet her.'

'No idea. When the divorce papers are about to be served, I expect. But my little sister Juliet is still at home occasionally, so Ma must make sure she's all right. Pa will be a nightmare once his philandering is broadcast. And yes, you'll love my mother. Everyone loves her – except for Pa, of course.'

'Is he violent?'

She shook her head. 'Not so far, but he's verbally abusive, full of himself and always in the right. Ma started to drink, then stopped, but carried on pretending to be an alcoholic.' Tia grinned. 'She's a great actress. Pretending to be drunk meant she didn't need to work with him any longer.'

'They did seem to come as a pair,' Theo commented.

He found himself relaxing. Her humour was similar to his, as were her story-telling skills. Apart from his father's family, this was the first person in Britain he'd told about Mom. Perhaps he was beginning to trust her; or was it because she lived here and would be working with him, too? Or was there a reason about which he preferred not to wonder? 'Will your mom go out while she's in Liverpool?' he asked. 'Or will she be a prisoner up here?'

Tia waited until her mouth wasn't full of food. 'She has wigs and sunglasses and all kinds of weird clothes. She'll be out and about, I dare say.'

Unsurprised, he grinned. 'Does she skiffle?'

'Not as far as I know, though nothing would surprise me.' She pondered. 'No, I can't imagine Ma with a wash-board and metal thimbles.'

'Well, if she overspills too much with her clothes and

wigs, she can keep some of her stuff in one of my spare bedrooms.'

'Thank you. You're very kind.'

Theo beamed. 'Colin Duckworth might not agree with you.' He set down his cutlery before regaling her with tales of his red-haired tormentor. The football on the roof was delivered first; after that came accounts of truancy to go fishing, roller skating and looking after our Denis. 'He seems to nurture the opinion that school is optional. He writes notes from his parents, all capital letters and misspellings. I knew there was no chance that Roy or Trish would leave Colin to care for a goldfish, let alone a younger sibling. But there's something about that kid . . .'

'You're fond of him.'

Theo nodded. 'There's a strange innocence about him.'

'In spite of the lies?'

'Because of the lies, Tia. Colin would make a terrific lawyer.' He stood up. 'Mind, he'd have to stop blinking. Blinking's his "tell"; it gives him away. He's not in your class, but if you follow the sound of trouble, he'll be closely attached to it.'

'Are you going now?'

'To see Jack, yes, then to Maggie's.'

She was about to ask if she might accompany him when her doorbell rang. 'Bugger,' she whispered. 'That'll be Simon. Oh, sh— shine a light. I've lost count of the times I asked him to stay in Kent.'

'He's in love with you, Portia.'

She blinked at him. 'Why do you sometimes give me my full name?'

He raised his shoulders. 'I like it. It's a beautiful name.'

'Oh. OK, abandon me and let him in on your way out.' She was scowling. 'Have you ever proposed to anyone?'

He paused for a few beats of time. 'Yes, but she accepted. I was young and foolish, far too young for marriage,

I suppose. But Hitler saw her off along with most of the rest of Bootle. Alongside other American, Canadian, Polish and Australian early volunteers, I was allowed to join the forces. By the time I was demobbed, Sally had been dead for over three years.'

Tia's heart lurched. His mother, then his fiancée – this was terrible.

Theo left and walked downstairs, opening the door to admit the very attractive young doctor. Simon Heilberg was dark-haired, blue-eyed, tall and handsome. 'Hello,' Theo said, stepping out to allow the visitor in. When he received no answer, he grinned and walked away.

The younger man almost ground his teeth; she often talked about Theodore Quinn. She seemed quite captivated by her boss and landlord. Was there something going on? And did he have the right to ask? After all, she'd told him often enough to bugger off.

Simon ascended the stairs. For six years, he had pursued Tia Bellamy. They had been close for a while, but she had drifted away from him, taking up with a series of adventurous males who had travelled with her all over the country and abroad. *She will come back to me. I've always known that she and I are meant for each other.*

He found her carrying dishes into the kitchen. 'Did you feed him?' he asked, trying in vain to keep his tone measured.

Tia sighed. 'Yes. We had a murder today, so everyone's upset.'

He perched on a stool, his mouth almost gaping. 'Murder? Do tell.'

She went through the story again while washing her dishes. 'The little girl will be a pupil of mine in September. It's been a difficult day.'

'So you're going into school without being paid? Surely you don't start work until September.'

Tia swallowed a quick and rather unpleasant answer about none of this being his business. 'I'm learning my job, Simon. Would a surgeon attempt a tonsillectomy without having watched someone else doing the operation?'

'That's different,' he almost snapped.

'More important?' She dried her hands. 'Well, let me tell you, Simon Heilberg – without good schoolteachers, there would be no surgeons.'

He held up a hand. 'OK, I give up.'

With her hands on her hips, she faced him. 'That's your problem. You don't give up, do you? Why did you follow me up here when I begged you not to?'

'Ordered me not to,' he actually snapped.

'I won't marry you. I'm not ready for marriage, and I'm not sure I ever will be. Whatever, whenever, it won't be you. And I made that clear before you chose to travel the length of the country. You're a dear friend, and if I could choose a brother, you'd be in the running.'

He gazed at her. 'When you say I don't give up easily, Tia, you're absolutely correct, because I love you.'

She walked past him into the sitting room, aware that he would be on her heels like a docile dog. 'For a clever man, you display quite a lot of stupidity.'

'I have a major flaw, a weakness,' he replied. 'It runs right through my core, and your name's printed on it.'

'Buy an eraser,' she almost hissed, 'or paint over me. I'm not available.'

Clearly deep in thought, he stared into the middle distance.

Tia picked up the evening paper.

'It's him, isn't it?' he challenged her. 'The boss, the landlord, who must be at least ten years older than you. You've changed since you met him.'

Tia peered at him over the top of Situations Vacant.

'Go back to Kent, please. Your father will be delighted to have you return to the practice.'

He snorted. 'I'm going nowhere until you come with me.'

'And I'm going nowhere, full stop. Right until the last minute, I hoped you'd show a bit of sense and stay where you were. You're a first-class doctor with a master's in stupid.' She threw down the *Liverpool Echo*. 'You know I care about you, Simon. But not in the way you want and need, and I can't make that happen, because it's impossible . . .'

He took himself off to the bathroom. Sometimes she annoyed him to the point where he felt like yelling and ranting, but he was too well bred for such behaviour. As he washed his hands, it occurred to him that his and Tia's roles were almost reversed, because she had reacted scarcely at all to the loss of her virginity, while he had taken the event very seriously.

He returned to the living room. 'Shall we go for a drink somewhere?' he asked. 'There's a decent pub just round the corner.'

'Not tonight, Simon. It's been a day and a half, believe me.'

He looked heavenward as if seeking divine guidance. 'Tia?'

'Yes?'

He cleared his throat. 'Was I no good at it?'

'No good at what?'

'Sex.'

'Ah, that. I can assure you that there were no faults in the mechanism. I just don't love you, that's all.'

Exasperated, he dropped into an armchair. 'Then why did it happen?'

'Well, I needed to find out what all the fuss was about, so I decided to do it with someone I knew and liked.'

His jaw dropped. 'And it didn't really mean anything?'

'Oh, but it did. I trusted you not to hurt me. Simon, that was five years ago – well, the first time was. And for a while I thought we might stay together, but I moved on, and so should you.' She rose to her feet. 'It's friendship or nothing, and you knew this already before you came north. Coffee before you go? I have things to do tonight.'

He stood up. 'No, thanks. I'll see you soon.' He kissed her cheek and left quickly. As he climbed into his car, he saw her leaning out of a window. She was shouting to Quinn; she was telling him that she'd be down in two minutes. Too tired for a drink with a friend, but not too tired for Quinn. Damn and blast that man. *This is not me being paranoid after all. Look at her face – she is glowing and smiling and . . . Drive off, Simon. Go back to your flat and think.* He revved the engine and sped away, burning rubber as he went.

Theo watched the black Ford as it turned onto the main road. She hadn't gone with the good doctor, because she had chosen instead to visit the afflicted in Isabel and Clementine Streets. What was more, Theo felt as if he'd won the bout on points, though he'd hardly categorized Simon Heilberg as competition. Was this a battle, then? The beginning of a war?

She arrived, hair in two plaits hanging over her breasts, blue ribbons on the ends of the braids, very little makeup, flat shoes, white socks, her skiffling jeans and a sleeveless blue blouse. 'Hi,' he said. 'You look about fourteen. Well, you would if you weren't so tall.'

Tia grinned. 'So if I fall to pieces in your hands, you won't need marinade to tenderize the flesh.'

'Hmmm.' He stroked his chin thoughtfully. 'Fresh asparagus and baby potatoes, I think. Let's go.'

They were nearing the city in his green MG when he next spoke. 'Your follower is following us.'

She nodded. 'It's all right, I'm used to it.'

'I'm not,' he said. He had no intention of becoming used to it. Pulling over, he stopped outside an off-licence, allowing time and space for Simon to park a few yards behind them. Without hesitation, Theo strode towards the black car. He pushed his head through the open window on the passenger side. 'Do you need to speak to Miss Bellamy?' he asked. 'You seem to be in pursuit of her.'

Simon heard and assimilated the double entendre. 'My flat's near here,' he said, his tone clipped.

'But you stopped driving when I did, so I assumed—'

'I'm going to buy wine.' The doctor's skin was suddenly flushed.

Theo stepped back. 'Right. I'll tell Miss Bellamy that she isn't needed.' He returned to his car.

'Well?' she asked.

He climbed in next to her, not bothering to use the door of the open-topped vehicle. 'Says he's buying some wine. Where's his flat, by the way?'

'Woolton.'

'So he's come out of his way, then. This must be a very good liquor store.'

Tia sighed. 'I should never have told him I was moving up here. He won't give up. But I was so excited that I opened my stupid mouth . . . Will I ever learn?'

Theo found himself hoping that she wouldn't learn. Like Colin Duckworth, she owned an innocence that appealed to him. She appealed to him. This woman was probably easy to love, and a part of him understood Simon Heilberg's dilemma. 'He's suffering, Tia.'

'As am I,' she snapped. 'Sorry. It's not your fault.'

'Seeing you with another man isn't helping him, though.'

She fiddled with one of her plaits. 'But you're not another man; you're my boss and my landlord and you're very, very old.'

He burst out laughing. She followed suit until they were both doubled over in pain. 'Jesus,' he managed. 'What the hell did you put in that shepherd's pie?'

'Body parts,' she gasped. 'A bit of cream in the mash and a tiny . . . oh, God, I'm going to cry . . .'

'A tiny what?'

'What?'

'It's your what, not my what. You introduced the what.' He dried his eyes with the back of his hand. 'A tiny what?'

She calmed herself. 'Oh, that what. A tiny bouquet garni and a bit of nutmeg.' A loud hiccup escaped from her throat. 'Now look what you've done.'

'What?'

'Don't start what-ing with me again, Mr Quinn. You've given me hiccups.' She took a deep breath. 'Why are we laughing, anyway?'

'I have absolutely no idea, but your boyfriend is walking back to his car with two bottles of red and a very deep frown.'

Tia held her breath.

'Why have you stopped breathing?' her companion asked.

'Trying to control my diaphragm,' was the answer delivered with difficulty from behind clenched teeth.

'He's driven off.'

At last, she breathed. 'Good. And he's not my boyfriend; he's a reject.'

'Poor Doc Heilberg,' Theo muttered. 'Such a cruel wench, you are.'

She offered no answer.

'Tia?'

'I'm trying to stop the hiccups. I don't want to be exploding all over Jack and Maggie and little Rosie, do I?'

It occurred to her that apart from the hour or so spent with her sisters playing on Chaddington Green, this was the first time in a while that she'd laughed uncontrollably. With luck and a strong following wind, Teddy Quinn was quite good fun. What was that saying of Ma's? Ah, yes. 'The way to a man's heart might be via the digestive tract, but to win a woman, a chap needs to aim for the funny bone' – that was the one.

'Are you composed now?' he asked, the tone innocent.

'Perfectly,' she answered. 'As long as I don't laugh, I'll be absolutely splendid. Drive on, please.'

Oh, yes, she was very BBC. Her accent, or rather the lack of it, enthralled him. It was as if she'd climbed out of the mesh on the speaker of his wireless, as the locals tended to name a radio. Yet she wasn't at all posh. For a reason he could scarcely explain even to himself, she belonged here. But she would probably fit in just about anywhere. 'Where did you get the body parts?' he asked, his tone remaining guileless.

'Shut up.'

'You didn't get into my secret room, did you?'

Had the car not been moving, she might have dug her elbow into his ribs. 'The butcher,' she replied. 'Bits of dead sheep.'

'I feel sick,' he groaned.

'Good. It's no more than you deserve.'

They pulled up outside number thirteen, Isabel Street. Theo reached into the back of the car and lifted out a shopping bag. 'Whisky,' he explained. 'Rumoured to be good for what ails him.'

Jack welcomed them into his parlour, which was spotlessly clean. He had clearly been glued to *What's My Line*, though he switched off his tiny television set before inviting them to sit.

Theo handed over the whisky. 'A drop before bed,' he

suggested. 'And I want to come with you to see your doctor.'

'But—'

'Don't argue with him,' Tia suggested. 'He's in a very strange mood.'

Slowly, Theo turned his head and glared at her. 'Miss Bellamy, would you mind having hiccups again? It's the only thing that manages to stop you talking.' He gave his full attention to the caretaker.

Tia, standing behind Theo, put out her tongue.

Jack chuckled.

'What's she doing now?' Theo asked without bothering to look at her.

Jack shrugged. 'Nothing.'

'Makes a change,' muttered the headmaster. 'Now, if you don't want me to come with you to the surgery, I need a letter from your doctor stating that you are fit for work. I refuse to allow any of my staff to be made ill by the job. Maggie Stone will take some weight off your shoulders by helping the other cleaners. You are the best janitor for miles, I'm sure, but your health comes first.'

Jack nodded.

'Do you need anything?' Tia asked. 'Washing and ironing, I'm your man. I'm sure we could manage shopping, too.'

'Thanks, both of you, but my neighbours will make sure I'm looked after. And I'll get you that letter, Sir — I mean Theo.' He chewed on a thumbnail for a few seconds. 'I'd better tell you; Sadie's drinking heavily. She found Tunstall's stash of money, and she's pouring it down her throat.'

'Is she at Maggie's?' Theo asked.

Jack nodded. 'And I know what she'll do when she runs out of money.'

Theo mirrored Jack's nod. 'So do I. Rosie needs rescuing from her mother, too. What a mess.'

'Can't you talk to that girlfriend of yours?' Jack asked.

'Which one?'

'Welfare. Every time she sees you, she looks like she needs a bloody knife and fork and a bit of gravy.' The seated patient glanced past Theo and looked briefly at Tia. She wasn't pleased. Ah, was this young new teacher to be the one for Mr Quinn?

'I'll have a word with her,' Theo said. 'And I'll talk to the education office, too. That poor child's already had enough to contend with.'

Tia made sure that Jack had no immediate needs before bidding him goodbye and following Theo out of the house. A tiny knife seemed to be performing a dance in her chest; perhaps she should have tried a little of Jack Peake's medicine. Or had there been something amiss with the shepherd's pie?

They sat in the car. 'What's wrong now?' he asked.

And in that moment, she knew. If Teddy had girlfriends, she wasn't happy. She wanted him; she wanted to be the one who would make him happier. 'Nothing,' she answered. 'Jack looks a little better.'

'He does, but I still want to hear from his doctor.'

Tia sat with her arms folded. It occurred to her that she might be the one closing shutters, guarding herself from life's uncertainties, bad memories, frightening thoughts. So he had girlfriends; or had Jack been joking? With deliberation, she uncrossed her arms as a sign that she had no intention of hiding from the world, of hugging herself in a corner like a child whose toys were broken.

'We'll go to Clementine Street now,' Theo said. 'I'd like a word with Sadie Tunstall.'

She remained quiet.

'Have you been struck dumb?' he asked.

'No. You should be so lucky.'

He started the car. 'You do realize that our relationship at school will need to be more formal?'

'Yes, Sir.'

He looked up to heaven before putting the car in gear. 'What's your problem now, Miss Bellamy?'

She couldn't say anything, certainly dared not tell the truth. *How many girlfriends do you have, Mr Quinn? Is the welfare woman prettier than I am? Am I not good enough for you? Perhaps I'm too tall. Many men prefer tiny women like china ornaments to be displayed and dusted from time to time.*

She glanced sideways at him. *Are you one of those inverted snob types who hate Roedean girls? And why am I talking to myself like this, even in my head? I don't just look fourteen, I'm thinking like a fourteen-year-old.* She sighed. 'I believe I must have put too much arsenic in the mash.'

Theo resisted laughter; he didn't want to give her hiccups again. This was ridiculous, though. Why should a girl as beautiful as this one be upset by Jack's joke about girlfriends? Oh, it wasn't necessarily that, he told himself, though part of him, a part he usually ignored, hoped against hope that this young woman liked him. Tia Bellamy was bright enough to understand his dilemma, yet could she live with it? But it was too early for this kind of thinking; he'd known her for just a few days. So why did he remember her from the future?

He stopped on Ivy Lane. 'We need to hatch a plot,' he said.

'Oh, goody,' she replied smartly. 'Do I get a gun and some bullets?'

'I'm serious.'

'So am I. Somebody was murdered here today.'

'Miss Bellamy?'

'Yes, Mr Quinn?'

She was adorable. A man might drown in those blue-violet eyes. 'You get Rosie and Maggie together in the front room. Or take Rosie out for a while. I have to handle Sadie.'

'I suppose she's been handled by many men of late. One more shouldn't be too much of a stain on her character.'

'Tia?'

'Yes?'

'Be quiet and listen.'

Like a child in reception class, she placed an index finger against her closed lips.

'I want Rosie out of earshot while I tackle her mother. Do you think you might take the child out to one of the late shops and buy her some chocolate? Maggie will be OK, because she's heard it all before.'

Tia nodded, the finger still in place over her mouth.

He continued. 'I understand that Sadie was a nightmare from her teens; it was a miracle that she got to twenty before giving birth to Rosie. She became pregnant again, probably by Tunstall, and had a back-street abortion that went horribly wrong, so her womb was removed in hospital to prevent her bleeding to death. She married Tunstall recently, and he became her full-time pimp. Maggie knows all this. Rosie has seen enough already, and I want to protect her from now on.'

Tia took the finger from her lips. 'You really care, don't you, Teddy?'

'About kids? Yes, I do. Of course I do. That's why I'm in a job that pays a pittance. I can make ten times more in the summer vacation than I earn in a year at Myrtle Street.'

'Body parts?'

'That's the one. Now, are we ready?'

'Tell me what you really do in that locked room.'

'No. You aren't old enough. And we've more important matters pending. Will you help with Rosie?'

She agreed readily. There was a stepladder in Teddy's shed, and she would use it to peer through the window of the body parts room, as its bottom half was usually hidden behind half-shutters. By fair means or foul – probably the latter – she would discover the secret that had enabled him to buy his enormous, beautiful house and turn it into two delightful flats. Body parts, indeed. 'I'm ready,' she told him. 'Let's see what can be done, Mr Quinn. That little girl deserves a chance, and her mother needs the opportunity to get sober.'

Maggie Stone was dabbing her eyes with a handkerchief when she opened her front door. 'Sorry,' she mumbled. 'I got something in my eye.'

'No, you didn't.' Theo ushered her into the parlour, a small, clean room spoilt only by shabby furniture. Maggie was clearly a woman who made the best of things, and her failure to make the best of her daughter probably sat heavily on her shoulders. 'Where's Rosie?' he asked.

'Back yard,' she answered.

Tia walked through the front room, the kitchen and a tiny scullery. In the paved yard at the rear of the house, she found Rosie talking to a doll. 'He's gone,' the child was saying, 'so we can make a noise now, and I don't need to go in the coal shed.'

'Hello,' Tia said softly. 'I'm your new teacher. My name's Miss Bellamy.'

The child blinked. 'Hello,' she said shyly. 'This is Dotty, my doll.'

'Dotty Dolly.' Tia squatted nearer to the ground. 'Is Dotty Dolly a good girl?'

Rosie frowned. 'She never got shut in the coal shed.'

Tia blinked hard. 'I don't like coal sheds,' she said. 'They're dark and dirty.'

The child nodded, her expression grave. 'He's dead now. He's dead and my mam's drunk. It's the gin.'

The knife returned to Tia's chest. Perhaps these horrible truths, spoken by an infant, were trying to escape from the child's soul before having the opportunity to take root.

'He put me in the shed when the jumping up and down men came.'

Tia closed her eyes for a few seconds. This little girl, this baby, had witnessed the act of sex, and was probably aware of money changing hands while she was locked in a miserable, dark hole. So here sat Teddy's reason for working in the state system; he could give a child a life better than the one he had endured himself. There were good people in the world, and he was one of them. 'Shall we go to the corner shop, Rosie?'

The child nodded and, when Tia stood, placed her trusting hand in that of her new teacher. The teacher sniffed back emotion, wondering how this beautiful child had managed to retain some faith in humanity. She made a game of going to the shop; they marched, skipped and hopped before performing the do-not-step-on-the-cracks-between-paving-stones competition. And Tia's opinion that women were the stronger sex was reinforced, because even this small, ill-treated female child retained her sense of fun.

They bought chocolates for Maggie, dolly mixtures for Dotty Dolly, a big lollipop for Mr Quinn, and a mixed bag for Rosie, whose eyes shone like jewels. 'What about you, Miss Bellamy?'

'I've no sweet tooth, Rosie.'

'Oh. Has it fell out?'

'I suppose it must have.'

The child frowned. 'I could ask Nana to make you a bacon butty.'

And there it came again, the attitude, the benevolence of northerners. No matter what, the kettle went on, tea was brewed, and even the poorest of pantries got raided. People who lived alone were seldom lonely, and the afflicted were almost always catered for. 'I'm not hungry, thank you. I had a meal before coming to see you. Shall we buy something for your mother?'

Rosie shrugged. 'She doesn't eat much. Food makes her sick.' The child studied her adult companion. 'You talk dead posh, Miss Bellamy.'

Tia grinned. 'I know. We all do. I have two sisters, Cordelia and Juliet. Cordelia plays drums in a band, and Juliet's a nurse.' She wondered how long Teddy wanted her to keep Rosie away from the house while he attempted to deal with Sadie. 'Shall we take a walk?' she asked.

'No,' Rosie said. 'There's only the park, and the police won't let nobody in yet. They have to find out who killed him, you see, cos it was murder.'

'Run back to the shop and get some chalk.' Tia handed over a sixpenny bit. While waiting for Rosie, she picked up a piece of slate from the pavement. She would return to Maggie's, but keep the child in the street out of harm's way.

It didn't work out quite as she had expected. She drew the hopscotch and showed Rosie how to play. Doors opened, and children spilled out into the street, all clamouring to join the game. Tia organized an orderly queue and, like a big kid herself, stood in line to await her own turn. She watched Rosie, noticing how well she interacted with others, the breadth of her smile, the joy when she won.

'Well done,' Tia said. 'You were the first to get all the way to number eight without falling over or standing on the wrong square.'

While Tia watched the children, Theo watched her from an upper window. With her plaits and ribbons and little white socks, she was just another child playing hopscotch. Behind him on her mother's bed, Sadie Tunstall lay almost comatose with drink. Two women of approximately the same age, one full of life and imagination, the other in danger of inhaling her own vomit.

He opened the sash window. 'Miss Bellamy?'

'Mr Quinn?'

'Take Rosie for a ride in my car, please. You can play another time.'

'Very well.'

'About half an hour,' he suggested.

The young of Clementine Street watched enviously while Rosie Tunstall was driven off in an open-topped sports car. They decided that she was a lucky girl, though opinion changed when the ambulance pulled up and Rosie's mother was carried into it on a stretcher. But they were soon engrossed in a new game of hopscotch.

'Where do you like to go?' Tia asked Rosie as they rode down Ivy Lane.

'Library and pictures.'

'The cinema?'

Rosie shook her head. 'Paintings. They're in a quiet place.'

'But you like playing hopscotch, too, don't you?'

'Yes. That's a different kind of nice.'

This was the point at which the teacher realized that she was in the company of an extraordinary child, one who, having endured abuse, had emerged with good humour, a strong sense of proportion and a more than adequate concept of her own intrinsic value. 'You can read, Rosie?'

'Yes, Miss. Big words are hard unless you can break them up. Some can't be broke up, so you just have to learn them.'

Tia blinked back some mixed emotions before taking Rosie to Otterspool, a place neither she nor the child had ever visited. Like most of the indigenous, Rosie clearly loved her river. After running back and forth near the railings for a while, she returned to Tia's side. 'I can do money as well,' she announced proudly.

'Good for you. You seem to be a very clever girl. I'll be pleased to have you in my class.'

When they returned to the house, Maggie put Rosie to bed. Tia sat in an uncomfortable armchair, while Theo stood with his back to the fireless grate.

'Where's Sadie?' she asked.

'Hospital. Alcohol poisoning. I'm happy to pay her fees for a private drying-out clinic, but she'd have to give written consent. Unless she can be certified insane due to alcohol, that is.'

Tia offered no reply. She was not in the mood for talking.

He studied her. 'Are you OK?'

'I scarcely know.'

'What is it, Tia? Do you think working around these parts is going to be too much for you?'

Again, she gave no answer.

He gazed down at her. She looked pale and drawn. 'Portia?'

She shrugged and continued to stare at the floor.

Theo walked through to the kitchen, the room from which the concealed staircase ran behind a door. 'We're leaving, Maggie,' he called up the flight. 'Miss Bellamy's rather tired, and I have a few things to do.'

Maggie shouted her thanks, as did Rosie.

He returned to the front parlour and took hold of Tia's hands, pulling gently until she was standing. 'Come on, now. Let's get you home.'

During the drive, she didn't say a word. Instinctively, he recognized her need for silence; sometimes, even a fool didn't set foot in a place avoided by angels. He parked the car next to hers on the villa's front courtyard between the lawn and the rockery. She didn't move, so he walked round to her side and opened the passenger door. 'Hey,' he said softly.

She looked through rather than at him. 'Hey,' she replied eventually.

'Come.' He took her left hand with his right and led her into his flat, placing her on a comfortable chair. He picked up Tyger and put the kitten on Tia's lap. If she wouldn't open up to a human, perhaps she might talk to an animal, just as he did when facing life's more difficult junctures.

She stroked Tyger, though her faraway expression remained in situ.

'What is it?' Theo asked.

Tia didn't know where to start. 'She's older than I am,' she managed at last. 'Five years of age, and yet . . .' Her voice faded away.

'That happens in areas like this one. Look, if you want to go home to Kent, I won't blame you for a second. I'd be disappointed, because I can see what an asset you'd be, but you mustn't stay if you're unsure.'

She leaned her head to one side. 'Look, I've never been near murder before, I've never seen people in real need, in houses so small–'

'Oh, stop this,' he said. 'It's not about you and what

you've seen; it's about them. If you're too precious to cope, so precious that your feelings are getting hurt, you shouldn't be here. They're needful. Not all of them by any means – most kids in these parts could run circles round you and leave you breathless. It's the odd one like little Rosie that stands out, because the rest of them are magnificent. I'm here because of Rosie and a few others. And I'm here for the rest, whose parents have climbed out of the quicksand of self-pity, found work, found pride, found ambition for their kids. I'm sorry.' He passed her a handkerchief. 'I didn't intend to make you cry.'

She handed over the kitten, grabbed the offered square of linen, dried her eyes, threw the handkerchief on the floor, jumped out of the chair and left the room.

He heard his door as it slammed home, heard her running upstairs to her own flat, flinched as her upper door banged. She was angry. He was angry with himself for making her angry. This was a whole new life for Tia Bellamy, and he should understand that, since he'd crossed the Atlantic to escape his past. And she was lovely and sensitive and . . . *God help me.*

Six

He woke at twenty minutes past six, his head banging, light streaming in through drapes he had forgotten to close, birds performing some sort of medieval madrigal with a few notes deformed by a fretful blackbird. Why were blackbirds so darned territorial? Fear, probably. But he shouldn't blame the birds or the light; it was Madam Sensitive upstairs who had deprived him of sleep, because he'd found himself worrying about her state of mind, about whether she would stay or go; he'd also reflected on her undeniable beauty, her downright cheek, her feistiness, her wonderful voice.

'This darn headache.' Just a minute – it wasn't a headache, as the sound was coming from outside his skull, from upstairs. What the hell was she up to now? He'd rented out a lovely, spacious apartment, and it sounded as if she was busy smashing it to pieces. Oh, God. He jumped out of bed, remembered that he was stark naked, pulled on pyjama bottoms and dragged a dressing gown from a hook on the door. When he'd grabbed the spare key from a drawer in the hall, he ran barefoot up the side of the house and let himself into his own property. *Why am I nervous? This is my house, my property, and I have every right to make sure it's in one piece.*

At the top of the stairs, he took a deep breath and knocked.

'It's open,' she called. 'Oh, wait a minute, I'm not decent.'

He entered the flat and found her in the living room on her hands and knees. She wore a cream silk night-gown that left little to the imagination, though she did wrap a dust sheet round herself just as he entered the room. Tia Bellamy was perfect, and she probably knew it.

'What the hell are you doing, Tia?' he asked. 'Sounds like Armageddon right over my head.'

'Building an extension, of course.' Her words carried the message that any normal person wouldn't have needed to ask so trite a question. She looked him up and down. 'Who got you ready?' she asked, the tone saccharine sweet.

He dropped into an armchair. 'Where did you get the work bench?' he asked.

'It's mine.' The tone was defensive. 'It came in Delia's van with the rest of my stuff. I usually keep it in this window draped in a floor-length cloth. It looks good with a plant on top. What's the problem? Am I breaking a rule of which you failed to make me aware?'

'The problem is the time, not to mention the noise.'

'It's Saturday,' she replied smartly, 'and you have men-tioned the noise. I always do woodwork when I'm stressed. Go back to bed; I'll soon be finished.'

He arched an eyebrow. 'Do you get stressed often? Because I'm darned sure I don't need a rude awakening like this on a regular basis.'

Tia rose to her feet and stood straight. 'Just a moment.' Clutching at the dust sheet, she left the room, found the robe that matched her nightdress and pulled it on. When she returned, he seemed to be trying hard not to laugh. 'What's so funny?' she asked, tying the belt at her waist. 'At least I haven't killed anyone in order to harvest body parts.'

He arranged his features into a more serious mode. 'Is the accommodation not big enough for you? Are you extending into the roof?' Her hair was so long, silk against silk, strands floating across the fabric of her clothing, seldom stilling unless she remained motionless, and she was almost always in perpetuum mobile mode.

A slippered foot beat a tattoo on the floor. 'The extension is for my dolls' house, not for your villa. I still need to learn plastering and tiling before I can do full scale renovations. Oh, and plumbing and wiring might be useful subjects for me to study. It's a double garage with an extra bedroom and bathroom above. Look!' She picked up a pair of small cardboard boxes. 'Our cars. Two MGs, one red, one green, both in perfect proportion to the house.'

Theo picked up the green one. 'Sweet,' he said. 'I love my car. But now, I'm going to make breakfast. Please try to be quiet for the rest of today. A man of my advanced years will need a nap to compensate for this disturbance to my sleep.' He studied her for a moment. 'Feeling better than you did last night?'

'Yes, thank you. Sorry I let things upset me like that. I'm usually tough, though I do seem to have inherited my father's temper and lack of patience, I'm afraid. Worry not, I keep both tethered in the bicycle sheds at school. Would you like some coffee and what I believe is named a bacon butty?'

He grinned broadly. The word 'butty' sounded strange in perfect English. 'Determined to feed me, aren't you? You spoil me, Miss Bellamy.'

'The elderly must remember to eat, Mr Quinn. When my grandmother began to lose the plot, we stuck a huge reminder on her kitchen door. It told her to eat, in capital letters, of course. She had a home help, but she, too, was senile. Growing old can be difficult in many ways, so do take care not to break any bones.'

While she cooked in the kitchen, Theo studied her dolls' house. It was almost certainly antique, and each room was furnished, wallpapered and lit by tiny torch bulbs fed by a battery. Little people were in almost every area; a baby looked ready to drown in a tin bath, so he righted the tiny figure. 'You could hide the battery in the back of your new garage,' he called.

'Good idea. You're not just a pretty face, then, Teddy?'

He puffed out his cheeks and blew gently. *She's goading me again.*

'Well?' she called.

He couldn't think of an answer. This was the problem. He had employed a probationary teacher who was probably cleverer than he was, and he was supposed to be the principal. The bossy creature was taking over his home life, too, and he felt . . . he felt happy. Feeling happy made him slightly bewildered, since he had sworn never again to take interest in a woman. 'Be quiet,' he answered her finally. 'I'm starving to death here.' He remained happily bewildered or bewilderedly happy – he wasn't sure which.

She bounced in with two bottles of sauce. 'I have learned about these,' she said smugly. 'This is red, this is brown. Which?'

'Neither. I like my bacon neat.'

'Do you want it soft or crunchy?'

'Well done.'

'Crunchy like mine, then.' She exited bearing ketchup, brown sauce and a huge smile. They shared a liking for well-cooked bacon.

She's used to looking after people, and that's why she's come to work in a city. Maybe she helped raise her two sisters, because she's the oldest. I guess if I were to write her down, I'd describe her as multi-faceted, so we're very alike. I am so drawn to her that I feel like a teenager trying to pluck up courage to invite her to a prom. Twelve years younger than I am, very young at heart and older than Methuselah in the head. If I make a move – and I'm shit scared of that – I could lose a great teacher, an inventive chef and a very interesting friend who builds extensions for dolls' houses in the middle of the damn night.

'Bugger,' she exclaimed.

'Are you OK, Tia?'

'I dropped some bread, that's all.'

Her voice alone is enough to seduce a man. My resistance is diminishing at a rate of knots.

She came in with a tray, two mugs of coffee and two bacon sandwiches. 'Here we go. That should help you get back to sleep. A full stomach attracts blood, takes it away from the brain.'

Theo's brain was on vacation anyway. He was hormonal, stupid and emotionally needful. And he'd done so well lately . . .

Tia sat opposite him and attacked her bacon sandwich with gusto. Building an extension was very hard work. 'Why aren't you eating?' she asked.

'I'm drinking coffee. Someone woke me before half past six, so I need the energy.'

She tutted. 'You must mind your heart, Mr Quinn. Caffeine can be lethal for a man in his dotage.'

This joke would run on and on, he decided. 'I am in the prime of my life, Miss Bellamy. Thirty-eight years of age and still ticking over. Any more of your clever talk and you'll get detention.'

'Is that a promise?'

Theo swallowed another mouthful of black coffee. She was communicating, wasn't she? 'You wouldn't like my detentions. We do geography and French, that kind of stuff.'

Je n'ai pas besoin de ces sujets, monsieur.

'*Oui, mais vous avez besoin de quelquechose, je crois.*'

Tia's appetite took a nosedive. She needed something, he believed? Oh, yes, she needed him to need her. Too early for courtship, too early for anything beyond liking his company, yet she knew he was winning her heart. Forcing herself to carry on as normal, whatever normal was, she turned to look at her dolls' house. 'I've had that since I was four years old.'

'It may lose value if you alter it,' he told her.

'The value was possibly slashed when Pa had it electrified. And my extension will be on a board that will take the house as well, so it should look like an extension without being one.'

'I see. You may use my shed for your future adventures with wood. Do you have any other hobbies apart from waking fellow residents at the crack of dawn?'

After chewing and swallowing, she gave him the list. 'Outsmarting my father, driving, flying kites, swimming, hockey, netball, archery, gun club, woodwork, swordplay, tormenting my sisters and cooking.' She inhaled deeply. 'In fact, I've scarcely time for teaching. You?'

'Body parts,' they pronounced simultaneously.

He decided to put her out of her misery. '*Take my Hand*,' he whispered, '*A Foot in the Door, A Finger in Every Pie, At Arm's Length, Two Hearts and a Spade, An Eye on the Money, Learning by Ear, Housemaid's Knee, Tooth and Claw, No Head for Heights, A Hair of the Dog, A Nose for Trouble, Heartburn, Hand in Glove.* I am currently out of titles.'

Tia seemed to be struck dumb, though not for long. 'Tom Quirke?' she screamed finally. 'Body parts?'

'Yes.'

'You're *the* Tom Quirke?'

'Guilty as charged.'

Tia clapped her hands like a child. 'I've read them. We

all have. They're the only truly hilarious crime novels on the market.'

'It has to be another secret, Portia.'

'Absolutely.' Her brow was furrowed. 'What about *Bad Blood? The Heart of the Matter? On Bended Knee?*'

'Write them down,' he ordered.

She jumped up and rooted out pen and notebook from her capacious school bag. 'That's three,' she said triumphantly. 'Tom Quirke. I am living in Tom Quirke's house. *Skin Deep? Feet First?* Oh, I'll just write whatever comes into my head, shall I? What about *A Toe in the Water? Six Feet Under? All Hands on Deck?*'

Theo nodded. He didn't want this from her, didn't want her as a fan. But she had to be told, because he needed few interruptions during school holidays. 'Perhaps you'll understand my desire for quiet now.'

She raised her head. 'Oh, I'm so sorry.'

'And don't tell anyone.'

She stuck a finger in her mouth, drew a cross on her gown and said, 'Cross my heart and swear to die if I should ever tell a lie.'

'Good title.'

'What?'

'*Cross My Heart.*'

'I'm on it.' She scribbled again. 'Mind, they might get confused if you use the same body part in more than a couple of books.'

'Yes, that's where the marinade comes in. The jacket. I paint my own.'

Her grin broadened. 'You're clever,' she announced.

'For a colonial person, I suppose I am.' Now, there would be too much respect, he feared. 'I'm just an ordinary guy who writes to pass the time and to fund my real hobby, which is teaching. Teaching in this country is not a good job. When war started, educators contributed by taking lower salaries, and they've never recouped the loss. You'll start on thirty pounds a month or thereabouts – am I right?'

She nodded. 'About that, yes – a pound a day. But I do have other money left to me by family elders.'

He shrugged. 'You'll need it.'

'Tom Quirke. I can't believe it.'

'Believe it.'

She pondered. 'You know the one called *Heartburn*?'

'I have vague memories, yes. Why?'

'Is it true that bodies can be found in that condition? Not a mark on them, but shaken to bits inside?'

'As the result of nearby explosion, yes.'

'Did you . . . did you see that?'

He nodded and told her a story he wished he could forget. Stationed just outside Hastings, he had been on the ground when the base had been bombarded by the enemy, who were going for the planes. 'My pilot,' he said. 'Outwardly peaceful, inwardly shaken apart by the blast. It happened.'

'Yet your books are fun.'

'Yes. Brooding does no good. And you'll notice I don't write about the war. I just use what I learned during those years.' He stood up. 'Thank you for the coffee and the bacon butty. See you later.' He left.

Tia remained where she was, remembering the nights when she and Delia had read aloud from the books of Tom Quirke. They'd been doubled over with laughter because of idiots who mapped out the perfect murder or grand larceny, only to carry out their plans so haphazardly that they killed the wrong person, or got stuck up trees, in chimneys, in locked safes or in prison for a different crime altogether.

Judges were cranky, deaf and incontinent, jurors scarcely literate, while lawyers were often inebriated, poorly briefed or out-and-out criminals whose misdeeds were greater than their clients' crimes. Tom Quirke took society and ripped it apart at the seams before stitching it back together in the wrong order, leaving an anarchic mess that was hilarious, impossible, yet strangely believable. Oh, she must read them all again.

She scrabbled about on her bookcases until she found a few of them. They were slim volumes, probably eighty thousand words at the most. But, for the first time, she looked at the dedication pages. *For Mom, who died too soon, For Dad – have a drink on me, For Sally; I saw the while cliffs of Dover, For Peter, Tim and Jamie, my half-brothers – read one third each.*

She couldn't tell anyone; she was unable to share this marvellous news. God, Delia would love to know about this, as would Ma and Juliet. *I can't betray him. He's my head of school, my landlord and . . . and something else. When I look at him, he often moves his eyes away from me, because he fears me, and I don't know why . . . and I fear him, and I don't know why. Madness?*

He was back, he was breathing hard, and here she sat with his books.

'Hello again,' she said, feeling like an eavesdropper because she was holding his work in her hands.

'She's escaped,' he achieved finally after regaining his breath. 'Sadie Tunstall got out of the hospital and it looks like she's taken Rosie from Maggie's back bedroom. Poor Maggie's a heavy sleeper.'

Tia leapt out of her chair. 'What? When did this happen?'

'Very early this morning. Get dressed,' he ordered. 'I'll go and do the same. Maggie Stone's in my apartment downstairs – Jack Peake gave her my address. Please hurry.' He ran downstairs.

Uncaring about how she looked, Tia had a quick wash,

tied back her hair, and donned the clothes she'd worn the previous evening. She was a good runner, so flats and jeans seemed best from a practical viewpoint. They had to find little Rosie.

She discovered Maggie sobbing her heart out in Teddy's kitchen. 'Come on, now,' Tia said, her arms wrapped round the weeping woman. 'They won't have got far. Did you go to Sadie's house?'

'I went, but nobody was there. They might be with Flo.'

'Flo? Who's Flo?'

'The other whore. Tunstall pimped for both of them.'

Theo stood in the doorway. 'Where does Flo live?' he asked.

Maggie shrugged; she had no idea. 'What I do know is that Sadie is the only one with a key to my house, and she has a load of cash, and she'll be drinking and my granddaughter will be watching . . . watching whatever's going on. Pimps are everywhere. Somebody will take Sadie and Flo on, and it'll be back to square one for Rosie.'

Theo addressed Tia. 'Do you have your car keys?'

'Yes.'

'You take Maggie. Go to Tom and Nancy Atherton – they live next door to Sadie's house. Ask if they know where Flo lives. I'm going to the police station. Meet me at the Pier Head in about an hour from now. If you get her address, do not go to Flo's place without me. Understand?'

Tia nodded.

'You know the Pier Head?' He asked.

'Yes. It's Liverpool's favourite meeting place, isn't it?'

'It is.'

'Right,' she breathed. 'Pier Head it is.'

He walked across the room, kissed Maggie on the cheek, then Tia on the forehead. 'We will find Rosie,' he said determinedly. 'Maggie, I am hoping that your daughter is drunk and that we can get her certified as incapable of remaining in society. The sooner Rosie is free of her mother, the better. I know that sounds harsh, but it's a fact.' He left the house.

Tia listened as his car drove away, her senses reeling slightly in reaction to the feel of his mouth on her face. 'Right, Maggie. Tom and Nancy Atherton's house. You're my guide.'

'The cops couldn't even question Sadie about the murder – she was three sheets to the wind and making no sense at all.'

'Come on,' Tia urged. 'The sooner we leave here, the better.'

Theo made for the police station on Ivy Lane. Speaking to the desk sergeant, he mentioned the murder of Miles Tunstall, and was led into a small room where, after a few minutes, a detective joined him. 'Mr Quinn?'

'Yes. I'm head teacher at Myrtle Street, and Miles Tunstall was stepfather to a little girl who joins my school in September. He pimped for his wife and for another woman named Flo. Did you find Flo?'

'We did.'

Theo told the tale of Sadie's escape from hospital, the subsequent disappearance of a five-year-old child and the distress of Rosie's grandmother. 'To be blunt, officer, some men may prefer younger flesh, so the child must be taken away from her mother. The Tunstall house was a brothel, and Rosie has seen enough. She spent hours locked in the coal shed while her mother, her stepfather and Flo carried out their business. I need to find Flo. Do you have her address?'

The man shifted uncomfortably in his chair. 'We do, but we can't divulge that information. This is a murder case, Mr Quinn–'

'And this is a child in danger of being contaminated simply by being in the company of her own mother, a known prostitute. What about when paedophiles discover that Sadie and Flo have a pretty little girl with them? How drunk will Sadie need to be before she sells her own baby?' Theo jumped up. 'If anything happens to Rosie because of your incompetence, I'll have your job, officer.' He slammed out of the room.

When he reached the Pier Head, Theo realized that he was very early. He dropped money into the cap of a man with no lower legs; the man sat on a wheeled trolley and played the mouth organ quite well. Theo gazed out at the water, thinking about his dad, who had often spoken about this part of the city. Here, and further up the coast, the women of Liverpool had stood over the years, watching, waiting for their ship to come in, the vessel that carried husband, father, brother, son or grandson. Now he was waiting for news of a five-year-old child.

He heard her before he saw her. She was shouting 'Harry' repeatedly as she approached the railings.

Harry grinned. 'My little songbird,' he said. 'I thought you weren't coming.'

Rosie threw her arms round Harry's neck. 'Mam got me. She put her hand over my face to keep me quiet, and I couldn't breathe hardly. She took me to Auntie Flo's. Auntie Flo lives over a tripe shop on Southport Road. Nana came knocking with Miss Bellamy, and Auntie Flo was in the bath, so Mam went to the front door and I ran out the back and down some steps while she couldn't see me. Then I heard the police bells. I don't feel like singing today, Harry.'

Theo stared at the child and the man with no legs. What the hell was going on here? 'Excuse me,' he said.

Rosie turned. 'Mr Quinn. Oh, hello. This is my friend Harry. He plays and I sing, and sometimes I help him to

134

sell papers. His sister is Martha, and she keeps my money in a box at their house and gives me jam butties. There's no stairs, cos Harry got his legs blown off, didn't you?'

Harry nodded before speaking to Theo. 'Rosie's had a hard life, sir.'

Theo studied the man and saw honesty and genuine concern in his face. 'I know it's not been easy. Thank goodness for people like you and your sister. Now, I have to try to get an emergency order from Welfare. Rosie needs to be away from the Lady Streets until her mother's dealt with.'

'Where will she go?' Harry asked.

'Wherever it is, her grandmother will be with her if I have any say in the matter.' He threw more coins into the cap. 'God bless you, Harry,' he said. 'I'll look for you next time I'm in town.'

Tia's red MG drew up. Maggie leapt out and ran to her granddaughter.

'She found her way here from Southport Road in Bootle,' Theo told her.

Harry chipped in. 'Every Scouser knows where the river is. We come with a sixth sense, I think.'

Maggie was in tears, as was Tia when she left her car.

'Don't cry,' Rosie ordered. 'My mam will be all right, Nana.'

'I know, love, I know.'

Theo put an arm round Tia's shoulder. 'I told you not to do this without me, but you did it; you made it happen. She was in Flo's place when you got there, and she ran out the back and down a fire escape, I imagine.'

Tia wiped her face with the heel of a hand. 'The police came and asked us what we were doing at Flo's door, so I told them, and they took Sadie away. She could scarcely stand. Rosie wasn't there. We drove round for a while looking for her.' *Nor can I stand while you're holding me.*

Yes, you've made me weak at the knees, Mr Quinn, and I can't tell you that. Oh, God, it feels as if I've come home.

'You take Rosie back to your apartment,' he said. 'I'll drive Maggie home to pick up clothes and so forth. Then I must see Emily Garner about an emergency order; we don't want Rosie in a children's home. Maggie is clearly her adult of choice, so they must be kept together. They will live with me until somewhere safe and more permanent can be found for them.' He tightened his hold for a second or two. 'You are one gutsy broad, Miss Bellamy.'

'Thank you, I think.' She pulled herself together and grinned. 'Come along, Rosie. Another ride in my car, you lucky girl.'

'We must hurry,' Theo whispered for Tia's ears only. 'If the police catch up with us, they'll take her and put her into care. I'll get Maggie back to our place as soon as possible. Rosie must be placed in her charge. Until she is, you are guilty of kidnap, so put your car in my garage and don't answer your door.'

Our place. He said our place. 'Right, I'm gone,' she said aloud.

She drove homeward in the company of a very serious, quiet child. After opening the door to her flat, she sent Rosie upstairs. 'Go and see my dolls' house,' she said. 'I'll put the car away.'

When she finally closed her own front door, Tia shot home a couple of bolts that she hadn't used before. Suddenly weary, she climbed the stairs and stood in the living room doorway watching Rosie as she played with the dolls' house. *I am a kidnapper. Maggie will probably get custody, perhaps temporary, but at this moment I am breaking the law. Where are you, Teddy?*

Rosie was talking to the miniature figures. 'Don't be frightened. There's no coal shed.'

Tia blinked back new moisture. Her hands were bunched at her sides; she felt ready to give someone a beating. 'Would you like something to eat, Rosie?'

The child turned and blinked. She was hungry. 'I can smell bacon,' she said.

'A bacon butty?'

Rosie laughed. 'Yes, please, but it does sound funny when you say it.'

'Oh, you'll just have to get used to me. And stay away from the windows. If someone comes to my downstairs door, carry on as you are. It's hide and seek. Mr Quinn has to guess where we are, and I like to win.'

'Are we being naughty, Miss Bellamy?'

Tia shook her head. 'We're just having fun and bacon, Rosie.'

Her hands shook as she placed bacon under the grill. How much longer was he going to be away? *He's the adult; I'm still a child because I've been so sheltered from the more disturbing elements in society. But this is why you came here, Tia. You saw a slice of this in London, and you chose Liverpool because London is too close to Pa. You are making a difference. You are breaking the law, so just live with that fact.*

Rosie was rearranging furniture in the dolls' house.

Tia handed her the sandwich on a plate. 'Wash your hands first. The bathroom's through there. Then wash them again when you've finished eating, because the dolls' house is my most special and precious possession.'

'Yes, Miss.'

How many items could be packed into the boot of an MG? How many bits and pieces might be fitted onto the shelf behind the seats? Where the hell was he? Time ticked on. Rosie fell asleep on the sofa, while Tia padded about in bare feet so as not to disturb her. She needed a telephone, and she made a note of that under the titles for Teddy's Tom Quirke books.

Were he and Maggie hurt; had there been an accident? Three hours? Three hours to collect a change of clothing for two people? She couldn't leave Rosie, didn't yet know any neighbours she might ask for help, had no phone, must stay hidden in case the police guessed where Rosie was . . . oh, God.

When she finally heard his car arriving, she stood at the top of the stairs and listened while he pushed his key into the lock of her ground-floor entrance. It had to be him, because she knew the sound of an MG's engine, and he was the only person with a key to her flat. She dashed down and drew back the bolts. 'Where have you been?' she asked sharply.

'Good God, woman – we aren't even married. Where's your gun or your battle axe?'

Tia reined in her nerves. 'Sorry. I was worried. You look exhausted, and where's Maggie?'

'Is Rosie OK?'

'She's asleep. Maggie?'

'In hospital. Let me in, please.'

She stood back and allowed him to pass into the small downstairs hall.

He took the stairs first, and she followed behind him.

'Coffee, please,' he begged when they reached the living room. The child opened her eyes and gave him a sweet smile. 'Hello, Mr Quinn.'

He sat at the bottom of the sofa and held the child's hands. 'Hello, Rosie. Did you play with the dolls' house?'

Rosie nodded. 'I had to keep my hands clean.'

Tia went into the kitchen to make coffee.

'You must be special if Miss Bellamy let you play with her dolls' house. She won't let anyone else near it. I asked if I could play with it, and all I got was a dirty look. Now, would you like egg on toast and a glass of milk?'

She nodded, wide-eyed. 'Where's Nana?'

'I sent her to bed because she was very tired. So you'll have to stay with me and Miss Bellamy for a short time. Just let me put your order in with the waitress. Stay there.' He followed Tia into the kitchen.

'Well?' Tia asked.

He closed the door. 'Maggie collapsed,' he whispered.

'Oh no, poor Maggie. Poor Rosie,' Tia said, her voice low.

'I got her to the hospital, and her heart's fine, but she's completely wiped out. They've stuck needles in her and taken about a pint of blood for this, that and the other – liver test, kidney function test, blood count, all that jazz – she's on a drip for rehydration, and can Rosie have scrambled eggs on toast with a glass of milk?'

Tia nodded and passed him a cup of coffee. 'Do you want anything?'

Yes, you, but I can't have you.

'Teddy?'

'Not yet, thanks. My stomach's in knots.'

She perched on a stool. 'How do we stand legally?'

Theo shook his head before telling her about his encounter with Emily Garner. An emergency order had been obtained for Maggie to act as guardian, but Maggie was out of the picture just now. 'I'll deal with this as soon as I can,' he said. 'Emily will vouch for me.'

'And meanwhile, when someone lets slip that Maggie's in hospital and no neighbour knows where Rosie is – what then?'

He scratched his head in the manner of Stan Laurel. 'The police need to know that the child is safe – that's the main thing. I'll talk to Emily again tonight, because I must come clean to her. She'll take up the slack, I hope. And I do have her home number.'

'Well, of course you do. Jack says she's your girlfriend.'

'Just one of them,' he said.

Tia picked up a couple of eggs and some milk. 'Did you see Emily before Maggie went into hospital?'

He shook his head wearily.

'So you knew Maggie was off the map and you said nothing?'

'That's right. Look, I'll take the rap for all of it.'

'But why? This is a sizeable risk and we could be in trouble for not following protocol—' She stopped, open-mouthed; he was lifting up his shirt to show her his back.

'This is part of the why. Fortunately, the RAF didn't mind my disfigurement – after all, I was only a rear gunner, so I didn't need to be a perfect model. The stripes are cuts made by a whip with a metal core. The prettier, more interesting bits are slash and stab wounds inflicted by a variety of knives. A broken rib pierced my lung, my arms have been fractured, and I have a metal plate in my skull. I tend to avoid strong magnets.' He pulled down his shirt. 'And that's why I take risks, why I never returned to live in America and why I put my neck on the line for kids like Rosie. And don't cry. I can't cope with weeping women.'

But she crossed the room and pulled him into her arms. A mere two or three inches shorter than he was, she looked him in the eye. 'Who did that to you?'

He gazed into those violet eyes. 'Masked men,' he answered. 'Probably the same group of cowards who killed my mom.' He pulled away from her and left the kitchen. She now knew more than anyone else; even his Liverpool relatives had never seen his back, had never known the full truth about his early years. And there was so much more, too much more . . .

'Yes, you will get some dinner,' Rosie was telling one of the tiny dolls. 'The jumping up and down men don't come any more, and the bad man got killed in the park.

What? No, he's never coming back. Nana's asleep, cos she's tired, so I'm in charge.'

Theo listened to her before creeping downstairs and returning to his own living quarters. Rosie Tunstall was organizing her own therapy through Tia's dolls. 'She is going to be OK,' he said as he entered his living room. He poured himself a double whisky for Dutch courage, took a deep breath, and phoned Emily Garner.

The whisky hit his head almost immediately, as his stomach was empty. 'Emily,' he almost purred, 'there's been a development.' He gave her an account of his very long day. 'So Rosie's in the upstairs apartment with her teacher. The cops need to know she's safe. Maggie asked us to keep her until she's out of hospital – just a day or two. Feel free to visit and examine Rosie's accommodation if you need to.' He paused while she ranted on.

'Yes, it's unusual and yes, I know you'll have to tell your boss, but Rosie is happy and occupied here.'

He allowed her to drone on while he switched to come-hither mode.

'Are you still there, Theo?' she asked.

He drained the glass. 'Emily,' he whispered, 'you and I have been friends for many years. In fact, I think we are very close friends. Please, I beg you, try to sort this out for little Rosie's sake. She needs continuity, not some anonymous bed in a place filled already by disturbed children. You won't regret it, I promise.'

'Theo, it's not that easy, I–'

'Go and see Maggie, then. Get her to sign something to the effect that her teacher is Rosie's babysitter for now. Please, Emily. Do it for me.'

'Your voice would seduce a saint, Theo.'

Inwardly, he agreed. 'It's the American edge, Emily. It makes women think of gangsters and cowboys.'

'You're smiling. I can hear your smile.'

'Yes, I'm smiling. Call me.' He replaced the receiver. Life was getting complicated, and he needed food. Canned soup and white bread were all he could find, so he heated the former and dunked the latter, grateful for the only nourishment he'd had since this morning's bacon sandwich.

Thinking about bacon sandwiches brought breakfast and Tia into his head. It was a strange situation, as he knew so little about her while knowing everything. Had he been waiting for her? Was she the one who could accept his past, his difficult future, the conditions that bound him even in this country? And how the hell did a person fall for someone as quickly as this? She'd given him a hug, and he'd run away faster than sand off a new shovel; he'd kissed her forehead, and she'd reacted . . . oh, bugger, as Tia might say.

With his stomach happier and the alcoholic haze dispersing, he went out to the car to fetch Rosie's clothes. Deciding not to disturb Rosie in case she was asleep, he used the key to let himself in. He tapped gently on the upper door to the apartment. Tia opened it. 'Ah, her things,' she said. 'She's in the bath playing with my ducks, and I was trying to find something of mine for her to sleep in.'

He told her that he and she were probably in the clear to babysit, since he'd managed to persuade Emily Garner to pave the way. 'It depends on how long Maggie is in hospital and whether her decision to entrust Rosie to us is enough. Welfare tends towards keeping all eggs in one basket, but I don't want our hatchling locked in a jail for kids.'

Tia took the clothes from him. 'Sit down,' she said. 'I'll just get her out of the bath and into bed. I've put the dolls' house in her room, because she's had a couple of naps today, and she may not be sleepy. Also, it will be the

142

first thing she sees when she wakes.' She pondered for a moment. 'And I've made a decision; I'll tell you later.'

While she was gone, he went to look at her bookshelves. He found an interesting and rather eclectic mix; Austen, Thackeray and Dickens rubbed shoulders with the Famous Five and Just William. She had *Beano* and *Dandy* annuals alongside Aristotle, Agatha Christie, Shakespeare, Wilde, George Bernard Shaw and, of course, Tom Quirke. There were hard-backed diaries dating back to 1948, when she had been in her teens, and several photograph albums on a low shelf.

She returned. 'Voices low,' she whispered. 'Our little charge misses nothing. We're going to play just suppose.'

'Just suppose what?'

'Just suppose Maggie is kept in hospital for days. Then just suppose your girlfriend moves Rosie into a children's home. Then bugger that, and just suppose Isadora Bellamy.'

Theo frowned. 'Go on.'

'Just suppose Rosie is a little pale and underfed.'

'Which she is, so I don't need to just suppose.'

Tia nodded her agreement. 'And just suppose that your foolish and inexperienced new teacher leaves you a note saying that she's taken Rosie for a holiday in Kent, or London, or both, depending on where Isadora is. Can you see the headlines? About Isadora Bellamy caring for a neglected child?'

He frowned. 'But you didn't want people to know who your parents are.'

'In your opinion, is that more important than Rosie's safety?'

'No,' he replied without hesitation.

'And I have little or nothing to lose, Teddy.'

'You could lose your job.' *And I could lose you.*

'I am very good at acting innocent and stupid. I'm very good at acting, full stop. And my mother could charm the

143

underwear off a monk. If we're discovered, she'll fix it. Pa is, of course, the fly in the ointment, but I can swat him.'

'And you'd do all this for Rosie?'

Tia smiled. 'And for you.'

He gasped audibly.

'Worry not,' she said, placing a hand on his cheek. 'There's something going on, neither of us is ready for it, and we're both terrified of it, so we slow down.'

His heart leapt about like a caged bird, and he knew the fear was showing in his eyes. This girl was far too clever for her own good. And too clever for him, of course. 'Sometimes I think you're older than I am, Tia.'

'My mother has said that for years, and she's even older than you are.'

He grinned broadly. 'Then she must be truly ancient.'

Tia agreed. 'Decrepit, yet still beautiful. Do remember, the world is putty in her hands. For years she carried my father, whose acting skills are nothing unless she's there to guide him.'

A thought occurred to Theo. 'What if she's on her way here?'

She raised her shoulders. 'She has her own telephone line. I'll call her tomorrow. If she's on the brink of leaving, all the better for us, because she can look after Rosie in my flat. I can't imagine my mother letting anything or anyone go without a fight. And Ma isn't fair when it comes to the protection of her girls. She'll stop at nothing to get her way.'

It struck Theo that while Tia might have inherited her father's lack of patience, she had also gained her mother's backbone, staying power and acting ability. 'We're in this mess together,' he said. 'While I'd hate to lose my job, I can exist on my writing.'

'And I should manage well on theatre and film work, so we are equal on that score.'

He turned sideways and studied her. 'I don't want to lose you.'

'I know.'

'How do you know?'

'I don't know how I know, but I know. And I know that you know that I don't want to lose you.' She frowned. 'Can we go back to just suppose? It was so much easier than I knowing.'

The doorbell sounded. 'You get it, Teddy. I'll go and make sure that Rosie's settled.' She left the room without giving him time to respond.

Theo descended the staircase. He hoped it wasn't a policeman or Emily Garner or someone else from Welfare, but he opened the door to find Dr Simon Heilberg on the doorstep. 'Is she in?' the visitor asked.

'Yes, she's caring for a child. Is there a problem?'

For the first time, Simon grinned at Theo. 'I think we share a problem, Mr Quinn. The hospital where Maggie Stone is a patient has let the police know that Rosie is here with Tia. I may need a tetanus injection, because Sadie Tunstall, mother of that child, bit me. Twice. The practice I'm with is attached periodically to Ivy Lane police station. She attacked two policemen, me, and a woman who was reporting a missing dog. Sergeant Nixon had to go for stitches. She was very, very drunk. And Tia has the child?'

'Yes, but the grandmother has custody, and she's in hospital, as you know.'

'A bit of a mess, then, Mr Quinn?'

Theo nodded. 'Go up. I've given Tia Rosie's clothes, so I can leave now.'

'Just a moment.' Simon placed a hand on Theo's arm. 'I want that child in outpatients at Alder Hey on Monday morning. Tia and I will take her and let the experts loose.

145

I'm aware that there's probably been neglect and psychological damage, but we need to look for injuries.'

Theo nodded. 'Good thinking, Doc. Thank you.'

'I promise you, Tia and Rosie that I'll do my best to get the little girl away from her mother. Some people are not fit to have kids.' He offered his hand and Theo shook it, then the doctor sped upstairs.

Tia was seated on the sofa. She looked tired, tense and beautiful. 'Hi,' she said.

He rolled up a sleeve to display a bandage. 'Sadie Tunstall bit me. I was called in to Ivy Lane, and she attacked several people. She'll be charged. Monday, you and I will take Rosie for a full examination at the children's hospital. She needs a proper, decent family to adopt her.'

Tia nodded. 'I'm going to bed,' she said.

'Do you want company?'

She glowered. 'Not with a child in the flat, no.'

'Sorry,' he murmured.

Tia rose to her feet. 'Anyway, that's all over between us.'

'Have you fallen in love with the little girl? If you want to adopt, you must marry.'

'Then I'll marry.'

'Really? Who?'

'I have absolutely no bloody idea. Thanks for coming to see me, and please support my intention to keep Rosie here till her grandmother recovers.' She walked to him and placed a kiss on his cheek. 'Some day, your princess will come, Simon.'

Crestfallen once more, he left. She was his princess, but she didn't want him. And they all lived happy ever after? 'Not me,' he mumbled, 'never me.'

Seven

Sunday was quite an adventure for Rosie. She was so excited that she started nibbling at her nails, and she'd already had the gentle, no-nail-biting lecture from her new teacher just yesterday. If she wanted to be a pretty young lady, she needed clean hair, unbitten nails and a spotless neck. Clothes were just the outer wrapping, and they didn't cover these important details. 'Shoulders back, and head up, Rosie. Not too far up, or you'll fall over something and give onlookers a free laugh. Oh, and always carry a handkerchief – I have some pretty ones somewhere. Just remember, you're as good as, if not better than other people. Walk tall.'

Miss Bellamy had decided to make her charge a whole new outfit of clothes. She took a dress of her own, measured Rosie, and made a pattern from brown wrapping paper before cutting out and tacking together a skirt followed by a lovely, grown-up style jacket. The little girl had to stand on a chair and stay still after her teacher warned her, 'I am lethal with pins, or so my sisters tell me. We all had to learn to sew when we were not much older than you are. Ma taught us to help with her costumes – she's an actress. Now, we take this off carefully, so that I can use my Singer to stitch it all together properly. Be brave, and try not to scratch yourself on pins. We don't want you to be full of holes, do we?'

Rosie was completely enthralled by the process and enchanted by Miss Bellamy; sewing was like magic, far cleverer than Mrs Atherton and her knitting. In a very short time, the sewing machine had flown over every seam and dart, and the resulting rose-coloured suit was amazing. 'Oh, thank you, Miss Bellamy. I never had nothing like this before. Dark pink. I like dark pink and light pink. I like red, too.'

But Tia hadn't finished the job. From a white nightdress scattered with roses, she produced a sleeveless blouse and a pretty hair band. 'Will you trust me to cut your hair? You seem to have more than your fair share of it.'

Rosie was pleased by the idea. 'It gets knotted up. Sometimes I can't get a comb through it. It's cos it's curly.'

Tia fetched the scissors. 'I noticed some marks when you were in the bath yesterday. How did they happen?' She kept her tone as casual as she could manage. Seeing so many bruises on such a small body had been disturbing.

'He did them. But I'm susposed to say I fell downstairs or tripped up in the street. But really, it was him.'

'Mr Tunstall?'

'Yes.'

'Did your mother try to stop him?'

'When she had no gin, yes, but he hit her, too. She couldn't get money off the jumping up and down men if she had marks, so he got really mad then. I can tell about him now, cos he's dead. Nana said nobody dead can hurt us.'

Tia swallowed. She felt sick and angry and extremely sad. Teddy was visiting Maggie in hospital, as were neighbours. As far as Rosie was concerned, Nana had been sent to bed in her own house and was being cared for twice a day by a nurse with a bike. Nana must not be disturbed except by the nurse with a bike. Meanwhile, police patrolled the streets, knocking on doors and talking to anyone over the age of reason and young enough to remain rational.

'Miss Bellamy?'

'Yes?'

'Why are some people nice like you and Mr Quinn and Mr and Mrs Atherton, and Martha and Harry, and some people not nice? What makes some of them to go nasty?'

Tia closed her eyes for an instant and swallowed. This was an infant who knew too much, too soon. 'Only God knows the answer to that one, Rosie. We're all made differently.' *I will not cry. Pull yourself together, Bellamy. Think of Shakespeare's Portia and show some bloody dignity.* 'You're a good person, Rosie, so add yourself to the list.'

A Constable Piggot was coming to see Rosie later today. So far, because of her youth, she had not been questioned, but the time had come, and Tia wanted her Rosie – yes, *her* Rosie – to look perfect. She cut the hair in layers, as it was too thick to manage en masse, before bathing the child, washing her hair and applying a conditioner to wilful curls.

Rosie stood in front of Miss Bellamy's cheval mirror, her mouth shaped in a perfect O. A beautiful girl, also with her mouth in an O shape, looked back at her. 'Miss Bellamy?' said both girls, one in the mirror, the other real.

'Yes, dear?'

'Thank you. Is Nana going to wake up soon?'

Tia squatted down and smoothed the child's hair. 'She'll be back, dear. You look wonderful. Run down and knock on Mr Quinn's door. He won't recognize you until he looks properly at your face. You are quite the prettiest child I ever saw. I did my best with your shoes, but we'll get new ones tomorrow or on Tuesday. You and I might have a day in town, do our shopping, then have a meal.'

'Pink shoes?'

'Sorry, but no. Sandals for everyday wear, black patent ankle-straps for best, a pair of gym shoes to play in, and a pair of wellies for when there's rain.'

'That's a lot of shoes, Miss Bellamy.'

'It is indeed. And when I was a little girl, I had two sisters, and we all had the wellies, the Sunday best, the play shoes and the sandals. But we'll get you some pink hair slides, pink beads and a pink bag and gloves if we can find them.'

When Rosie had run off to strut about in front of her headmaster, Tia sat on the floor among debris. Paper pattern pieces, bits of fabric, some scraps bigger than others, Rosie's dark, cut-off curls, a colouring book, two reading books, crayons, plasticine and paints all cluttered the living room. It was a living room now, because it looked alive, vibrant and colourful. And it hit Tia in that moment: she wanted to keep Rosie for ever.

Take your time, O stupid one. Simon is right, you'd need to be married. The only person you could marry quickly is Simon, and you don't want him, so that would make an unhappy home. Anyway, it will take a while to get the poor child away from Sadie in the legal sense, and Rosie has a lovely grandmother who's still in her forties. Yes, you'd adopt Maggie, too, wouldn't you? Your silliness knows no bounds, Portia Bellamy.

Face it squarely, idiot. You want to pledge your troth, for what it's worth, to the man downstairs, a chap you scarcely know, a fellow with a handsome face, kind eyes, and a back that looks like a relief map of a volcanic region where earthquakes and eruptions rule. He has problems. He has girlfriends. He probably has your foolish heart, too. He may not want you; not every man is as susceptible as Simon Heilberg when it comes to you and your charms.

The door opened and Rosie bounded in. He was with her, of course. Was little Rosie playing matchmaker?

'Miss Bellamy,' he said solemnly, 'who is this gorgeous young woman you sent to my door? Something about her seems familiar, though I can't quite put my finger on her identity. Is she selling household goods or encyclopedias, perhaps? Or might she be from the RSPCA, sent to see if I'm caring properly for Tyger?'

Rosie skipped round him. 'Mr Quinn, Mr Quinn, it's me – Rosie.'

'There was a Rosie yesterday, but she had untidy hair and she didn't skip and didn't say much. I can't shut this one up. We've had money tables, two-times and three-times tables, a lecture on the Viking invasion of the Mersey—'

'I read that in the Picton Library,' Rosie announced proudly.

'She read that in the Picton Library,' he repeated, his face expressionless. 'Go and look at yourself in a long mirror, child. Make sure you know who you are, because I need convincing.' He winked at Tia.

'I saw that,' Rosie said, hands on hips.

'She looks good,' he said when Rosie had left.

'She looks happy for now,' was Tia's reply. 'Let's hope it lasts.'

When the little girl was completely out of earshot, Theo grabbed Tia's hands. 'Emily Garner's on her way – welfare woman. I'll see her downstairs, but she may want to talk to you. Any chance you can make yourself look plain?'

Tia cocked her head to one side. 'Whose daughter am I? And may I ask why I must look plain?'

He grinned. 'Emily wants my body, so I took a drink or

three and almost made love to her over the phone in order to make sure we keep the little one until Maggie gets out of hospital. I'll tell Rosie you're playing the same joke as she did by making yourself unrecognizable.'

'Is this in my job description, Mr Quinn? Or are you adding a codicil?'

'Indeed. I added a couple of clauses, actually.'

'Bugger. Sounds like the Treaty of Versailles.'

Seconds ticked by while he hung on to her hands. For the first time, they gazed into each other's eyes like a pair of lovelorn loons. 'Portia,' he whispered. 'Beautiful name, beautiful woman. What the hell is happening here?'

Tia inhaled sharply.

He grinned at her. 'Well?'

'Theodore,' was her eventual reply. She gave him the sexiest of her collection of smiles. It involved mobile eyelashes, brilliant teeth and a gentle exhalation of breath. 'Stop it,' she murmured. 'Stop, because I like it.'

'I wish I could stop. And I wish you'd keep that smile to yourself, because you light up the room, and you know it. Now, go and get scruffy while I pay court to Emily Garner. She's not my kind of woman, but I think she's a man-eater dressed in Marks and Spencer clothing.'

'Is she pretty?'

'Yes.'

'Prettier than I am?'

'No.'

'Give me ten minutes and she'll look like Greta Garbo and I'll be one of the ugly sisters.'

'OK.' He released her hands. 'Rosie?' he called. 'Or whatever your name is? Come along, because we have to meet a pretty lady, then you may come back up here for lunch if you wish.' He looked again at Tia. 'I can't wait to see you looking wrecked.'

'Oh, go away, Teddy.'

'I'm going, I'm going.'

She grinned like a teenager this time. 'I shan't go over the top.' She would, of course. Rosie arrived. 'Go on, the pair of you – shoo. I have tidying to do, and I must put my face on.' She blushed when he winked at her again before leaving with Rosie. 'Damn it, I don't blush any more, do I?' she mouthed to herself as the door closed behind them.

Alone at last, Tia raided her makeup box. She applied a full green mask, covered it with a mixture of grease-paint numbers five and nine, drew pale pink lines around her eyelids and slightly dark smudges under each eye. After combing through some hair-grey, she fastened abundant and deliberately greased locks into a net perched on top of her head. Circular spectacles with clear glass completed the picture. She looked fortyish, not very well and decidedly unattractive. 'He'd better warn Rosie,' she muttered. 'God, I look like something that fell off a dust-cart.'

Clothes. She found a washed-out blue blouse that had seen better days, probably in the latter part of the nineteenth century, a grey skirt and some black slippers. In the cheval which had so recently reflected a pretty child, there now appeared a woman of indeterminate age. The green mask, her first application, had been used by her father, who became flushed and overheated on stage. Although covered by more conventional tones, it lent a pallor to Tia's skin, and she now added the final touch, which she knew would amuse Teddy. Collingford's Toothbrown, applied by most who played the witches on the heath, had been used quite recently by the Bellamy sisters in the Scottish play for Chaddington Green's amateur dramatic group. Toothbrown resisted saliva and took half a tin of tooth powder to remove, but she couldn't resist. She looked absolutely ghastly.

Downstairs, Theo was preparing Rosie. 'Miss Bellamy is going to dress up in something weird. It's because I pretended not to recognize you, but we'll turn the joke on her by treating her as if she always looks terrible. Can you manage that?'

Rosie nodded.

'No laughing?' he asked.

'No laughing,' she agreed, her eyes dancing.

'No acting surprised?'

'I won't act surprised.'

'Good girl. Here comes the welfare lady. I call her Emily, but you must call her Miss Garner. Be polite and happy. OK?'

Emily Garner arrived armed and dangerous. Wearing a short-sleeved blue dress, she had applied her war paint and tottered on high heels that made her legs look great. 'Emily,' he gushed. 'Isn't Rosie pretty in her new suit? Miss Bellamy made it for her.'

She cast an eye over the child, nodded and said, 'Very nice indeed.'

Theo winked at Rosie, who smiled prettily. 'Miss Garner,' she said. 'Thank you for coming to see me.'

The invader sat on the sofa's edge, scarcely glancing further at the child she was supposed to be visiting. 'Lovely. Do you like Miss Bellamy, Rosie?' He looked wonderful in a short-sleeved shirt and moleskin trousers.

'I love her, Miss Garner. We do painting, counting, reading and jigsaws,' Rosie said, 'and I play with a great big dolls' house. It has lights in it, real lights that can be switched on and off.'

'Good!' Emily continued to stare at Theo. 'Mrs Stone is doing well, you'll be pleased to hear. Anaemia. She'll probably need to take iron tablets, that's all.'

'That's great news,' Theo said, not troubling to remind her that he'd visited Rosie's grandmother in the hospital.

He turned to Rosie. 'Your grandmother's not as tired as she was, child, and she'll be back with us soon. See if you can find Tyger, but don't dirty your new clothes.'

The little girl abandoned him to the tender mercies of a female predator whose find-a-husband antennae had probably been on red alert for over a decade. She was not his type, but he was definitely hers. It was time to speak. 'Miss Bellamy and a doctor friend of hers are taking Rosie to Alder Hey tomorrow. She shows signs of non-accidental injuries. When will Maggie Stone be home?'

'A couple of days, Theo. She's happy for you and Miss Bellamy to keep her granddaughter until then, and I've cleared it with the powers.'

'Thank you, Emily. Would you like to visit Miss Bellamy?'

'I'll take your word for her, because Mrs Stone will be out of hospital very soon. The woman upstairs is good with Rosie, I take it?'

He nodded. 'She's turned her apartment into an activity centre. A very homely type, she is. I'll vouch for her. In fact, Miss Bellamy will be in charge for a couple of hours today, as I am lunching with my cousins.' With this untruth, he prevented the issue of an invitation to lunch with Emily Garner.

She cleared her throat. 'We might have a drink one weekend, or even a meal, perhaps?'

'Yes, that would be nice,' he replied. 'And you'll be at the end-of-year party.' He stood. 'I must rescue Rosie's clothes from my kitten's talons.'

Emily rose gracefully to her feet. 'Of course. I'll be in touch.'

Relief flooded his veins as she walked out of the room.

She turned just once to offer him a brilliant smile.

Theo followed her to the outer door, leaning on its solid surface once the woman had left. 'Being so handsome is a difficult occupation,' he muttered. Opening his eyes, he saw Rosie walking towards him.

'Your cat is mad,' she complained.

'Really?'

She nodded, her face solemn. 'Going round and round in circles.'

'Is he, now?'

'Yes. Why does he do that?'

'He's trying to work out which is his front end and which is his behind.'

The child shook her head. 'Why do grown-ups do that?'

'Do what?'

'Give daft answers to children. We aren't stupid, you see. He knows where his mouth is, cos he eats with it, but he's still working out why he has a tail. He thinks it's another animal following him, so he bites it, then howls cos he's hurt himself. Mad.'

'Sorry. Would you like some lemonade? Don't drip it on your clothes, or we'll have to apologize to Miss Bellamy.' He walked to the kitchen. *Oh, she's gonna kill me. Try to look plain, I told her. I bet she's up there now in wrinkled lisle stockings, curlers and a headscarf done up like a turban.* He went outside and sat in his deckchair for half an hour, one eye on a she-must-stay-clean Rosie, the other on a clinically insane kitten. *And now my blessed phone's ringing, and that policeman will be here later this afternoon. Will I live till this afternoon? Bugger, as Tia would say . . .*

He picked up Rosie's half-finished glass of lemonade and went to answer the phone. 'Hello, Theo Quinn here.'

'Mr Quinn?'

My God, it's Isadora Bellamy. The same voice as Tia, but older. 'Yes, I'm Theo Quinn,' he repeated.

'Isadora Bellamy,' she said. 'May I speak to my dau-ghter?'

'Of course. I'll have to go and get her from the upper apartment. Will you wait, or shall I get her to call you?'

'I'll wait, thank you.'

He placed the receiver on the table, turned round and saw Rosie. 'Your nana will love your new suit.' He smiled when Rosie clapped her hands. 'Now, please go and get Miss Bellamy. If the outside door's locked, ring her bell. Tell her there's a telephone call for her. I'll take care of your lemonade.' When she had left, he took care of the drink by adding a double dose of whisky and swallowing the lot. To hell with it; a man had needs. The trouble was, he tended to mislay his inhibitions after a double Scotch.

He combed his wayward hair, paced about, wondered about his blood pressure, heard Rosie returning. 'She's coming now, Mr Quinn.'

'Thank you.' He picked up the receiver. 'She's coming now, Mrs Bellamy.'

'Good. Is she well?'

'Er . . . yes.'

'Are you unsure?'

'No, I believe she's in good health.' He moved away and felt his jaw drop. A picture of health and beauty stood before him. Portia Bellamy, dressed in a fitted, bright red dress with a peplum that emphasized her shape, and with murderously high-heeled shoes to match, glared at him. 'You owe me one tin of tooth powder,' she hissed. Her hair was still damp. She smelled of sunshine and flowers and summer rain, and he was no longer making sense, even to himself.

Tia took the call. 'Hello? Oh, darling Ma – how are you? Yes, yes, he's my landlord and my headmaster. What?' She looked him up and down. 'Well, he's not as ugly as Mrs Melia, but not as pretty as we are. Right. Fire away.'

Grinning broadly, Theo took Rosie out to the rear garden. *That was a close call. I think I got off lightly, all things considered. She must have seen Emily leaving, and she's cleaned up her act just to make a point. This is part of her charm, part of your reason for liking her. Was liking a strong enough word?* 'There's Tyger,' he told Rosie. 'Look, he's trying to catch a bird thirty feet up in the sky. You're right, after all. He's as mad as a hatter.'

He watched the little girl chasing his kitten. *I suppose Isadora and Nanny will arrive soon. Rosie and Maggie can stay with me; I'm not letting them go off home in case Sadie reappears and starts playing tricks again. Oh, God. I'll be sharing my house with five females, three up and two down.*

'Mr Quinn?'

'Yes?'

'Why are hatters mad?'

'I believe they used to put lead in the brims of the hats. Too much lead makes people ill and causes them to act strangely.'

Rosie blinked up at him. 'Do you know everything, Mr Quinn?'

'Definitely not,' he answered. He seemed to know very little about women, and he was about to be invaded. Panic threatened . . .

Tia joined them. 'I saw your girlfriend leave, and I had made a real effort to be dowdy. You would have left me in that state, wouldn't you? And I ran out of toothpowder. Have you any idea of the damage I am doing to the enamel? That stuff's like scouring powder.'

'What are you talking about?' he asked.

'I browned my teeth,' she announced haughtily. 'I browned them to make me old and ugly.'

'In the oven? Like browning a joint of meat?'

Tia looked round; Rosie was out of earshot. 'You are

lucky not to be on the receiving end of a Bellamy Burn. As for your silly question, we have something to paint on our teeth when we want to look old.'

'We?'

'The Bellamys. Actors. Shakespeare, mostly. Don't you remember him? He was in your class at school. Wore tights. He did all those plays with people running onstage, talking a load of hogwash, and running off again. No actor sits unless he or she is dead. Some do soliloquies with daggers in their backs or while talking to a human skull. Freud would have had a field day with Shakespeare.'

This is why. It's not just the way she looks and speaks; it's who and what she is. 'Yes, I remember him,' he said. 'He sat at the back scribbling with a feather, ink up to his armpits. Never got a smile out of him, and he was thumped by one of our baseball stars who had huge muscles and no brain.'

'Why?' Tia asked.

'Well, Shakie asked could he compare him to a summer's day, and all hell broke loose. It was like the Alamo all over again. We all joined in, and our teacher made for the hills, never to be seen again. All because of an ink-spattered playwright and sonnetist.'

'Poor Shakespeare.' She shook her head sadly.

Theo continued. 'Even his mom despaired. She always said he'd come to nothing if he didn't clean up his act and stop dressing like a woman at weekends. She thought he was uncertain about his gender, but men had to play all the parts. He was the back end of Richard Three's dying horse, too. Made a real hash of it, no sense of direction.'

'And who was the front end?'

He shrugged and told her he was pleading the Fifth Amendment.

'Just as I thought.' She giggled. 'Yes, your face fits the part.'

'Glad I wasn't the rear end, then. So, is Isadora on her way?'

Her face entered serious mode. 'Yes, and she's nervous. Ma is a complicated character, and Pa will go volcanic. The ash will cover most of Europe and half of Africa. My mother is a very good woman, so sweet and kind, but under the icing sugar and the marzipan she can seem as cold as steel. Beyond the steel is a heart of gold, which she does her best to ignore. It was the steel that got her through the pretending to be drunk time, but the precious metal's still there.' She sighed heavily. 'If that twenty-four carat comes to the surface, she might give in and stop proceedings out of pity for him.'

'And which metal is she today?'

'Steel with a thin layer of gold plate. She's bought a flat in Canterbury for Juliet. Pa's on a tour, so Ma's denuded the house of furniture, because she bought most of it. That's in storage. They are packing personal stuff, and Delia will use the van to bring it here. Ma and Nanny will travel by train.'

'When?'

Tia raised an eyebrow. 'Your guess is as good as mine, but within days, I believe. The divorce papers and all pieces of evidence are filed with her lawyer, who is waiting for her nod, as is her agent. She's intending to buy Bartle Hall from Pa, because it's his only asset, and it's crumbling. The money he earned went on wine, women and London clubs where actors meet. Without Ma, work may dry up for him, because they used to come as a pair like Hepburn and Tracy, the difference being that Tracy can act, while Pa needs scaffolding – my mother.'

'Bugger,' he whispered.

'Stop upstaging me, Quinn. That's my line.'

160

'You have copyright?'

'Absolutely.'

'Bugger,' he repeated. 'What happens now?'

'I sue, or . . .' she blushed and turned away.

'Or what, Tia? The Bellamy Burn?'

And there it was between them, a roaring, snarling animal that would not be tamed, an elemental force of nature that belonged to neither of them, and ruled both. Theo, who had been in love eighteen years earlier, recognized the symptoms, while Tia, whose experiences had scarcely got past the lust stage, remained confused. This was different. What the hell was going on? She'd known him for a few days, yet she couldn't imagine life without him. It was very silly. She walked off to find Rosie.

Theo watched as she attempted to stalk through the room, her gait unsteady. She probably needed a pilot's licence to drive such shoes; she was now taller than he was. *Trying to stop this would be fruitless. It's like the idea of training iron filings to stay away from a huge magnet. It was the same with Sally, but I was young and foolish then, a stranger to England and a slave to the RAF's Brylcreem boys. Do we never learn? I've survived almost nineteen years without the pain of love; now, I'm losing my reason, my strength, but not my memory. Damn, this hurts.*

Tia returned and sat in the deckchair he had left in the garden. She'd already told him once that something unusual was happening. What was happening lay well outside the scope of her experience. He was a dozen years older than she was, so was she looking for a father figure? No way was he old enough to fill that role. Older brother? She shook her head almost imperceptibly.

Closing her eyes for a few minutes, she allowed her mind free rein. *What is it about Theodore Quinn, aka Tom Quirke, aka Teddy? Ticks a lot of boxes, I suppose. Attractive, tanned, dark-eyed, a lunatic, loves children and*

161

animals, creative, industrious, protective of Rosie, very aware of me. Aware, but afraid, I think. Why? What troubles him? Am I too forward, too pushy? Ma certainly thinks I am. 'Let a man lead on the dance floor, and grant him the delusion that he is leading you through life,' Ma had suggested years earlier. But what did Ma think now? On the brink of divorce and . . . A shadow loomed over her, and she looked up.

Holding Rosie's hand, Theo looked down at the young woman who occupied his chair. 'Is this the Bellamy Burn? Do you pinch a man's seat?'

Double entendre yet again. She kicked off her shoes. If sparring continued, she needed to stop towering over this poor, frightened, delightful creature. 'Rosie, thank you for staying clean. A policeman is coming to talk to you very soon. Tell the truth, don't be shy, and try not to be cheeky.'

The child frowned. 'Am I cheeky, Miss Bellamy?'

'I should be worried if you weren't, and so would Mr Quinn. You're a clever girl. As you grow older, you'll learn to be cheeky silently, inside your head.'

'Colin Duckworth didn't learn,' Theo grumbled.

'He's a mere male,' was Tia's swift reply to that. 'We mature more quickly and learn when to keep our counsel. My father's still a teenager, and he's fifty-something. Throws a tantrum if he's given the wrong toothpaste.'

'Lend him your tooth powder,' Theo suggested.

Tia awarded him a look designed to cause a large war in a small country.

Rosie bent to pick up Tyger's miniature teddy, the gift bought by Tia. 'Here he is,' the child shouted triumphantly.

'Great,' Theo said. 'Tyger hates sleeping alone.' He turned and looked at the ridiculous kitten, who was

162

engaged in battle with a geranium. 'Look at that,' he muttered. 'My money's on the plant.'

They walked into the house, each holding one of Rosie's hands. It occurred to both that any casual onlooker might see them as a family, a mother and a father with their daughter. In Tia's heart, hope fluttered like a fledgling bird, up in the air, then down to earth, repeatedly. But all Theo felt was fear. Unless this heat died down, he would need to tell her things about which he had seldom spoken thus far.

Rosie put Tiny Ted in Tyger's basket. She was happy. Nana would be better soon, and Mr Quinn and Miss Bellamy were ... happy, too. They were happy together. 'Can I go up and play with the dolls' house, Miss? I'll wash my hands first.'

'My front door isn't locked. Yes, go up and help yourself.'

Rosie skipped outside. They could talk in private now.

Tia knew that she was the braver one. Something held Theo back, and she intended to break through the barrier. Boldly, she placed a hand on his face; bugger the male lead, she told her mother silently. This was the dawn of a new age, and women were moving on, no vapours, no declines, no Victorian females waiting for orders from husband or father. 'Why did you never marry?' she asked.

The power of speech seemed to have deserted him.

'Teddy?'

He cleared his throat. 'Genetics,' he achieved finally.

'Genetics?'

'Genetics,' he repeated. 'There's a fault in the line that shows up from time to time. I care too much for children to risk producing one of my own.'

She didn't remove her hand. 'I'm so sorry,' she whispered.

'As am I, Tia. But it's a fact. No matter who or when I married, the danger would be there. Yes, I was engaged almost two decades ago, but I was young, foolish and careless – you know that stage you go through when nothing can touch you, when the world's your playground?'

'Oh, yes. The recklessness of youth.'

'Then life changed for all of us, Tia. We matured quickly.'

'The war?' she asked.

He sighed, the air shuddering its way out of his lungs. 'War in the sky is a desperate and terrifying experience. It aged me. I killed so many people, and after several sorties I saw countless unoccupied seats at breakfast. One night, we lost fifty-six men, each and every one a friend and colleague. The mess would be silent, because we felt guilty about being alive. The Battle of Britain was also a battle of conscience. Now, my conscience forbids me to reproduce.'

'Oh, Teddy.' She placed her hands on his shoulders. 'Talk to Simon.'

'He doesn't like me, Tia.'

'Only because he knows I'm . . . fond of you. He can enquire about vasectomy.'

Theo shuddered. 'Look at me. I've stared death in the face, and I've looked briefly into the eyes of young Germans just before shooting them down. You've seen my back with all its scars. I survived all that, yet I remain terrified of surgery.'

'But it's not major surgery,' she told him.

'I'm a coward.'

'Good,' she declared. 'I was beginning to worry that you might be perfect. I'm not keen on perfect; it's a bit too Roedean and Oxbridge for me.'

Tia continued in charge, pulling his head down an

inch or so, since she had remained barefoot. But the kiss, which began life as her property, was quickly taken over by him. She was his oasis after a long drought, and he drank long and hard.

No one had ever kissed her in such a way, but perhaps none of her ex-boyfriends had been starving. She stopped thinking and lost herself in the moment, the minute, the quarter-hour – she had no idea how long the embrace lasted. He played with her hair, touched her throat, an arm, her behind, and it wasn't enough for either of them. When they finally separated, each had to fight for breath.

'What the hell was that?' she managed eventually. 'It tasted of whisky.'

'An American special,' was his answer. 'Learned at drive-in movies while making out.'

'In your teens?'

'Yes, we colonials start early. Not sex, no whisky, just kissing and stuff.'

'More like vacuuming,' she giggled.

'Are you complaining?'

She shook her head, but said nothing. Her brain was on fire. *He never married because a child might be affected by some fault, some handicap. How do I feel about giving birth to a disabled son or daughter? No bloody idea. He seems physically and mentally unaffected by whatever it is, yet he could possibly be a carrier, as could his offspring. The damage to him is probably emotional, too, and it's the root of his fear. I don't know what to say to him. But he's letting me in. I have the feeling that he's never before allowed anyone in.*

'Tia?'

'Quiet, I'm thinking. With my paucity of brain cells, it's a difficult process.'

'Don't be silly; you have twice my ability, as you know very well, Mother Superior.'

'Bollocks.'

'Another Roedean word?'

'No. Oxford. Shut up.' *Shall I ask him for the name of the disability and how it affects the unfortunate ones? Are they blind, unable to walk, mentally afflicted? No, I must wait. Whatever's happened belongs to him, so it's his to keep or tell.*

'Still thinking?' he asked.

'No, I've used up all my energy. After a kiss like that, it's understandable.'

'Ah, so I'm too much for you, then?'

She stared straight at him, her face expressionless. 'Best kiss ever, Mr Quinn. But we need to put you through all the paces, see how you follow through.'

'Is that a challenge?'

Tia raised her shoulders. 'Perhaps, though there is a child in the house at present, and I'm expecting Bellamys. Bellamys can be exhausting.'

'I noticed.'

'Juliet's the prettiest and quietest, but she isn't coming.'

'But Delia is?' *Six women. Four up and two down. Maybe I should take time off from writing and go for a cruise up the fjords. I've been promising myself that for years. There's only a week to get through at school, and I'd enjoy the fjords. Can I separate myself from this amazing woman?*

'Yes, Delia will drive their stuff up here,' Tia was saying. 'But she'll come a couple of days before or after they do, I imagine. And she won't stay, because she'll want to get back to her girlfriend. She's lesbian. Teddy?'

'What?'

'Stop worrying.'

He swallowed. 'It was my best ever kiss too, Portia. You're lovely.'

'So are you.' She shrugged. 'Don't worry. These things

happen, don't they? And always when we least expect them.'

He searched her face for clues, but found none. She did deadpan better than anyone he had ever met. That would be the drama training, damn it. 'So it's just another of life's hiccups?' *What are you hoping for, Theo? A yes, a no, a perhaps?*

At last, she awarded him a cheeky grin. 'I rather suspect it's more, but what do I know? The first time I met you in the school doorway, I thought yes, I'll be working for this man and yes, he's attractive and challenging. I think fate drove me towards Maitland and the other chap at the lettings agency, fate sent me here, to Crompton Villa and your body parts.' Her smile broadened.

'Another double entendre?' he asked.

'You do more of those than I do, Teddy.'

'Sorry.'

'Don't be sorry. You're the most interesting person I've met for a very long time. But there's a lot of stuff going on – Ma and Nanny Reynolds, that murder, Rosie and Maggie and Sadie. There's no time for us to be ourselves.' She blew him a kiss before going up to check on Rosie and prepare a late lunch.

She decided on a picnic. Mr Timidity could bring the drinks, but she hoped he'd leave the whisky alone. After all, the police were coming.

Meanwhile, several emotions fought for space in Theo's chest. He felt fear, exhilaration, need, impatience, loneliness and happiness. Near-insanity threatened; was he courting disaster?

Upstairs, Tia wore a silly smile and a sensible dress, since scarlet clothing and shoes seemed too flippant for a meeting with police. Rosie had managed a great deal of tidying; it was as if she were trying to pay for the privilege of staying here. 'You are not just a good girl, Rosie. You are the best.'

Rosie beamed; she was unused to praise. She was also unused to regular meals, cleanliness and a pleasant environment. 'I like it here, Miss Bellamy. It doesn't smell bad and there's a garden.'

It occurred yet again to Tia that children like this one appreciated stuff that had always been taken for granted by many, including herself. On the Bartle Hall estate, there were barns and cottages, stables, fields, gardens, summer houses, woods, ponds, a tree house, and many wild animals, including deer and ponies. For some people, life was a near-holiday; for others, it was prison, and it wasn't fair, wasn't designed to be fair.

The visiting policeman was a woman, and she brought a man with her. He was a policeman, though he wore an ordinary suit. They arrived early and found themselves picnicking in the rear garden with Mr Quinn, Miss Bellamy and Rosie Tunstall. The uniformed female explained to Rosie about her mother being in hospital, about Nana needing a rest, and about Miles Tunstall having been murdered. 'Do you know what that means, Rosie?' she asked kindly.

Rosie nodded. 'My mammy got sick because of all the gin, my nan's very tired, and that's why I'm staying here with Miss Bellamy. I heard Mrs Atherton telling Mr Atherton that my mammy loves gin more than she loves me, and Mr Atherton said it was a disgrace. Uncle Miles adopted me and I had to call him Daddy, but I kept forgetting. He got murdered on the park. That means somebody killed him.' She lowered her head.

'Rosie?' Constable Piggot touched the little girl's hair. 'The adoption wasn't completed when he died, sweetheart, so he wasn't your stepfather. You're still Rosie Stone.'

Up came the chin. 'He hit me when I wouldn't call him Daddy. He threw me in the coal shed and my head banged on the wall. That was when the jumping men came, and I had to stay outside.'

'Sadie and Flo's clients,' Theo interjected.

The man in the suit got out of his deckchair and sat on the ground with Rosie. 'My name's Dan. My children call me Dan-Dan the cop shop man.' He smiled. 'Did you know any of the jumping men?'

'No.' She shook her head. 'But they made a lot of noise. I saw some of them. I saw one hitting Uncle Miles.'

'Was the man who hit Uncle Miles very tall, with a beard?'

Rosie closed her eyes. 'No. He was fat and going baldy. He had a bit of hair low down. It started at his ears and went all the way round, but the top of his head was like a big boiled egg, but shiny.'

The plain clothes detective mouthed at his uniformed companion, 'Photographic memory?'

Rosie continued. 'Then my mam got beaten up because she wouldn't let a black man play jumping up and down. Uncle Miles hit her so hard, she slept for three days.'

Tia placed her sandwich in a piece of greaseproof; her appetite had gone. 'Concussion,' she said quietly.

'Mammy said she wouldn't go with men like him.' Rosie opened her eyes. 'She wouldn't go with the black man, and he was nice.'

'How was he nice?' Constable Piggot asked gently.

Rosie closed her eyes again. 'I was sat on the front doorstep, and he gave me a shilling. He had very white teeth and a big smile, but no beard. He had a green jumper and brown trousers with lines in the cloth. Black shoes and big feet, he had.' Her eyes flew open. 'I never saw a man with a beard, but that doesn't mean there wasn't one. I could have been in the coal shed.'

'So you've no idea who killed him, Rosie? We were wondering if it might have been one of the jumping men.'

Rosie nodded. 'It might have been, but I don't know.'

'It was a big, strong person,' Dan-Dan the cop shop man said.

'I'm sorry.' Rosie bit her lip. 'I wasn't allowed inside, you see. The men came in the front way, and I was out at the back, so I never saw nothing. You'll have to ask my mam.'

The officers stared at each other; Sadie Tunstall had said scarcely a word. She was drying out, and she was making no sense when she did explode with vitriol. 'We'll ask her when she's a bit better,' Dan said.

In the near distance, a phone sounded its bell. Theo ran in and picked up the call. Within seconds, he was out again. 'It's from Detective Constable Fallon,' he said.

Dan jumped up from the ground and went inside. He listened, frowned and wrote on a pad. 'Thanks,' he said, before ending the call. For a few minutes, he stood in Theo's living room and watched the neighbours mowing grass, dead-heading roses, sweeping paths. 'Just an ordinary Sunday,' he muttered.

On heavy feet, he went back through the dining room and reached the back garden via open French doors. He smiled at Rosie before handing the torn-out note to Theo, who scanned it quickly.

It said, *Sadie Tunstall tried to hang herself last night. Condition critical.*

Eight

Exciting was not an adjective Isadora Bellamy might have applied to this particular Sunday. Confusing might have come near, though. Terrifying was a step too far, since she refused to be any more than slightly afraid of a man whose heart was cold, who felt no obligation towards his own wife and children, whose talent had died due to neglect and self-indulgence. She could not bear the idea of living or working with him again; as for any physical contact – well, the very idea turned her stomach. She and Richard no longer had anything in common, so conversation had been off the menu for months, even years. And she was sick to her wisdom teeth of acting drunk, so . . .

Yet more than anything, she feared herself, because he'd worn her down so many times before when she'd hovered on the brink. 'Come on, Izzy,' she whispered. 'Your duty days are over; it's your turn now.' She was too tired for further adjectives, though a few expletives sprang to mind when she thought about him, and she needed to hang on to her anger. 'Time to exit stage right followed by a bear with a sore head if you don't get a move on. Oh why, why did he have to choose now to become ill? I'm sure he does these things deliberately.'

She clung to her anger like a baby with a ragged comfort blanket. After a heavy sigh, she jumped to her feet, trying hard to keep up with her brain, which was doing a hundred miles an hour along an unpaved road that led to . . . that led away from here. Richard was on his way home to convalesce after an infection, and his home was rather deficient in the furniture department. His home was no longer a home, was it?

She was supposed to be an alcoholic, yet she had just spent an hour or more unpacking her personal belongings and placing them back on her dressing table. While preparing to arrange herself in a stained robe on her chaise longue, she had wondered vaguely whether fate had stepped in with an unwelcome message. Richard had lost his voice, so an understudy would play his role. Was this really a suggestion that she ought to take him back? But very suddenly, she stopped dead in her tracks. 'Do not weaken,' she ordered herself now in a low voice. 'Let him come; do not be nervous. Get out. Get out now. Collect some people first . . .' She went into reverse, collecting things she had just unpacked, the same things she had packed last night. Was this the onset of premature dementia? Lord, how she wished Portia could be here. Portia, like her namesake, could manage people.

Joan Reynolds, often known as Nanny, was busy secreting suitcases and bags in priest holes. Occasionally, her screams could be heard travelling along corridors and through rooms, because the poor woman was terrified of spiders and cobwebs. The children no longer played in the priest holes – children? Isadora's girls were twenty-six, twenty-three and twenty-one, so hide-and-seek was no longer on the agenda – and the secret cubicles made in Cromwell's time were left to wildlife, and spiders thrived. Poor Joan. It was time to put an end to all this nonsense, surely? *Come on, Izzy. Pull yourself together and get out of here now, immediately if not sooner.*

'Bugger,' she mumbled, borrowing her eldest daughter's favourite swear word. She opened her bedroom door and yelled. 'Joan? Joan? Come out, wherever you are. We can't do this; we mustn't do this. Throw yourself into reverse, please.'

The ex-nanny emerged on hands and knees from the smallest of holes behind the panelling. 'Isadora?' she squeaked, blowing dusty hair from her eyes. She was hot, bothered and furrowed in the forehead department. 'Yes?'

'Stop. I've had enough and you've had enough. I've spoken to Portia on the telephone, and we're not expected today. I shall call Delia to find out which day is best for her to collect our things, after which I shall speak again to Tia. Now, get on your bicycle and go to the Punch Bowl, because the personal touch is required when begging. Ask Mr Jenkins to summon any or all available cars in the village and to send them here. Book rooms for us and an extra room for our belongings. Tell the truth – say we're leaving. If Richard finds us, we'll be in a safer place with plenty of company.' Yes, there was some fear, she finally managed to admit to herself; just a little bit, a mere frisson . . .

Joan closed her gaping mouth. 'Are you sure?' She didn't relish the idea of yet another change of mind.

'Positive. There's nothing else I can do, is there? Do we want to be here when he tries to eat from a non-existent dining table while sitting on an invisible chair? I'll leave a note for him. The time for honesty has come at last.'

'But what if he comes while we're still here?' Joan asked, her face ashen under smears of aged dirt. 'He'll hit the roof.'

Isadora shrugged. 'Just go, please.'

When Joan had rushed off to the inn, Isadora divested herself of the stained gown and dressed in a decent suit. She wouldn't bother just yet with makeup, because another task needed to be performed.

Armed with pen and pad, she wrote the message carefully.

Richard, I am leaving you. Joan will come with me and we shall settle somewhere eventually once the business of divorce is completed. I intend to make an offer for Bartle Hall, since you have not the money required to save it. The furniture is in storage, though we have kept essentials like beds. Table and chairs in the morning room remain, but all valuable pieces bought by me are securely kept under lock, key and vigilant guards in a facility far from Chaddington Green. I expect you are now apoplectic with rage, but do read on to the end before throwing your weight about.

Mrs Melia, who is due to retire, has been paid two months' wages in advance and has promised to stay for that length of time to ensure that you are fed. She will live out her remaining days in Lilac Cottage, as promised in her terms of employment. I have arranged a pension for her. Mrs Melia will have no dailies to help in the Hall. If you want the rooms you use cleaned, you must pay those who are prepared to stay on. That also applies to garden workers.

My agent is aware that I refuse to work with you. He also knows that I am not, and never have been, dependent on alcohol. Our doctor can verify that, too. As I lay in my supposed stupor, I heard every word you said, every piece of nastiness that emerged from your throat. You are a sad, vicious man who will end life alone and bitter, since very few will tolerate your rages and your verbal abuse.

My legitimate reasons for seeking divorce are lodged with my lawyer, but the truth of the matter is that I hate the way you have treated me and my daughters. Perhaps your other children (I know of two) might

tolerate you better. Tia will make an excellent teacher,
Juliet a wonderful nurse, and Delia will find her way
to a settled future. You are not their master; nor are
you mine.

Perhaps you should warn your more recent
'conquests' that you have been followed and
photographed and that the stories will hit the press
sooner or later. I have wanted to do this for years,
but was forced to wait until my daughters had escaped
your reach. Twice in recent times you have persuaded
me to stay, but I am depending on this third time to be
lucky and beyond reach. Do not try to find me; be
aware that nothing could possibly induce me to live
with you or work alongside you ever again.

She re-read it twice and signed her given name only, since she intended to cease being a Bellamy in the very near future. Just as she penned her signature, she heard the village entering the front courtyard. Several cars pulled up, and Joan could be heard guiding drivers towards various priest holes. 'Stay away, Richard,' Isadora said aloud. 'Just half an hour or so, and we'll be gone.' After sweeping bottles and jars into a vanity case, she applied a smear of lipstick and a small amount of powder before placing the note on Richard's pillow in the dressing room. There. It was done.

She returned to her own room, picked up her handbag and the medium-sized suitcase. 'I'm not abandoning you,' she told the house she and her girls had loved. 'I'll make sure you're put to good use, I promise. Have a rest in the meantime, stretch your timbers and listen to the birds.' She dropped her bags, picked up the phone and left a message for Delia, asking one of the housemates to remind her to phone her mother at the Punch Bowl. 'It's important,' she stressed to the one person who was awake. 'Please pass the message on.' Skifflers seemed not to go to bed before six in the morning.

For now, there was no more to be done, so she left her much loved home and went out to thank all who had come to help. Most of the luggage was on a flatbed lorry, so matters had been hastened.

Cases wearing a red spot would be stored somewhere or other, probably in Liverpool for a while; the rest contained enough clothes for herself and Joan Reynolds, and they would be kept at Tia's place once Delia had transported them upcountry. *Oh, please hurry, my friends. Collect the luggage and throw it in your cars and get me out of here. The self-elected Grand Master will be back at any minute, and I want to be gone before he shows his smug countenance. I married an idiot, so what does that make me? Why did I carry him for so long, especially after he became rigor mortis weight? Oh, I can answer that one: you're a fool, Izzy.*

Mrs Melia waved goodbye, a handkerchief mopping up her tears. Isadora, seated with Joan in one of the cars, waved back before staring deliberately forward, because the house was, for now, a part of the past. It was all horribly sad, yet it had to be done as smoothly as possible and without a show of emotion.

Like a wagon train in the wilds of America, the cars pulled out of the estate and proceeded in an elegant convoy towards Chaddington Green. Fortunately, there were no Indians about, though they did have to slow down for a few stray deer whose sense of direction was confused, to say the least.

It was fiesta time when they reached the Punch Bowl. A late lunch had been prepared for the two women, and two rounds of drinks for everyone were on Isadora. There were cheers and whoops of joy when villagers learned that she was leaving Richard at last. Bill Jenkins delivered his imitation of Richard Bellamy, a stiff, stilted and very gung-ho World War Two flight lieutenant from some black-and-white movie of that era.

Polly Jenkins proposed a toast. 'To freedom,' she called, 'and the absolute emancipation of women.'

The men pretended to boo, while their female companions cheered.

Isadora stood. 'Deadlier than the male,' she shouted. 'It would be in the best interests of every man to bear that in mind.'

Polly Jenkins raised her glass again. 'I'm coming with you,' she joked.

Isadora sat and clinked her glass against the one held by her children's nanny, now her best friend. 'To us, Joan. I haven't been to – you know where we're going – for years. We did Priestley's *When We Are Married* there, I seem to remember.'

Bill Jenkins approached the table. 'Phone call for you, Mrs Bellamy. It's Delia from London.'

'Thank you.' She stood.

'And your cases are in our dining room. My Pol thought that would save carrying them downstairs when you need them picking up. I hear you're going to stay with Tia.'

'That's right.' She would tell nobody where Tia was. Even Mrs Melia at Bartle Hall knew nothing of Isadora's immediate plans. She picked up the phone. 'Delia, darling. Thank you for calling back so quickly.'

'Hi, Ma. Sorry, I was asleep when you rang. Have you run away from home at last?'

Isadora could not manage to contain a chuckle.

'Have you, Ma?'

'I have, but Joan and I are staying here tonight. Our belongings are taking up space in Mr and Mrs Jenkins' living quarters, so they need to be shifted soon. When you pack the van, put the red spot cases in first, because we need to store them somewhere in . . . somewhere close to Tia. When can you come?'

'I'll try for tomorrow, but it's more likely to be Tuesday. I have to be back in London by Thursday afternoon. You're taking some stuff with you on the train, I expect.'

'Yes. We have to get out of Chaddington very soon, because your father's on his way home with a sore throat. Villagers brought our luggage to the inn; they all seem delighted to hear about my leaving him. Now, don't rush, because we want no accidents.'

'OK, Ma.'

'Joan and I will go to our rooms now; we need to be out of sight. Can you telephone Tia and tell her I'll be on the afternoon train tomorrow? I think it reaches its destination at about six o'clock. And if you are able, will you tell Juliet what's happening?'

'Of course I will.'

'Cordelia?'

'What, Ma?'

'You've met someone. Your voice is lighter. Take that slowly, too; as I said a few seconds ago, we want no accidents.'

'Right, Ma.'

After a few beats, Isadora spoke again. 'Are you perchance laughing at me, Cordelia Bellamy?'

'Yes, Ma. Good luck and God bless. He never deserved you.'

'Oh, he wasn't always as he is now. Or perhaps I was more tolerant, but I don't like the way he's treated his daughters over the past few years. So, what's her name? Your young lady, I mean.'

'Too early for that, Mother dear. It's like any other relationship, and introduction to family doesn't happen for a while. She's pretty, she's learning bass guitar and is a good cook. Oh, she does knitting and crochet, too, and she's teaching me to make blankets for African children. It gets cold at night even in the tropics, or so I'm told. That's all you need to know for now, Ma.'

'Shhhhh,' Isadora whispered. A sudden silence had descended on the public area at the other side of the bar. He was here. A shudder raced through Isadora's body when a crash broke the quiet in the snug. She dropped the receiver and rushed out to find Joan Reynolds on the floor with Richard standing over her, one foot raised as if he were preparing to stamp the life out of the slender woman. 'Where is my wife?' he rasped.

'I'm here,' Isadora answered, her voice low and threatening. She knelt beside her friend. 'Did he throw you to the floor, Joan?'

Joan nodded.

Men leapt forward and dragged Richard Bellamy to the outer door.

'Keep hold of him, please,' Isadora begged. 'Joan, stay where you are.' She returned to the phone, said a hurried goodbye to Delia and dialled the three nines, asking for police and ambulance at the Punch Bowl, Chaddington Green. When she walked back into the bar, her husband was tied to a chair. Three large farmhands stood over him, while Polly Jenkins squatted near Joan. 'I don't think anything's broken,' she told Isadora, 'but I'm no expert.'

'Keep her on the floor in case there is something broken,' advised Polly's husband. 'Don't move her. He was so quick coming in, Mrs Bellamy, that we didn't realize what he was up to until it was too late. I've never seen him move so fast. Being ill must suit him.'

The farmhands began to translate Richard's hoarse whispers. 'He says you've left him with no furniture. He says you can't go away while he's ill.'

179

'He's made me sick for years,' was her response. 'And I'm not going away; I'm leaving him.'

'She's an alcoholic,' the prisoner said hoarsely.

'No, just a good actress,' Isadora snarled. She looked down at Joan. 'We've plenty of witnesses to what happened here today. Bill, do you have a camera? Will it do indoor shots?'

He nodded. 'I'll get it.'

'Good man. I want a couple of him tied to the chair, and a couple of poor Joan on the floor. Let's give next week's newspapers something to chew on.'

By the time the snaps had been taken, a locum doctor had rolled up. He examined Joan, shining a light into her eyes, asking her for the day, date, month and year, asking had she banged her head and did she feel sick. He placed her in a chair, said he was satisfied, but that the ambulance folk should have a look anyway. He then spoke to Richard. 'Your wife acted like an alcoholic so that she wouldn't need to work with you. It's all in Dr Heilberg senior's records.' He left the scene muttering darkly about people who didn't appreciate others, and raising his voice to wish Isadora and Joan good luck when he reached the doorway.

The ambulance arrived next, and Joan was once again declared out of danger.

'She wouldn't have been if Mr Bellamy had followed through,' said the biggest of the farm labourers. 'He was going to stamp on her till Mrs Bellamy stopped him.' During this accusatory declaration, the police entered the scene. They questioned Joan, Isadora, Polly and Bill before talking to other witnesses. Richard had little to say due to his damaged throat. He was taken away to the police station while villagers cheered raucously.

Exhausted, Isadora and Joan went up to their rooms. Once again, Richard Bellamy had managed to wear out his wife simply by being there, on the attack and . . . and breathing. 'No,' she muttered, 'it isn't that I want him dead. I just want him away from me.' *And how could he pick on Joan after all she's done for us? She's such a small woman, so breakable, so loving and kind. Without her, I could not have worked; without her, I would have been in poorer financial health. She made the partnership possible, and I carried him as far as I could. Once the idiot started to believe the publicity machine, he became too big for his boots and too small for his co-performers. He's earning so little, has never saved . . . but he's no longer my problem.*

Exhausted, and chilled to the bone in spite of the warm day, Isadora drifted into sleep, dreaming of happy days when children played in Bartle Hall's grounds, when rain drove them inside and hide-and-seek with its accompanying shrieks and footfalls echoed through the ancient building. Plays written by Portia and Cordelia were performed in the great ballroom to an audience of people from the village, and Christmas had always been wonderful.

At about nine o'clock that evening, the extension telephone rang. She woke, temporarily disorientated, taking a few seconds to remember where she was and why. It was Bill from downstairs. 'Mrs Bellamy, I have Tia for you. Polly came up to see you a few times, but you've slept for hours.'

'Thank you, Bill.'

'Ma? Is that you, darling? Did I wake you? So sorry if I did. Mr Jenkins told me just now about Pa's behaviour. Is Nanny hurt? Oh, Delia asked me to call you, by the way.'

'Portia, Joan is well, sweetheart. Is it convenient if we come tomorrow? Delia can definitely bring our luggage on Tuesday.'

'Of course. There are complications . . .' Tia told her mother about the murder, the abused child, the attempt at suicide by Rosie's gin-dependent mother, and about Maggie. 'Teddy got permission to bring Maggie out of hospital today and she and Rosie are staying with him. They could go home now, because Sadie's in a coma and no threat at present, but he feels they need a break. Rosie doesn't know everything about her mother's condition, you see. Maggie does. We can only hope that this latest tragedy won't leave Rosie's nana open to further health problems.'

Isadora listened carefully. It occurred to her, not for the first time, that evil spread its tentacles across the whole of society, missing no sector, rich, poor, or middle of the road. Had Richard stamped his foot, Joan would now be in hospital or in the morgue, and that would have been a huge blot in the pristine copybook of a great acting family. No one was immune when it came to the nasty streak in the human animal. 'I am so sorry, Portia,' was all she managed to say. 'You seem to have been through the wars, and you haven't even started work yet.'

'I'm using Teddy's phone, Ma. I've ordered my own line, but goodness knows when it will arrive. As for what's happened, I'm sure this sort of thing goes on in Manchester, London and Birmingham. Most people here are wonderful.'

Isadora heard Mr Quinn in the background. He was telling Portia to talk for as long as she needed, and he awarded her the full name. The mother of Tia smiled. Teddy was falling in love; it was etched into every syllable he spoke. 'Tell him hello from me, darling.'

'He's wandered off, Ma. I think he's a nomad at heart. He's probably looking for his camel.'

'He sounds pleasant.'

'He is. He's a half-American lunatic. I'm waiting for him to build a totem and do rain dances.' She lowered her tone. 'He's lovely, Ma.'

'Delicious voice, Portia.'

'Hands off, Mother. He's also halfway in love with you, and he's the only name on my maybe list. There isn't one of your films he hasn't seen, but he's too young for you.'

'Darling, no man is too young for me.'

'But I saw him before you will, so I get first dibs. You can't go around picking up innocent young men just because you've ditched Pa.'

Isadora smiled into the phone. 'You're falling in love, my darling.'

'Perhaps. As far as I'm concerned, he's the lone ranger on the definitely interesting list. See you tomorrow, Ma.'

'Be careful,' Isadora warned. 'Don't jump too quickly into a relationship. I did that, and look at the state of me now, on the run from home.' She paused. 'How is the little girl?' She listened while her daughter delivered the rest of the tale. What she said and the way she said it betrayed the affection Tia had developed for the child, too. She had always been an open-hearted girl, but she now seemed to be offering bits of herself all over the place.

'I love Liverpool,' Tia said.

'You love Liverpool, Teddy and Rosie, don't you?'

'Perhaps I do.'

'I hope they deserve you, my precious girl. Though I must say, that poor child has had a very rough introduction to life. How could a mother decide to take her own life and leave a daughter behind? That's what I can't understand. I suppose the drink addled her brain. Oh well, we'll talk tomorrow.'

'Is Pa in jail, Ma?'

'I haven't the remotest idea. Good night, Portia.'

Tia replaced the receiver. She heard him entering the hallway, knew he was standing very near to her.

'What's your father done now?' Theo asked.

'He's just being a pillock.'

'Pillock? That's a new one for me, Portia.'

She faced him. 'It's a hillock with a P on it.'

'Ah.' He nodded gravely. 'So he's been done for depositing a pee on a small hill? Surely he's not so undignified as to urinate in public? Isn't that a breach of the peace?'

She grinned. 'How are you spelling that, P-E-A-C-E or P-I-E-C-E?'

'Mind like a sewer, Miss Bellamy.' He sat in a Victorian rocker. 'Maggie's telling little Rosie now. Unfortunately, it will have to be the truth, because it will be all over the Lady Streets, and children are cruel.'

'Shit,' Tia mumbled.

'He didn't do that as well, did—'

'Shut up, Teddy.' She gazed at him. 'Do you always talk rubbish when you're nervous?'

'Yes, I do,' he replied. 'Is your mother coming tomorrow?'

Tia nodded. 'And she's gone silly, too. She likes your voice. I'll sit next to you on the floor. No, no, don't stand up, I prefer the floor. If I'm on the floor, I can't fall.' She slid down the wall. 'Do you think Maggie will have told her yet? Will she know how to tell her? I feel a bit wobbly.'

He left the chair and sat next to her on hard oak floorboards. 'This is not comfortable, Portia. And there's no right way to tell a child that her mother wants to be dead. Telling her that Sadie almost died by her own hand will be hard, but it has to be done before Rosie hears it at school in September.' He shifted. 'My backside's already defunct on this floor.'

'It's not supposed to be comfortable. Maggie won't be comfortable telling Rosie that her mother's critically ill. And Maggie has all the gossip to face. They both do, I suppose, because Rosie will suffer, too.'

'And my butt will go gangrenous if we sit here much longer.'

Tia took hold of his hand. 'Pretend you're Catholic and think of it as penance.' A pleasant tremor travelled up her arm, her neck, her face and into her hair. Had her crowning glory been less abundant and shorter, it would probably have stood on end. But she said nothing. This might be the right time for distracting jokes, but romance was off the cards. Rosie was learning one of life's sadder lessons, so flirtation would be inappropriate. But Tia propped her head on his shoulder. 'You should go in, Teddy. Take them a drink or something and see if you're needed.'

'You think?'

'*Ergo sum.* I think, therefore I am.'

'You go in,' he suggested. 'You're female.'

'Glad you noticed,' she said drily. 'But why should the task fall to a woman? Would I be better at dealing with bad news just because of my gender? You're the ex-perienced teacher.' Then she remembered – his mother had been murdered in America. 'Sorry. I didn't forget; I just wasn't thinking while this is going on. Someone had to give you similar news, I expect.'

'No.' His fingers tightened their hold on hers. 'I was there. I heard her screams and saw the flames, breathed in the smoke, watched my father trying to claw his way through hot metal to get to her. His hands were banda-ged for weeks.' Theo turned his head and looked at her. 'No one else knows that, not from me, anyway. I can trust you, yes?'

She nodded and tried to swallow the lump in her throat. He still hadn't told her everything – of that she felt sure. 'Always trust me, Teddy. I've lived in a war zone for long enough to know unhappiness.' She told him about Ma and Pa, the former having nurtured and im-proved her talent, the latter continually neglecting his and becoming lazy. 'Father was dragging her down, so

185

she pretended to be unfit for work due to alcoholism. He became righteously indignant, and she turned into a mess, stinking of gin and saying little that was sensible. We had no trauma like yours, of course, but it was hard, especially on Juliet, who's the family's token Christian.'

'Your mom was sober?'

'Oh, yes, though we discovered that only recently. She and Nanny fled to the local inn, and he came in and threw Nanny – Joan Reynolds – on the floor. The police took him away.' She awarded him a rueful smile. 'You have a comfortable shoulder, Mr Quinn.'

'My ass is dead.'

'Poor creature. Do you mean arse?'

'Probably.' He paused. 'I heard you telling your mother that I was a nomad and a half-American lunatic.'

Tia wagged a finger at him. 'Eavesdroppers hear no good about themselves.'

'I heard good,' he whispered. 'Did you mean it? Because if you did, we shouldn't work together.'

She shrugged. 'Get rid of me, then.'

'I can't. You know I can't, and you know why.'

'Do I?'

The front door opened quietly, and both turned to see Simon in the porch. He stepped into the hall and apologized, explaining that he had tried Tia's bell first. 'I came to tell you I've cancelled the appointment for Rosie at Alder Hey tomorrow. The poor child will have been through enough, I imagine.' He studied the pair on the floor for a few seconds. There had been other men in Tia's life, and he knew it, though he'd never met any of them. Something was happening here, and he felt as if he had been kicked hard in the belly. Oh well, she had warned him often enough, so he could blame only himself.

He sat on the floor opposite the two of them. 'Is her grandmother telling her now?'

Theo sighed. 'Yes, and it must be damn hard for both of them. God, how does a person describe attempted suicide to a five-year-old? It's no use wrapped up in jargon, because children from school will be hearing their parents talking about it. Shall we go into the living room? Maggie and Rosie are in a spare bedroom.'

As he stood up, Simon noticed that Tia's right hand was holding Quinn's left. So it had happened, then. First prize to the swarthy-looking fellow who looked as if he needed a good shave and a hot bath. *I should have stayed in Kent. She was right. She's always bloody right. Her sisters are the same. No, hang on, Simon, that's not true. Juliet's sweet. Delia bats for the other team, and she's plain, but Juliet has the real looks . . . Perhaps.*

They went into Theo's living room and sat like three dummies in a shop window, frozen and silent. 'They're not talking,' Tia whispered after several minutes. 'Shall I go in?'

Simon decided to save his beloved from that. 'If no one emerges within ten minutes, I'll go in. It's all right for me, because I'm a non-person, a doctor. It gives me a professional edge, though I'm not looking forward to it. That poor, innocent child deserves better than all this. She needs decent parents.'

'Thank you,' Theo said.

Tia announced her intention to make tea.

When she was safely out of earshot, Simon spoke to Theo. 'Are you two an item?' There was no point in beating about the shrubbery; he wanted an answer, and he wanted it now.

Theo shifted in his chair. 'We seem to be growing fond of each other.'

Simon waited, as he sensed that there was more to come.

'But if she wants children, it can come to nothing,' Theo said softly.

'I see. Why is that? I'm a doc, so you can talk to me.'

Theo shook his head almost imperceptibly. 'I'm not impotent and, as far as I know, I'm not sterile. There's a genetic fault on my mother's side. Tia knows about it, though not in detail, not yet.'

Simon frowned. 'Is your mother affected by it?'

'She's dead.'

'I see. Sorry about that – was she affected?'

'To an extent, yes. I could be a carrier. For that reason, I have remained a bachelor. Portia breezed into my professional life first, then into my home life. She's quite a character, isn't she?'

'She certainly is. I've been in love with her for years; I think her heart belongs to you, though.'

Theo offered no immediate reply. For the first time in many moons, he felt truly alive, and she was the reason for his joie de vivre. There was something different about her, and it wasn't just her fascinating accent or her stunning good looks. She was mischievous, intelligent, unpredictable and warm. 'I'm sorry, Simon.'

'Not your fault. She made it plain that I was swimming against the tide. I just wouldn't listen.' He gazed at Theo. 'Do you love her?'

Theo shrugged. 'It's a bit early for all that kind of jazz. Love at first sight isn't to be trusted in my book. But I do have a lot of admiration for her – affection, too. As I said before, it depends what she wants out of life.' He pondered for a moment. 'For myself, I was wondering about vasectomy.'

'Because of the genetic problem?'

'Yes.'

'It could be arranged.'

The conversation was cut short by Tia's return. She

passed a cup and saucer to Simon. 'Drink that before you go in,' she said. 'It's still very quiet, isn't it? I wonder whether Maggie managed to tell her?'

Simon put down his cup without taking even a sip. 'Which door?' he asked Theo.

'Second on the left after the little morning room.'

'I'll be right back.' The young doctor squared his shoulders, ran both hands through his hair and went off in search of Maggie and Rosie. He returned within a minute or two. 'They're not here,' he said. 'I looked in all the rooms, bathroom included – no sign.'

Theo and Tia leapt to their feet. They left the flat by the front door; there was no one in the garden. Dashing round the back, they ground to a halt when they saw two figures on a bench. Grandmother and granddaughter sat very still. On a table in front of them, candles flickered in a light summer breeze.

'Thank God,' Tia whispered. 'Come on, Teddy – we're not wanted here. Maggie seems to be handling the situation well.' She turned to Simon. 'I think they're having some kind of prayer ceremony – let's leave them to it.'

When they returned to Theo's sitting room, Simon began to feel like a spare part or even a spy. They wanted their privacy, and he needed to get the hell out of here. After a swift farewell, he left and sat in his car for a few minutes, his mind wandering back through the years.

He remembered getting bored one wet summer when all his friends seemed to be away on holiday, and he'd picked up some books of Mother's. The stuff hadn't been his cup of tea, but he'd persevered through Louisa M. Alcott's works. The guy next door to the March family had been stuck on Jo, but Jo had rejected him, so he'd turned to ... Amy? Juliet was sweet. She was a nurse, too, wasn't she? Doctors often married nurses, so could he switch sisters as easily as the Alcott character had managed to do? It all sounded so slick and simple, just as it had when he'd read the novels. Surely that sort of thing didn't happen in the real world?

Tia's always been the one for me, despite the attitude of her prejudiced father. I've been raised C of E, because Mother's a Christian, so why should my surname matter? Now my thoughts are out of order. They've been all over the place since she said she was moving to Liverpool. Perhaps I should return to Dad's practice, and to hell with all this northern business.

He started the car. One thing was certain: he should get away now, at this moment, from the house where two newly hatched lovebirds were starting their courtship. Well, the arrival of Mrs Bellamy and Nanny should put progress on hold. With this thought in mind, he selected first gear and drove towards another lonely evening in a city he scarcely knew. Perhaps he should get out more.

'He's gone,' Tia said. 'Poor soul – he's a good man, Teddy, but I just can't love him. God knows I tried, even if only to drive my father wild. Simon's dad's a Jew, lovely man, a well-respected family doctor. My father's a bloody Nazi!'

'Sounds like a charming chap.'

'He was very good in post-war films, mostly RAF. The problem is that he's remained stiff and stilted, because he thinks he knows it all, and he hates what he terms relaxed acting. Realism isn't for him, but the world has moved on while he stands still in the middle, rigid and posed. The only one who can gee him up is my mother, and she wants to fly solo from now on. Juliet's the only person who feels sorry for him.'

Rosie wandered in, her grandmother following. 'We said prayers,' the child said. 'My mammy wanted to go to Jesus, but she got saved.'

Tia reached out a hand and was pleased when Rosie took it. Sadie was in a coma, and there was a possibility of brain damage due to oxygen deprivation. The new reception class teacher made a sudden decision. 'How would you like a holiday, Rosie? There's this little house called Rose Cottage. It's a bit of a mess, and we have to put buckets and bowls all over the place when it rains. There are fields and woods, and there's a village nearby with shops and a green where children play. Oh, and a duck pond with mallards on it. You could feed the ducks.'

Rosie's eyes were round. 'Yes, but what about my mam?'

Maggie placed a hand on her granddaughter's shoulder. 'She's asleep.'

'Like you were asleep?'

'No,' Theo said. He believed in giving children the absolute truth. 'Your nana had tired blood and needs more tests, but Mom is more ill, so she could be in hospital for some time. She can't even have visitors yet, so why not go to Kent with Miss Bellamy?'

Tia thought for a moment. 'School finishes on Friday. Why don't we all go, just for a few days? We can telephone the hospital every morning and ask about your mother, Rosie. And if Bartle Hall's empty, I can show you a terrific game of hide-and-seek.' She turned to look at Theo. 'Shall we try to borrow a four-seater with a luggage rack?'

He stared hard at her. No matter what, Madam would always be in charge, the maker of decisions, the boss. The crazy thing was that he didn't mind, because all around her were caught up by her enthusiasm and energy. Yes, she would take some keeping up with, but he sure as hell was willing to give it a try. 'How many bedrooms?' he asked, his face a picture of innocence.

'Three,' Tia answered. 'Well, two and a cupboard with a window. We adult females will have the larger one, you will sleep in the middle-sized, and Rosie will have the tiny room. Even a person of her size may need to open the window and sleep with her feet outside.'

'Gee, thanks on her behalf.'

'She could use the sofa downstairs, or the gypsy caravan in the wilderness that used to be the back garden.'

'Who owns the cottage?' he asked.

'Ma does. She bought them all from Pa when he ran out of money. There's Rose, Lilac, Honeysuckle, Geranium and Holly, all cottages. They used to house the servants from the big house, and each cottage specialized in the growing of trees, flowers or bushes that matched its name. At Christmas, we all went to Holly Cottage for our holly. Rose and Geranium won masses of prizes, and the lane outside Honeysuckle smelled like a perfume factory. In the spring, Lilac Cottage was wonderful. It's all changed now.'

'Why?' Rosie asked.

'Everything except Rose Cottage and Lilac Cottage is rented out to people who work in Canterbury. Ma kept Rose Cottage for when she wanted to paint or read. And Rose Cottage has your name, doesn't it?'

Rosie nodded. 'Can we go there, Nana?'

Maggie was tired. 'Let's see about that tomorrow, shall we?'

Tomorrow Tia was supposed to be taking Rosie for new clothes, but she didn't mention that while Maggie was here. Some people objected to charitable deeds. 'We all need a rest and a change,' she declared. 'What about Tyger, Teddy?'

'Your mother and her friend will look after him, won't they?'

'Yes, he'll be ruined. Ma will take him upstairs and feed him only the best. He'll be spoilt.'

Theo sat back and watched his tenant writing a list.

She had lots of lists. He wondered whether she kept a list of lists. If she lost her list of lists, she'd be lost.

Maggie took Rosie off to bed. 'I think I'll lie down with her,' she said as she left the two lovebirds together. She might be lacking iron in her blood, but she could still read the signs, the body language, the expression on his face. Would Miss Bellamy become Mrs Quinn?

'Why don't you get a hardback notebook for lists?' he asked. 'That's what I had to do with all my English pronunciations and Scouse idiom. Keep all the lists in one place.'

She eyed him sternly. 'Are you trying to get on my nerves?'

'No need to try – it's easy. You're a controller, aren't you? Am I OK to be letting you loose on my new intake in September?'

'Sorry. There's a lot of Pa in me, which is why he and I clash so often.'

'Will he be at home?'

She shrugged. 'No idea.'

'Your home's Bartle Hall, right?'

'Yes. It's huge, decaying and beautiful. If he's there, we'll be fine. I can deal with him.' *The press, however, might be a different matter if they come looking for members of his family, for him, for local gossip. Oh, God, why does life have to be so difficult? When will this mess hit the newspapers? Will Maggie be willing to leave her daughter? Should Rosie be here in case her mother gets better or dies, or–* She ordered herself to stop thinking.

It was Theo's turn to ponder. He'd already bought an ambulance that was being converted so that small groups from school could be taken out on trips. It all dovetailed so nicely, didn't it? *I want to be with her. Tom Quirke can take a rest for a while. Wherever she goes, I shall want to be with her. Is this insanity?*

Nine

I wonder who the hell did that to his back, who flogged him and cut him and why? Was it because his mother was slightly handicapped, a bit different from everyday, run-of-the-mill folk? Who assumes the right to decry and murder the afflicted and to beat their children? I have read about the southern states of America with their weird slants on the Bible, their many little churches, their invented hell's-fire-awaits-you religions, so fierce and unforgiving. But what kind of Christian beats a child and burns his mother to death? Oh, pull yourself together, Tia Bellamy, because you have things to do.

Did no one comfort him when his mother was murdered? I have to know all these things. Why? Oh, I don't now why I have to know, because my mind is full of him, full of empathy and something that bears a close resemblance to love. Maggie and Rosie seem relaxed, so that's good.

Child and grandmother were fast asleep and sharing a bed in one of Theo's spare rooms. Tia closed their door quietly and rejoined Theo in his living room. She dropped into an armchair and kicked off her shoes, because her imprisoned feet had begun to ache.

Theo glanced up from his newspaper and grinned. She was making herself thoroughly at home, and that idea pleased him. 'What's your problem?' he asked. 'Your brow is furrowed and your smile has died.'

She sighed dramatically. 'I've still two beds to dress for Ma and Nanny. Tomorrow's no good, because I'm taking Rosie out for the day – I promised. In view of all that's happened, the murder and her mother's condition, I can hardly let the poor baby down. We're going for shoes and perhaps a little handbag before having lunch in a restaurant. Oh, and she wants to see Harry the Scoot, her friend without legs. We'll probably have afternoon tea out, too. That child is bright, and she needs stimuli.'

Theo chuckled. 'She'll get plenty of that in the fall; her new teacher's quite an unusual and illuminating woman.'

'Is she now? She sounds marvellous. Do I know her?'

'Perhaps. I've heard it said that only a wise man knows his father, though I think that's connected to possible adultery. I maintain that it's a wise person who truly knows him or herself. Shall I help you with the beds for your mom and her friend? I don't mind, and I'm thoroughly domesticated.'

Tia smiled. 'Please. And we'll need both cars to pick up the ladies from the station at six o'clock tomorrow evening. The MGs will suffice, because my visitors will have just one suitcase each.' Her smile broadened. 'You'll get to meet your film star at last, Teddy, though you may not recognize her. My money's on a dark wig, a brown coat and an accent of some sort. Nanny is slender and short with greying hair; she'll come as herself. Shall we go upstairs and get things together while we have the chance?'

He blinked a couple of times. Tia Bellamy made just about everything sound like an invitation to sin. He was guilty of the same, of course, though he was unused to women as forward as this one. 'To dress beds? Certainly. We've had a busy day, haven't we? Police, Welfare, dragging Maggie out of hospital, Tyger coming second in a fight with a geranium. I swear that cat has mental issues.'

'Indeed,' she concurred, 'so he's come to the right place, what?'

'If you say so, it must be true.'

Tia grinned. 'At least Rosie's visit to the children's hospital is postponed. Thanks for letting me use the phone yet again. Simon knows we're going to Kent and not to the children's hospital. He's popping a note through your letterbox. We're to give it to his dad, Dr Heilberg Senior. Oh, I must warn you about my mother.'

'Oh?'

'Never eat anything she brings to table. Whenever Mrs Melia, our cook and housekeeper, was ill, Ma ventured into the kitchen on the occasions when she wasn't away at work. We all fled, suddenly remembering invitations to dine or lunch with friends. When we turned up at the local cafe, the owners knew exactly why. They were very sympathetic and generous with portions.'

'Oh dear.'

Tia shook her head gravely. 'Nanny's not bad, though she does what she calls good, plain cooking with everything simmered to death, but she's not a total write-off as a cook. She can do scrambled eggs – Ma manages to produce scrambled pans, absolutely uncleanable. To label my mother adventurous would be like referring to Everest as tall. She's totally bloody lethal. Her mulliga-tawny soup takes the top layer off your tongue, and you could sole your shoes with any joint she lifts out of the oven. We bought her some vouchers for cookery classes in Canterbury, but she went just once and said it was boring because they started off with Windsor soup and croutons. I think she was expecting Cordon Bleu.'

'Bugger,' he said softly.

'Hey, I've told you about pinching my script,' she chided playfully. 'If she invites you to dinner, plead insanity, world war or bubonic plague. I'm serious. She has the ability to make your stomach feel like a battlefield from the Napoleonic Wars.'

'Yes, Miss.'

Tia stood and pushed her feet into their shoes. 'Right, come on, Mr Quinn. Beds.'

'Yes, Miss.'

'Are you taking the pi– the piffle?'

He nodded gravely. 'What's a piffle?'

'It's a Delia word, a cross between urine and skiffle – it means they've had a bad night in a club.' She held out a hand. 'Come along, boss.'

Theo took her hand. It was becoming plainer than ever that she was the leading player, and he wondered how this would work out at school. The bloody woman was worming herself into his affections, and he simply couldn't manage to worry too much about that here, in a domestic situation, but his professional life mattered. He decided to address the situation as she led him along the side of the house. 'Portia Bellamy,' he began, 'I hope you're not going to try leading me by the hand or by the nose at school.'

She stopped so suddenly that he shunted into her. 'I wasn't born yesterday,' she said haughtily. 'I shall know my place, Mr Blackbird. You'll be my superior and my mentor, and I'll be an asset. This is home. You told me to treat it as my home, so you're my neighbour. Get used to it.' She looked him up and down. 'Are you afraid of me? Am I utterly terrifying?'

'Not exactly. You're pushy, that's all.'

She dropped his hand, folded her arms and stood with her back to the door to her flat. 'And you're moody. I think you're scared of what might happen between us, but fear not, I have yet to be charged with rape. I like you. I more than like you. And you're interested in me –

197

that kiss betrayed you, Teddy. We're adults, so what's wrong with any of that?'

'Babies,' he replied.

'But there are ways of prevention, as I'm sure you know. Those thick, washable and reusable articles are history – we now have throw-away sheaths. What's the matter with you?' She tapped a foot. Always outspoken, she wasn't about to begin couching her opinions in duck plumage. 'This is our one and only chance, Theodore. I am a hundred per cent safe today, and we may not get another opportunity for weeks, depending on how long we both have guests.'

'Safe?'

She nodded. 'I am safe. Now, are we dressing beds or using one?'

Theo inhaled deeply. Pushy was not the word for this precocious madam. 'You are a member of my staff, Tia. In a few weeks, we'll be colleagues.'

'And?'

'And it could be awkward.'

'OK. Good evening, then.' She opened the door, went inside and slammed it in his face. This was the first time she'd been turned down, and it didn't feel good. What was the matter with him? She wasn't ugly, wasn't shy or stupid or undesirable. But she was like her father, wasn't she? Over-confident, determined to have her own way, selfish, ill-tempered on occasion. She was a damned fool, because the loveliest, handsomest, funniest, wittiest man was a few inches away on the wrong side of a door. Well, she thought he was still outside on the path.

She bent down and lifted the letterbox flap. 'Are you still there?'

'No, I've gone.'

Tia grinned. 'When did you leave? Is there a forwarding address?'

'Open the damn door, Portia.'

'Please?' she said.

'I don't beg, Portia.'

She shook her head. *Well, you asked for that one, Tia. Why can't you be a bit more delicate, more feminine, more vulnerable? Why does everyone have to dance to your tune, idiot? Who are you? Wolfgang Amadeus bloody Mozart?* She opened the door. 'What can I do for you? If you're a salesman, we don't buy at the door. If you're a gardener looking for work, I already have a man who looks great in shorts. Or are you peddling some strange religion where you stand on the tops of mountains waiting to be saved?'

'Go find the linen for the two beds.'

She widened the gap to allow him in. 'Standing well back,' she declared, hands held aloft. 'I'll make you a flash card, Sir, like those I use for word recognition. Yes. *Do Not Disturb* says it all, what?'

'I knew you'd get on my nerves,' he answered, standing rock-still facing her. 'You're a spoilt rich kid, never deprived, Roedean, Oxford, three-day eventing, hunt balls, debutante occasions—'

'And an eighteen-bedroom house on a huge estate – don't forget that. It's falling to bits, but it's still beautiful. I am anti-hunt, by the way. If a farmer wants to shoot a chicken-killer, fair enough, but a pack of starving dogs tearing a fox to pieces is not my idea of fun. You're the snob. You're carrying not a chip but a boulder on your shoulder.'

He agreed. 'I have trouble trusting people.'

'Why?'

'Childhood,' was his brief reply.

'Tell me.'

He moved and leaned against a wall in the small hallway. 'Tia, you're right, as I suspect you usually are.

199

You know I'm growing fond of you, very fond. Talking about my life in America isn't easy for me. The loss of my mom devastated me and drove my dad to drink more heavily than ever. The story is bigger than I am, and it cuts me up. I dream it quite often, so don't try to force anything out of me, please.'

'Sorry.' And she meant it. His disabled mother had died in an arson attack, and Teddy had never recovered from the shock. Then there were the marks on his back, the stripes of a whip, the slashes made by knives. 'I just don't think, and you're probably right – I'm spoilt, and you can blame my parents.'

'We can all do that, Portia.'

She shrugged. 'When I arrived, Ma's firstborn, she treasured me and heaped love and attention on me. By the time she'd had two more she'd come to her senses, but by then I was Pa's little rising star. He dragged me all over the place, dance lessons, acting classes, got me to perform at the local church, the school, the inn. We put on plays in the ballroom, and I began to make up the stories before I started real school. That's pretty normal for any lively child. A person doesn't need to be the product of two acting dynasties to want to play.'

Theo inclined his head in a gesture of agreement. He understood her well enough. Children born into relative poverty had attended university, gained good apprenticeships, had even become actors or comedians on radio and television. 'Few of us follow our parents in the world of work, Tia. My father was an itinerant who went where labourers were needed, and we had to go with him. He planted and gathered crops, herded cattle, learned to tame wild horses. All I wanted was a permanent home rather than one on wheels, so when the war ended here I took the British Higher School Certificate, went to university and even did a semester of teacher training after that. We are both born teachers, and there's no cure for the condition.'

'Try telling my father that.'

'He wouldn't listen.'

'How right you are, Teddy.'

Upstairs at last, she taught him to make hospital corners on sheets and blankets, a skill she had been forced to learn during Juliet's cadet year. She also reached a decision about herself and her own behaviour, because he was right, she was pushy, spoilt and arrogant. Changing was impossible, so it would have to be a matter of will-power. She needed to calm down, slow down and think of someone other than herself for a change. Above all, she should be careful not to alienate this very special man.

When the rooms were prepared, he demanded a light supper as payment for his time. 'Prove you can scramble eggs rather than pans,' he suggested.

'Certainly. Coffee, tea or cocoa?'

'I'll let you choose.'

He sat in the evening light near the front bay window, watched the sun as it prepared to disappear behind a horizon formed by sky and Mersey. Because of the water, Liverpool sunsets had a special, luminous, almost magical quality, even here, away from the river. Theo loved the city. Even now, with a murderer on the loose and Rosie's mother trying to check out of life, this was his home, his happy place.

He thanked God for the existence of the Athertons, who had visited Maggie during her one day in hospital. Rosie had been kept away from Sadie and led to believe that Maggie had been having complete rest at home under the supervision of a district nurse. People were good. Well, most people were good.

Madam was making noise in the kitchen and in his heart. She brought in a mug of cocoa and placed it on a table mat. He took a sip. 'That's creamy,' he said, almost smacking his lips.

Tia looked at him down her aristocratic nose. 'A pinch of salt in the milk.'

'You're kidding.'

'No. Some of us know how to run a kitchen.' She went away to butter toast, almost dancing because he was pleased with her cocoa.

'Well,' he mouthed to himself, 'that's me put in my place yet again.' It was a pity there were no clams in the sand here; he could have made her drool over Mom's clam chowder . . . Ah, here she came again. 'Yes?' he asked when he noted her furrowed brow.

'Teddy, you don't think Maggie hired someone to kill Tunstall, do you?'

He shook his head slowly. 'It's not in her, Tia.'

'How do we know what's in someone when a beloved granddaughter's in danger?'

'No,' he insisted. 'She wouldn't be able to live with what she'd done.'

'How can you know that?'

'I just can. Or maybe Tom Quirke knows it.'

'Your alter ego.'

'Owner of this house and every stick of furniture in it. He makes twenty times Theodore Quinn's paltry salary. There are many good teachers in this country who can't afford to do the job. You are a rare animal, Tia. Money left to you by grandparents and so on will make up the shortfall. Most with real talent will not come into the profession, and the result might be that only also-rans will apply. The quality will deteriorate, and we'll get inferior staff who will bring down standards.' He chuckled. 'End of lecture, Miss Bellamy.'

They ate perfect scrambled eggs on golden brown toast, their conversation covering union membership and the possibility of strike action among members of so essential a profession. 'Would you cross a picket line?' he asked.

'No,' was her brief reply.

'Why not?'

Tia frowned. 'Pa calls me a lefty, but I'm not. If the leaders of our union say we're out, then we're out. What about you?'

'The same.' He put down his knife and fork. 'Well, Miss Bellamy, thank you for supper. Please note that I use my cutlery correctly, none of that changing hands performed by most colonials – such an untidy way of eating, don't you think? Me ma brung me up proper, like.'

'Are you taking the piffle again?'

'Definitely. Oh, and wherever you and I are going, nothing can happen until I have the confidence to give you the whole truth, and God alone knows when that will happen. And we may need to work together first.'

'OK.' She piled used dishes on a tray. 'No messing about, then.'

He thought about that for a few beats of time. 'I suppose a little messing about will be fine as long as it's here rather than at school.'

Tia couldn't help herself. 'Then let's mess about in my bed.' Immediately, she wished she could bite back the words. Hadn't she already had a conversation with herself about this type of behaviour? She was selfish, manipulative, greedy and . . . and she wanted to get close to this difficult, confused man. She tried to improve matters. 'I'm falling in love with you,' she explained, yet again failing to process the thought before allowing it to drop out of her mouth. *I have a brain, a good enough brain, yet I seem not to have the sense required to kick it into gear.* 'Sorry,' she said quietly.

'It's OK,' he said. 'I'm in the same predicament.'

'Shall I find somewhere else to live, Teddy?'

His answer arrived immediately. 'No. I don't want you to leave here. You cheer me up, you annoy the hell out of me, and you make me feel alive.'

Tia sat down suddenly, as her legs felt uncertain. She was in the presence of an unusual creature; this was an honest human who simply had trouble accounting for his past. 'We'll wait, then. As long as I know you like me, I'll be fine. It hasn't happened to me before, you see. I'm no angel, but this is different.'

'I know.'

She looked hard at him. He had almost black hair, and plenty of it. It was rather disobedient and slightly wavy. Locks tumbled onto the forehead, stopping above eyes that were a warm, chocolatey brown with laughter lines at the outer corners. His skin was unusual, tanned, but with a scattering of freckles here and there, while the odd glint of red-gold showed in sideburns that needed attention. He had a straight nose, beautiful lips and a cleft in his chin. Ma might want to put him in a film . . . 'How do you know?' she whispered.

'Hard to say. It's a primal kinda thing, isn't it? Probably born in the id rather than in the ego.'

'Animalistic?'

'Yes, it's hormonal. The brain can't get a hold on it.'

'But it's real?'

He grinned at her. 'It's how all life began, Portia. The first time I saw you at the school door, I had a quiet word with myself. I didn't want you to go to St Helens or Southport, and was afraid of you coming to Myrtle Street. Confusing? Oh, yes. And you blushed. It's my guess that you seldom do that.'

'True,' she said. 'And for my part, I have to say that those feelings have grown stronger. You?'

'The same. Which is why Maggie and Rosie and your visitors will provide a barrier, and I figure we need that.' He stood, walked to her chair and perched on its arm. 'One step at a time, eh? Oh, I forgot to tell you, I've bought an ambulance.'

Her jaw dropped. 'Why? Are you opening a hospital?'

'Not just yet, no. It's been converted and it seats up to eight people with room for luggage. We can take out small groups of children once I get insured for that. I can drive it now for personal use—'

'To Kent?'

'Yes.' He threaded the fingers of his right hand into her hair. 'Can we take the Athertons, Tom and Nancy? They've fed Rosie since God knows when and I don't know when they last had a holiday. You say there's an inn?'

'Yes.' Tia loved having her hair played with, but this time was different. It was an intimate moment with the first man towards whom she felt something approaching honest passion. 'The Punch Bowl,' she added, pulling herself together. *I'm not a loose woman; there have been only three men, Simon included. But this is shattering. I feel as if I don't own me any longer. Teddy doesn't own me, either, but something does.* 'Love is outside us, isn't it? It's a bit like invisible shackles.'

'Is this messing about?' he asked, rubbing his fingers against her scalp.

'Yes.' Her voice was untypically soft.

'How do you know you're safe from pregnancy just now?' The timbre of his speech matched hers.

'A woman knows these things. But I've never before been afraid of a relationship, Teddy Bear. What if we want more? What if we can't stop?'

'Exactly. That's why we should wait, but it's not easy, is it? I knew you'd be trouble. When I saw you and heard your voice for the first time, I even considered going back to America.' He grinned. 'You're a rather tall bundle of mischief with so many talents and so much silliness ...' His voice faded. 'We need a period of good, old-fashioned courtship, back row at the movies, drives to the seaside, a day in the country, a week in Kent.'

'My father may be there.'

'Are you afraid of him?'

'No.' She was one of the few people who didn't fear the bumbling, bombastic clown who strutted about like the only cockerel in a run filled with hens. That was exactly what he was, she reminded herself. Apart from staff who attended to the grounds occasionally, he was surrounded by females. 'We all deal with him in our own way. Ma pretends to be drunk, Nanny Reynolds ignores him, as does the cook, Juliet is sweet and kind to him, Delia tells him to piffle off, while I just disobey him.'

Theo sighed. 'I'm surrounded by women, too. Tyger and I will soon be the only males in Crompton Villa, and he'll be useless; he even lost the battle with a geranium.'

'Poor baby,' she said, the words trimmed with sarcasm.

'Do you mean me or the cat?' His fingers spread across the back of her head and drew her towards him. 'I'm just messing about,' he whispered before kissing her.

The unexpected contact went through her like electricity, but without the bite of pain. This wasn't just a man; this was her man, her forever other. When the pressure decreased, she spoke, her lips still on his. 'You're amazing,' she mumbled. 'It's as if I remember you from somewhere in another time.'

'I know,' he replied without moving away. 'We're doomed.'

For some inexplicable reason, both found this statement amusing. They clung one to the other, chuckling and laughing like a pair of teenagers on their first date, embarrassed yet happy, young yet growing older with each heated heartbeat. 'I like messing about,' he managed eventually, 'but my hand's kind of knotted in your hair.'

Tia reached up and pulled pins and clips from her abundant tresses, which had started life earlier in the day in a very tidy French pleat. The mane tumbled from its small metal anchors, and his hand was freed, though he used it now as a comb. 'Like silk,' he said. 'How can such a beautiful, clever girl be interested in me?'

'Very easily.'

'I'm twelve years older than you.'

'I know you're geriatric, but I don't care. The elderly are deserving of attention.'

He laughed again. 'Careful, or your attention will land you in detention.'

'Any time. So tell me, how long did you study for your School Certificate, Mr Quinn? I've been trying to work it out, and you must have moved at the speed of sound when the war ended.'

'I didn't study. I just took the exams and passed.'

'After living a nomadic life in America and being a rear gunner in the RAF?'

He shrugged. 'I went to some schools and I found libraries, too. My memory was photographic for a while.'

'Like Rosie's?'

He nodded.

'Degree?'

'First with honours, then a master's, then a doctorate.'

'In how many years?'

'Four. Are you interviewing me?'

'I am, Dr Quinn. After all, you and your posse grilled me for long enough.'

'That posse is your Board of Governors, Portia.'

She stroked his face. The man clearly had no idea of his own genius. Tia had been crammed at prep school, force-fed at Roedean, and polished at St Hilda's College, Oxford, but this man had walked his own walk with no privileges and probably without much money. To achieve so much against all odds would have needed an unusual brain and a massive amount of determination. There was cleverness in his books, too, intelligence, wit and complicated plot. He was a completely self-made man, an admirable example of humanity. What happened to him in America?

'What?' he asked, noting the strange expression on her face. 'What?'

'I'm proud of you, and of Tom Quirke. You did the whole lot by yourself, hardly any help. Some of us had every advantage . . .' Her voice died. 'Tell me, Teddy. Tell me about the genetic business and who hurt you and who killed your mother.'

He inhaled deeply. 'I will tell you if and when things are clearer between us. There's no point in heaping my woes on your shoulders unless this . . . relationship of ours develops into something serious. You don't need to hear it, and I don't want to relive it during hours of wakefulness, because dreaming it's bad enough. I may write it for you, give myself time and a chance to get it all in the right order.'

They stayed together in near silence for a length of time neither cared to measure, since it didn't seem to matter. He carried on combing her hair with his fingers, while Tia continued to wonder about his troubled past. When night began to cast its shadows, he picked her up and carried her into her bedroom. 'You're heavier than you look,' he complained.

'I have a big brain.'

'Really? I look forward to seeing the results of that. There's been little evidence so far. Your taste in men is questionable.' He placed her on top of the covers and stretched out beside her. 'You may be safe from conception right now, Portia, but just messing about, no more than that. OK?'

She smiled at him. 'I'm fit for nothing more,' she giggled. 'I have a very wearing neighbour, you see.'

He kissed her. It was the only way to stop her talking . . .

Maggie Stone was in the kitchen when Theo crept in like a thief through his own front door. She smiled broadly, keeping her face angled towards the window. There would be wedding bells soon, unless she was very much mistaken. Losing the grin before turning round, she spoke. 'Hello, Mr Quinn.'

He paused, guilt etched into his features, a hand rising to smooth his hair. Some people were out of bed earlier than necessary, and they were all named Maggie Stone. 'It's Theo or Ted when I'm at home, Maggie. No need for formality here.'

'Oh, all right.' She looked him up and down. He bore a strong resemblance to a pile of dirty washing on legs; she tried hard not to react. 'It's a good idea going for a walk before breakfast, like. Gives you a bit of an appetite.'

He glanced down at yesterday's crumpled clothing. 'I'll just get a shower,' he told her before dashing down the hallway.

Maggie carried on cleaning; she was determined to find a way of repaying Mr Quinn's kindness. She'd had a rude awakening at six o'clock in the form of an excited granddaughter who was going shopping with Miss Bellamy. Rosie had rattled on for ages about welly-boots, sandals, gym shoes and shiny black ankle-straps-for-best shoes. 'Are you coming with us?' the little girl had asked.

'Not in that car, love,' Maggie's reply had been. 'I'm not having you travelling on a parcel shelf. No, I'll get my hour of rest like the doctor said I should.'

Rosie continued excited, but at least she was excited in a different room. Maggie's little princess didn't seem to miss her mother, and Maggie understood only too well the reasons for that. Rosie had never had a real mother. Rosie's mother was a mess, and God alone knew with certainty who or where Rosie's father was.

Maggie gazed once more through the kitchen window. All that grass with flowers in beds, sheds to shelter in, a greenhouse and a vegetable plot. Would she ever have a place like this where Rosie could play? Would Sadie come out of her coma all right, or would she need constant care? For the moment, Maggie was all the child had to depend on, but would the authorities allow a tired, anaemic, middle-aged woman to take care of a five-year-old? The doctors suspected that Maggie had weak bones, too, so what would happen to her grandchild?

She pushed the worries to the back of her mind, because she, too, intended to go out. 'Sod the bloody hospital,' she mumbled. 'I'm going to see my daughter, and just let them try to stop me.' What if Sadie came out OK and went back on the game? Bugger these negative thoughts; she was going to clean the sitting room. Sitting room? The best the Lady Streets had to offer was a bit of space in the middle of the kitchen.

Oh well, never mind. As long as things with Sadie weren't too bad, a week in a place called Chaddington Green was on the cards. There was even a possibility of visits to Ramsgate, Deal or Broadstairs so that Rosie could play on a beach. Mr Quinn and Miss Bellamy were such kind people, and they made a lovely couple. 'Mind,

I won't buy a hat just yet,' she whispered under her breath. 'I might not get an invitation, anyway.'

'Talking to yourself, Maggie?'

She swung round to see a shiny, clean-shaven and all-dressed-up-for-school Mr Quinn. He still didn't look quite right, though, as he wore a plain white pinafore over his shirt and trousers. 'Yes, I was,' she replied.

'It's the only way to be sure of an intelligent audience. Would you like a bacon butty?'

Maggie grinned. His accent clung like a limpet to some of his consonants, and 'butty' sounded a bit like 'buddy'. 'I would, thanks,' she said.

'No cleaning yet,' he warned, wagging a finger at her. 'I'm the boss, so I'll tell you when to clean.'

She fixed him with a steely eye. 'If you think I'm going to park meself on me backside all day while Rosie's gallivanting, you'd best think again. I'm going to see Tom and Nancy, cos they visited me when I was in the ozzie. Then I'll go and find out about me daughter. I'll see if that fracky ward sister will let me anywhere near our Sadie.'

'Fracky?' He raised an eyebrow.

'Short for fractious, I think.'

Theo grinned. These bloody Scousers were always a step or three ahead of him with ready answers, plenty of cheek and a wisdom that seemed to be born in them, because even their young led him a merry dance from time to time. 'I'll go cook,' he said.

Maggie followed him and sat on a stool, watching as he made his way through the preparation of breakfast. She couldn't remember when she'd last seen a man having a hand in producing a meal. 'You'll make somebody a great wife,' she told him.

'Mom taught me the basics,' he said, 'and I can read. Anyone who can read a recipe can cook. Would you like to try one of my cheese dreams?'

She nodded. 'Go on, then, as long as it's not poisonous.'

He lit the burner under a frying pan.

'There's nothing in that pan,' she said, 'no fat, no nothing.'

'I know.'

He buttered two slices of bread and put cheese between them, leaving the butter on the outside of the bread. When the sandwich hit the hot pan, it sizzled, and he flipped the whole thing over with a fish slice so that the other side fried quickly. 'Now we go low to melt the cheese,' he said, turning down the gas.

'That's simple, but clever,' Maggie exclaimed.

'Just wait till the bacon goes in.' He grinned at her, peeled back the top slice and inserted strips of well crisped streaky bacon. 'Get a knife and fork, Maggie. Two of the things you Brits do well are bacon and Cheddar cheese. And, of course, your shop-bought cakes and pastries are great. America has you beat when it comes to steak, though.'

Maggie cut through the cheese dream; it was delicious. 'You're not just a pretty face then, Ted.'

He crossed his eyes and stuck his tongue out of the corner of his mouth.

'Stop it, I'll choke. You look like something that fell off the back of a circus.'

He made monkey noises and pretended to scratch his armpits.

'Behave yourself. You're supposed to be in charge of a school.'

He stopped and sat on the second stool to eat his toast. 'When you've finished, get your coat and I'll drop you off at the Athertons' house. I'll pick you up at lunchtime and take you to see Sadie.'

Rosie bounced into the kitchen in her new pink suit.

'You're a beautiful girl,' Maggie told her.

'I'm having breakfast with Miss Bellamy. I'm having

dinner and tea with her, too. And I'm getting shoes and sandals and wellies and–'

'We know.' Maggie felt slightly uncomfortable about accepting charity, though she soothed herself with the knowledge that Rosie would be the real recipient. 'You go up and see your teacher. I'm off with Mr Quinn to visit Tom and Nancy. She's on the last piece of your cardy, by the way. It'll be ready before we go on our little holiday.'

Rosie's eyes almost brimmed over. She was going to Kent, which was, according to Miss Bellamy, the beautiful garden of England. She was going to the seaside, and to woods and fields and wild ponies and deer. She was going to see a massive house with eighteen bedrooms and holes in the walls where priests used to hide. 'I'm happy,' she said, sniffing away her tears. 'I'm all excited inside.' She ran out through the front door.

'Thanks,' Maggie said gruffly. 'I wish you and Miss Bellamy were her mam and dad.'

'So do we,' he muttered to himself, though he could tell that Maggie had heard him.

'You look good together, you and Miss Bellamy.'

'Do we, now?'

She nodded. 'She's lovely.'

'Yes, and she's a bossy madam, a bit of a dictator. Or would that be dictatress?'

'No idea.' Maggie swallowed the last bit of her cheese dream. 'Women got bossy while you lot saved us from Hitler. We made planes, we made bullets, we made bombs, we made dinners and we made do. We dug back yards up, got two tons of topsoil and grew spuds. We hatched little fluffy chickens in our kitchens, fed them, ate their eggs, then ate the chickens. Women are tough, Ted. We became the makers of decisions. Thank Germany and Japan for that.'

Surprised, Theo raised both eyebrows. She was right,

of course. Maggie was yet another of those females who hid a wealth of knowledge and opinion behind a pronounced accent and under day-to-day drudgery and worry. 'Do you read?' he asked her.

'Course I do. I go to the library and borrow. See, if you look at that Jane Austen, the girls sat about sewing ribbons on hats or staring cow-eyed at the men they fancied. There was no going about and saying "How's about it, then, lad?", because women had to pretend to have no brains in them days.'

She lowered her tone. 'Her upstairs,' she raised a hand towards the ceiling, 'she's what they call liberated. We're not inferior to men, like, but we're different, that's all. And it's only the . . . the embroidery that's different. Underneath all the trimmings on the hats, we've the same spirit with the same . . . er . . . the same rights. She's a cracking girl, Ted. I know she talks funny, but so do you and so do I. You could do a lot worse and no, I won't say nothing to nobody.'

He already liked Maggie, but now she was warming his heart. While women like this one were in the world, the planet was safe enough. 'Where were you educated, Maggie?'

'Myrtle Street and the seniors down the bottom of Ivy Lane.'

She reminded him of himself, since he'd gained most of his knowledge outside school, in libraries, in his parents' trailer, reading in cornfields and talking and listening to the elderly on benches outside saloons. There was wisdom to be had from the aged, if only youth would stand and listen for a while. 'Come on, Maggie, get your coat. I'll be in detention if we hang about here. The headmaster's what you might call a stickler.'

She laughed and went to get her coat and bag. Mr

Quinn was a character, well fit to manage Miss Fancy Nancy upstairs, God love her.

Theo went out to start his car. He found himself looking forward to the proposed trip; Tom Quirke could spare a week or two, surely? But he did have a niggling worry, and he needed to talk to his passenger.

As they reversed out of the driveway, Maggie waved at her grandchild. Rosie was standing at Miss Bellamy's sitting room window, grinning and waving goodbye. She turned to Tia. 'Can we go soon? I've never been proper shopping in town. Mam never paid for nothing. I had to hide things under my coat, cos I've got an angel face, she always said.'

Tia joined the little girl and waved at the couple in the car. He'd been rather good at messing about . . . She stopped waving and turned to face Rosie. 'Your mother had you shoplifting?'

Rosie thought about that. 'Not a whole shop, because it wouldn't have fitted under me coat. Bars of chocolate, socks, knickers, just small things, they were. It's all right, I don't do it no more.'

'Good. Because it's wrong, Rosie.'

'I know, but you have to do what your mam tells you.'

There was no arguing with that. And she'd almost missed it altogether, because she'd been basking in delightful memories . . . 'Come on, Rosie. Breakfast, then town, and we pay for everything.'

Maggie wasn't comfortable. 'It's like sitting on the floor,' she complained.

Theo grinned. 'You're in a sports car. Saturday morning, you'll be in an ambulance.'

She turned her head and glared at him. 'I bloody

won't. No more ozzie for me; I had enough of lying in bed for one day like wet fish on a slab.'

'It's been converted,' he began to explain.

'A Catholic ambulance? I'm Methodist.'

He laughed. 'Don't get cute with me, Maggie. It will seat eight, driver included, so we can take Nancy and Tom if they want to come.' He paused. 'But you must all keep quiet about it, or say you're going to Blackpool for a few days.'

'You what?'

He parked outside the Athertons' house. 'This may sound cold and calculating, and I don't want to upset you, but if Sadie wakes soon, she may want Rosie back. If your daughter returns to her old ways, new pimp included, we need to keep the little one safe. Dr Heilberg is giving us a letter to take to his dad, who is Tia's family doctor. As a temporary resident, Rosie can be looked at, examined for old injuries. We get the evidence and take Sadie to court.'

Maggie's face blanched.

'It has to be considered,' he added seriously.

'Are you talking about kidnap, Teddy?'

He inhaled deeply, puffed out his cheeks and exhaled slowly through his mouth. 'In effect, yes, I suppose I am. It would be short term, hopefully, just until we get the evidence we need.'

'Then what?'

'Then you are awarded custody.'

She swallowed audibly. 'I've got this anaemia thing, Ted. And one of my arms has been broke twice and healed up wrong, cos I didn't know it had broke. They think I'm weak-boned.'

He processed her reply. 'OK, we get her fostered near the Lady Streets until . . .'

'Until what?'

I must be mad, because I'm thinking until Tia and I are ... are married, then we'll try to adopt her ... 'Until we work something out. Be aware that both Tia and I could lose our jobs, but we feel so strongly about Rosie that we are prepared to be prosecuted as accessories. That child will not spend another day in the company of a pimp.'

'God!' Maggie put her hands over her face.

'Don't cry,' Theo said softly.

'Perhaps we'd better not take Tom and Nancy.'

'Don't you trust them to keep quiet?'

'Course I trust them.'

'Well, then . . .'

He was the sort of man few people looked at twice, because he was part of the scenery, a sight as familiar to most as were the birds perched on top of the Liver Building. The tools he'd needed to bring about the death of Miles Tunstall were now smashed to pieces and drowned beneath the greyish depths of the River Mersey. Lads from the Grenadier pub had seen to that, and little Rosie Tunstall was safe for a while. She wasn't Tunstall, he reminded himself; she was Rosie Stone.

He sat in sunshine, his face raised to enjoy the warmth exuded by Earth's mother star. A man without legs needed to stay warm, as he couldn't walk about to keep the blood flowing. A man without legs owned very strong arms and a well-muscled upper body, since self-propulsion depended on the torso. He could still hear the snap of bone in Tunstall's neck but, as an old soldier, he had become inured to killing during the Great War.

So Tunstall was dead, but the music went on. Harry took the mouth organ from his shirt pocket and began to play 'Molly Malone'. Perhaps little Rosie would come today . . .

Ten

Theo always took assembly on Monday mornings. Other teachers were on a rota system, so their pupils were trained to take their turn to pick a theme, read, sing and perform in front of the whole school. But on the first working day of every week, Mr Quinn, commonly known as Blackbird, took the stage. He placed his notes on the lectern, flapped his 'wings' and cleared his throat. This was one of his favourite times, because he got to teach, to make them think, to make them laugh.

The children from Standard Three seemed rather giggly and agitated, so he raised a hand and waited for the excitement to dissipate. Colin Duckworth, a pupil in the class, was usually at the centre of any giggling or agitation, but a hard stare from Blackbird did its usual trick, and things seemed to grow calmer after a few seconds had passed. The chattering was reduced to whispering, and the whispering stopped when Blackbird's expression grew more stern.

He looked at the whole school, over three hundred faces, some clean, some not-so-clean, most of them alert, a few pale and possibly hungry, an Alsatian dog, Colin Duckworth . . . a dog? After doing a double take, he glared at Colin and his large, furry companion. As he did, he noticed that Miss Cosgrove was gazing adoringly at him yet again.

Damn it, Friday night's end-of-year party promised to be interesting, Emily Garner, Miss Cosgrove and Tia Bellamy, the probable love of his life; oh, what a mess. Being so irresistibly handsome was such a burden . . . Who was he kidding? 'Miss Cosgrove,' he said, 'could you explain to me why a German Shepherd is among your flock? Are we going to need the dog to keep order among the ranks?'

She simpered. Simpering didn't suit her long, thin, freckled face. 'Mr Martindale died,' she explained. 'The dog was howling, and Colin rescued her. We're looking for a new owner. Colin brought her in to see if anyone wanted her. He didn't know what else to do.' She blushed, the colour of facial skin suddenly clashing loudly with her tight-curled ginger hair. Taking a handkerchief from the sleeve of her blouse, Miss Cosgrove mopped her fevered brow. 'Sorry, Mr Quinn, but I hadn't the heart to throw the poor dog out.'

Theo opened and closed his mouth twice. Occasionally, words failed him.

Colin rose to his feet. His hair, similar in colour to the peel of a slightly decayed orange, had taken another walk on the wild side. The crowning glory stuck up on top of his head like a semi-halo, though the sides were flatter, darker, and showed signs of having been treated with hair cream. 'Sir, it's a shame, Sir. It's not Miracle's fault, Sir, but Mr Martindale died and Miracle's got nobody, Sir.'

Sir glowered. 'Is this the right place to find a new adoptive owner, Colin? The dog does not belong in a school. Come here.'

Colin, plus dog with a rope tied to her collar, arrived at the front of the school hall. Children fidgeted and whispered while the unusual scene arranged itself. Dog and Colin looked as miserable as mortal sin, heads drooping, hair messy, silent as the grave. Theo squatted down and stroked the dog's head.

'She's called Miracle, Sir. She rescued a lad from the river when she was only one year old. I think she's about six now, and she's all on her own since Mr Martindale died. She hasn't got nobody nowhere, Mr Quinn.'

'Miracle, eh?'

'Yes, Sir. She's a miracle cos all her brothers and sisters was drownded, and she's the only one what stayed alive. And she must have remembered nearly getting drownded, and that'll be why she saved the boy. When he first got Miracle, Mr Martindale never slept proper for weeks, cos he had to feed her all the time, little drops of milk and stuff. Now she hasn't got nobody, and she's lonely. She wants somewhere to live, Sir.'

Theo ran a hand through his own hair. 'Go back to your classes, children,' he ordered. 'Assembly's cancelled for today. Colin and Miracle, my office – now.' Theo turned right and opened the door.

He strode down the corridor, black gown billowing behind him, one sad child and one sad dog following in his wake. He was good with animals. He could make peace between Tyger and Miracle, but did he have the time to train a cat and a dog to be civilized? Isadora Bellamy plus one more female would arrive this evening, then Delia would fetch the rest of their stuff as soon as she got use of the van, probably tomorrow. He was trying to keep Rosie and Maggie calm and happy, was busy falling in love with an annoying woman who allowed messing about, was going to Kent on Saturday with afore-mentioned-in-thought exasperating female. And now, a dog had added herself to the ingredients. She was a beautiful animal with soulful eyes and a depressed tail, no lift in it, no life, not a hint of a wag.

An idea struck as he sat at his desk staring at one upset lad and one grieving canine. 'How old was Mr Martindale, Colin?'

'About eighty. I used to walk Miracle for him, Sir. We can't have her, because Mam coughs near animals; she's adjerlic to them.'

'Allergic.'

'That's what I said.'

Theo sighed. 'Stay here. If the phone rings, don't answer it.' He dashed off, leaving Colin with the bereaved animal.

After knocking on the Athertons' door, Theo opened it wide enough to poke his head into the room. 'Tom, Nancy? Hi, Maggie. May I take up a few minutes of your time, people?' He entered the house and explained about the dog and how she was used to living with a mature person. 'If you'll give her a home, I'll buy her food and Colin Duckworth will walk her for you. And if you can't manage her, I'll find an alternative home for her, I promise.'

Maggie stood up. 'Oi, Mr Headmaster,' she said, 'we're going on holiday on Saturday, aren't we? What happens to the dog then?'

Theo shrugged. 'She gets a long ride in an ambulance. It'll take her mind off her loss. She can run round in Kent for a change, chase a few rabbits and ducks.'

Nancy and Tom stared at each other in silence. The only clue that they were taking notice lay in the fact that Nancy had actually stopped knitting and Tom had ceased to suck on his empty pipe. They both blinked a few times, but said nothing.

Maggie shook her head and sat down again. 'Does the dog have to keep quiet about Kent in case our Sadie comes round, goes back to her old ways, and tries to get hold of Rosie? This bloody plot thickens by the minute. Don't say where you've been or who you've been with, kidnap your granddaughter in case your suicidal, alcoholic, whoring daughter wants her back, tell Nancy and Tom to say nothing, and look after a great big dog. It's a grand life. I'm supposed to be having a rest, you know.'

Theo stood in front of the empty grate. 'Look, I've a school to run, and I've left a young boy in my office with a very sad German Shepherd bitch. Colin Duckworth could start a war in a garden shed, so will you let Tom and Nancy speak for themselves, Maggie, then I can get back to my job?'

Tom opened his mouth at last. 'We could give it a try,' he said.

Nancy was her predictable self. 'You're right, love. We could give it a try.'

'Thank you,' Theo said, heaving a sigh of relief. 'I'd better get back and see if Colin's managed not to destroy my school.' He left in a hurry.

'Do you like dogs?' Maggie asked the bemused couple.

'No idea,' Tom replied.

'That's right,' his echo chimed, 'because we've never had one. We never had kids, neither, but we like them.'

Maggie blinked. Coming from Nancy, that sentence equalled a full paragraph. 'What if it bites?' she asked.

Tom sniffed back some emotion. 'Sammy Martindale was a good lad. Older than me, he was. At school, he stopped Chuffy Briggs kicking the shi– the life out of me. He was a bully, Chuffy Briggs. Collected train numbers; that's why we called him Chuffy. Well, Scruffy Chuffy, because his neck was always as black as the fire back. Me mam always said she could have grown spuds on Scruffy Chuffy's neck. Sammy Martindale stuck up for me, because he was on the side of bullied kids, so I can pay him back now by looking after his dog.'

'That's right, love.' Nancy picked up her knitting. 'This green's hard on my old eyes.'

*

Rosie and Tia happened upon Dr Simon Heilberg in Free-man, Hardy and Willis; he was over on the men's side paying for a pair of shoes. With his transaction complete, he joined Tia in Ladies and Children. He sat next to Rosie, who was wearing brand new black shoes with ankle straps, but her gaze was fixed on the same shoes in red. They were in the window, and she couldn't take her eyes off them for a second.

'Can we try them in red?' Simon asked. It was clear to him that the child was head over heels with the scarlet footwear.

Tia stared at him. 'Black goes with everything,' she advised him.

'She can have both, can't she? Why are you looking at me like that? Have I committed a criminal offence?'

Tia dragged her gaze away from the ceiling. 'Have you any idea of how quickly a child's feet grow? They get new shoes not because the old are worn out, but because feet grow like weeds at her age.'

'Yes, I'm a doctor, so I know all about growth rates, thank you.' He asked the assistant to bring a pair of red ankle-straps. 'She deserves them,' he muttered at Tia. Smiling at the child, he said he had an idea. 'Set a trend, Rosie. Wear a right red one and a left black one, then a right black one and a left red one.'

'That's daft,' Rosie told him. She seldom accepted silli-ness from adults.

'Listen to the child,' Tia suggested. 'She's wise for her age.'

'I've already got wellies and sandals and gym shoes,' said Rosie, pointing to a bag.

'Good,' he said. 'Wellies are good; they let you jump in puddles.'

'Miss Bellamy's spent loads of money.'

'No more than you deserve.' He stroked the child's

head. 'I shall buy the red shoes. There's a film called *The Red Shoes* and a fairy tale with the same title. Red shoes are for dancing.'

Rosie studied him. 'Is that true, or is it something grown-ups say to kids, like "Be good or a bogeyman will come and get you"?'

Simon's face almost split in two, so wide was his grin. 'You are a bright little one, aren't you?'

'She has the measure of most,' Tia said. 'Will you do us a favour, Simon?'

He nodded. 'If at all possible.'

Rosie realized that this man liked Miss Bellamy; so did Mr Quinn.

The assistant arrived and fitted the shiny red patent leather shoes to Rosie's feet. 'Can I keep them on?' the child begged. 'Please, please let me wear them. I won't scrape my toes, I promise.'

'Walk up and down the carpet, love,' suggested the saleswoman.

Rosie did as asked. 'They fit,' she pronounced. 'Please let me keep them on. Please, please,' she implored again.

Simon gave his permission, and Rosie flung her arms round his neck.

Tia grinned. Why couldn't she love this special man? He would make a great husband and father, an ideal care-giver for children.

Rosie finally released him. Her face shone like Christmas, twinkling eyes and glowing cheeks. She was going to be a great beauty, Tia believed.

'Your favour?' Simon asked.

'Ah, yes. Come for supper tonight, about seven. Ma and Nanny Reynolds will be there. They'll be pleased to see someone they already know.'

'She's finally done it, then?'

'She has. I just hope he isn't running round like a bear

with a sore head. Don't forget the letter for your dad.' She glanced at Rosie. 'We have to get the examination done for old . . . old damage.'

He nodded. 'Is Sir going south with you?'

'Yes. We won't all fit into the cottage, so some will stay at the inn.'

'I see.' He saw, all right. She had finally fallen, but not for him; she was perilously near to the brink with a man who wanted no children.

Rosie was trying to dance in her red shoes. They were no different from any others when it came to dancing, so doctors made up stories, too. But the shoes were so pretty . . . Miss Bellamy and Dr Heilberg paid while Rosie skipped about in red shoes outside the double-fronted shop.

The adults found her and took her off for lunch in a hotel. They had wine, while she had pretend wine made from blackcurrant and apple juices. She had it in a proper wine glass with a stem, and she made up a story in her head about these two people being her mam and dad. This made her feel slightly guilty, because her real mother was ill in hospital, but Mammy hadn't looked after her properly, so making up a story about belonging to nice people wasn't really bad, was it?

They had cream of chicken soup, poached salmon with Jersey potatoes and sauce, and a cold salad on a side plate. The bread was flaky on the outside and soft on the inside, and tonight she would have more good food with Miss Bellamy's mother, who was a secret film star.

For pudding, she enjoyed vanilla ice cream with hot chocolate sauce, and she had never tasted anything so wonderful in the whole of her life. She saved a bit and mixed it round with her spoon until it was a thick, tepid, chocolate and cream sort of custard. Delicious.

Simon watched her, humour in his eyes. 'Adorable,' he mouthed at Tia.

She inclined her head in agreement. If Sadie wanted her daughter back, and if the mother and grandmother should both be judged unfit, Simon would probably be looked upon as a very suitable adoptive father. But was that reason enough for Tia to marry him? No. He would make a lovely daddy, though.

'You have a lot of parcels,' he commented as they left the hotel.

'I bought fents to make Rosie a few more dresses.'

'Fents?'

'Come north and embrace the culture,' she said, smiling at him. 'A fent is the end of a weaver's run, sometimes with a tiny flaw, often perfect.'

Simon took the packages and spoke to Rosie. 'Miss Clever Clogs, isn't she?'

Rosie found no answer. Miss Bellamy was clever, but she didn't wear clogs. 'We're going to see Harry,' she told him. 'He's got no legs. When they got blowed off, he could still feel his feet itching.'

'That's quite common,' Simon told her.

'He's not common,' was Rosie's swift reply. 'He has nice furniture and a big plant nearly fifty years old called an aspiduster and a sister called Martha and no stairs. I sing with him and get pennies and Martha keeps them for me.'

Simon's grin widened; the child was beyond price. How had she survived thus far? He squatted down. 'You are precious,' he said, his voice thickened by emotion. 'One day, I'd like a daughter just like you.' He walked with them and placed the parcels in Tia's boot. After locking it, he handed the keys back to Tia. 'See you later,' he said. 'Is the plan in place?' He mouthed the word 'kidnap'.

Tia nodded just once.

'Good luck with it. I know nothing, of course.'

'Thanks, Simon. You're precious, too.'

Rosie looked them up and down. 'She loves Mr Quinn,' she stated baldly. 'Nana thinks so, and Nana's always right. She never told me, but I heard her talking to herself in the kitchen, and she called them the lovebirds.'

Simon chuckled; he'd never before seen Tia blush. 'Don't try to keep a secret from this one,' he said. 'I'm throwing in my cards, Tia; I'll probably be back in Kent by Christmas.'

'I'll miss you.'

'Not as much as you'd miss Quinn, the lucky devil.' He walked away to his own car. Although the day was sunny and quite warm, he felt as if the main source of heat and light had been removed from his life.

Rosie slipped her hand into Miss Bellamy's. 'He loves you, too, doesn't he? Can you have two husbands?'

'No. It's a crime.'

'Is it? Like killing Uncle Miles was a crime?'

'Not quite. Come on. Now we'll visit the library and the gallery.'

'Then Harry?'

'Oh, yes. Then Harry. I have a little picnic for him.'

When Theo returned to his office after delivering Miracle to the Athertons, the dog was already back and waiting for him. Oh, God, it was happening again. All his life, he'd been a magnetic force as far as animals were concerned. Even the crazy horses in America's southern states had slowed down to avoid trampling him or knocking him over. 'Miracle? Did they leave a gate open? OK. In the office and sit. Stay there.'

The dog sat, her eyes fixed on him, her tail wagging hopefully. It was clear that she had adopted a new master. How did she know? Did he have something printed on his forehead, a message visible only to animals? 'I have a kitten,' he announced. 'He's small and useless when figh-ting geraniums, but he'll go for you, I'm sure. Very territorial creatures, cats.'

Theo left his office and locked the door, marching briskly to the deputy head's class. Miss Cosgrove was his second in command, so she was sent to inform the Athertons that Mr Martindale's dog was sufficiently intel-ligent to require formal education and had returned to school.

'What happened, Sir?' Colin Duckworth asked.

'I seem to have won a dog, Colin, and I didn't buy a raffle ticket.'

'Oh.'

'Oh is right. I have a feisty kitten who will scratch poor Miracle. Thank you for bringing trouble to my door yet again, Colin.'

He sat with the class and waited for their teacher to return. Colin looked so crestfallen that Theo awarded him a wink. 'What are you all working on, class?' he asked.

Colin was self-elected spokesman, of course. 'Project, Sir. The slave trade and Liverpool. Loads of black slaves died, Sir. They got buried at sea – that means chucked over the side, Sir.' Colin shrugged. 'Really interesting, it is. We done some terrible things, didn't we?'

The girl next to Colin used an elbow to dig him in the ribs. 'It was Bristol, too, and London.'

He rubbed his injury. 'Girls have dead pointy elbows,' he complained. 'Liverpool done the most. Miss Cosgrove said it wasn't nothing to be proud of.'

'We're not responsible for the sins of our ancestors, Colin. Carry on with the work.'

A flushed Miss Cosgrove re-entered the fray. 'I met Mr Atherton. He was looking for the dog, Mr Quinn, so I told him that you were looking after her.'

'Thank you, Miss Cosgrove.' He left while the going was good. If she started batting her eyelids at him again, he would probably blow a fuse, bust a gasket or throw a box of chalk.

Things were stacking up somewhat. His feelings for the beautiful Portia were stronger than he had been prepared to admit to himself, and it had all moved too quickly. Visitors were arriving; he already had Maggie and Rosie as guests, and he now had a large dog standing next to him holding her own makeshift lead. She pushed the end into his hand. 'OK, Mickle. If you think I'm going through life shouting "Miracle", you can think again. Let me ring the playtime bell.'

When the bell had sounded, Theo Quinn, head of Myrtle Street, allowed himself to be led out of school by the dog. They reached Mr Martindale's house and passed it, because Mickle wanted the next door, which opened after a couple of woofs. 'There you are,' cried the woman of the house. She picked up a box. 'Her lead, her blanket, her toys and some tins of food. Are you looking after her, then, Mr Quinn?'

'She chose me. I've had no say in the matter.'

'Well, she knows what she's doing. Had her photo in the paper when she was just a pup, saved a drowning boy.'

'Yes, I know.'

'I'd keep her meself, but she'd be sad here right next door to where she's lived all her life. Hang on.' She disappeared for a moment. 'Here's the list he left; he knew he was dying. Miracle likes egg on toast for her breakfast. At night, she'll eat just about anything, and he's written down her most favourite foods. Our cat will miss her. Best of friends, they were.'

Mickle took Theo back to school, led him back to the office, dragged blanket and bone from the bag and settled in a corner. Flabbergasted, the head of school sat at his desk and watched the wise dog watching him. 'Why me, Mickle? I've never done anyone any real harm since I stopped killing Germans, I go to church occasionally, keep my hands clean and the garden tidy most of the time, I'm good with kids, help old people cross roads, change shirt and underwear every day – why me?'

Unimpressed, the dog yawned noisily.

Theo closed his eyes. *Tyger and I are being marginalized. This evening, there will be five human females plus one canine female in my property. The odds are stacking against me and my cat; we will be buried beneath the weight of the tons of accessories that seem to accompany all members of the fairer sex – even Mickle has her box of stuff – and our personalities will be flattened.*

I am so . . . happy. For the first time in my life and in the life of Tom Quirke, I feel hope taking root somewhere in the region of my diaphragm. Portia will understand; perhaps I'll tell her everything if we can get some time to ourselves in Kent.

'I have an ambulance,' he told Mickle. 'It's been adapted and I'm having it painted blue, so I hope you don't suffer from travel sickness. Right. You stay here, and I'll go raid the teachers' biscuit tin for you. It's in the staffroom, so I won't be gone long. Don't say a word.'

Mickle sighed and settled down for a rest. She wouldn't say a word.

Maggie was glad to have something to do. Up in Miss Bellamy's flat, she was making a huge amount of scouse in two large pans. Southerners needed to learn that folk north of Birmingham knew how to live. Pickled beetroot and red cabbage were already on the dining table, and a stool had been brought in for Rosie, as there could be as many as seven or eight diners. It was possibly going to be a funny do, because Miss Bellamy had said last night that both Mr Quinn and her ex-boyfriend might be attending if she could contact Dr Heilberg. Maggie wondered why the girl didn't collect something sensible like stamps or dried flowers, since men were difficult to store even in a place as big as this.

When she heard a car arriving, she turned the flames to simmer and looked through a front window. Ah, here he was in his little green MG with that big dog sitting in the back on the seat-level shelf that allowed no legroom for humans, though it seemed to be OK for a dog. Miracle had run away from Tom and Nancy this morning; she clearly wanted to live in better circumstances, with posh rugs and a garden.

Oh, God, the cat, the bloody cat. Is my hair all right? He's one of those beautiful men who make every woman of any age want to look her best. I'll take this pinny off. The scouse should be fine; I'll just give it a stir. A squirt of Miss Bellamy's perfume on my wrists – ooh, that's nice – and I'm off. No, a bit of lippy and a dab of powder. Pull yourself together, Maggie Stone. You're not on a date and you're not eighteen, you hussy.

She dashed downstairs and along the side of the house, letting herself in through Mr Quinn's – Theo's – front door. As a guest on both levels, she could come and go as she pleased in either flat. When she entered the living room, Theo was standing in front of the fireplace, a finger to his lips. Maggie froze. A scrap of spiky, furious fur was clawing at the dog's nose. Behind needle-sharp teeth, Tyger's face was distorted into the very embodiment of absolute hatred and anger.

The Alsatian remained unmoved for a while before flattening the kitten under one huge front leg. Tyger blinked and hissed, though his enthusiasm for the task appeared to be diminishing fast. It was clear that the deceased Mr Martindale's faithful companion was in no hurry. The bitch seemed to be smiling, pink tongue on show, ears pulled slightly back as if trying to create a non-threatening frontage.

When the hissing and spitting stopped, that same pink tongue began to wash the kitten. A few half-hearted swipes were attempted, but the canine rose above such innate nastiness. She knew cats, was familiar with their aggression, and had made lifelong friendships with several of the unpredictable bundles. This was a baby that missed its mother, and she would act as surrogate.

'Aw,' Maggie breathed, a hand on her chin. 'Look, Theo!'

'I'm looking,' he whispered. 'Mankind could learn a lot from this.'

Mickle edged her face forward, moved her foot slightly and picked up the kitten in her mouth before lifting her leg off his little body. She carried the tiny creature to her blanket, placed him on it, and began a thorough grooming of her new pupil.

'Peace in our time,' Theo said. 'Five minutes, that took. We fought for six years, and I don't know how many young Germans I killed to get to this stage. The planet would be a happier place without people. We fucked it up – sorry, Maggie, excuse my lingo.'

'You're right, though,' she said. 'We do fuck things up. There's her at number four for a start, carrying on with him at number twelve while her husband's on nights. There'll be blood and guts from Ivy Lane to the Albert Dock one of these days. Yes, we make a mess.'

A soggy kitten curled into the dog's neck and fell asleep.

'Well, that was fairly quick,' Theo said. 'Have you done the scouse?'

'I have. And I made a cake with *Welcome to Liverpool* wrote on the top. It's a bit wobbly, cos I'm not much use with icing, but I done me best. The music's ready – I just have to click a doodah on the wotsname, so we're all right.'

'You've done well, Maggie. Would you mind staying here in a supervisory capacity while I take a shower?'

'Eh?'

'Be the zoo keeper. Watch them.'

'Right.'

While he showered, he found himself feeling a child-like excitement. For years, he'd lived in this magnificent house, all alone except for his cat. Suddenly, because he'd done the sensible thing by turning the villa into two apartments, the curtain had finally risen on the Theodore Quinn Show; he had a life. Tom Quirke had never provided that, because writing was done by isolated and often eccentric people who communicated through paper and ink and a typewriter. He'd met several, and some were socially inept, while many spoke only via their characters, choosing to step back and accept people's love, admiration, praise, criticism, condemnation or whatever by proxy. *At least I have my real life, my school, my children, my Portia. If I can just draw a line below . . . under all that went on before I reached the age of reason . . .*

So Maggie thinks Simon Heilberg might be on the guest list if Tia can get in touch with him? I suppose he'll be turning up, booted and suited in doctor mode, so I must wear my Sunday best. No, she wouldn't like that. Not a suit, then. Slacks, white shirt with open neck, no tie, casual shoes and I wish I'd had a haircut. Still, I'll look OK, won't I? But so does Simon, and it never seemed to get him anywhere.

He dried himself, put on a robe and returned to the living room. Tyger was playing with one of Mickle's ears. Maggie blushed. It was a while since she'd seen a man's bare legs. They weren't hairy, and he had nice feet, and she should pull herself together and get down to the Derby and Joan night at her local, find somebody nearer her own age and class.

'Go and mind your scouse, Maggie,' he advised. 'I'll open the red wine before I go to the station, let it breathe for a while. Exciting, isn't it?'

Maggie nodded. 'Oh, it is that, all right. And we can't tell nobody. I remember seeing her a couple of years back in that film, *Marking Time*. Broke my heart, she did, and what a lovely dancer. When her husband got sentenced to death, our Doris ran to the ladies' room until it was all over.' She paused for breath. 'Has she left him? Has she left Richard Bellamy?'

'Yes.'

'And this Rose Cottage – is it near their house?'

'Yes.'

'Won't he be in a bad mood?'

Theo grinned. 'Yes,' he repeated, 'but he's being in a bad mood in London. Anyway, even if he comes back, Tia can deal with him. She's afraid of nobody.' He failed to remove the pride from his tone.

'She's lovely, isn't she?'

He nodded. 'Quite a catch for Myrtle Street. She'll enliven us.'

Maggie smiled; the enlivenment had already begun, and it showed in his eyes whenever the lady in question was mentioned.

The subject under discussion shouted from Theo's hallway. 'Nine for food,' she yelled. 'I'm going up for a bath.'

Rosie ran in. 'Look, look, red shoes, Nana.' The little girl immediately turned into a happy chatterbox. Theo, used to disentangling the excited outpourings of the young, managed to separate shoe shop from lunch with

Dr Heilberg plus pretend wine in a posh hotel, the Walker Gallery from a picnic with Harry My Friend Without Legs, and the tide beginning to turn while tug boats pulled in a ship from oh, you've got a dog.

Maggie and Theo stared at each other. The child had been so quiet, so cowed and afraid. It was almost like a renaissance, because this was how she might always have been had her mother protected her from the likes of Tunstall.

Theo whispered to Maggie, 'This is why we have to do it, Maggie. If Sadie makes a complete recovery, well . . .' He needed say no more.

Maggie inclined her head in agreement. Sadie was her daughter, but betrayal was necessary, since the betrayal of Rosie was the bigger sin.

'How is she?' he mouthed.

'No change; still in a coma.'

Rosie had now become the third occupant of Mickle's blanket. With her head on the dog's side, she fell asleep. This had been the happiest day of her life so far, and her dreams were pleasant.

Maggie's pain and gratitude poured down her face. 'I don't know what we would have done without you and Miss Bellamy.'

'Tia, Maggie. Miss Bellamy's the schoolteacher.'

'Yes, right. Don't know how we'd have managed without Tia, then.'

'And without whoever killed Tunstall. The police have hit a brick wall, I think. Now, stop weeping. You've enough on your plate with all that scouse. I'll get dressed.'

'She's always wanted red shoes.'

'Shut up, Maggie, or you'll have my eyes leaking, too.' He patted her shoulder before going into his bedroom. Leaning against the door, he closed his eyes. In five days, he would be enabling kidnap by driving Rosie and Maggie to Kent. He would be accessory before, during and after the fact. 'It's the only way,' he whispered to himself. 'She needs to be safe.'

They walked hand in hand down the platform while the huge metal dinosaur breathed its last until turn-around time, as Theo termed it. While the brakes were fully applied near buffers, smoke and steam filled the air. 'Ma will be in Class One,' Tia murmured, almost to herself. 'She has her priorities right.'

'We're going diesel soon,' Theo grumbled. 'I'll miss these monsters.' He stared at his companion; she was a sight worthy of attention. 'Class One?' His eyebrows shot upward. 'Can't she read?'

'Do you want a thump?'

'Don't answer a question with a question. And leave your hand in mine, because she knows. When she phoned to ask me to inform you that your dad was last seen screaming in Wardour Street, I told her about us.'

'Us? What about us?'

'That we're beginning the mating ritual.'

She clouted him with her handbag. 'She's my mother. I should tell her when there's something to tell.'

He grinned broadly.

'You're lying, aren't you, Mr Quinn?'

He nodded, smile still in place. 'I'm not lying about your father sacking his agent. The effluent hits the press this week – nothing will stop it. If the man has any sense at all, he won't contest the divorce.'

'Sense is a lot to ask, Teddy Bear.'

The grin remained in situ. She cared. The pet name she'd chosen for him, the facial expression when she looked at him, half shy, part happy, part confused, such clues presented no problem to either Theo Quinn or Tom Quirke. This precious and beautiful girl was growing closer to him, and her kisses were becoming greedy. '*Hand in Hand*,' he said. 'Quirke's next book.'

'Romantic?'

'Depends.'

'On what?'

'On whom would be a better question. When I've unburdened myself to you, when you know the details—'

'Ma!' she screamed. 'Nanny!'

Determined, Theo held on to her hand while they ran towards Isadora Bellamy and Joan Reynolds. He released Tia only when he picked up two small suitcases. The three women hugged each other for at least thirty seconds. As predicted by Tia, Isadora had dressed down, brown wig, brown jacket, brown skirt, brown bag and brown shoes.

Tia released her loved ones. 'Ma, Nanny, this is Teddy or Theo. He's my head teacher and my landlord.' She paused. 'And he's my boyfriend, too, I suppose.'

Isadora looked him up and down. He was solid, broad-shouldered, tall, dark-haired, dark-eyed and very handsome. She held out her right hand while he put down the luggage. 'I believe you're a fan of mine, young man. It's clear that you have good taste in women, because this daughter of mine is extraordinary.' She shook his hand and introduced him to Joan. 'Joan is responsible in part for the fact that my three daughters are brilliant, kind and lovable. She raised them while I worked my way up through the ranks.'

He felt the heat in his face; he had just shaken hands with a star. 'I've met Delia,' he said. 'The only one I've missed is Juliet.'

'You'll meet her next week if you go to Kent.' She

turned to her daughter. 'You do realize that Richard will leave London and run home to lick his wounds.'

'I'm not afraid of him,' Tia said for what felt like the hundredth time.

'That's because you have his stubborn streak.' Isadora smiled at Theo. 'You'll do,' she told him. 'Just stay one step ahead of her, because she's quick. We lost count of the number of occasions on which she went missing for hours at a time. When the other two were growing up and getting about, she used to take them with her.'

Nanny Joan agreed. 'She was naughty, but interesting.'

'I'm pleased to report that there's been no improvement whatsoever,' Theo replied. 'Come along now. Maggie's scouse awaits us.'

Isadora smiled. 'I'm travelling with this gorgeous young man, Joan. You must make do with my daughter.'

On the way home, Theo told Isadora about the welcoming committee. 'They all know who you are, and none of them will talk.' He reminded her about Maggie and Rosie and the plan to keep them in Kent until the child's mother's future could be assessed. 'You already know Simon Heilberg. That should make seven, but Tia said nine, so I've no idea who the other two are.'

Isadora thought about poor Simon. He had altered the course of his life for Portia, and he would be heartbroken, though Madam had told him not to relocate to Liverpool. 'Is Simon aware of the plan to abduct Rosie?'

'It's hardly abduction; she'll be with her grandmother.'

'All the same, the comatose mother is still the mother.'

'I know,' he sighed. 'Yes, Simon's aware. We shall throw ourselves on the mercy of his father. We need to know what happened to Rosie while her mom was entertaining clients.' He pulled into the drive, leapt out of the open-topped car and rushed to open the passenger door. They walked towards Tia's entrance to the property.

Maggie's dulcet tones floated down the stairs. 'Is that yous lot?' she cried.

'It is indeed,' Theo shouted.

'Wait there,' Maggie ordered, 'while I press the doodah on the whatsitsname.'

'The which on the what?' Isadora enquired.

'No idea, sorry.'

Handel's 'Arrival of the Queen of Sheba' crashed down to ground level.

Maggie came down with the noise. 'Sorry,' she said, taking fingers out of her ears. 'It was Miss . . . it was Tia's fault. She's got that bloody gramophone turned up to gas mark nine.'

'Where's Rosie?' Theo asked.

'She's zoo-keeping.'

Isadora beamed. 'What a fabulous accent.'

Maggie bobbed up and down as if curtseying to royalty. 'I seen you in the films,' she said.

The second MG arrived. Tia jumped out while Theo opened the door for Joan.

Isadora mouthed at Maggie, 'Call me Izzy while I'm here. Remember I'm in hiding, as will you be quite soon. That music! She does this to me every time, though occasionally we get the "Ride of the Valkyries".' She glared at her daughter. 'Look at her, Maggie – butter wouldn't melt. Now, take me upstairs and I'll turn Handel's handle to simmer, then I'll get washed and changed.'

By seven o'clock, Tia's flat felt smaller. Maggie fussed about with sherry and glasses, while Rosie played on the floor with one solid, sensible dog, plus one lunatic kitten. Isadora and Joan shared the sofa, and Simon stalked about like a spare part. Theo and Tia had vanished. 'Where are they?' Isadora asked. 'You see, Joan? She still does the disappearing act.'

Simon walked to the window and looked down at the

front garden and pathway. Owner and tenant were standing together, his arm round her waist, her eyes looking into his. *I am a damned fool, standing here looking at them standing there. He has my life in his hands, literally. I needn't have put myself through any of this. She warned me repeatedly, but did I listen? No. I heard what she said, but didn't heed it.*

A *Liverpool Echo* van hove into view. The driver alighted, opened the rear door, and three other men jumped out. A middle-aged female left the van by the passenger door. She waited near the vehicle while four men carried a fifth up the path; the fifth man's legs came to a full stop at knee level. Theo Quinn reached into the van and lifted out a flat piece of wood with a wheel at each corner.

When all had entered the ground-floor flat, the driver plus three men left in the delivery van. Eventually, Theo appeared in Tia's flat. 'Downstairs, everyone,' he ordered. 'We have a visitor who can't walk. My table is set, and I'll transfer the food. Rosie, take Mickle and Tyger down first.'

Rosie was delighted when she reached the lower flat. She hugged Harry and Martha before showing the red shoes to the latter. 'Harry seen them this afternoon when we had a picnic at the Pier Head. I had the bestest day in my whole life.'

When the others had arrived, Harry took his mouth organ from a pocket and played while Rosie sang 'On the Good Ship Lollipop'. Her pitch was perfect, and she dressed the lyrics in Shirley Temple's easy-to-understand Americanese.

Here came the point at which Isadora Bellamy fell in love. This baby was only just five years old. How many like Rosie were buried under sin all over the place, London, Birmingham, Manchester, Liverpool? She watched the grandmother wiping away tears, saw Portia closing her eyes, Theo blinking away emotion. Everyone in this room probably supported what was about to happen. Simon just smiled and nodded at Isadora. He knew.

Isadora had a contract that needed just her signature. It would keep her in England for the foreseeable future, and the real money was in Hollywood, but she would stay and work in British studios. A series of comedy films was on the cards, all entitled *Don't Look Now, the* (whatever) *is Coming.* Potential whatevers included thus far Vicar, Policeman, Mother-in-Law, Judge and Teacher. She now had plans for her earnings. Her life's real work began in this moment, in this flat, in Liverpool.

Bartle Hall and all cottages would be owned by her, and Richard could live on what she paid him for the property, plus a small annuity, plus any earnings he might gain from those prepared to employ him without her. While a beautiful child sang, the Bartle Hall Home and School was founded in Isadora's head. The cottages might provide shelter for those whose mothers or fathers needed somewhere to live, and there would be enough outdoor space for young ones to enjoy.

Eighteen bedrooms would be put to good use, as would the large ballroom. Divided, it could make two or three classrooms. *My life has meaning. Simon can be the hall's doctor, Juliet might be matron, while Theo and Portia should provide education for the needy. I think I have finally come of age.*

Eleven

I am happy, happy, happy. I am so happy, it's making me tired, nearly as tired as I used to be after long times in that coal shed. New shoes, red ones and black ones, brown sandals, white gym shoes and black wellies. I am with Nana and Mr Quinn and Miss Bellamy and her mam and Joan and Harry and Martha and Dr Heilberg's here, too. Happy feels so good it nearly makes me cry, which is very silly. I want to sing and shout and laugh and cry all at the same time.

I think it's because they all like me. There's no coal shed and no jumping up and down men and nobody hits me. My mam is in hospital asleep cos she wanted to go to heaven, but it wasn't her time, Nana said. I am singing now. Miss Bellamy says I have an angel's voice. Her mam looks a bit sad. Joan, the lady with Miss Bellamy's mam, has grey hair and twinkly blue eyes. They are kind eyes.

I'd like to stay here for ever and ever. There's a shed in the back garden, but I've never been in it. It isn't a coal shed. Mr Quinn says it's for sawing and hammering and making things. He has a vice in there, but I don't know what a vice is. And there's a last. He mends his own shoes on the last because it's cheaper and he remembers being poor in America, so he's careful with money.

Rosie stopped singing and received a hearty round of applause from an appreciative audience. Tia handed her a package wrapped in tissue paper. 'It will match your red shoes and your black ones,' she said. 'I really hope you like it.' It was a small offering, yet the child reacted as if she'd been given the Star of India. *A present! It's a present for me!*

The little girl inhaled sharply, thanked Tia and tore at the wrapping; it was clear that she was unused to receiving gifts. She pulled out a small clutch bag, scarcely bigger than a woman's purse, but it was in black patent leather with red trim. Her face lit up. 'It's the same red,' she cried. 'Look, Nana, look. My very own shiny bag.'

Maggie smiled. Seeing her granddaughter so lively and happy strengthened her determination to stay firm. If Sadie got well and went back to her old ways, Rosie must be protected no matter what the cost to any adult.

'It's not new; it was mine,' Tia told Rosie, 'and I've dropped in a florin for good luck. Now, pass it round, and we'll all put in a bit of spending money for your holiday. You'll be able to have a lovely time in the shops when we go to the seaside.'

Rosie smiled and blushed. She was being treated like a special person.

The bag did a tour of the room while Theo fetched his guitar. There was no percussion, but he produced a good enough bit of skiffle. All who knew the song delivered words referring to a very tall woman who slept with her feet in one room and her head in another. Those unfamiliar with Lonnie Donegan's lyrics clapped in an attempt to imitate a rhythm section, and Rosie dashed about in her red shoes while adults put money in the bag.

Harry the Scoot winked at Theo when the song ended. 'How much, Rosie?' he asked. 'Watch,' he mouthed silently at the other adults. 'Add it up, little princess,' he said.

The child tipped her spoils on the rug. She separated a ten shilling note from the coins, then silver from copper before lining up denominations and working it out. 'Two pounds, nineteen shillings and elevenpence halfpenny,' she said triumphantly. 'I am very, very rich.'

Harry threw another halfpenny in her direction. 'How much now, queen?' he asked.

'Three pounds,' Rosie shrieked joyfully. 'I've got three whole pounds.'

Theo summoned her and made his contribution. 'And another ten shillings. At this rate, you'll be able to buy shares on the stock market.'

'And sweets?' she asked. 'I hope there's some left for sweets. Do they sell butterscotch at that market? Oh, thank you, Mr Quinn.'

Isadora suddenly couldn't look or listen any longer. The beautiful, clever Rosie was one of the threads that would weave the tapestry of the future, and she had suffered already. That such young shoulders managed to support so old a head was the sobering, terrifying fact that made Isadora's breathing irregular. Using Bartle Hall was a decision she'd made in her brain, but the reason had wrapped itself round her heart. 'Excuse me,' she muttered.

She dashed off into Theo's bathroom and sat on the cork lid of a linen basket. This wasn't a play, wasn't a scene from some overworked tragedy in which a much maligned king offers his throne in exchange for a horse, or a handkerchief leads a man to insanity. She held no script, and no prompt lingered on a stool in the wings, because the action was real, just one run, no director to call for an extra take on film. 'We arrive in this world without a map or a book of instructions,' she whispered. 'The scene is set, and we just have to learn from those who've been here a bit longer. At the final curtain, we are still apprentices, because there's not enough time, not enough strength, too much cowardice—'

Someone tapped on the door.

'Who is it?'

'It's Joan.'

After over two decades together, these two women could almost read each other's thoughts. 'Come in.'

Joan entered and closed the door quietly.

Isadora raised her head. 'I should have stayed with my girls when they were growing, but I didn't, and none of us has the ability to change the past. The future is a different matter. Rosie's just one among many, Joan. Did you see her joy at being given Portia's clutch? Her mother's pimp kept her in a coal shed. She hasn't even started school yet. There are others like her, so many of them.'

'I know.' Joan's reply was carried on a whisper.

Isadora smiled wanly. 'I'm also acquainted with a lot of influential people, and that's the plus side of being famous. I'm staying in England and doing those comedy films. If they fold, I'll think again.'

Joan breathed an audible sigh of relief. 'They won't fold with you as the star, Izzy. If you lead, other good actors will jump on board.' She sighed happily. Joan had no desire to move to California and live among the beautiful people in permanent sunshine and compulsory happiness. 'What are you thinking, Izzy?'

'I'm not sure, but I may need to throw Isadora Bellamy's weight about, dear. We're going to save some children.' Her smile reappeared, but it was real this time. 'What's the point in having money stashed when it can be doing some good? I must talk to my girls, of course, since they'll inherit whatever I leave, though I have a feeling that they'll agree to my plan.'

'Plan?' Joan raised an eyebrow.

'Still in the formative stages,' Isadora said. 'Let's go back and act as if we're normal.'

Joan chuckled. 'That's asking a lot of me. I'm just re-lieved not to be going to America.'

'Theo's American,' Isadora said, apropos of next to nothing.

'I'm aware of that. And where does he live? He's half English and that's the half he chose. The American Dream is really the American Blind Optimism, invented after the Wall Street crash and now heavily supported by the Republican Party. No, I like being English and misera-ble. We value sunshine, because we get so little of it. I should hate having to pretend to be happy all the time.'

Isadora turned and gazed at her companion. 'Normal Americans aren't like that, but you're right about California, and Hollywood in particular. So you wouldn't have accompanied me?'

Seconds passed. 'I might have gone with you, but I fear I wouldn't have stayed. It's too big a country for the likes of me. I'd be a weed in a garden of orchids.'

'Of course you wouldn't, silly girl. However, it's just as well I'm not going to California if that's how you feel.'

'Indeed. Let's get back to the party.'

On the whole, it was a happy band of people who sat at Theo's table and ate Maggie's scouse. The quietest member of the group was Simon Heilberg, who watched as small signals passed between Theo Quinn and Tia, fleeting glances, smiles, the shaking of his head, a flush along her cheekbones. It was agony for the young doctor, who offered an apology before pudding arrived, making his goodbyes as early as possible, keen to be away from the lovers.

Harry, on the floor and propped up on cushions, ate apple crumble and custard from a tray on his abbreviated legs. Tyger found himself fascinated by this unusual human, and he sat on an arm of the chair made of cushions, while Mickle wondered if there might be a chance of a spoonful of something for herself at some stage. 'I'm surrounded,' Harry said. 'I'm not so much Custer's Last Stand as Foster's last sit. Do you ever feed these animals, Mr Quinn?'

'They'll get some of the spare stew when I've fished out the potatoes. Dogs can't digest them very well.'

Across the table from him, Isadora Bellamy, star of stage, screen, radio and her own bedroom in which she'd played drunk for months, watched the silent messages floating between her daughter and Theo Quinn. The pair had known each other for a very short time, yet there it was, love in bloom. She felt a fleeting pang of pity for Simon, who had worshipped Portia for years in spite of her lack of love for him. Portia liked him, but Portia's real Waterloo sat here eating his crumble after polishing off a large amount of a dish the locals called scouse. *My eldest is already lost to this man; I never before saw her like this, shy yet bold, happy but needful. She should be careful; my love for Richard arrived express, two nights out followed by a diamond ring.*

But the more she stared at them, the more she suspected that this was a match made in heaven, not in hell. Portia and Theo were made for each other, so where did time come into that? They would marry, probably sooner rather than later, and the thought pleased Isadora.

The meal ended, and the cavalry returned in the *Liverpool Echo* van, which had to be delivered to its legal owners before nightfall. Harry and Martha, both grateful for the rare invitation, thanked their host repeatedly before being whipped away into the gathering dusk. Because Harry had for years sold many copies of the local newspaper, transport had been provided to give him a chance of visiting friends.

When all eating had finished, Tia and Theo carried the debris into the kitchen and fed two animals who were plainly demanding legal representation from the RSPCA, citing malnourishment, dehydration and neglect as their reasons for seeking retribution.

'You're definitely an animal person.'

Theo smiled. 'Yes, it started in America. My father's good with them, too. He emigrated twice, you see, once from Ireland to Liverpool, once from Liverpool to the United States, but he was born to a farming family in Mayo. He has a fascinating accent, with the brogue of Western Ireland mixed with a bit of Liverpool and the whole cake iced with inflections from many states. We travelled. I think he had the soul of a tinker until the second wife got him a job as a school janitor.'

'So she planted him?'

'Oh yes, she made him take root. A powerful woman, also Irish.'

'Do you like her?'

He smiled again. 'Yes, I do. I learned to love her. She would probably kill me if I didn't. I like strong women.'

'Good.' Tia left him in the kitchen. She found Rosie asleep on the floor and Maggie snoring in an armchair, while Ma and Joan nodded in a more-or-less ladylike fashion on the large sofa.

She picked up the child and woke Maggie. After placing Rosie on the bed she shared with her nana, Tia left Maggie to deal with bedtime details. Ma and Joan were her next victims; they were kissed good night and evicted without ceremony. 'Go up to my flat,' she ordered. 'Theo knows you've come a long way today. I'll say cheerio for you.' She rubbed her hands together. Right. Dishes, then cocoa for herself and the man she had chosen by accident.

By accident? *It's a special occurrence, Tia, not an acci-*

dent. This stuff happens all the time to ordinary, everyday people, to princes, to beggars, to teachers who have festered for years in an academy for young ladies, to gypsies and beggars and presidents. It's called love at first sight, or perhaps love outside Junior Standard One, Two or Three. You haven't had an accident, Portia Bellamy. You've tumbled into love with a man you don't know, a man you remember, though you never met him before. Perhaps you don't know his past, but you sure as hell know his future. You know his present, too. You know he's washing a mountain of dishes with no help, because you can hear him clattering. Stop daydreaming; go and help him.

She re-entered the kitchen, took up a tea towel and dried. 'Hello, you,' she said. 'I got rid of the stragglers.'

He stopped washing and removed his butcher's apron. 'Come on,' he ordered.

'What? Where?'

Theo chuckled. 'Why?' he finished for her.

'Don't laugh at me, Teddy Bear, or I'll have your growl removed and replaced by a very rude sound.'

'We have two guests each, no privacy,' he explained. 'If we're going to have a relationship, even a messing-about-only affair, we need to be elsewhere.'

'Where elsewhere?'

'Somewhere elsewhere. Get into my car and shut up.'

'You ordering me about, Mr Quinn?'

'Get used to it. Blackbird is your boss, OK?'

Tia placed her hands on her hips. 'At school, yes. Out of school, it's anyone's game. You can't lead me by the nose when we're in the civilian world.'

'You wanna bet? Are you questioning my authority, Miss Bellamy? Because I own your apartment, too. I can turn you out whenever I feel like it.' He chuckled. 'Not while your mother's here, though. She's kinda special.'

'So gentlemanly of you, Sir. Lend me a sweater or a

cardigan, please. If I go upstairs, Ma might collar me and make me unpack.'

'Is she diva-ish?'

'No, just lazy.'

'I don't believe that,' he muttered.

Tia snatched the proffered cream-coloured jersey and led the way out of the house. She climbed into the passenger seat of Theo's MG and waited while he closed the car's folding canopy. For some inexplicable reason, she felt elated, like a child preparing to go somewhere exciting and new. He seemed more relaxed today, as if he might be coming to terms with whatever made him tense and preoccupied for much of the time. She also felt strangely shy and rather like a sixteen-year-old on her first date . . .

He opened the driver's door.

'What's our destination?' she asked as he sat and started the engine.

'Are you going metaphysical on me?' he asked, an eyebrow arched in amusement. 'Is it one of those poetic purpose-of-life questions or a matter of simple geography?'

Tia shrugged.

'Automatic pilot,' he replied. 'God's supposedly in charge of the dimensional probabilities, and this car will take us where it wants to go. OK?'

'You need treatment,' was her tart reply.

'Shut up, or Tom Quirke will put you in his next book. You'll be a double-barrelled spoilt kid with too many toys and an attitude problem. Making you comedic would be no difficult task.'

A smile tugged at her lips, but she didn't give in to it. Was feeling flustered a compulsory factor when it came to falling in love? *I have no idea, have I? Twenty-six years of age, and I've never before suffered from this condition. It seems I've been waiting ten years for this strangely sad man with genetic problems, a back like a relief map of West Yorkshire and a doctorate in humour. His books are so funny and . . . ah yes, that's it. His books are his escape. Where are we going? And yes, I want the long- and short-term answers to that question.*

'You're quiet,' he said. 'Are you cogitating?'

'Only in the privacy of my own home,' was her smart reply.

It was Theo's turn to squash a grin. She was a handful. She was several handfuls, tall, energetic, beautiful, naughty, talented, adorable. Very little would faze her. At last, he'd made close contact with a woman who might understand, because she had the intellect and generosity of heart to cope with his past and his future. He parked the car.

'Where are we?' Tia asked.

'Belle Vale,' he replied.

'Why?'

'My alter ego Tom Quirke owns property here. He's richer than I am, and he lets some out to families, some to students at the university, some to medical staff from the hospitals. Money standing still is worthless, so it's invested and doing some good.'

Tia scanned the street's substantial Victorian terraced houses. 'Why are we here? Are you throwing me out?'

'No,' he said emphatically. 'The students have dispersed for summer vacation. Two houses are empty. There will be no audience here. Before we go any further, before we move south in more ways than one, I'm going to introduce you gradually to me, the me I tried and failed to leave behind.'

She swallowed. Her heart was suddenly in fifth gear, and breathing was becoming a luxury. She felt the colour creeping across her cheekbones. Even as a teenager, she had seldom blushed. *It's Roedean's fault, Tia. When it comes to love, you get to analyse* Sense and Sensibility *and write a report about the radical differences and similarities between Elinor and Marianne Dashwood, both of whom were hysterical females. Why are you trembling? It's not as if you're about to lose your virginity, for goodness' sake.*

'Shall we go inside?' Theo asked.

Her mouth lacked moisture. With a tongue as dry as unused blotting paper and a throat that seemed to have narrowed, she felt unable to give birth to language. She was going to meet a child disguised as a man, the man she loved.

'Portia?'

She didn't even mind when he used her full name, because he had a way of coating it in honey. *Stop this now, Bellamy. This is the first time, because you've never teetered on the brink of love until now. Are you sorry that you didn't save yourself for him? He's no virgin, either – remember that.*

'Portia?' he repeated.

'What?' At last, she managed to force a syllable from the depths of her lungs.

'Are you nervous?'

She nodded just once.

'So am I. This falling in love is bloody hard work. I haven't written a word since . . . for a while.' That wasn't true; he'd worked on no body parts, but he'd started to write an account of his own life, and it was draining. Seeing it pouring out of his typewriter, page after page of his own absolute truth, made the whole mess revive itself to the point where nightmares were a distinct possibility. Yet it was cathartic in a sense, as if the process were a cleansing agent. She was sitting as still as a lovely statue. 'What is it?' he asked. 'Are you afraid of me, Portia Bellamy?'

'I'm afraid of me,' she admitted, honesty etched into the statement. 'I'm no innocent, but I haven't felt like this before.' *Keep talking, Tia. Don't sit here like a block of that Wall's ice cream, solid, rectangular and slow to melt. Where's your confidence gone? Back to Kent to hide in a priest hole? You've always been in charge, even where Pa's concerned. Keep calm. Stick with the truth.* 'I feel odd,' she admitted. 'Fascinated by you, needing to know everything about you, leaping off the edge, but afraid – do you understand that?'

'Absolutely, because there's no parachute, no safety net. We seem to be suffering from the same disorder. It must be communicable, either infectious or contagious. Don't worry, I can assure you that I haven't brought you here to have my wicked way with your delightful self. To be truthful, I wouldn't eat in a place that's been occupied by students, let alone . . . anything else. Just privacy, a place to talk – it's what we need.'

'OK.'

They left the car and walked up the short path to the house. He opened the door and breathed in sharply. 'There's the student eau de toilette,' he told her. 'Heinz beans and testosterone – a heady combination.'

Tia laughed. 'You should put that in one of your books.'

'Don't worry, I will.'

'How many live in here?' she asked.

'Four pay rent, but the rest are nomadic. I don't mind, because I remember my own time at university. I was older than most, and I had part-time jobs, although I know how poor the youngsters were. Someone has to house them.'

'You're a kind man, then.'

'Maybe. I think of myself as pragmatic – the houses gain value.'

They entered a large living room which was rather frayed at the edges, but spectacularly clean. 'I thought it would be a mess,' Tia said. 'It seems quite tidy, too tidy for students.'

'It was in a bad way, but a Mrs Venables comes in during vacations to fight the good fight. She'll have shifted decayed food and filthy clothing, and she keeps rodent life at bay, though even she can't eliminate the under-smell of confined young manhood.'

They sat on a cleanish sofa, and his arm crept across her shoulders.

'We're supposed to talk,' Tia said, a huge smile fastening itself across her face. At last, she was relaxing.

He repaid her with a grin. 'We've done everything apart from *the* deed, so don't be coy. About Saturday – the ambulance is garaged and ready. Tom and Nancy are close enough to walk to it, and I'll pick up their luggage this week. Officially, they've bought raffle tickets and won a couple of weeks in Blackpool. You take Rosie on Saturday morning, and I'll take Maggie. We'll get the ambulance out, and put our cars in the garage.'

A few beats of time strolled by before Tia spoke again. 'So we are definitely kidnapping a child and putting our jobs in jeopardy?'

'Would you rather leave Rosie's life on the line?'

'No,' she answered with vehemence.

He kissed her gently on her forehead. 'Think about Maggie. Her daughter is ill in hospital, and no matter what Maggie might say, she loves Sadie. But she knows that Rosie is more important, so she's taking her away to Kent. The poor woman is in danger of making her own condition worse, yet she will risk her health for the sake of that child's safety. I like Maggie.'

'I'm growing fond of her, too.'

'She's prepared to abandon her sick daughter for

Rosie's sake. What are a couple of teaching posts compared to that?'

Tia nodded. 'You're right.'

'I'm always right.'

She pursed her lips. 'So am I. What an interesting relationship this is promising to be.'

'Just don't challenge me at school.'

Tia giggled. 'Not even behind the bike sheds or the air raid shelter?'

'Especially not in those places.'

'OK.' She rested her head on his shoulder and breathed him in. This was her safe place; this was where she wanted to be.

In a quiet voice, Theo told her some of his past, the easier bits. He described stepchildhood as vicious, as a cavern deep and bottomless and lonely. The isolated hole, cold and damp, was created by the interloper, the invader who separated a child from his own blood, from his dad, gradually removing all evidence of her predecessor and fighting a ghost while trying to create her own family from her own belly. 'It's a meeting of precariously united nations in miniature, feelings buried behind stony masks until a fault near the surface erupts and battle commences, and some fool – usually me – puts his hand on the button that makes a new Hiroshima. I was twelve, confused, and I missed my mother and wanted my father back,' he said quietly.

Tia had to remind herself to breathe.

He told her that he'd felt excluded when half-siblings arrived. He described a teenage where corners had been cut from his life; he opened up about feeling like a satellite whose orbit was denied any warmth from a sun, recounted the many occasions on which he'd run from the diapers, the screaming kid in the pram, the crawling, alien infants, the 'wrong' smell of a house that was *hers*.

'Then one day when I was almost fifteen, Timmy made a break for it. He was just about two years old, unsteady on his feet, no wisdom, no street sense. Dad was at work. He hated city life, but my new supposed-to-be-mother was a city girl and she called the shots, so we were suddenly New Yorkers.

'I saw the truck bearing down on the child, and in that moment he became mine, my little brother. I ran like the wind, knocked Timmy to the sidewalk and took the blow from the slow-moving vehicle, whose driver had braked. No bones broken, just my shoulder out of joint. She screamed blue murder at Timmy, the way a mother does when her offspring terrifies her. She then put a grateful arm round me and held me like one of her own. "Come home with me," she said. "You're our big, brave boy, and your mom must be real proud of you, wherever she is right now." After apologizing to the ashen-faced driver, she took me and Timmy back to the house, pulled my arm back into its socket and gave me coffee with a shot of brandy in it. A nurse, she is, and she still works in a hospital. She loved me, Portia, though she didn't know how to say it, and she loves me to this day.'

'How could she not? Tia asked.

He shrugged. 'I was traumatized and difficult. Hearing the screams of my mother burning to death left me angry at the world, at God, at myself. Then my dad shut down like a safe whose combination was lost. He was silent until he got drunk, at which point he became loud and stupid. Till he met her. And as I grew older, I saw the love between them and allowed myself to be drawn in. I had to want to be loved, you see.'

'Yes, I do see.'

'And she made me go to school. High school was easy, and I made friends. Without my stepmom, God alone knows what I might have become.'

'You had a tough life, Teddy.'

He stroked her silky hair. 'There is no light without dark. I've had a rich life, Portia, colourful like a rainbow, each hue spilling into the next. The only difference was that my indigo darkened to black for a while.' He turned and smiled at her. 'And if you are my prize, then I am well compensated.' He kissed her long and hard on the lips. 'Will you be my prize?'

'Probably. As long as you'll be my prize.'

He laughed. 'You have to read the rest of it first.'

'That's fine. I learned to read a few months ago. But just in case, make sure there are no big words in it.'

'OK.'

They sat for a while, touching, kissing until breathless, both wanting, both needing, both knowing that Theo, like the man in the truck, must apply the brakes. Tia owned no stopping mechanism. She could control a class of children, but herself? She indulged and spoiled herself. She was a naughty child; no gold stars for Tia Bellamy.

When they reached home, Theo kissed his darling good night before locking himself in the body parts room. He began to write, his head bent over the typewriter, fingers flying until keys locked in a tangle on the page.

Although I was young, my bones seemed older, colder, gone to mould, even becoming weak. I could not bear the smell or the sound of fire, hated to be touched or spoken to. Memories depended from my framework, the still vulnerable flesh drooping raw from sinew and cartilage, since I virtually stopped eating. I was a bag of skin, bone and hurt. Somewhere within the shell I had become, a parasite embedded itself and sucked me dry from within. Its name was, I think, hatred, and its close companions were fury, sadness and despair.

Surrounded by life with all its colour and sound, I remained alone, locked in, isolated, yet still searching for a true solitude into which I might scream louder than the noise of flame and crackling wood and swollen metal as it pops and buckles in the path of white-hot flames . . .

He stood, rubbed his eyes and went to bed. He was making so many mistakes, which could be corrected on the top copy, but the carbon, supposed to be for Isadora, was beginning to look like Swahili . . . Why Isadora? Because she, like her wonderful daughter, owned a heart big enough to hold his truth and keep it safe in this land that was no longer foreign.

Tia crept up the stairs, anxious about waking two women who had travelled all the way from Kent to Liverpool before enduring a supper party with strangers.

She opened the door at the top of the flight, surprised to find Isadora waiting for her. 'Shouldn't a woman of your advanced years be in bed, Ma?' She kissed the top of her mother's head.

'You were out with Theo?'

'Yes. We went to look at some of his other properties in the city.'

'Ah.' Isadora glanced down at newly painted finger-nails. 'There's something going on, then?'

Tia shrugged. 'I think I love him. And he thinks he loves me.'

Isadora nodded. 'I see. That was quick.'

'Being quick doesn't have to mean mistaken or wrong.'

The older woman pursed her lips. 'Dip your toes before taking the dive, sweetheart. For some men, it's a takeover bid, a dabble in mergers and acquisitions. He's older than you, about halfway between my age and yours.'

Tia grinned. 'You're definitely not having him. I saw him first.'

Isadora giggled. 'I like him, Portia. I like him very much. There's intelligence, talent and humour in the man, and he clearly thinks that you are his main source of light. I'm sure you will take care to disabuse him of that mistaken concept.'

Tia could not contain herself. 'This is a secret, Ma, though he finally gave me permission to tell you. Theodore Quinn retained his initials and became Tom Quirke, and he wrote the Body Parts series of books. The writing allows him to indulge his hobby, which is teaching.'

Isadora blinked several times. 'Goodness gracious, and his dialogue's excellent.'

'Yes, it is. Are you thinking what I've been thinking for days? Theatre, film, radio, television in the long term?'

'From an acorn, the heart of England grew. That was a line in . . . oh, I forget, but it was in a play long ago, when I was a mere sapling.' She stared at her daughter, as if assessing her. 'I can get something done with those little acorn books of his, Portia. The man is clever; he has forced me to laugh until I was too sore to read on, yet there's solidity in his characters. What a find, my love.'

Tia grinned. 'He's a treasure.'

'You may be right there.'

'Not a word, Ma. He'll talk about it openly in his own good time.' Tia sat next to her mother. It was all going to happen tomorrow; Pa would receive his divorce papers if he could be found, while the national newspapers would be full of it.

But Isadora's mind was on other things. Roughly half of Quirke's books were set here, in Liverpool. The mistaken of the southern counties probably believed that the only culture to be found in the north would be in neglected refrigerators or in mould on bedroom walls. How wrong they were. Having met Maggie, Rosie, Martha and her injured brother, Isadora had already experienced the wit and wisdom of this beautiful, vibrant city. She could do some good here; her money might multiply and yield sufficient to turn Bartle Hall into a refuge for children, and the north, too, would benefit. 'I won't say a word, Portia.'

'Thanks, Ma.'

They clung together for a while. 'Did you love Pa?' Tia asked eventually.

'Yes, he dazzled me. I thought he was my way forward, a torch in the darkness. That's the other thing, my precious girl. We change.'

'Fortunately, some grow closer with age, Ma.'

Isadora kissed her daughter's cheek. 'Just take care, Portia. Marriage can be a difficult journey, so make sure you tread softly, because you tread on dreams. Who wrote that, or something like it?'

'I forget.'

'Well, don't forget to call me Izzy as from tomorrow. This evening's guests will not betray me, but some penniless soul might be happy to take payment from the press. Guard me well, baby.'

'Always, Izzy; I shall always guard you.' In that moment, the daughter's love for her mother was too big to be contained, and it spilled down her face like summer rain. 'Always,' she repeated, her voice strangled by tears. 'My mama, my best friend in the whole world.'

'Don't weep,' Isadora whispered. 'Marry him. You've changed because of him, child. Yes, you should marry him. Stop crying now.'

Tia smiled. 'These aren't tears, Ma. They're just overflow.'

ENGLISH ACTOR IN DIVORCE SCANDAL

ACTING DYNASTIES AT WAR

RICHARD BELLAMY TO BE SUED BY ISADORA

NO FUTURE FOR THE MARRIAGE,
SAYS ISADORA'S AGENT

They will never again work together,
the same source insists.

Theo picked up the newspapers at seven o'clock before returning to his ground-floor apartment to prepare for school. He climbed the stairs to the first floor and placed the four copies on a table in the upper hallway. A young Isadora stared up at him from a front page; Tia was the image of her mother, though taller. 'I get better value for money if this works out,' he whispered. 'More pounds for my pound.'

The door opened. 'Good morning, Teddy Bear.'

He smiled. Her hair was sleep-disturbed, her eyes hooded against the invasion of light, the nightdress crumpled. She seemed not to be a morning person. 'Don't dare to call me Teddy Bear at school.'

'Mr Quinn,' she amended.

'That's better.' He handed her the papers. 'It's happening. I'm worried about your younger sister. Few will know where Delia is, because she's an itinerant anyway, and she's supposedly on her way here with your mother's things. But Juliet is a fixed point in that hospital. She'll be easy to trace. I'm also wondering whether we should go to Chaddington Green after all. There'll be reporters and photographers looking for Bellamys.'

'We'll talk about this later. Remember, my father will be prey for the media, too, and every reporter in the country knows that Bartle Hall is Pa's home, so he'll probably be elsewhere. I'll sort out something with our housekeeper, Mrs Melia. I promised Rosie a priest hole, and a priest hole she shall have.'

'I'm concerned for Juliet, Tia.'

She nodded her agreement. 'Delia's tough, as am I; she'll tell them to go away and urinate, but Juliet . . . You're right. I'll telephone Matron. Incidentally, my own phone will be installed some time today, but I must beg to use yours this morning.'

'Everything I have is yours, baby.'

'Not until we're married, Mr Quinn.'

'Presumptuous, aren't you?' he said, his face split by yet another wide grin.

Tia shrugged. 'It's inevitable.'

He cocked his head to one side. 'Really?'

'Oh, yes. Despite your worries about matters genetic, we belong together. Now bugger off while I get dressed.'

He buggered off happily, fed his animals, showered, shaved, cleaned his teeth and dressed himself in decent clothes. This was the last week of the school year, possibly even his final week at Myrtle Street. Would he be here in September? He might well be arrested for kidnap, abduction, or whatever the wording might be in the statutes of Britain. Maggie and kidnap victim were still asleep, and he moved quietly in order not to wake them as he left the house.

Am I to lose all this, my dream since the end of the war? Will my Portia's name and reputation be sullied because of what must be done for little Rosie? But the machine is already rolling, and I cannot, will not, stop it. He went to his office where he penned a letter to his solicitor, telling all he knew about Sadie's history, about her dead pimp and his habit of shutting the child in a coal shed, about Sadie in a coma and Rosie's maternal grandmother's need to remove the little girl in case Sadie reverted to type when she recovered.

The phone rang. It was Tia. 'Hello, sweet man. Ma's agent has spoken to Pa's agent. My father is leaving the country today, and that will be broadcast tomorrow, so we can use Rose Cottage. Maggie, Rosie and I will stay there, but you and the Athertons might get rooms at the Punch Bowl, though Mrs Melia has offered to lend you Lilac Cottage if you prefer that.'

'You'll be seen, Tia.'

He almost heard her shrug. 'I'm afraid of very little, Mr Quinn. My parents' business is not mine, so it matters not at all if I'm approached. The main thing is that we keep Maggie and Rosie safe. Happily, there are many places where Rosie can play, but she and Maggie must remain on the estate unless we go out in the ambulance. When we do go out, we use back lanes and stay away from the village.' She paused. 'Actually, I have an idea, Mr Quinn.'

Theo groaned inwardly. 'And Juliet?' he asked.

'She'll be here in my flat with Ma and Joan. Matron released her from duty as soon as I delivered the warning; she doesn't want the rubbishy press crawling around in the hospital grounds and corridors. I spoke to Juliet, too. She's tougher than she looks, yet she remains the baby of the family, and we guard her well. See? I think of everything, Mr Quinn.'

He smiled. 'I think of you all the time.'

'Yes. I suffer too, you know.'

'We're diseased, Portia.'

'Probably. See you later.'

Theo sat back, a silly smile plastered across his face. She was worth it, as were Rosie and Maggie. Should proceedings take place, Portia's name would be kept out of . . . No. She wouldn't agree to that, because Madam was as stubborn as the proverbial mule, and she probably had a kick to match, too. *What is it about her? She's difficult, opinionated, mercurial, crazy. She's lovely. Don't question this, you fool. You can trust her, and that's the main thing. Write down all your rubbish and cleanse yourself; she will take you as you are in spite of your lineage.* He placed the letter for his solicitor in an envelope.

After tapping on the door, Colin Duckworth poked his head through a small gap. 'Sir?'

'Yes, Colin?'

The rest of the child crept in. 'You know in America, Sir?'

'I know a few things about America, but not every-thing.'

'Why do they have Indians? Indians should live in India, shouldn't they? Was they brung over from India like the slaves from Africa?'

'No.'

'So is there another India as well as the India what used to belong to our Hempire?'

'No.' Theo squashed a laugh. *Hempire?*

'So what happened?'

Theo sighed heavily. 'Where does your teacher think you are, Colin?'

'Toilet, Mr Quinn.'

'We have to stop meeting like this, son. Rumour has it that Christopher Columbus thought he'd found India. The people labelled Red Indians are indigenous.'

'Oh. Is that an illness? Is that why they're red?'

'They're not red, Colin, they are brown. And indige-nous means they were there first.'

'Oh, I thought it meant indigestion. My mam suffers with that and says it's my fault.' He paused, though not for long. 'So it's their country?'

'It used to be until people from Europe took over and made them live in reservations. Those among us who are decent are thoroughly ashamed of that.'

Colin made a decision and voiced it. 'Right, Sir. Next time I go to the fleapit and they're showing a cowy, I'll cheer for the Indians.'

'Cowy?'

'Cowboy film, Sir.'

Theo couldn't contain the chuckle that escaped from his mouth. 'Colin, you're a long time at the toilet.'

But Colin had an answer for that, too. Digging in a trouser pocket, he pulled out two sheets of lavatory paper. 'She thinks I've gone for a number two, Sir. She'll think I'm conspitated.'

That was the last straw. Theo burst out laughing, his head shaking from side to side. He loved this terrible kid, loved his deliberate Spoonerisms, his cheek, that enquiring mind, the silly hair, the deepening frown that had arrived through too much thinking. 'Go, Colin,' he gasped. The boy was definitely university material.

Colin went. His true hero, Mr Blackbird-Quinn, liked him. For some time, Colin had suspected this, but he now had proof. Mr Quinn was the true seat of learning in this place of education. He rid himself of toilet paper and returned to class, one hand clutching his belly. 'Sorry I took so long, Miss. I must have ate too many chips last night . . .'

Twelve

We were staying in our trailer on the ranch owner's land about seven miles outside Atlanta, Georgia. It was 1930, and I was almost ten years of age, a skinny kid with too much hair and very little flesh on my bones. Mom used to say I looked like nobody owned me, though Dad always told her I would fill out in a few years. I still hear his wicked laugh from all the times he chased me with a wooden spoon, threatening to play a tune on my ribs. We had fun. I try to think about the fun, but nightmares still haunt me. My life may seem strange when you read this, but I was happy most of the time, and I was loved.

Dad was working early mornings and evenings with horses, his favourite job, and I went with him occasionally. My father respected the noble beasts (his lovely Irish term) and refused to run them in the heat of the day. When it was hot, he did general jobs round the ranch. I recall occasions on which he took wet cloths and used them to cool down 'his' horses. There was an ice house under the ground in a kind of cave, and the ice man filled it twice a week.

Mom stayed inside the trailer for most of the time; the reason for that was something I would come to understand fully quite soon. It was hot, so hot, and the air was wet and clammy; any clothing was soaked in sweat within minutes. There were baths in a shed. Sometimes, Dad and I took two or three quick baths a day, but Mom waited until the middle of the night to go and get clean.

She was different, and I was finally beginning to understand what that meant. Mom didn't act like other wives and mothers on the trailer park. They spent time together when chores were done, chatting over lemonade or iced tea, but my mother kept herself to herself. Sometimes, I stayed with her and we read together. Dad and I taught her to read.

I loved her so much. She was gentle, kind, funny, an avid reader and a very beautiful woman. She was also terrified of other folk, so she kept herself very much to one side and was always delighted when Dad and I came home, because we were her whole life. She had a limp. Whenever I asked about the weakness in her left leg, she told me it had happened as the result of a fall when she'd been at school. She left school after the injury.

I still hear Dad almost growling at me whenever I spoke about Mom's limp. He was very protective of his Lily-Mae, and she was clearly the love of his life. The chattering women sometimes spoke about us; I knew that, because they would occasionally stop talking when I passed them. Our trailer was parked away from the others, so I figure people thought we considered ourselves to be a cut above them. That was not the case at all. Mom needed to be some distance away from the rest because she was afraid, not proud.

I've spent twenty-eight years wishing we'd never gone to the Bella Vista Ranch. It had been a toss-up between two places, and this one was the nearer. Dad's love of horses might have been a factor; one of the beasts he tamed went on to win the Kentucky Derby. Dad backed it and won a bundle, but he'd rather have had Mom safe instead. He used his winnings to buy a marker for her grave, white marble and beautifully engraved. Although he was preparing to remarry by then, he still adored my mother. She'd loved calligraphy, so we had her details on the stone done in *copperplate. I detest the weather in Georgia, but I visit her grave every time I go to America.*

The ranch owner paid for her funeral and shot dead two of her killers. When I discovered the identity of those murdering bastards, my faith in humanity was seriously corroded. That day, I saw two men dead and two crying; one weeper was my dad, the other was his employer. These were tough men, skin etched in deep furrows caused by sun and wind, well-muscled limbs and chests, teeth stained by tobacco and beer, both harsh of voice, clear of eye, deadly with a gun. Yet they sobbed like babies on that day, the day my mother died.

I didn't cry, or so I'm told. I just absented myself and was almost catatonic until some specialist or other snapped me out of it weeks later. So my inner pain was postponed, as was Mom's funeral because Dad, a far-seeing and somewhat primitive genius when sober, insisted that his son should see Lily-Mae buried. She was kept on ice, though not under the ground at Bella Vista. The boss paid for all that, too.

So now, I approach the climax, the crux of the matter. Fortunately for me, Delia has just pulled up in that battered van, so I am reprieved once more. But I will get to it soon, Portia. I love you, and you deserve to know the truth about my beginnings. And it is time for me to let this out anyway for the sake of my sanity, because anger isn't healthy, especially when it stretches over decades . . .

Tia was already on the driveway when Theo arrived. 'Hello, stranger,' she said to him. 'I thought you'd left home.'

'Home is wherever you happen to be,' was his whispered reply.

She shivered in spite of the warm weather. Sometimes, the man of her dreams said the loveliest things. 'Quite the romantic, aren't you, Mr Quinn?'

A red-faced Delia climbed out of her metal Turkish bath. 'I've been roasting in that thing,' she complained, kicking the van before hugging her older sister. 'I feel like a Christmas turkey ready for the table. Where's Juliet?'

'Simon's collecting her from the train. She'll need help with luggage, and he has a bigger car. Izzy and Joan have gone shopping. And yes, you smell sweaty, my love.'

Theo opened the rear doors of the van and looked at its contents. 'Hell's bells and bloody murder,' he exclaimed. 'What have you got here? The contents of wardrobe from Stratford-upon-Avon?'

Delia fixed him with a steely glare. 'I don't know, do I? I'm just the bloody courier, bring me, fetch me, carry me, Delia.' Her hard stare disappeared, but it was replaced by a wagging finger. 'I've already helped to lift their junk at home when we packed the van, so I am now on strike, and that is official. My labour is withdrawn, and I need to pee.' She marched away.

'See? It's not just me, is it?' Tia asked innocently.

'What isn't just you?'

'We all have a tendency to misbehave, though Juliet's not as confrontational. She says little, but does as she pleases.' She paused. 'Hey, do you have ten rooms? I have only nine.'

'No, I don't have ten rooms, madam. If you'd open your eyes, you'd notice that my dining furniture is in the living room, so don't start with the complaints, because Mr Quirke needs a room for his body parts. I'm thinking of using the other bedrooms for something or other so I won't need to have guests,' he grumbled.

Tia looked into the van. 'There are many items here, Teddy.'

He scratched his head. 'I need to buy another house for this lot.'

'Don't worry.' Tia held his hand. 'Most of it will be in

storage – it's all arranged. Anything with spots doesn't come into your house.'

'I should think not. We've enough to manage without breaking out in German measles.'

Tia awarded him a look fit to curdle milk. 'Get carrying,' she snapped.

'You're too bossy,' he complained.

'I am not.'

'And stubborn,' he added.

'I am not stubborn.'

'You are.'

'I'm not.'

He stepped away from her. 'See? That's stubborn. You stick to your guns even when they aren't loaded.'

A decision was reached. Non-spotty containers would go into Theo's spare bedroom, since Maggie and Rosie were sharing a room. Izzy and Joan could unpack at their leisure while he was at work. 'I don't want to interfere with ladies' underwear,' Theo explained.

'No comment,' Tia snapped.

'I mended the thing,' he muttered. 'And I did a very good job.'

'After you broke the clasp. I was one up and one down for most of that evening.'

'Don't be coarse,' he advised, and they both burst into gales of laughter.

Tia dried her eyes. 'Are we leaving the spotty ones in the van?'

'Bet your bottom dollar we are. I've been invaded, haven't I? If I get a hernia, you can pay for the truss. OK?'

But Tia was too busy dragging out a couple of suitcases. 'Shut up and take those in,' she ordered. 'Are Rosie and Maggie in the rear garden?'

'With the animals, yes. Izzy and Joan will be back soon. Izzy's feeding all of us.'

Tia dropped a heavy case. 'I warned you. Don't eat anything prepared by her. She's lethal with food.'

He chuckled again. 'It's OK, she's bringing a fish supper.' He disappeared into his flat.

Tia threw out the last of the spot-free luggage. Members of her family were becoming a liability, and she hoped with all her heart that Teddy wouldn't run out of patience. Until very recently, he'd lived in a huge house with just a cat for company. Now, he had Maggie and Rosie downstairs, while she had three Bellamys including herself plus one Joan Reynolds upstairs. Delia would be gone soon, but Ma and the rest might be here indefinitely. Oh, and Jules was on her way . . .

Theo returned. 'Shall I send them to a hotel?' she asked.

'No. I haven't had this much fun since VE day in London. I started off near the palace, but woke the next day in a house in Bow, no idea of how I'd got there, and no memory of the householders. My father used to do that sort of thing quite often, and I was worried about becoming an alcoholic. But I failed alcohol and got a degree instead.'

'Good,' she said. 'The occasional glimpse of a pretend drunk was difficult enough.' She stepped out of the van. 'That's it,' she announced, 'just six cases. The rest have spots. The keys are in the ignition, so just secure the van while I visit my sweaty sister.'

She's gone bossy again; would I like her to change? Not at all.

'Why are you staring at me?' she asked.

He shrugged. 'Just imagining what fun taming you is going to be.'

'Get a whip and a chair, Teddy. I'll pick up my shotgun when we go to Kent.' She turned on her heel and walked inside.

No, she mustn't improve, because I would hate that. I'm sure the consummate actress within will come to the fore at school. She'll be a great teacher, and I'll be Mr Quinn, the busy blackbird. Before all that, we've a small matter of kidnap to think about, and the essay I'm writing for my Portia and her lovely mom . . .

Martha Foster closed the door of their ground-floor flat. Reclaiming the ability to breathe, she stared at her brother. He was sitting on his low divan, the wheeled trolley abandoned, as he had finished selling newspapers for today. Next to him lay his mouth organs, the instruments that earned him and young Rosie extra coppers for playing and singing at the Pier Head.

'Make us a cuppa, queen,' he begged. It had never occurred to him that he might be questioned. Who would suspect that a man in his condition could be capable of murder? 'They won't come back,' he said as he stared at his sister's ashen face. 'Put the kettle on.'

She didn't trust her legs. 'Me legs have gone funny,' she murmured.

'I'll swap you for mine,' he answered. 'If yours are funny, mine are bloody hilarious.'

'Sorry, Harry.' She leaned against a wall to steady herself. Two policemen had questioned them about Rosie. Had they known she was a victim of cruelty, that she'd been shut in the coal shed, that her mother was a prostitute? Did they know a strong, tall man with a black beard, had they heard anything about the murderer? Did they know of anyone who might have hired such a man to kill Miles Tunstall? Martha staggered into the kitchen and set the kettle on the hob.

'They know nothing,' Harry shouted from the living room, which also served as his bedroom. 'They're clutching at straws, Martha. It's only because Rosie sings with me and helps to sell papers sometimes. Half this city knew what Tunstall was, so there's a long list of folk who might have killed him or hired someone to do the job. He was vermin and he needed shifting.'

Martha arrived in the doorway, a hand clinging to the jamb in search of steadiness. 'They asked about false legs,' she said. 'Everybody in your condition gets false legs. I know you're not the only one who didn't manage to wear them regular, like, but the fact is that you used them and killed him, love.'

'Apart from practising in here for Rosie's sake, I never needed them except for ... except for that day. My stumps were red raw, and they're still a bit sore.'

'The police know you have unusual strength in your arms and chest, Harry. They said it took a remarkably powerful pair of arms to do what was done to Tunstall. You're powerful. I'm an accessory and so are your mates Billy and Jim. They took your legs down to Billy's house on Ivy Lane. They picked you up and got you ready in Billy's house. And I knew everything.'

'Stop this now, love.'

'I'm scared.' She was near to tears.

Harry shook his head. 'Martha, I have no prosthetic legs. They went in the muck cart years back.'

'They didn't, though. And that sergeant looked straight through both of us. Your legs are weighted down in the river or under a road somewhere.'

'Yes, so they're no longer here. There was no rain, and I stayed off the grass and the soil, so I left no prints in the park. Can you imagine what a laughing stock Liverpool police would be if they accused me of murder? I put the legs and the beard on in Billy's back kitchen, went to keep my date with Tunstall, did what I had to do, then walked as fast as I could back to Billy's. I even wore surgeons' gloves. We dressed my poor old stumps and an hour later I was back in the middle of the city. The legs are gone, and my stumps are healing well, thanks for asking.'

'Sorry,' she said again, turning towards the kitchen where a whistling kettle demanded her presence. Her brother had pretended to have access to cheap alcohol and tobacco; Billy and Jim had arranged the hush-hush meeting between Harry and Tunstall. Martha scalded the pot and made the tea. Harry had saved Rosie by killing her evil stepfather, and he could hang for that.

They drank tea and sat staring into an empty grate. 'She's worth it,' Harry said eventually. 'Neither of us has a kid, and Rosie's a real little star. I reckon Quinn and Miss Bellamy will take over now, so she'll be safe. Just try not to worry, and don't get flustered if the cops come back. I can tell you this much, our little girl won't forget us, Martha.'

She offered him a slight smile. 'Let's hope the police forget us, Harry.'

Juliet threw herself at Simon Heilberg, kissing him on his cheekbone. Behind her, a porter struggled with a trolley bearing the weight of four large suitcases.

'Simon!' she exclaimed, 'I have never in my life been so happy to see anyone. Pa says he's leaving the country, but one never knows. Have the newspapers found Ma yet? They were certainly looking for me in Canterbury.'

'I think not. You are instructed – we are all instructed – to call your mother Izzy. For the time being at least, you must be an almost orphan. Delia will be there, too, so you'll be the Blyton Three for a few hours. It's a case of heads down and attract no attention, I'm afraid. The press has been very noisy about your father's behaviour and the pending divorce.'

She shook her head sadly. She was beginning to see

her mother's point of view, since Pa seemed to have behaved very badly. 'How's Tia?' she asked as they walked along the platform with the porter on their heels.

'She's head over heels in love,' he replied, trying to erase bitterness from his tone. 'Not with me, needless to say. I was just her fallback chap in case she needed a partner and didn't meet someone more interesting. Still, at least she was honest about it. She ordered me not to come up north, but I'm as wilful as she is.'

'Delia and I suspected as much. It's her boss, isn't it?'

'Boss and landlord. Nice enough chap, born in America, but volunteered at the beginning of 1940 and joined the RAF, rear gunner, survived the Battle of Britain. After the war, he trained as a teacher and was soon head of a school in Liverpool. He's about twelve years older than Tia.'

'So you moved here for no good reason?'

He looked at her. 'I wouldn't say that. Things have a way of working themselves out. There's something about this city that winds round your heart like a tight rubber band. It's not a lonely place the way London can be; it's magnetic, pulls you in and holds you. I work in a practice not far from Tia's school, and one of our duties is to take turns in police stations if anyone gets ill in the cells. Even their criminals have charm. Yes, I like Liverpool.'

'Won't you go back to Kent?'

He shrugged. 'If my father needs me, I'll go back.'

A single tear made its lonely way down Juliet's face. 'My father will soon need me, Simon.'

He stopped and held her arm, forcing her to stand still. The porter ground to a halt behind them, and Simon turned to give him a pound note.

'Thanks, lad,' the man said, backing off slightly.

'Juliet, don't cry.' Simon handed her his handkerchief, as that single tear was now in the company of others. Compared to Tia, this Bellamy girl was like a little doll, as beautiful as the eldest sister, but a miniature version. He lowered his tone to an almost-whisper. 'Your mum wants you all safe from him and from journalists. It will be a nine-day wonder before press attention wanes and they go off and find someone else to crucify. Journalists have poor long-term memories, thank goodness. By next week, it'll be "Richard who? Isadora who?", so be strong. Be strong for your mother and for your sisters.' He looked down at her. 'And for yourself, too.'

'I'm sorry,' she sniffed. 'Travelling by train always tires me.'

'Don't apologize. When things settle, you and I might go out for a meal one evening. I can show you why I love this city. There are some decent restaurants and pubs in the centre and on the outskirts.'

'Thank you.'

'You're most welcome, Juliet.' He led her out of the station to his car.

Juliet looked up at him. 'Simon, I pity the poor reporter who gets hold of Delia. She'll separate him from his breath, his notebook and his pen. Delia takes no prisoners. She'd perform one of her drop-kicks.'

Simon laughed. 'I know where she'd aim, Juliet. Tia's similar, though she'd emasculate a man with words.'

The porter, well pleased by the generous tip, loaded the suitcases into the boot and the rear seat of Simon's car. He spoke briefly to Juliet. 'I know you're not from here, love, but listen to him.' He waved a hand at Simon. 'All are welcome in Liverpool. The other bits I heard, I didn't hear.' He touched the neb of his cap, winked, and disappeared into the bowels of the station.

'He was nice,' she remarked.

'He was typical,' Simon told her. 'There are places a damned sight worse than here. Come on, do your face up a bit and I'll take you to Tia and Izzy.'

'And Delia and Nanny.'

'Yes. A full house.'

'Do I get a prize for a full house?'

'I'm afraid not.' *No, I hope to be your prize, Juliet. Tia and I noticed when you were young, how you watched us, how you envied your sister. You had a teenage crush on me, Baby Doll. Maybe Louisa M. Alcott wasn't so wrong after all. We'll give it a whirl and see how it works out. You are lovely, quieter, a nurse and a clever little soul. Time will tell.*

Theo sometimes did playground duty, thereby giving all his teachers a break. He often had several from reception class hiding under his cloak, but he didn't mind; he was Mr Blackbird looking after his brood. After a few minutes, he would send them away while he chatted with the older children. He loved each and every one of them, the ugly, the pretty, the well-behaved and the cheeky.

Colin Duckworth invariably fastened himself to Theo. He wore an air of ownership, as if the boss belonged to him and only to him. 'Sir, you know smallpox?'

'I've heard of it, yes.'

'Can you have bigpox or largepox or massivepox?'

Theo sighed. Colin had recently added 'doctor' to his list of careers, and he was heavily into diseases. 'I think not.'

'Then why is it smallpox?'

'Because it isn't chickenpox.' Oh, no; he knew what was coming next.

'Chickens don't get that. Why is it not peoplepox?'

The head teacher had to admit that he had no real idea. 'It may be because the skin of a sufferer from chickenpox resembles a newly plucked chicken ready for the oven, but I'm not sure.'

He had a ready answer for Colin's next query. 'The appendix is part of the bowel we don't use any more.'

'Then why do we have them, Sir?'

'To digest chlorophyll.'

Colin cocked his head sideways. 'Is that what puts people asleep?'

Theo had suspected for some time that young Master Duckworth was playing games with him. 'No, that's chloroform. Chlorophyll is green stuff. It's in green vegetables. I believe a rabbit has a working appendix, but there again, I'm not completely sure.'

'My mam makes me eat green stuff, Sir. Why do I have to eat green stuff if me appendixes don't work?'

'Appendix. You have only one. Greens are good for the system.'

'But what if it splodes, Sir? Mr Pilkington's sploded—'

'Exploded.'

'That's what I said. And he got poisoned in his belly. See, if you eat too much chloro-stuff, your appendix might try to work and burst like Mr Pilkington's and get septic seams.'

'Septicaemia.'

'Is it?'

Theo nodded solemnly. 'The green stuff we eat bypasses the appendix, so don't use that as an excuse for not eating your vegetables and salad. That's enough for now, Colin. Help me to break up this small squabble near the prefabs.'

Thus Colin became a sort of prefect, assistant to the teacher in charge of playground. From this day, he would deputize himself to any of the supervising staff and keep an eye on children who were misbehaving or in danger. His attendance had improved in these final weeks of the summer term, and he even brushed his hair occasionally.

Theo blew the whistle and lined them up, before

sending each line back to class. Colin was growing up, and Theo didn't know how he felt about that.

As he turned to follow the stragglers, he saw Tia coming through the gate. 'Mr Quinn,' she opened, straight-faced. 'Delia has gone, Pa's in Ireland so there are no photographers or reporters in Chaddington, Juliet is settled and . . .' she looked round as if making sure no one was listening, 'and she has a date with Simon tomorrow night. I am so pleased, because they're perfect for each other and she's always had a crush on him.'

Why was she here? 'Why are you here, Miss Bellamy?'

'For next term's hall timetable, a look at your physical education equipment,' she offered him a winning smile, 'and I need to check out the reading scheme for my flash cards and wall work.'

'OK. Follow me.' He led her into the main building. As they passed through the hall, which doubled as gymnasium, he felt Miss Cosgrove's heated gaze pursuing them across the floor. Her class leapt about on the apparatus while she stared at her beloved. Friday night's end-of-year party promised to be interesting, one deputy head, one welfare worker and the new reception class teacher all vying for his attention.

He closed the door of his office, dug out a timetable for use of the hall, gave Tia the published precis of the school's reading scheme and pointed to the door through which they had just entered. 'I think you'll find the hall is yours for two periods each week.'

'I need drama time, Mr Quinn.'

'Fine. I'll bring in some men from the building sites and get them to stretch the length of our working day. I'm sure they have suitable tools.'

'Permission to speak, Sir?'

'Fire away.'

She tutted. 'I forgot my gun. May I ask permission to institute an out-of-hours drama class?'

'I'll put it to the parents, though depending on numbers, you'll need extra supervision.' He took pity on her. 'I'll stay behind if you like.'

Tia pursed her lips. 'Thank you, Mr Quinn. And the gym equipment?'

'Miss Cosgrove will show you the gym equipment, Miss Bellamy.'

A new smile played at the corners of her mouth. 'She doesn't like me. When you invited me to that staff meeting, she was giving me daggers. Miss Ellis says that Miss Cosgrove has designs on you.'

'We'll discuss this elsewhere, yes?'

Tia made no reply.

'Miss Bellamy?'

'I'm going, I'm going.' She left.

I am grinning like the Cheshire Cat. If I leave this room now, the smile will linger here, hovering over my chair. She's even pushing poor little Juliet into the arms of Simon Heilberg, one of her rejects. In three days, I'll be in Kent hoping to hide Rosie and Maggie from the glare of publicity right where the glare of publicity may well be burning at its brightest, though the pack of rabid dogs might pursue Pa Bellamy to Ireland instead. I am annoying myself by doing as I'm told by Madam Gorgeous.

He walked to the window and watched Standard Four playing rounders, which was a bit like baseball with a flat bat. The children in this top class would not return in September; they would move on to Ivy Lane Secondary, and very few would return to visit the 'baby' school. Next year or the year after that, Colin Duckworth, self-elected head boy, would go to 'grown-up' school. Would it be a case of *et tu, Brute?* Theo hoped not. Theo hoped that

Colin would pass his eleven-plus and gain a place at grammar school. *And he must visit us.*

What is it about that child with his rusty hair, accidentally lost adult teeth, Spoonerisms and silly questions that charms me? What is it about Portia? Is it her cut lead crystal voice, her face, her body, her silken hair, her naughtiness? Or is it all of the above?

At his desk, Theo sat and opened the books sent to him by Miss Cosgrove. Colin Duckworth had skipped a class. In mathematics, the lad was now doing algebraic equations and some geometry. His composition book was incredibly untidy, since the writing failed to keep pace with the boy's speed of mind, but misspellings were few, and the construction of English betrayed him as a keen reader. Theo, realizing at last that Colin's Spoonerisms were deliberate, smiled broadly. Two could play that game.

It was clear that the roof-ball-drainpipe saga had been a huge joke. There was a possibility – no, a probability – that the crudely presented notes from home had been deliberately malformed. And in this precious moment, Theo smiled and shook his head. Colin Duckworth was treating Blackbird like one of his family. 'He likes me,' Theo whispered. 'He tries to keep me occupied.'

He found proof. *In the long holidays, I miss school. Mostly, I miss Blackbird, who talks to me and listens. My dad is Roy and he's a good dad, but if I didn't have him, I'd choose Mr Quinn. He laughs at me and tries to hide it. I know he likes me.*

Further on: *It was deliberate today when I told him I'd been sleepwalking. He knew that I knew I was making it up, and I knew that he knew I knew. I hate geography and history and French, but detention with him is a laugh a minute. He's not like the other teachers.*

He scared me a bit when he mentioned my dad, but he

said he wanted to see him about something else. Mr Quinn doesn't hit children, doesn't believe in it. My dad and mam are the same. I wonder if kids can adopt an uncle? Uncle Theo, Uncle Blackbird, Uncle Quinn.

A few pages later: *Sitting on the stairs, I listened to Mam and Dad talking. The new teacher in Infant One is very pretty. Dad said nobody else stood a chance because compared to Miss Bellamy, other faces looked like smacked arses, so he may have meant that Miss Bellamy might marry Blackbird. I hope she's nice. I wouldn't like to adopt a not nice auntie.* Theo chuckled. It was plain that Miss Cosgrove hadn't bothered to read Colin's diary portion of the compositions book.

He kept the dog and called her Mickle. The dog chose him, just like I did. That dog has brains. The educational psychologist Dad saved up for . . . What? Theo shook his head to clear it. 'What happened to cycle-ology, Colin?'

He says I'm roughly top four per cent for brains and should do well. My reading age is sixteen and I have something called a high IQ. He did tests and Mam and Dad were proud until I went fishing last Saturday without asking first.

Miss Cosgrove is sending my books to Mr Quinn to show how clever I am, so the game is over. Are you reading this, Sir? I didn't done it, I did it. I never got borned, I was born. It's a game, you see, because you never make me bored. If I'm clever, you done it for me, Sir. (DID IT.)

Theo's eyes were suddenly wet. Once or twice in a teacher's life, a miracle happened, a happenstance that tossed a genius from poor streets into the educational arena. This impossible boy was just that, a rare orchid in a bed of pretty wildflowers. Thus far, most of the precious ones had been female, since a girl's learning speed was usually faster than that of her male counterpart until the teenage years. But when a true two-percenter male popped up – and

Colin was no mere four-percenter – the result was amazing. 'I suspected you, Colin, but you're cleverer than I am. Well done, you. But boy, am I gonna getcha.'

The restaurant was small, though each dining table had its own permanent screens, wooden at the bottom, decorative stained glass privacy panels in the upper half.

Prices were geared towards the select few who could afford the cost of food prepared under the guidance of an imported French chef, and the business was situated in the village of Woolton, a part of Liverpool coveted by all who wanted to keep pace with the Joneses. Most Joneses were professional people with decent salaries and substantial properties, though the self-made man in property development or retail was beginning to encroach. This factor made for the beginnings of a happy mix, most on nodding terms, at least.

After the nods, groups of two or four settled into the privacy of a booth. Larger parties were catered for upstairs in a room large enough to provide for a wedding breakfast or a Christmas office get-together, so the Par Excellence was a success story, certainly good enough for Simon's first date with Juliet.

She looked beautiful, of course, in an emerald green silk suit with navy blue accessories. Like Tia, this youngest of the sisters knew how to dress; like Tia, she wore very little makeup. As the pair walked the central aisle overlooked by the open end of all occupied booths, Simon noticed male heads turning to gaze at the little princess, while female companions of these men did not look best pleased by their partners' ogling.

Simon and Juliet were shown to a table for two in one of a pair of alcoves nicknamed lovers' nooks. When they faced one another across the table, Simon noticed a faint blush staining his companion's perfect cheekbones. She wasn't Tia, would never be Tia, but she was a nurse, more than easy on the eye and usually better behaved than his ex-beloved.

He dragged his eyes away from his companion. 'Caviar?' he asked nonchalantly.

'As long as they cut the crusts off my toast. Mrs Melia used to tell us that eating crusts would give us curly hair, but I prefer straight and manageable, so I've never eaten them.'

Simon grinned – she sounded just like Tia. 'And for the entrée, mademoiselle?'

J'aime beaucoup le steak au poivre, monsieur.'

'That's hot stuff, Juliet. Fresh peppercorns battered to dust, all that cream and Dijon mustard – you'll be very full.'

She smiled sweetly. 'Then crème brûlée as dessert.'

'Is this your way of informing me that you're no cheap date? Shall I need a bank loan?'

'Oui, vraiment.'

'Your sister is similar, though she has been known to enjoy fish and chips served on the *News of the World*, no fork, just fingers.'

'Yes, I do that, too, but I insist on *The Times* and no peas. Fingers weren't made for peas, or perhaps peas weren't made for fingers.'

He settled back to read the wine list, his feelings dichotomous, because this young woman *was* Tia until he looked carefully at her. She used the same phraseology, the same body language, the same laugh. Yes, this was just a first date, but would it be right to follow on after tonight? The sisters were close, and he might see more of Tia if he dated Juliet regularly. He would see the real Tia, and this miniature version. Could he bear that?

But he liked Juliet . . . she was a great girl.

He gave his order to the sommelier before speaking again to his lovely companion. 'You'll get a good reference, I'm sure, so why not continue your midwifery at Liverpool Women's Hospital? You can return to Canterbury when all the fuss has died down.'

'I don't want to impose on Tia. She has enough guests with Ma and Nanny.'

'There's plenty of room in my flat,' he told her. The blush paid another visit to peaches and cream skin. The blush pleased him, though he didn't dig too deeply into his psyche to work out why.

'That wouldn't be right,' she answered softly, before raising her chin. 'Ma bought me a flat in Canterbury, so I could let that and use the money to pay for a flat up here.'

He grimaced. 'Still the same girl, aren't you? Determined not to dig too soon into your legacy. Talk to Quinn – he owns property, I believe.' *He also owns your big sister, and do you want to associate with me after my longstanding affair with Tia? I need you here for a few months so that I might work out what's good for me, whether you maintain interest in me and how I might feel about partnering the Bellamy baby. You are so sweet, though. And I am a selfish bastard.*

'What's on your mind, Simon?' she asked.

That was typical Tia behaviour, digging for the truth, asking too many questions, addressing a point when the point hadn't yet been raised. 'I'm thinking of food, wine and the companionship of a very beautiful woman.'

'What else? Are you hoping that Tia will become jealous because you're with me? After all, you left an established family practice in order to pursue my sister.'

'No.' The single syllable was delivered strongly.

'No, you didn't leave home to follow Tia, or no, I'm not a scrap dropped from the top table for dogs on the floor?'

'We're just having a meal,' he whispered.

'Wrong,' she replied. 'You're having a meal, and I'm going to the ladies' room before phoning for a taxi. Nobody uses me, Heilberg.' She leapt to her feet and walked the length of the restaurant to the facilities near the front reception area.

He shook his head almost imperceptibly. Juliet had power and backbone and determination. *That behaviour was definitely Tia-ish. Oh, God, what am I going to do now? I still haven't ordered the food . . .* He placed the price of the red wine, which had no doubt been uncorked to breathe, on a side plate together with a tip and followed as casually as he could in Juliet's footsteps.

She emerged a few minutes later, tear-stained and drying her eyes on a very small handkerchief.

'Here,' he said, passing his man-sized and monogrammed square. 'Let's go. I haven't had a drink, so we can retrieve my car from the restaurant's car park.' He had intended to make use of a service offered by Par Excellence, who allowed customers to leave vehicles overnight if they preferred to take a taxi.

Simon drove in silence to the Pier Head and parked nearby. 'Come on,' he said. 'A bit of fresh air and a conversation is my prescription, Nurse Bellamy.'

She stood by the railings, twisting and turning Simon's handkerchief in nervous fingers. 'You knew. Both of you knew. I managed to convince Tia that it was just a crush, but I've never had a boyfriend. I've never had a boyfriend because of you. So don't mess me about, Doc. Stay away from me and don't moon over Tia, because she's found her man now. I may seem quiet, but do not mistake me, don't think of me as weak. Ever.' There was weight behind the final word.

'But I—'

'But you what?' She rounded on him, her eyes seeming to blaze shards of blue fire. 'I gave you my truth, so you must give me yours. After all, fair exchange is no robbery, or so people say.'

The Mersey was skittish tonight, and a breeze whipped up over the water, causing Juliet to shiver.

Simon removed his jacket and placed it round her shoulders, leaving his arm in place and pulling her closer when he had covered her back. 'Yes,' he began, 'my turn for truth. It's all the fault of Louisa M. Alcott, American writer, associate of many famous authors, feminist, abolitionist and spinster, died in Boston, I believe. I read *Little Women*, *Little Men* and *Jo's Boys* one summer when I was bored. The chap next door to the March sisters fixed his eyes on Jo, but his affection was not returned, so he married a younger one, Amy, I think.'

'And?' She shrugged away his protective arm.

He paused, noticing that Juliet's eyes were nearer to grey at the moment; perhaps they attempted to echo the odd colour of the water. 'And I thought you might be my Amy.'

'Just because my sister rejected you.'

'Just because you're beautiful, intelligent and sweet.'

'I'm not sweet,' she almost growled. 'Merely quieter than Tia.'

'And than Delia,' he said.

'Delia's different, Simon. I begin to believe she may be lesbian.'

'She is. But I beg you, give me a chance.'

Juliet stared into his eyes. 'And damage myself even further? All the way up from Kent, I had one thought in mind because I was going to see you that day. From time to time, I thought about my mother and my sisters and Nanny, but you have been . . . I always wanted you. Perhaps I should have grown out of it, and I certainly wish I had, but I am not playing second fiddle. I lead the orchestra or play a different tune.'

'But—'

'Take me back to Tia. Now.' She stalked off towards the car.

As she walked away, he noticed that his jacket was almost a full-length coat on her.

He opened the passenger door for her, took his time while walking round to the driver's side, climbed in, and placed his hands on the steering wheel. 'Juliet, what can I say to you? I brought you out for a meal to show you that Liverpool is a worthy place. Behind that intention lay the hope that you might still like me and that we might find some kind of future together, professional, personal – whatever.'

She sat with her arms folded, as if hugging the inner child.

'Think of me as a man who has imperfect vision and is taking measures to correct it. She dazzled me, Jules. She claimed all my senses, because I lived only to see, hear and breathe her. I had to come all this way to realize that it was simply a recurring dream, and I must not allow it to become a nightmare. She is not the sun, and you and I are not mere satellites. You're a very beautiful woman, and I'm a starving man because I haven't eaten since break-fast, and I hope we can be friends.'

Juliet uncrossed her arms. 'Can we get fish and chips?' she asked.

'Of course.' He grinned. She had turned down caviar and steak au poivre for cod and fried spuds.

'Dandelion and burdock?'

'Possibly.'

'And might we eat outside somewhere near the river?'

'That can certainly be arranged.'

'OK, Doc Hunter-Gatherer. Go forth and find food.'

He turned the ignition key. This was going to be fun.

Thirteen

Maggie arrived at the school just as Theo was leaving his office to deliver the Last Post, as he had named the final assembly of every school term. Today's Last Post was to be truly final for Standard Four pupils, as they would not return in September. For six years, these had been his children; Myrtle Street School was their foundation, while Ivy Lane would build their walls and roofs. 'They'd better do a good job and use the finest of materials,' he was muttering as he left the office and collided with Rosie's beloved nana. 'Maggie?' She was clearly distressed, a handkerchief held to her face, upper body racked with sobs. 'Maggie, what the hell happened? Come on, tell me.'

'Sadie's come round from her coma,' she wept. 'She's not right in her mind, Theo. They said she might improve in time, but she didn't know me. She doesn't recognize her own mother. She strangled all the oxygen out of herself and her brain might be all wrong. I can't leave her like that, can I? I can't go dashing off to Kent while Sadie's ill – it wouldn't be right.'

'Maggie, if she doesn't know you–'

'She's my daughter, Theo. She's the only child I ever had. When her dad died, there were just the two of us, so we used to be close until she started . . . You know what I mean.'

'I do know. And Rosie is your only grandchild. We

have to give her the holiday we promised her. That child must be shown that she has value, that we care. Have you packed? Did Tia finish making Rosie's new dresses?' He needed to distract Maggie, to get her to focus on her real precious burden – little Rosie.

'Yes,' was her whispered reply. 'And she bought her a new coat.'

'Sweet lady, remember that the young come first in everything. Sadie is in good hands, expert hands. She won't miss you, but Rosie would. She'll have Tom and Nancy from next door, but you're the person she truly needs and loves. You're the last stable ship afloat on the stormy waters in which she's been flotsam or jetsam so far. Sit in my office while I do the final assembly before dismissal until September.' He leaned in closer to her. 'There's a drop of whisky in the top left hand drawer of my desk. For medicinal purposes only, you understand. Calm yourself, but don't get drunk, or you'll be in detention.'

She opened the door, turned and looked at him. 'I feel torn in two,' she said. 'I don't know what to do for the best.'

'Wait in there for me.' He walked off towards the hall, no notes in hand or pocket, his stride purposeful, though part of his mind was occupied by thoughts of Maggie, Sadie and Rosie, three people whose futures were uncertain at best, ill-fated at worst. He took hold of a good thought and held it at the front of his consciousness. This year, eleven leavers were going to grammar school, eleven scholarships, eleven chances of a career rather than a job. In Theo's sector of the city, Myrtle Street School was top of the class.

He stood before the lines of children, his hands holding the front edges of his black gown as usual, a smile on his face. It was time to say goodbye. Of course he wanted them to move on and do well, but he found it difficult to let go, because this was probably as near as he would ever get to having children of his own. Pausing for a moment, he looked along the lines of faces. *She will want children, and I know she's capable of overruling me.* He shook the thought from his head and smiled.

'Well, the pupils in Standard Four have already endured my yearly lecture without falling asleep, and I thank them for their attentiveness. Here in Myrtle Street they are the big boys and girls, but they will start all over again at the bottom when the new school year begins. We will miss them, and I'm sure we all hope they're going to behave themselves and be a credit to us.'

He delivered a sad, heartfelt message of goodbye for Miss Ellis, who was presented with a set of cutlery, plus a Royal Doulton china figurine to add to all the others in her glass-fronted cabinet at home. She managed not to weep after her forty-odd years in the same classroom, and Theo was grateful for that. This was an admirable woman and a splendid teacher, but he was losing her, too. Yes, and he was gaining— He squashed a smile. *Oh, Portia. God help me; God help both of us.*

Much to Theo's surprise, this year's leavers had organized a collection. With their spoils, they had bought for him a collar and lead, both leather, and the collar was studded to make Mickle look 'dead hard'. He blinked back emotion while offering his thanks and then leading them into 'All Things Bright and Beautiful', followed by the National Anthem. Miss Cosgrove, who played the piano, gazed at him lovingly while he sang. *Oh, bugger. See? Tia's taking over my unspoken words now. I wish that poor woman would stop staring at me.*

And, after three cheers, it was supposedly over, yet the leavers' class came to the front and stood in front of younger, smaller children, blocking their view of the head teacher. After singing 'For He's a Jolly Good Fellow', they applauded him loudly, turned, and got the whole school to join in the hand-clapping. Theo maintained his composure before dismissing school. Sometimes, these kids almost broke his heart.

Standard Four remained until the end, as if reluctant to leave. He shook each hand before shooing them out of the hall. But they finally filed out in good order towards a summer of freedom, though their sedate behaviour changed when they entered the yard. Whooping, whistling and shouting, they ran towards liberty and uncertainty, leaving behind the protective shell that had contained them for so many of their formative years. Never again would they receive the same level of pastoral care; next year might well be obedience, homework and not a great deal of fun.

Staff began to prepare for the evening's party before their students had left the yard. Anxious to get away to make the best of themselves, the teachers moved swiftly to change the hall/gymnasium into a meeting place for a few adults. Theo left them to it and returned to his office and Maggie.

She was at a window, staring out at the escaping throng. 'You're not wrong,' she said after glancing over her shoulder. 'They come first, and Rosie's one of them. It's a bit late for Sadie, no matter what happens. She'll either go back to her old ways, or she'll be brain-damaged, or even both.' She shuddered. 'Rosie's told me she wants to stay with me, because her mother hasn't looked after her. She didn't say Sadie hadn't saved her, but that's what she meant.' She turned completely and faced him. 'Yes, we'll go and give Rosie a nice holiday and a look at a different part of the country. It's educational, isn't it?'

Theo smiled, though his eyes remained sad. 'You can

keep in touch with the hospital, ask daily about Sadie's progress.'

'On the phone?'

'Yes. I'll get the details for you. Come along, young lady, let's get you home.' She, Nancy, Tom and Rosie were in for a huge surprise when they reached Kent, because Tia had come up with a rather splendid idea.

'Young lady?' she asked, an eyebrow arched.

'Don't worry, I'll tell you when you're old, Maggie. Now, I need time to change into my best frock. Shall I wear the pink gingham with the sweetheart neckline or the strapless black with a boned bodice and sequins? Don't laugh. For all you know, I might be serious. How do you know it isn't going to be fancy dress? I rather fancy myself as Little Bo Peep.'

Maggie actually giggled. 'You're as mad as she is.'

'She?' he asked, though he knew the answer.

'Miss Bellamy, Portia, Tia, or any other name she's using today.'

'Oh, her,' he grinned. 'Yes, she's unusual.'

Maggie shook her head. 'No, unusual is Nella Fishwick from the bottom end of Ivy Lane. She's about six foot tall and about eight foot wide. She looks like a gasworks with a hairnet. Tia's special, and she's a special kind of clever with a special idea of fun. I never know what to expect when I get back from visiting Sadie. Yesterday, she had your dog dressed in a frock. A bloody Ally in turquoise with spots. My poor Rosie was rolling about on the floor in pain cos she'd laughed that much. Oh, I don't know whether you noticed, but Mickle has nail polish on her claws. Candy pink, it is, if she hasn't chewed it off. Tia says she's trying to bring out the dog's feminine side. Fortunately, she couldn't catch Tyger.'

He nodded, still grinning. 'I took her down to the river where it's begun to eat its way inland. She did a Canute and got quite wet. She says we all have Canute wrong, because he sat there on his throne while the tide came in just to prove that no man, not even a king, can hold back the inevitable. Oh, and she taught me that although he couldn't stop the tide, Canute managed to hold back Viking invaders.'

'She's brilliant, Theo.'

'Oh, yes. Most good teachers are a fount of totally useless information.'

Maggie was quiet for a mile or so. 'You get on well together, don't you?' she asked as they neared Allerton.

'Yes, we do.'

The next bit was difficult and intrusive. 'She can't take her eyes off you. And you can hardly take yours off her. We can all see you're made for each other. I know it's early days, but there's something going on. Izzy and Joan think so, too.'

'Then it must be true.'

That meant she should shut up and mind her own business. Oh, it was lovely round here, trees and bushes, big houses with gardens, cars parked outside and everything clean. Although she wasn't one for jealousy or envy, she wondered how or when people from the Lady Streets would get out and move to a place such as this. Education was the basic need, she decided. Rosie had to win a place at grammar school, then at college, then in a decent career. 'You're right,' she said.

'About what?'

'Children and education being important.'

'The young are going to become the warp and weft of future society, Maggie, so we need to strengthen that fabric. There will always be worker bees, but we need leadership, too. Unfortunately, members of my profession are very badly paid, so the foundation of a child's learning lies in the hands of people who are prepared to accept poor pay and difficult conditions. Standards will slip.' He pulled into his driveway.

'How did you afford this house, then?'

'Because I have another job, and teaching is my very important hobby.'

'Oh.'

When the car was parked and its engine silent, he looked at his companion. 'Portia will earn just one pound per day. She has a legacy from her grandmother, and that helps. But other probationers have to pay rent, gas, electricity, water, food and clothing out of that. Until some government realizes the true value of teachers, we'll get nowhere.' He sighed. 'Let's go and see what our two children are up to.'

They found Tia and Rosie in the back garden, both flat on their fronts, chins resting on hands, elbows deep in grass.

'Mine's winning,' Rosie yelled. 'Look, he's nearly there.'

'Mine has staying power,' Tia said.

'Yes, it stays where it is, Miss Bellamy.'

Tia laughed. 'See? I told you. Your Albert has turned left, because he has no sense of direction, so my Victoria will be victorious.'

'What are they doing?' Maggie whispered.

'They're racing snails.'

'You what?'

'It's a snail race.'

'Isn't that a bit daft?'

'You hit the nail square on the head, Maggie. Let's go make some tea.'

In Theo's kitchen, Maggie collected a couple of biscuits, an apple and a glass of milk for Rosie. 'She's not used to a lot of food, so I give her four small meals a day.'

'Good plan. Maggie?'

'What?'

'I'll have three women chasing me tonight. Any sugge-stions?'

'Thank your lucky stars and take some Aspros in your pocket,' was her quick reply. 'Or start running for the hills now. If you go fast, you might reach Yorkshire by tomor-row.'

'Isn't Yorkshire the enemy of Lancashire?' He scratched his head.

'Listen, lad. If you have to choose between three needy women and the anger of Yorkshire folk, pick Yorkshire. You'd have a better chance with a load of sheep-shearers and wool-weavers than you would with our women. Anyway, my money's on Tia.'

'So is mine,' he replied softly.

'I knew it!' She went to give Rosie her afternoon snack.

Theo watched her as she wandered off. *Every woman in this house is always right. Therefore, because I am merely male, I am always wrong. There are several women in this building; as a result, I am guilty times five, as there are five of them. Little Rosie's young, so she, number six, doesn't yet qualify as a tormentor. Maggie sees straight through me, as does Izzy. No idea about Joan, since she's quiet. Portia drives me wild with desire, as messing about ain't enough. Where do I buy bromide?*

He went to find his suit for this evening. *Juliet grilled me yesterday, probably trying to judge me as unfit for her big sister. This is my house. I feel like standing outside in the front garden screaming THIS IS MY HOUSE.*

You have never felt so alive, Theodore Quinn. You are in love, in good company and in a mess. There will be three women wanting you tonight, then tomorrow you are kid-napping a child. Somewhere out there, perhaps in Ireland, perhaps not, a raving lunatic is sharpening his wits in an effort to fight his wife, his daughters and the rest of the world.

The grey suit looked good, as did the new shirt and dark tie. What would Madam be wearing? That stunning scarlet dress? Oh, he hoped not. Advertising wasn't always a good thing.

When he reached the living room, Rosie was chewing thoughtfully on her apple. She looked at him and grinned. 'You look nice, Mr Quinn. Miss Bellamy's wearing silver-grey, so you'll match. When are you getting married?'

Oh, God. He shook his head slowly. Rosie was joining the ranks. There were six of them now, four upstairs, two downstairs. Tomorrow, there would be Nancy as well. Arithmetic. He was leaving behind Izzy, Joan and Juliet; they would mind Tyger-Two and both apartments. So that was minus three and plus one, as Nancy You're-Right Atherton would be joining the coven. Four. There would still be four. 'Eat your apple, Rosie,' he said.

'My mam woke up,' she told him.

'Yes, your nana told me.'

'When we get back from holiday, I can go and see her, Nana says.'

'Good.' Would Rosie be coming back, or would she stay where she was with Maggie after examinations of old injuries? Oh, what a mess. This adorable child with her broad accent and good intellect might be at a Kentish school. Would her way of talking provide the cabaret for several days?

'You're worried,' the child told him.

'I'm fine,' he replied. 'By the way, who won?'

She gave him a quizzical look.

'The snail race,' he explained.

'Miss Bellamy did. But I think she cheated when Nana came out with my milk and biscuits. I turned away, and when I looked back Victoria was at the edge of the stone. That snail would have needed to run to get all that way.'

'Did Victoria have a bicycle, Rosie?'

She shook her head and grinned.

'Then Miss Bellamy cheated.'

'But she's a teacher.'

'I know. We just can't get the staff these days.'

Tia wandered in wearing the air of somebody who owned not just him, not just the villa, but the whole street. She was not clad in silver-grey; her dress was violet, with a full skirt and a moulded top half that showed off her magnificent figure. The welfare woman and the deputy head would be defeated from the start of play.

'You changed your mind,' Rosie accused her.

'This dress matches my eyes,' was Tia's reply.

'Do you have a licence to drive those shoes?' Theo asked. Because of the underpinning, she was easily as tall as he was. The shoes matched the dress perfectly. Her hair was in a chignon, with a small, crystal-encrusted barrette pinned at the front. An echo of this adornment sat on her left shoulder, and she looked delicious.

He gave her a hard stare. She knew what she was doing. Miss Garner from welfare was pretty, and Miss Portia Bellamy was at war. So this was the female equivalent of a testosterone rush. Men fought and argued over partners; women simply painted and decorated themselves. But oh, she was lovely.

Rosie wandered off to sit with Maggie and Mickle in the garden.

'Portia?'

'What?'

'Stay away from me during this party. Emily Garner could take Rosie away just like that.' He snapped fingers and thumb.

'I'll stay here if you wish.'

'No. I want you to meet your colleagues socially.'

'Miss Cosgrove hates me already.'

'Then court her friendship. She's already suffering some kind of crush, and it's directed at me. Behind the raw facade, she's a vulnerable and lonely woman. Erotomania can be painful. As the subject of her scrutiny, I hurt, too.'

'OK. I'll get my engagement ring.'

'Thank you.'

She left.

Theo picked up Tyger. 'Just the two of us *contra mundum*, little kitty. I am dreading this evening. I can't let her drive her car in those shoes, so I'll have to arrive with her as my passenger. I'm going to get you neutered, because females are deadly, and you need to keep your distance.'

Tia returned, flashing her blindingly huge diamond in its ornate Victorian setting. 'Will I do?' she asked innocently. She showed him her heavily layered underskirt, fold after fold of virginal white tulle. 'You should wear a Teddy boy suit, Teddy Bear, then we'd match.'

'Miss Ellis would have a heart attack, and she retired only today. Just behave yourself, Portia.'

'Yes, Sir. Will you be wearing your blackbird wings?'

'No, it isn't fancy dress.'

'Pity.'

'You would have gone as Lady Godiva, and I couldn't risk that. Now, Miss Adams and Miss Bailey from the infants department will be bringing boyfriends, fiancés or whatevers. Heads will turn when you walk in, so leave the men alone and concentrate on your fellow teachers.'

'Sir.'

'And those stiletto heels will damage your spine in later life.'

'Sir.'

'Stop with the Sir.'

Tia sniffed. 'I shan't wear them in later life.'

He gave up. She was determinedly naughty, unreasonable and amusing. 'Let's go, then.' His tone was suddenly resigned. She would do as she pleased and when she pleased. 'Were you ever well behaved?' he asked.

'Once, at Roedean, I gave in an essay on time. I got double bread-and-butter pudding, which I loathe, and a twenty-one gun salute at sunset.'

'God help me,' he muttered.

'You don't need God; you've got me.'

They left, he in a state of worry, she in painful shoes. It was a hard life.

Miss Lydia Cosgrove had pencilled in some eyebrows and was wearing lipstick, mascara and a yellow dress that served only to emphasize her pallor and the bright red corrugated hair with which she had been endowed. At the piano playing background music, she accidentally allowed her fingers to hit some wrong notes when Tia glided in behind the boss.

Tia smiled at her enemy and sent her a little wave of greeting before crossing the room to join her. Standing behind the upright instrument, she curled her left hand over its top so that the engagement ring would be on display.

'You're engaged,' said the pianist partway through a bit of Chopin.

'Yes, but separated until after Christmas when he moves north. We shall probably marry during the Easter holidays, in Kent.'

'What does he do for a living?'

Lying was so easy, too easy. 'He's a doctor.'

Lydia Cosgrove smiled. 'I see. Well, welcome aboard.

It's a happy ship on the whole, and the children are well behaved for the most part.'

'Colin Duckworth?' Tia smiled.

'There are always exceptions, Miss Bellamy. He's very lovable and a mile ahead of most just lately. At last, he's accepted the fact that school is compulsory.' She finished the piece with a flourish Frédéric Chopin would never have touched with a bargepole. 'Will you and your husband-to-be continue living in Mr Quinn's flat after the wedding?'

'I expect so, until we find somewhere to buy.' Tia bit her lower lip. She was digging a pit out of which she might find it impossible to climb.

The first hour was fine, people talking in small groups, eating sausage rolls, sandwiches and little homemade cakes that were more or less edible, though rather dry. There was punch containing very little alcohol, and soft drinks were provided for the dedicated teetotallers. Theo spent much of the hour with Mr Cross, teacher of Standard Four Juniors. Two satellites named Emily Garner and Lydia Cosgrove orbited them, but the pair of males, clearly not interested in the plumage of their female counterparts, seemed thoroughly engrossed in negotiations of global importance.

Tia decided to be glad that there was to be no skiffling tonight. Had she and Theo sung together, Cosgrove and Garner might have exploded with envy. Cosgrove and Garner sounded like a building firm or an estate agency or a chambers full of lawyers . . .

Theo kept the corner of an eye on two situations – the pair of prowling predators and men who gazed hungrily at Tia. Miss Bailey had told off her boyfriend twice, while Miss Adams was admirable, since she ignored her fiancé's wandering gaze. *I have to get used to this. Men will always covet her, and I shall follow Miss Adams's example, I hope.*

'So what do you think?' Paul Cross was asking.

Theo's brain clicked into gear. 'Montessori? Nonsense. We're supposed to let kids swing from the light fittings instead of reading and writing? We'd have a riot on our hands, and that would be organized by the parents. If our lot went home and did as they pleased, it would be our fault. Discipline matters, as long as it doesn't involve corporal punishment.'

Emily Garner homed in. 'Mr Quinn? Sorry to interrupt, but how is Rosie?'

'Ah, Emily. She's very well and happy, thank you. She'll be able to see her mother soon. I understand that she woke from her coma today, so all seems to be well. You know Mr Cross, of course.'

'Oh, that's good news about Rosie's mother.' The young woman glanced over her shoulder. 'Who's that?' she asked. 'The one in purple, I mean.'

'Miss Bellamy,' he replied.

'Your new teacher? The one who lives in your upstairs flat?'

'She's there until she marries, yes.'

Relief shone in Emily's eyes. 'So she's spoken for?'

'Yes, she is definitely off the market. Ah, Miss Cosgrove wants me. It's quiz time.' *Women, bloody women. I suppose they constitute fifty per cent of society, so they can't be avoided. But Portia is not for sale, I hope. And we might very well live somewhere else and let out the two apartments if or when it happens. Ah, Miss Garner seems to have taken a liking to Paul Cross. He's a widower, but he comes with baggage in the form of three children. Emily Garner doesn't seem the maternal type, though you can never tell ... Thank goodness there were no skifflers available tonight. On top of all this, I couldn't have coped with performing.*

Miss Ellis was plucking names out of a hat. When the three teams were picked, Theo found himself parked at a table with Tia, Emily Garner and Miss Bailey's other half, whose name was Joe. Joe, almost salivating, sat opposite Tia, and Theo wondered whether to get him a knife, fork and condiments, since he looked just about ready to consume the vision of loveliness across the table.

Things went from difficult to impossible when Tia dropped her pencil, bent to retrieve it, and lingered a moment to caress her head teacher's shin. While the minx made love to his lower leg, he plastered a fixed smile onto the lower half of his face and promised himself that he would deal with her later.

She knew all the answers, of course. When Joe-At-The-Other-Side-Of-The-Table heard her 'mouthful of plums' accent, he reddened and lowered his eyes as if in the presence of royalty. Theo's grin was no longer false. He was proud of her. She was lively and uninhibited in company. If he could just climb over his stumbling block and get a vasectomy . . . He swallowed. The idea of surgery terrified him still. Being sewn up and dragged about after the attack by those freaks in Georgia had left scars on his mind as well as on his skin.

Joe spoke to Theo. 'Is there anything Miss Bellamy doesn't know?'

Theo shrugged. 'Her Russian isn't good, but she's OK with scrambled eggs.'

'Stop talking about me as if I'm not here,' Tia snapped.

'Good manners, too,' Theo announced. 'Roedean and Oxford, yet she chooses our little school. We are blessed. Ouch!' She had kicked him.

'What's the problem?' Tia asked sweetly.

'It's just an old injury from way back. Baseball.'

'You must take care, Mr Quinn. These things have a tendency to catch up with us in later life, rather like stiletto heels.' Tia awarded Joe a dazzling smile. 'I like quizzes. They usually contain the sort of nonsense I collect.'

Theo glanced at the next table; Miss Bailey was glowering. There would be trouble for Joe and for Tia later this evening.

Emily Garner, too, was staring at Tia. There was something about the girl's attitude to Theo that seemed rather comfortable and almost disrespectful. It was probably because they shared a building . . . And Miss Bellamy was wearing a huge engagement ring which, according to Lydia Cosgrove, was from a fiancé in the south.

'Question twenty – this is the last one.' Miss Ellis's voice, which had remained strangely young and clear, travelled across the hall. 'Who killed Abraham Lincoln?'

'It wasn't me,' Tia called out. While people laughed, she watched Theo as he wrote *John Wilkes Booth* on their answer sheet. 'I knew that,' she said.

'What was Booth's job?' Theo asked.

'Actor,' she replied. 'Do we get extra points?'

'No.' She would get extra marks – black ones. He wrote a short note on his pad. YOU ARE DEAD.

'So is Abraham Lincoln,' she whispered.

Emily Garner's lips tightened into a straight line. These two were more than just friends or neighbours. If they were dancing the light fantastic in Allerton, perhaps Rosie should be elsewhere. Miss Know-it-All in the purple dress was almost as bad as the child's mother.

Theo's table won, of course. Their prize was a packet of lollipops, three yellow plastic ducks for a bathroom, a box of coloured chalks and half a pound of dolly mixtures. These spoils were divided more or less equally between team members, though there was some infantile squabbling when it came to the pretty red chalk.

Everyone but Miss Bailey and her boyfriend stayed behind to clear up. Joe was pushed out by his girl like a man being frogmarched towards a firing squad. Theo looked through a window and watched while Anne Bailey read the Riot Act to her captive audience of one.

Jack Peake, caretaker, noticed Theo's tense expression. 'Go,' he said.

'But there's all this stuff to be moved—'

'I've six weeks to shift it, Mr Quinn.'

Theo shook his head in despair. 'Are you sure you're fit for work?'

'You saw the doctor's letter. Go home and look after Rosie and her nan.'

Theo stood still for a moment with a man who had become a close friend and occasional drinking partner in recent years. 'I've had an accident, Jack. A fall, you might call it.'

'I know,' came the quiet reply. 'You've been floating on a cloud for over a week, daft lad.'

'It shows?'

Jack nodded. 'And it's two-way traffic. She's fallen, too. It's not going to be easy for either of you come September.'

'I told her to behave herself tonight.'

'Yes, but you didn't tell yourself, did you? I watched you ignoring her deliberate, like, and I saw your face when she ended up in your team for the quiz. See, she attracts attention from everybody, male and female. Just slow down a bit; it's early days.'

'I'm stupid.'

Jack grinned. 'If you're stupid, God help the rest of us, Theo. I wouldn't mind being your kind of stupid, all them letters behind your name. Go home. Go on, bugger off.'

'She's driving me crazy, Jack, and it's not a long journey because I was halfway there. From the first time I saw her—'

'I know, lad. We've all been there. Take her home.'

Theo drifted to a corner where Tia was stacking chairs. 'Wait for me in the car,' he muttered.

'But I'm—'

'Now.'

She turned and looked at him. His eyes were glacial. 'Yes, Sir,' she said softly before stalking out of the hall. *I shouldn't have touched his leg. I shouldn't have batted my eyelashes at Miss Bailey's other half. I shouldn't have smiled so saccharine sweetly at the welfare woman. I shouldn't have come to the damned party. Oh, someone help me, here he is.*

He climbed into the passenger seat, angry with her, angry with himself, worried about Rosie and Maggie, worried about Kent.

'Aren't you speaking to me?' she asked.

'I'm not talking to either of us.'

'Where are we going?'

'To some place we're not known. Shut up.'

The some place they weren't known was the seafront in Southport. It wasn't so much seafront as sand-front, as the tide was so far out that it was a thin, silver ribbon across the far horizon. Because of the run of local waters, Southport was stealing Blackpool's sand, with the result that Blackpool had the more spectacular tides.

He parked the car and sat in silence, staring at the desert spread before him. To hell with writing it all down and giving the essay to her in Kent; he would tell her now, and be done with it. So where were the words? Was he, like Tom Quirke, hidden beneath a thousand printed chapters? Was he a coward?

'It was a social situation,' she said finally after a silence that had lasted for some twelve miles. 'We were supposed to have fun, though I should be suing the person who baked those concrete fairy cakes.'

He glanced at her. Why did she have to be so wonderfully pretty? 'Having an affair with my right leg was wrong.'

She shrugged. 'Right or left, or right or wrong, I'm sorry. It won't happen again.'

Theo sighed heavily. 'The next time you walk into my school, you come as the teacher of innocents, little five-year-olds entrusted to you. Can't you control yourself?'

'It's difficult near you.'

He shook his head almost imperceptibly. 'It's not just you. I go to the other extreme by trying to ignore you. Now, because Emily Garner has designs on me, we could lose Rosie.'

'No. Oh, God, no.'

'Oh yes, Portia.'

She stared at him with tears in those huge, violet eyes. 'We can't lose her, Teddy.' After pulling herself together, she asked, 'How many women are there in your queue?'

'Hundreds. I don't want Maggie to lose Rosie because of our stupidity.'

'Then perhaps we should go along with Ma's plan. She has real faith in us, even after so short a time. I've told you, Ma has arranged it all. She really is magic, you know, and she's used her charm to talk to officials in Canterbury. I'm so sorry if I've put Rosie and Maggie in danger.'

'The fight ain't over yet, baby. I'm still in the corner putting my gloves on.'

'Good for you. I'll be your second.'

Theo sat stock still for several minutes before plunging into territory he hated to visit. 'Have you been to London lately?' he asked. 'I don't mean the smart areas or the slums – just ordinary London where bed and breakfast is affordable.'

She shook her head. 'I usually stay with Aunt Rachel, Ma's sister.'

'There are notices in guesthouse windows or doorways, usually in capital letters and often spelt wrongly; they say *No coloureds, no Irish, no dogs*. You've never seen those?

Still, at least they have the courage of their twisted convictions, I suppose.'

'No, I haven't seen them, but I've heard about them.'

He stared through the windscreen at mackerel clouds illuminated by the setting sun. So beautiful. 'My father is an Irishman who emigrated first to Liverpool, then to America. He met and fell in love with my mother, who was a quadroon. She was one quarter black, and her skin was dark, darker than mine. She had tight curly hair, too.'

Tia regarded him quizzically. 'So what does this mean? Is it your so-called genetic problem?'

'I am an octoroon, one eighth black,' was his reply.

'OK.'

'An octoroon married to a Caucasian can father or give birth to a child who is completely black.'

Her jaw dropped slightly. 'And this is your genetic fault? This is what you fear?'

He laughed, though the sound he produced was grim. 'It's the attitude I fear, Portia. It's the notices in windows, the unequal opportunities, the sheer bloody snobbery of pale-skinned people.'

'Oh, fuck them,' she spat.

'Language, Miss Bellamy.'

'Sorry, Teddy.'

He waited until she had calmed down. 'Be quiet,' he advised. 'This isn't easy for me.'

'Right,' she whispered. 'Go on, spit it all out.'

'The hieroglyphics on my back were executed by the Klan, who wanted me marked as unclean. I am the product of a mixed marriage. Even in the hospital, I was treated as less than human, so somebody there was a member or a supporter of the Ku Klux evil scum. I don't look coloured, yet they knew I was.'

Tia remained silent while he searched for words.

'I was sore for weeks after being whipped and knifed.'

He took a deep but unsteady breath. 'When I got back from the hospital clinic that evening, the trailer was on fire and . . . and I heard her screaming. Dad received terrible burns from trying to rescue his Lily Mae, my mom. Mr Delaney, who owned the ranch, shot dead two of the masked killers. One was the sheriff of a nearby hick town; the other was one of his deputies.'

Tears rolled down Theo's face, though he did not sob. 'My mother's limp was from an attack she'd endured as a child, since she didn't belong anywhere, because she wasn't completely anything. And that is why I can't have, mustn't have, children. The world isn't good enough for any son or daughter of mine, Tia.'

A tangled mass of words sat in her mind, though she prevented them from reaching him. Indignation and sympathy almost choked her as she fought to remain outwardly tranquil; at this moment, she realized how much she truly loved this furious, frightened man. But she had to tell him, must say it now. 'Teddy?'

'What?'

'It makes no difference to me, to how I feel. I know we're right. Even after so brief a time, I know we're right.'

'Yes. So do I.'

'Then for Rosie's sake, we think seriously about doing this Ma's way.'

He shrugged.

'Think about it, Teddy.'

'We'll see.' He paused for a while. 'When I saw those notices in London, I felt like blacking my face, shouting with an Irish accent, or barking like a dog. I got a bed, but what about others who were real "niggers"? That's the word. That's the word they wanted to write on their signs, because it's easier to spell than "coloured". But I must say this – they're honest. They don't hide behind masks and silly dresses – they write it down and display their antipathy.'

She felt his frustration and his fear. Because of some faulty commandment invented by stupid, prejudiced people, Teddy was denying himself the third innate right of man. The right to have a family and to raise that family followed close on the heels of the right to life and the right to bodily integrity. Because his mother had been dark, she had suffered a cruel death, while he had been badly scarred.

'So there you have it,' he said.

Tia pointed south. 'No, there you have it. Liverpool is built on the bones of your African ancestors.'

'That is an over-simplified view, Tia. Remember the poverty, the primitive cellar dwellings with no windows and water running down the walls, the rate of infantile mortality, the pain of hunger. Yes, the big, bad money boys made a pile, but the people of Liverpool began to get jobs and were slightly better housed and better fed. What the hell did they know about Africa?'

He paused for breath. 'Yes, boat crews knew what their cargo was, but they, too, were struggling to feed children, so what should they have done? Refused money, refused the work, remained in dire poverty – was that feasible? Africans weren't people. They were thought of as something unusual, a missing link between animal-and mankind. The whole mess was built on ignorance. America wanted cheap labour, and America got what it wanted. Now it's stuck with a lot of angry descendants of those slaves. If it hadn't been Liverpool or Bristol or London, if it hadn't been England, some other country would have complied.'

She wondered how he could be so generous, so in love with a city that had traded in human souls. His distaste for the southern states of America was more than justified, yet he forgave Liverpool?

He spoke as if reading her mind. 'Here, they learned, Portia. When slavery ended, merchant ships from this great port simply switched to different cargo. They were excellent sailors and brilliant navigators. Yes, African lives were lost at sea in conditions that were beyond primitive. They were fed thin gruel and they perished in their own effluent. But it stopped. In America, it never stopped. The whites go to church and read their Bibles, then they put on their pure white gowns and their pure white pointy hats and they kill black people.'

She was quicker, angrier this time. 'It hasn't stopped here if people won't give rooms to those of mixed race.'

'There's no Klan in Britain.'

'What do you think Mosley was about? Boy scouts and jamborees?'

'I think he was wrong, yet open. He wore no mask, Portia. It's the Klan's attempts at anonymity that get to me. Yellow-bellied cowards to a man, they are. North America isn't too bad, but the southern states are steeped in prejudice and religion that has no moral base. I just had to get out, and my father's people are here, in Liverpool. What? Why are you studying me so closely?'

'Does your father have red hair?'

Theo managed to smile at last. 'Yes, though most of it's gone now.'

'There's red in your sideburns.'

'I know.'

She shook her head. 'Right, that's my mind made up. I don't want a red-haired child. See? I can be as silly as you are. Come on, let's go home, Teddy.'

'What if it's just infatuation, Tia?'

'I've done infatuation. This tastes different.'

He nodded his agreement. 'Just because it's happened

at the speed of light doesn't make it any less real, I guess.'

'Then we must follow our star, Teddy.'

'You're my star, you terrible woman.'

It was too early to tell him that she wanted his children, that she held the opinion that all would be equal within twenty years, that colour and creed would cease to matter. 'Yes, follow me, baby. I have a terrific sense of direction.'

'Good, because we'll share the driving tomorrow.'

'Bugger.'

'Yes, that too.'

Having asked and been granted permission, Tia told Ma, Joan and Juliet the life story of Theodore Patrick Quinn as soon as she reached home. When she delivered the part about the burning trailer, Tia's mother and sister were both in tears. Joan, the quiet stalwart, kept her cool, though her eyelids were more mobile than usual.

'He manages not to blame Liverpool,' Tia said. 'He insists that it's all historic and that the city opens its arms to most incomers. Not once has he seen here notices banning certain people from asking for a room. As you're aware, he doesn't look like a person of mixed race, but he insists that any wife of an octoroon might give birth to a coloured baby.' She snorted in a very un-Roedean fashion. 'If he thinks he'll get away with that nonsense, I shall put him right.'

Juliet dried her eyes. 'Pa was bad enough when he thought you'd set your sights on Simon – this would drive him crazy.'

Tia nodded sorrowfully. 'I wonder how he'd feel if you married a half-Jew and I married an octoroon? He is one prejudiced man. He struts around the stage blacked up as Othello, but–'

'We have coloured actors now,' Izzy reminded her eldest daughter.

'Good,' Tia said. 'That should save a few pounds on greasepaint.'

'Pa's fighting back,' Juliet said. 'He's counter-suing Ma for unreasonable behaviour and mental cruelty because she pretended to be drunk for months.'

Izzy shrugged. 'I'm not Ma, darling. I'm Izzy. Richard is purchasable. I'm having Bartle Hall valued, and I shall buy it from him by offering a little more than is strictly necessary.' She turned to Tia. 'Look after Theo. Don't hurt him emotionally, since he's already had enough of that. If your minds are made up, keep the appointment I made for you; if you're unsure, cancel it. I realize it's all been very quick, but if you're both sure about protecting Rosie, you need to be in a stronger position.'

'Oh, Ma, I . . .'

'Oh, manage him,' quiet Joan said, her voice stronger than usual. 'Men are uncomplicated creatures.'

'Nanny, he isn't easy to deal with. He's a determined soul with a dark history. His mind is set.'

'Then change it for him,' Joan almost shouted. 'We can all see that you'll settle only for him and that he feels the same. Follow your heart and give your brain a rest. Let him chase you till you catch him. I'm serious. You'll never forgive yourself if you lose him. Izzy, tell her.'

Izzy shrugged. 'You know my girls better than that, Joan. They do as they please no matter what you or I say.'

Tia sat back and closed her eyes. Tomorrow promised to be one hell of a day. Tomorrow night would be . . . different, too.

Downstairs, Theo listened while Maggie read the story of Sleeping Beauty to her granddaughter. *Well, you did it, Theo. You finally managed to tell a woman why you're such a mess, such a sad man. And it was cathartic, cleansing,*

313

though difficult. Yes, you haven't known her long and yes, commitment is a huge step and yes, she'll want children. We might adopt eventually. There are hundreds of them out there in need of a settled home, and Rosie is just the start.

Maggie entered. 'Did you have a nice time?'

He shrugged. 'Like the curate's egg, it was good in parts.'

She had no idea what he meant by that. 'And Tia?'

'She played to the gallery, as usual. She and I are similar, both in danger because of our sense of humour. Let's just say she was naughty, shall we?'

'Oh deary me. She looked lovely, didn't she?'

Again, he raised his shoulders. 'Yes, she had some of the men salivating like hungry hounds. Speaking of which, where's Mickle?'

'She's asleep with Tyger in the basket. That cat will miss her.'

'I am not taking the cat to Kent. Let the ladies upstairs spoil him for a while. I'll just pack the last of my things.' He left her listening to the radio.

After closing his suitcase, he took a bath before going to bed. Sleep eluded him until the early hours; all he could think of was the long drive south, Rosie and Maggie, the fuss that might be caused by Emily Garner when she discovered that the child and her grandmother had disappeared.

The plot thickened. Would he and Tia keep that appointment on Thursday? Would they win Rosie by keeping that appointment? Would she be safe from her own birth mother and all potential pimps? Questions, questions. He slept fitfully and was woken at dawn by birdsong. It was time. Today was just the beginning.

Fourteen

On Saturday, Nancy Atherton discovered something new about herself. Riding in a converted ambulance put paid to knitting if she gazed down at her work. As long as she knitted without looking, as long as she wasn't counting stitches or reading a pattern, all was well, but she couldn't lower her eyes without feeling ill. She needed to get out of the vehicle several times, as did Tom, because he would not leave his wife's side, especially when she felt sick.

Rosie, who had started the day in a quiet but happy state, fell asleep after the first hundred miles. Her night had been restless due to anticipation and excitement, so she had to be woken now whenever they stopped for food and drink. 'You're missing some pretty places,' Maggie told her, but the child continued to fall asleep. Her temporary nickname was Dozy Rosie, though it didn't matter, as she wasn't awake to hear it.

Mickle took it all in her majestic stride. She lay on her special blanket next to luggage in the back part of the van behind an open-work metal screen, very relaxed and happy to go along with whatever these peculiar creatures expected of her. She was fed and watered regularly and given a short walk, after which she was allowed to sleep. What more could a dog want from life?

Maggie's eyes were wide with wonder; she had never

before been out of Liverpool except for the odd day trip to Blackpool, Southport, Morecambe or North Wales. 'It's so green,' she said repeatedly. 'There's loads of space with no houses,' she announced once or twice.

'We're taking the scenic route,' Theo called to her. The scenic route meant a journey in excess of three hundred and fifty miles, so Tia had to do her share. As she'd driven farm vehicles along narrow lanes from the age of twelve, the extra width of the van didn't worry her.

With her thick mane of hair in a pony tail and her legs clad in those abbreviated jeans, Tia Bellamy looked like a very tall five-year-old except for her rather magnificent upper body. She felt Theo's eyes on her. He put her in mind of a starving child whose nose is pressed against the window of a baker's shop; his experiences of physical love were probably few and far between. She had plans for him, and he had been untypically quiet of late.

Theo tried hard not to stare at her while she drove, but his disobedient eyes were clearly riveted to her by some irresistible force, and he found it impossible to concentrate on the lush green beauty of England. 'What about London?' he whispered. 'Rosie's asleep, so she wouldn't see much.'

'Later in the week or on our way back,' was her reply. 'My arms ache.'

By the time they reached their destination, dusk had begun its descent. Theo parked the van and heaved a heartfelt sigh of relief. 'Come on, sleepyheads, we're here,' he called, mischief in his tone.

Maggie blinked and stared through the window. 'You never said Chaddington Green was at the seaside.'

Theo and Tia grinned at each other.

Nancy woke. 'I've dropped a stitch,' she grumbled.

'You never said it was seaside,' Maggie repeated.

'That's because my home isn't at the seaside,' Tia told

her. 'This is beautiful Broadstairs. Your hotel, the King's Albion, is here on the front. Everything's paid for, and your spending money is in Rosie's case. You are expected. The manager will tell you about the sights and how to get to Deal or Ramsgate or Margate. There's even transport to Dover and the famous cliffs.'

The hotel was massive, white, and lit up from the outside as well as on the inside. 'That looks a bit expensive for the likes of us,' Maggie mused quietly.

'It's a lovely place,' Tom said, looking out at the harbour. He wondered whether there might be fishing trips, though he wasn't sure about leaving his Nancy to worry in case he fell overboard and drowned.

'You're right.' Nancy had apparently ceased to worry about a dropped stitch. 'Yes, you're right, Tom. It's so pretty.'

'We'll pick you up on Thursday morning,' Tia announced, 'because we may have a meeting in Canterbury on that day. You'll love Canterbury.'

'Have you been here before?' Tom asked Theo.

The American-born Anglophile frowned. 'Yes, I have been here before, but I had a limited aerial view. Battle of Britain. This was known as Hellfire Corner. I was flat on my belly pumping bullets into Nazis. Make your own memories of Kent, because mine aren't all happy. I killed people on the ground, too. If I took a German plane down, it didn't always fall into the water. Grim.' He shook his head as memories of war filled it. 'Still, I got my medals. Some people below got a casket and a funeral. I was one of the lucky ones.'

Tom disagreed. 'You were one of the few, according to Churchill.'

Rosie opened her eyes at last. 'Is it Blackpool?' she asked. 'I can smell the sea – I can hear it, too. It's licking the sand.'

A glance passed between the two teachers; this little child was probably going to be one of Theo's miracles. Licking the sand? That was surely a symptom of a good imagination.

Maggie held her granddaughter close. 'No, Rosie, this isn't Blackpool. It's warmer, better weather down this end of the country. We're sleeping here for five nights – it's a surprise from Mr Quinn and Miss Bellamy.' She spoke to Theo. 'Are you and Miss Bellamy staying?'

'No.' His eyes slid momentarily towards Rosie. 'We're seeing Dr Heilberg's father about that check-up and making sure that a certain actor isn't on the loose. But Rosie will see Bartle Hall and the priest holes, we promise. Come along, folks, let's get you inside.'

A liveried young man with a porter's trolley took the suitcases while Tia prepared to book in Mr and Mrs Atherton and Mrs and Miss Stone. As Tunstall's attempt at adoption had ended with his death, Rosie had reverted to her mother's maiden name. She was wide awake and smiling now; she was at the seaside.

Tia led the way into the hotel.

Little Rosie, awestruck by such opulence, walked into the foyer and stood on thick, royal blue carpet. She was the last of the group to enter, because her eyes and ears had been concentrated on the sea. She stood very still and took in her new surroundings. It was the most beautiful place she had ever seen.

As well as the reception desk, there was a bar, and tables with chairs were dotted about the huge space. Two opposing staircases, both curved and both covered in the same blue carpet, rose out of the entrance to the first floor. There were paintings and gilded alcoves with little statues or vases of flowers in them. Every table had a posy in a white pot, and the chairs were painted gold, their upholstered seats the same blue as the carpet. 'It's like a film,' she said, 'really, really posh.'

Tia squatted down. 'You can play on the sands, go for coach trips all over Kent, have ice cream with raspberry sauce, take a ride in a boat.'

'But you won't be here?'

'No, I have things to do. Now, come with me. We're going with your nana up in the lift to your room. Nancy and Tom will be next door to you. Teddy, will you go in the other lift with them?'

Rosie loved the lift and wished she could go up and down a few times, though she doubted that grown-ups would accept that as a good idea.

Her mouth dropped open when they reached their destination. It was all pale blue and cream with twin beds and thick, soft, cream towels piled in the small bathroom, and toilet paper folded to a point, all fancy, and tiny soaps shaped like flowers or butterflies, and sweets on a little dining table in the bedroom, and the sea just across the road, and a bowl of fruit next to the sweets, and fat pillows on the beds, and reading lamps, and towelling robes to wear after a bath, and she was happy. The happiness almost spilled down her face; this was as good as Buckingham Palace, she felt sure.

Tia blinked hard and smiled at Maggie. 'I think Rosie likes it,' she said. 'Mr Davidson, the manager, says you may phone the hospital as many times as you like – Teddy and I will pay the bill. We want you relaxed, Maggie, for your own sake as well as for Rosie. Tom and Nancy are right next door in number seventeen.'

'It's lovely,' Maggie said at last. She was afraid of touching anything, since it all looked brand new.

Of course, Rosie had to dash into the next room to give it the once-over. It was the same as hers and Nana's except for the double bed. This was how rich people lived. Rich people had baths with taps and didn't need to get a wash and clean their teeth at the kitchen sink.

Mr Quinn was smiling at her and telling her that if she left her shoes outside the door, someone would clean them during the night. They had a table in the dining room downstairs, or they could have food delivered to their rooms if they preferred. Rosie didn't prefer; she wanted to look at the rich people. She had five new dresses, two pairs of posh shoes, a handbag, a suit, two blouses, a very pretty skirt and two cardigans knitted by Mrs Atherton. Oh, and if the weather went cold, she had a brand new coat, so she could look pretty and well dressed, and nobody would know that she was poor.

Tom emerged from the bathroom and grinned at Theo. 'This is the life, eh? Rosie, you'd best pass your scholarship exams and get a proper job, then you'll be able to live like this all the time.'

'Is that how they do it?' Rosie asked.

'Sometimes they inherit money,' Theo explained. 'It gets left to them when people die.'

She thought about that. 'We haven't got nobody to leave us money. I'll have to make money for me and Mam and Nana.' This, she decided, would involve hard work and huge responsibility. 'I'll be a doctor. Our doctor's got nice clothes and a car, so he must be well off.'

Theo groaned inwardly. Colin Duckworth's latest career path was meandering down the medical route. Could a headmaster cope with a pair of them? 'Miss Bellamy and I are leaving now, Rosie. She's given your nana the telephone numbers of Rose Cottage and Bartle Hall, so if you need us, call. If we're out, a Mrs Melia at Bartle Hall will take a message.'

Tia and Theo returned to the van. 'You know the way,' he said. 'You drive.'

For once, she found no clever reply, as she was too

busy thinking about Rosie and the others. 'Do you think we've overwhelmed them, Teddy?'

'They'll get used to it. Very few Scousers become overwhelmed by circumstance. From what I've heard and read, they were magnificent during the war. That city carried every bullet and every bomb through its transport systems. Oh yes, they had their own Hellfire Corner. You know, they never cease to amaze me. Somebody gets ill and ends up with enough food to cater for the whole street. Very few die alone, because it isn't allowed. Neighbours sit round drinking tea and eating biscuits, talking about everyday matters and making death a part of life. It's heart, Portia. Liverpool has a strong heartbeat and a healthy gut.'

She nodded her agreement. 'Yes. It's almost impossible to feel lonely. Right. Rose Cottage, here we come.' When the engine was started, she glanced at her companion. 'Nervous?' she asked.

'Yes.'

'Are you equipped?'

'Yes.'

'Afraid of me?'

'No.'

She drove off. If he was going to become monosyllabic, she would ask no further questions. Yet she couldn't resist having the last word. 'Why couldn't I fall in love with somebody uncomplicated?'

Theo managed a grin. Madam Portia, a multi-faceted jewel, was far from uncomplicated, a mile away from predictable. She was a precious nuisance; perhaps they were designed for each other.

Jack Peake drained the last drops from his tea mug, which, when full, held a pint of the drink to which he was addicted. He raked his fingers through thinning hair, shoved his feet into old brown slippers and answered the door. When he looked at the unexpected visitor, he rolled down his shirt sleeves and wished he'd had a bit of a wash, because the man facing him was very smart. Jack knew the face, but couldn't place it immediately.

'Mr Peake? Caretaker of Myrtle Street School?'

'Yes, that's me.'

The man looked up and down the street. 'May I come inside for a few minutes?'

Jack hesitated for a second or two before opening the door properly. His house wasn't in too bad a state, though it lacked the decor usually enjoyed by people as well dressed as this fellow.

'Thank you,' said the elegant, middle-aged intruder as he entered the front room. 'I'll come straight to the point. I'm looking for my daughter, Portia Bellamy, often known as Tia. I found out through Civil Service contacts of mine that she's accepted a post at Myrtle Street.'

Jack shook his head. 'I'm just the dogsbody,' he said. 'I don't have anything to do with the teaching side of things.'

'I understand that. But have you met my daughter?'

Jack's mind was spinning. 'There's a new teacher starting in September, but I don't know the name.' He recognized this bloke's face now that he'd studied it for a few moments. Like the rest of the population, he'd read the lurid tales about his behaviour, about his wife leaving him after pretending for months to be dependent on drink.

'The head teacher's name is Quinn, I gather.'

'That's right. You were in that film, *Forty Braves*, weren't you? Mr Quinn was in the real thing, Battle of Britain.'

Richard Bellamy sat down without asking permission.

322

'Yes, I'm Richard Bellamy. Do you have Mr Quinn's address?'

Jack had no alternative but to follow instructions. 'Yes, I have his address, Mr Bellamy, because if anything happens at the school, he is my first contact. But I can't give out that information. The fact is that the school is closed now till September. Oh, and another thing, I happen to know that Mr Quinn set off on his travels early this morning. He sometimes goes home to see his family during the summer.' That wasn't a lie.

'Where?' Richard asked.

'America. New York, I think.'

Richard Bellamy's expression darkened. He had been used to getting his way in most situations, though he was beginning to suspect that Isadora had been the key. The country, the industry and possibly the world had turned against him. He tried a different tack. 'My health is deteriorating,' he said.

'Sorry to hear that.' Jack, inured to the top-drawer accent employed by Tia, was not fazed by her father's gobful of plums. 'You should go and see a doctor, or try outpatients at a hospital.'

The unwelcome actor rose to his feet. 'A sick man needs to see his family,' he stated.

Jack shrugged. 'From what I've read in the papers, your family might not want to see you. Sorry I can't help you, but Mr Quinn's address would be no use, because he isn't there.'

'And who do you contact in his absence?'

'I can't tell you. I can't tell anybody.' Miss Cosgrove, Theo's deputy, would probably swoon if Richard Bellamy landed on her doorstep. She was man-hungry, and this particular man probably knew how to play on a woman's weaknesses.

Richard thanked Jack, though there was sarcasm in his

tone. He left, closing the door none too quietly in his wake.

Jack dashed to the window and watched while the adulterous menace drove away. 'Right,' he said to himself. 'Pull yourself together, Peake. Bike, Allerton, Miss Bellamy's flat.' He dashed out to the back yard and collected Old Faithful, a ramshackle mode of transport he had used for years. Bellamy might well be lying in wait or parked round a nearby corner, so Jack pedalled through alleyways and back streets too narrow for cars, doubling back on himself and taking a circuitous route to his destination.

When he finally reached the villa, he knew he was alone. Wheeling his bike up the side of the house, he sprayed medication into his mouth before hiding Old Faithful and pushing Miss Bellamy's doorbell. 'Stay calm, Jack,' he murmured. He heard footsteps muffled by carpet, followed by a voice similar to Tia's but younger and more lightweight. 'Who's there?'

'It's Jack Peake, caretaker from Myrtle Street School.'

'Just a moment.'

He heard bolts being drawn back. When she opened the door, Jack stared above her head for a fraction of a second. She looked very like her sister, though she was tiny. 'Hello,' he said, after lowering his eyes to her level. 'Sorry to disturb you, but I need to speak to you and your mother.'

Juliet widened the gap and allowed him to enter the small ground-floor hallway. 'I'm Juliet, Tia's sister,' she told him before leading the way upstairs. 'A visitor, Ma,' she announced. 'This gentleman is Theo's caretaker at the school.'

Jack stood in the presence of Isadora Bellamy. A thin woman sat beside her on a sofa; she was holding Tyger-Two, the kitten that had replaced Theo's old cat. 'Sorry to disturb,' he repeated, 'but as your daughter said, I'm care-taker at Mr Quinn's school, and I've just had a visit from your husband.'

He noticed that the thin woman's face blanched, while Mrs Bellamy gasped and put a hand to her mouth.

Jack continued. 'I am one of the few who know you're staying here. Theo left my address for you, I understand, in case you need any help. Well, your other half found me about half an hour ago. Some crony of his, probably at government level, managed to find out that your daughter will be working at Myrtle Street from September. I told him nothing.'

Isadora closed her eyes for a moment. 'How can anyone learn about Portia being in Liverpool?' she asked, her voice almost a whisper.

'My guess is some big-gob pen-pusher in the Ministry of Education, Mrs Bellamy. So, however it happened, the fact is her dad knows that Miss Bellamy is starting work at the school. I suppose somebody from the Lady Streets told him where I live, and he knocked at my door. He has a car.'

'Rented, probably,' Juliet said. 'Please sit down, Mr . . . sorry, I'm hopeless with names.'

'Jack Peake.' He sat in an armchair.

'Were you followed?' Isadora asked.

'I don't think so. I used back alleys and lanes too narrow for cars. Oh, and he says he's ill and needs to see his family.'

'Did he look ill?' Juliet was genuinely concerned.

'No, he's a picture of health.' Jack paused. 'I can get rid of him easy if you like. I can tell the *Echo* he's in Liverpool.'

'No,' the kitten-holding woman muttered. 'He'll go south and start looking for Portia if he's chased from Liverpool. London's no hiding place for him just now; even his agent's been fired.'

'He'll find another, I'm sure,' Isadora whispered.

Juliet perched on the sofa's arm and held her mother's hand. 'Try not to worry, Ma.' She turned to Jack. 'We thought he was in Ireland.'

Isadora made a decision. 'We mustn't tell Theo or Portia or any of the others that Richard's here. Rosie and Maggie need that holiday, so we can't have them dashing back just because Richard has resurfaced. With any luck, he might disappear until September.'

Jack shifted uncomfortably. 'Some in the Lady Streets know where Theo lives, and they might know that Miss Bellamy rents this flat. It's only a matter of time.'

'You're sure he isn't ill?' Juliet asked.

'I'm as sure as I can be, miss, though I'm no doctor.'

Joan, having had a short rethink, spoke again. 'Then let him find us, Mr Peake. He'll rant and rave like the child he's always been, but he won't dash back to Kent immediately and disturb the others. I am in a privileged position here, because I can threaten to sue him for attacking me in front of many witnesses. The magistrates bound him over to keep the peace, that's all. If anyone needs to know why I didn't sue him there and then, I shall tell them I needed to get away from him, that I feared him. Now that he's here, I'm terrified. He and I can create a stand-off situation with Izzy acting as peacemaker.'

'My father hurt you?' Juliet was clearly incredulous.

'Yes, Juliet, he did.'

Juliet closed her eyes as if trying to block out thought.

Isadora spoke. 'Darling, he threw her to the floor at the Punch Bowl – how apt that name is – and was about to stamp on her. The locals tied him down. He was drunk; Joan and I were not.'

The youngest of the Bellamy girls swallowed hard; it was indeed a bitter pill. 'How will you stop him going back to Kent?' she asked. 'How will you keep him here?'

Isadora smiled enigmatically. 'Joan and I will cope if he isn't imprisoned,' she said. 'He needs us far more than we need him, my love. It's just a case of allowing him to believe that he's getting his own way. We praise him and placate him.'

'But how?' Juliet asked.

Joan gave the answer. 'By pretending to negotiate, by pretending to be reasonable. He can stay in Theo's flat, then we can keep an eye on him. He needs to be contained like the wild animal he is.'

'I told him I thought Theo had gone to America,' Jack said.

'Good man. We'll convince him that Portia is touring in France with a friend,' Isadora said. 'I don't need to ask you to keep quiet, do I?'

'No.' Jack stood up. 'My boss is a good man, and your daughter's a lovely young woman, Mrs Bellamy. They need some time, too.'

Juliet agreed, though she made no remark. Tia and Theo were clearly drawn to each other, and Juliet was glad for them and for herself, since she was now able to spend time with a man she'd loved for years. 'Will you still divorce Pa?' she asked her mother.

'Yes, but like Mr Peake, I'll take a detour up a few dark alleys. Whatever it costs in terms of time, we need to ensure that the visitors in Kent are not disturbed. Things may change after Thursday. I've arranged a meeting for Portia and Theodore. They will, I hope, take the first step towards securing a safe future for Rosie. She'll be having X-rays and so forth, because we need to keep her away from her mother by finding evidence of old injuries.'

'So what must we do now, Ma?'

'Nothing. Someone will point your father in the right direction. He will come here looking for Portia, and we must manage him for a while.'

Joan shivered. 'Can't we just put arsenic in his food?' She winked at Juliet in an attempt to take the sting out of her words.

Izzy laughed. 'No, we must be clever, lull him into a false sense of security for a while. I know it may sound cruel, Juliet, but we need to get our priorities right. Theo and Portia want to keep Maggie calm and Rosie happy. In order for that to happen, your father must stay away from Kent. So I'll pretend to consider reconciliation while Joan behaves as if he terrifies her. He's easily confused and easy to please. The way to that particular man's heart is not through his stomach – it's via his narcissism, which needs regular massage.'

Juliet shook her head. She disliked lies, hated dishonesty of any kind. But Pa had lived the dishonest life, so she had to appreciate her mother's position in this situation. Two actresses and one journalist were purported to have given birth to Pa's children. His professional life was suffering because he was unwilling or unable to keep up with trends in the job. Deep down, Juliet knew why; it was because he appeared to have no sense of humour whatsoever. When it came to laughing at himself or responding to jokes directed at him, he froze.

Jack stood up. 'I'd better get back,' he said. 'The lights on my old boneshaker don't always work. If you have any problems, come and get me. You have my address?'

'Yes, thank you very much,' said Isadora. 'See Jack out, Juliet.'

'This is just day one,' Joan said when the two women were alone. 'It's almost as if he timed it, as if he knows Theo isn't here to protect us.'

Isadora laughed, though the sound was far from happy. 'You know I can manage him. Why do you think he went to pieces when I played the alcoholic? He needs a strong-minded woman behind him, not a dipsomaniac. We have to keep him here, Joan.'

'For Rosie, yes,' Isadora's faithful companion said.

'And for Portia and Theo. They are blinded by infatuation, and they need this time to decide whether or not it's love.'

'I think it is, Izzy.'

'So do I. Oh, I do hope it is, Joan. He's a very special man, and she's a precious girl. They look right together.'

Rose Cottage looked completely different. The outside sported a fresh coat of paint, and all ancient roses had been removed. Tia lingered for a while in the rear garden. It would be years before the house might live up to its name, because new roses seldom thrived where old ones had been recently removed. To compensate for this, tubs containing miniature roses and tumbling lobelia had been placed at each side of exterior doors front and back. The rest of the land was laid to lawn with little paths running hither and yon. The gypsy caravan remained, all freshly painted and colourful. 'Rosie will love that,' she said. 'She'll want to sleep in it.'

Theo yawned, as did Mickle.

'Am I boring the two of you?' she asked.

'No, I'm just exhausted, though I can't speak for my dog. It was a long drive, I'm ashamed to say. As an American citizen, I know of people who drive over a hundred miles to work. Maybe living here has made me nesh.'

'Nesh?'

'Scouse to describe a moaner.'

She shook her head. 'It's like a totally different language.'

'Language develops almost of its own accord,' he advised her. 'Wales is near – perhaps that's where we got the guttural sound at the end of words such as black or sock. Many incomers were Irish, and foreign travellers from all over the world moved to Liverpool. A Birmingham accent came from God alone knows where, and what about Cockneys? It's the same in America, where accents change every couple of hundred miles or so.'

She was laughing.

'What?' he demanded.

'You. You're a zealous lecturer.'

'I'll shut my mouth, then.'

Inside the cottage, all buckets and bowls for collecting rainwater had disappeared. Mickle, presented with her famous blanket and an old bolster from Theo's flat, settled down and fell asleep within seconds. All she needed was her master and, since he had chosen to travel to this place, it was good enough for her.

'The roof's been mended,' Tia said, almost to herself. The little house was so pretty. Ma had made sure that everything would be ready for them. There was a new cottage-sized suite, and all soft furnishings were clean and fresh. 'My mother's a clever girl,' Tia mused. 'It's a honeymoon cottage.'

'We're not married.'

She laughed. 'You just lost your lecturer status, Teddy Bear. You should be teaching me stuff I don't already know.'

She knows everything, Theo. She knows what she wants, and she wants to try you like a new shoe. Here you are with a box of French letters stashed in your case, because she's going to put you through your paces. Are you ready?

He got the feeling that Madame Guillotine might give him marks out of ten or a gold star if he came anywhere near top of the class. He wondered vaguely which part of his body might be removed by the sharp edge of her wit if he didn't come up to scratch.

'Light the fire, Teddy,' she suggested. 'It's the only source of hot water, I'm afraid. I'll dig about in the kitchen, see if I can find something to eat. We both need a good bath, I think.' Having left the sitting room, she called from the kitchen, 'Everything's clean or new in here, too.'

The fire had already been set. He grabbed a fancy matchbox from the mantelpiece and set the flame to light newspapers. It was a good flue, and the wood was burning within seconds. After claiming the small sofa, he lay down, bent his knees, put his head on a cushion and fell asleep almost immediately. Just before nodding off, he allowed himself a slight smile. She would not be pleased.

But she was pleased. She knelt by the sofa and stroked his hair, smiling when light from the fire illuminated the red-gold bits in his sideburns. *I'll have a bath tonight, and he can get clean in the morning. Just look at those disgraceful eyelashes, Tia; such a tragic waste on a chap. And it's a strong face on a strong man who needs love; you have a lot of love to give, madam.*

What will happen on Thursday, I wonder? Oh, go and have a bath, you lovelorn loon. He'll still be here in the morning. God, please make him want to be with me every morning. He has captured my heart. Look at it this way, God. If we take each other out of general circulation, we won't damage any other people, and that has to be a good thing. Think about it, please. Oh, yes – Amen. I almost forgot that bit . . .

When Maggie woke on her first morning in Broadstairs, there was no sign of her granddaughter in the bedroom or bathroom. A note on Rosie's pillow announced, *I gon for brEkfuss, lovE form ROsiE.* Form was probably from, and Rosie would be mithering folk downstairs, making a nuisance of herself, no doubt. Oh, God. The child was probably interviewing the rich about how they got their money, or talking to the hotel staff, or running across the road to watch the sea. Running across the road? She was probably running the bloody hotel by now. Theo had warned Maggie that intelligent and gifted children were often unpredictable and that Rosie might be hard work from time to time.

She threw on some clothes, dragged a comb through her hair and went down the stairs – she didn't trust lifts. As she descended one of the sweeping staircases that led to the large reception area, she spotted her only grandchild perched on a stool between two young women at the reception desk. Early risers on their way out were stopping and handing keys to Rosie, who passed them on to one of the staff. Maggie failed to suppress a giggle. Little Lady Rose had been in town for five minutes, and she already had a job.

As she got nearer, Maggie heard her clever-mouthed key-grabber talking to a guest. 'I'm Rosie from Liverpool and I hope you have a lovely day.'

'What is she like?' Maggie mumbled to herself. 'She's showing me up something terrible – I'm ashamed.'

The two young women on the desk were delighted with her. 'Mrs Stone? She's had us doubled over laughing. So sweet, and what a wonderful accent!'

Rosie eyed her grandmother. 'I'm not being a doctor any more; I'm going to have a hotel like this one. Your key, Mrs Stone?' she asked, her expression deadly serious.

'I haven't got it, Rosie. I came looking for you, didn't I?'

The child shook her head slowly. 'You can't go outside. You can't go out without giving your key in. It's hotel pollisty.'

Maggie sighed and spoke to one of the real receptionists. 'Sorry,' she said. 'She's a bit . . . precocious, I think the word is. Come on, Rosie, let's get some breakfast. And it's policy, not whatever you said, princess.'

Rosie led her nana towards the dining room. 'You have to get your own breakfast from the sideboard. That's because posh people in posh houses do that. The other meals get served by servants, but you let the servants go and eat their brekky while you have yours.'

Maggie chuckled quietly. When Rosie got her stately home, she would know how to run it. 'What's this?' she asked, lifting the lid from a dish.

'It's kedgeray or a word something like that,' Rosie replied. 'I had some, and it's horrible. There's kippers further down, then bacon and eggs and porridge and toast and there's two kinds of marmalade and some jam on the tables and—'

'How many breakfasts have you had, Rosie Stone?'

'Two,' was the reply. 'I had bacon and eggs with Mr and Mrs Beresford. They sell jewellery in London and I think she was wearing most of it. Then I had toast and jam with a lady called Miss Forrester. She's a private sacristary for the Foreign Sacristary.'

'Secretary,' Maggie said.

'Oh, right. I'll just get some more toast. Tell me what you want, Nana, and I'll fetch it for you.'

Maggie watched her precious charge as she walked the length of an endless sideboard filling a plate for her grandmother. Everybody spoke to her; it was clear that word had spread and that people were looking out for a pretty little Liverpool girl in a red and white gingham dress and shiny red shoes.

Tom and Nancy joined Maggie. 'Hello, love,' Tom said. 'Is this our table?'

'I think so. But our Rosie eats at any table she fancies. People like her.'

'That's right,' Nancy pronounced. 'Everybody likes

Rosie!' She placed her badge of office – her knitting bag – on the floor.

After serving her nana, Rosie told Tom and Nancy what was available. She didn't mention the kedgeree, but she went off to bring their bacon and eggs. At a hatch in the far wall, she shouted, 'Tea for four, please, table sixteen,' before returning with Nancy's plate. 'It'll be a big pot,' she told Tom. 'Somebody will bring it for you. I'll go for my bro-chewers. If you want coffee as well, tell that lad in uniform. He's the only one not having his own breakfast. His name's Alan, and he gets his breakfast when the dining room closes.'

Maggie wondered who hadn't been interviewed by her granddaughter.

When Rosie had left the table, the remaining three looked quizzically at each other. 'She's organizing us,' Tom chuckled.

'You're right, love. I must make her a red cardigan.'

Maggie blinked rapidly as she remembered the frightened little girl who had run for Tunstall's baccy after spending half the night in a dark shed. 'I know this sounds terrible, but I don't want Sadie to have her back. If my daughter's head is buggered, she won't be fit to have her; if she gets back to normal and goes on the game again . . .'

Tom patted her hand. 'Sadie neglected her while the bad bugger knocked her about. You have a strong case, love.'

'And anaemia,' Maggie muttered.

Their little imp returned with 'bro-chewers' containing photographs and literature. 'A king called Charles landed here after hiding somewhere. Another king called Henry cut people's heads off. There's an archway built for him somewhere.' After announcing that anybody who cut people's heads off didn't deserve an archway, she led them to the white cliffs of Dover, Bleak House, another house once owned by Dickens, eighty miles to London by train, and to various beaches and harbours in Kent. 'And there's lovely countryside,' she concluded.

Tom and Nancy chewed on bacon.

'Who's Charles Dickens?' Rosie asked.

'A writer,' Maggie told her.

'Where does he live now?'

'He's dead, love.'

'Is he?'

Maggie nodded.

'Well, that's a shame, Nana, cos I wanted to talk to him. He knew all about Broadstairs.'

Nancy swallowed her bacon. 'That's right, Rosie. He was a very clever man. He wrote *A Christmas Carol.*'

'Did he? Which one? "Silent Night"?'

Nancy chuckled. 'He wrote a story called *A Christmas Carol.*'

Rosie frowned. It was becoming clear that she had a lot to learn.

Richard Bellamy shaved off his moustache and used brown dye on his hair. The result was rather patchy, but he certainly looked different. He dressed in casual clothes, cavalry twill trousers, open-necked shirt, fawn cardigan and brown shoes. A panama hat completed the picture before he prepared to sally forth in search of lunch. Thus far, this hotel's food had not kept up with his Epicurean standards.

Liverpool. Why on earth would anyone choose this place after living a good life in the garden of England? Why would Portia work in a worn-out Victorian building after teaching daughters of the elite in a college for young ladies? Why teach infants and juniors when she was trained to work with older children? Had Simon Heilberg accompanied her on her travels? So many questions, no sensible answers.

Leaving the hired car behind, he strolled towards the city. Even as far north as this, England was enjoying good weather. Donning his hat, he ambled forth in search of a decent restaurant or a public house where food was on offer. There was thinking to be done, because he felt sure that Portia would know where Isadora was. Surely someone living near Myrtle Street would know where Portia was living? After all, his oldest daughter left a mark wherever she went.

He hadn't believed the caretaker. The eyes had held secrets, while the mouth had opened and closed rather rapidly before lies had dripped from the man's lips. Joining the line of thinkers at the Pier Head, he stared at calm water, bright blue sky and a future that threatened to contain little promise. *We came as a pair, as Richard and Isadora. We worked well together. Yes, I'm guilty of philandering, but I never abandoned my real family. Oh, what a mess.*

The man next to him was weeping quietly. A woman standing at Richard's left side was staring blankly into the water, as if the solutions to life's problems swam just below its rippled surface.

She glanced at Richard. 'You all right, lad?' she asked.

'Thank you, yes. And you?'

The woman shook her head. 'Me boy died,' she said. 'Measles went to his brain. His legs died first, and they cut them off, like. But it never stopped it. He was only twelve.'

'I am so sorry,' he said.

'We come here and talk to strangers when it gets too much in the house with the family all suffering. Know

336

what I mean? It's easier telling somebody you don't know. You're not from round here.'

'Kent,' he told her. 'My wife left me. I think she's somewhere in or near Liverpool.'

She touched his hand. 'Pray for my lad, and I'll pray for you.'

Richard watched as she walked away, her shoulders rounded, her steps small, because she had to get home but didn't want to go there. He could have stood at the Thames embankment for hours, and no one would have spoken to him. Was this enough to entice Portia to move north?

Isadora was not in Canterbury, of that he felt sure. Had she been there, the press would have tracked her down. Delia was of no fixed abode, while Juliet was not answering her phone, so God alone knew where she was. Lunch. Yes, he had come out here to find something worth eating.

He found a newsagent and bought several papers, including gutter press publications. The Bellamys were no longer front-page news, thank goodness.

In the most popular and noisiest newspaper, he found a small headline.

ISADORA TO BE KNOWN BY
HER FIRST NAME ONLY

Fury filled his chest and his stomach, threatening to scream out through his mouth. God, the bitch knew how to play her cards well. She knew how to play the drunk well, too. She was dumping him, his name, their joint history on stage and film. Could she cut any deeper? Oh yes, she could steal his daughters, too.

He marched into a public house and ordered a double whisky. There was a menu on the bar, and he picked it up. Ah, they had a full beef dinner including Yorkshires and vegetables.

'Dining room's through there, sir. We're open till two.'

'Thank you.'

He stayed for a while in the bar, where he perused the latest article relating to the collapse of his marriage. Isadora and her agent were clearly intent on taking no prisoners. What the hell was this? Isadora Films? She was planning her own company? Christ, what next?

He read on. She intended to use new writers, new actors, young crew. Furthermore, she would be signing up to star in a series of silly comedy films, because she didn't want to leave England, and the funds would be useful for other projects and for . . . *what?* A children's home? Had she lost her mind completely?

Angrily, he screwed up the newspaper and walked through to the dining room, where he opted for a small table near a window. More furious than ever, he threw back the last of his whisky and picked up the wine list. Isadora held the purse strings. Soon, he wouldn't be able to track down a decent burgundy, as such luxuries would be beyond his shortened reach. Yes, he could have saved, no, he hadn't saved.

Then he heard the laugh and almost froze in his seat. Diagonally opposite him, in another corner, Juliet sat with . . . God, no! She was with Simon Heilberg – did that man intend to work his way through the whole Bellamy family? This was too much. In a trice, he crossed the floor, dragged the unprepared doctor from his seat and slammed him against the wall. With a sickening thud, Simon's head made contact with the hard surface, and he folded on the floor, unconscious.

Juliet leapt to her feet. 'Police and ambulance,' she cried before dropping to Simon's side. Other diners jumped up, some leaving the battle zone, others remaining to see what might happen next. The manager ran in from the bar, calling over his shoulder, 'Mike – nine nine nine, police and ambulance.' He threw Richard into a chair. 'Move, and I'll bloody deal with you, mate.'

Shaking, Richard stayed where he had been thrust by the muscle-bound master of the establishment.

The manager knelt next to Juliet. 'Let's keep his airway in a straight line, love.'

'Yes,' she agreed. 'I'm a nurse. Recovery position, I think.'

Between them, they rearranged Simon's limp body.

Juliet stood up, steadying herself by placing a hand on the helpful manager's shoulders. In an unprecedented show of anger, she spoke to the remaining diners. 'This article here is my father. You have all witnessed his attempt to kill my . . . the man I love. He may be successful, because Simon is out cold.' Tears threatened, and she had to pause for a few moments before continuing.

'Pa was bound over recently in the sum of three hundred pounds because he attacked my nanny, the lady who raised me and my sisters.' Slowly, she turned to face Pa. 'If Simon dies, I'll hang you myself. As things stand, there isn't a court in this land that will let you mix with normal humanity. For the rest of my life, I will not speak to you, ever.'

The police arrived, and removed Richard after listening to Juliet's claim. They promised to enquire and keep him under lock and key until the answers came. His rights were read, and suspicion of causing actual bodily harm was mentioned before he was shoved out of the dining room.

'Where's the ambulance?' Juliet wailed. The bell clanged outside before her last word was fully formed. When the ambulance staff rushed in, the manager led her and all the other diners into the bar. 'Free lunch for all of you

whenever you like – get your tickets from Mike.' He pointed to the barman. 'A small cognac for this young lady,
please.'

Dazed, angry and tearful, Juliet found herself riding in
the ambulance with her beloved. He lay on a hard board
with a surgical collar round his neck. 'Are his pupils dila-
ted?' she asked. 'Are they equal? What's happening?'

She was told to hush. 'Take it easy, miss. Looks like a
fractured skull, but calm down. He's breathing well, and
that's always a good sign.'

Juliet closed her eyes and prayed. There was nothing
else she could do.

Fifteen

'What are you doing now, Portia? Will we need the fire
brigade?' Theo rearranged his pillows and propped his
upper half into a vertical position. She was leaning perilously off her side of the bed. 'You'll fall,' he said just
before she fell. Sighing in an exaggerated fashion usually
reserved for the likes of Colin Duckworth, he pushed
back the bed covers and moved across into her territory.
'What the hell are you up to now, Baroness Tia? Is this
part of some exercise routine? Do we get fifty push-ups
and ten minutes' running on the spot in the nude? It
should be an interesting display.' He laughed. 'Talk to me.'

Tia continued to lie in an untidy, crumpled heap on
the floor. She had taken a pillow with her, and she was
beating her head against it. 'Bugger,' was her sole bequest
to the conversation. She pummelled her pillow with both
fists.

'Never mind,' he said. 'If you landed on your head,
you mustn't have felt a thing. You're a fortunate girl.'

She stood up, gloriously naked and completely
unashamed. 'I've lost my thread now. You are always
making me lose my thread.'

'Ah, you were sewing. Are you embroidering a badge
of office for me? Was I so wonderfully successful in the
sack? Will you stitch it to my Boy Scout's sweater?'

'You're not wearing a sack, and the Scouts wouldn't

have you, I'm sure.' She could be as childishly obtuse as he was. 'No. I'm taking notes. And losing one's thread means a breakdown in a train of thought.'

'So you're playing with trains? I didn't know you had a train set. Is it a Hornby? Do you keep it under the bed?'

Portia Bellamy rearranged her features in an effort to appear calm and as unamused as Queen Victoria. 'I was about to make a comment in my notebook about body parts,' she said without a smile. 'I thought it might help Tom Quirke with his writing. The pen is mightier than the sword, but if one omits the gap between pen and is, one has a body part.'

He burst out laughing so hard that the bed shook. His glee proved infectious, and she threw herself on the tangled mass of sheets and blankets, and laughed with him. She was happy. She was happy because she was his, and she wanted to feel like this for the rest of her life. 'We're silly, Mr Quinn,' she managed eventually.

'Thank God,' he answered, wiping his eyes on the sheet. 'Did you mark my pen is?' he asked, grinning widely. He pondered yet again on the fact that he loved her vulgarity. Even when she was coarse, she somehow managed to remain refined. Impossible? Yes, she was. 'Well, the marks, Portia?'

'Gave it an A plus for presentation and an A for performance skills.'

'Where's my second plus?'

'It's probably under the bed where I dropped my notes. Shall we search? It's a very small plus, and it could be anywhere.'

He simply could not deal with the woman when she was in so feisty a mood, which was most of the time. 'No, we need food. I'll go rustle up brunch and, when we've eaten, we'll have round two. You get the buckets and the

342

gum shields while I find hand strapping and gloves. Oh, and a towel in case you want to throw it in.'

Tia sat on the edge of the bed and watched as he swung out his legs and stood up. 'Teddy?'

'Yes, ma'am?'

She swallowed hard before continuing. 'What does A K mean?' It was there on his back, stark white scar tissue where he'd been stitched.

'K is for Klan. Not sure about the A. It could be Atlanta, Arransville, Auguston – no idea. There were plenty of hick towns, but the sheriff and his deputy didn't come from any place beginning with A. Maybe it's for amalgamated, I'm not sure. Where Klan numbers dwindled, chapters re-formed.' He turned to face her. 'Poached or scrambled, baby? Don't cry.'

'I'm not crying. My eyes are leaking.'

'Dry them on the sheet.'

'The evil things they did to you—'

Theo tutted and blew her a kiss. 'Shush, it's over, kiddo. I survived that *and* the Battle of Britain.' He pulled on a robe and went downstairs. 'I'm a tough cookie,' he called over his shoulder. He loved her and couldn't bear to see her upset. Perhaps, when new love grew older, he would be able to comfort her without resorting to his own tears.

Tia sat in the middle of the bed. Her sweet, tender and gentle lover could be heard talking to his dog about farm animals and how to resist chasing them. 'Eat your breakfast, Mickle. And steer clear of geese and swans,' he was saying. 'They are dangerous. As for farmers with guns, they can be lethal.'

Lethal? He was so right, Tia mused solemnly. The most dangerous animal on earth was human. How could grown men carve letters into the flesh of a ten-year-old boy? And the stripes on his back were still there, so the whips must have torn at skin and sunk into his body. Such a slight child he had been, too.

Furthermore, which breed of animal incinerated a woman because of darker skin and curly hair? 'I will have your children, Theodore Quinn. In twenty or thirty years, no one will care about colour and quadroons and octoroons and mulattos, because it won't matter.' She had vague memories of being told by someone that after the Second World War, before American servicemen were shipped back home, the question of a possible colour bar in Britain had been aired. And it had been dropped, of course, though a few extreme right-wingers continued to champion the cause.

Was it true that in southern states, coloureds and whites had to sit in different parts of a bus, that they were segregated during childhood and sent to all-white or all-coloured schools? Was that the land of the free, then? Was it the home of the brave? Oh yes, as long as they were Caucasian.

'What are you doing?' Theo called.

'Cogitating.'

'Do you have a licence?'

'Get cooking and I'll show you my qualifications.'

He laughed and returned to the kitchen.

Tia managed a grin. The only problem with the main part of Rose Cottage was its size; a person could scarcely think without being overheard. She pulled on underwear, a skirt and a blouse. Her hair she left loose, because he loved it, called it a golden waterfall, as the sun had bleached it with blonde streaks. Theo was an unexpectedly romantic soul; he was also the lover she had sought for some time. And they had three clear and private days together after today.

Although now fully clothed, she suddenly felt shy when she joined him at the kitchen table. It was something about the way he looked at her – no, he looked through her, as if he read her mind, her heart and her soul. God, she was thinking like some pathetic, elderly and disappointed writer of sixpenny novellas.

'You are beautiful,' he said.

'So are you. This is splendid; I'm starving.' He had made toast, fluffy scrambled eggs and crisp bacon. 'I like being here with you,' she said. It was a massive kitchen which had once been a piggery. Although it lacked the charm of the original house, it was a place big enough to contain a large family. This was the only part of Rose Cottage that offered a bit of privacy, since the dining area was at the far end of the piggery, well away from the main part of the building.

'I like your blush,' was his reply.

'I do not blush.'

'I like your pink cheeks, then.'

'Shut up, Mr Quinn. I am pink because the weather is already warm. And before the day really heats up, we should take Mickle out and show her the size of the Bellamy estate.'

Theo frowned. What had happened to round two?

'Rose Cottage is mine now,' she told him. 'I have the deeds. Ma bought a brand new flat for Juliet and she's looking for a London pied-à-terre for Delia, so I got Rose Cottage. She's planning to take on Bartle Hall and sell the farms to tenants. A very astute businesswoman, my mother.'

He offered what was left of brunch to Mickle, who sucked it up like a vacuum cleaner before asking for more. 'I suspect that you got the best deal, Tia. It's beautiful. Real old England,' he said as he followed her into the living room.

Tia remembered fondly her mother's instructions when most of the third room upstairs had been converted

345

into a bathroom, leaving space in which only a single bed could be housed. The bath itself was plonked – Ma's word – in the middle of the room. It had clawed feet and brass taps and it made rude noises when emptying. The washbasin was massive, easily big enough to provide a bath for a six-month-old baby, while the lavatory tried to hide coyly between two stout, vertical oak beams.

'You like Rose Cottage, don't you, Teddy?'

'It's wonderful.' This was his favourite room. Doors were oak planks held together by diagonal stretches of the same material, walls and ceiling were lumpy between vertical and horizontal beams, while the floor, covered in places by faded rugs, was flagged and worn. Logs were stashed under an oak settle, and the fireplace had an oven attached to it. Ancient pewter plates and tankards sat on a rack near the ceiling, and a wooden pulley clothes-dryer was currently parked high in the air until required. 'I could live here,' he said. The kitchen was big enough to contain him and Tom Quirke. 'I could work here.'

Tia laughed. 'I wish you'd seen Ma when she got the cottages electrified. "Discreet" was her constant cry. Until we got used to it, we needed an oil lamp or a candle to find switches and sockets hidden in cupboards or between shelves. We got many a bump in the dark, especially if she moved furniture. She paid for the mains to be laid between the village and here. There's no gas on the estate. We depend on coal, wood and electricity. Come on, I'll show you some decadent splendour. You are going to love Bartle Hall.'

Isadora was at war with a chicken, and she wasn't winning. The giblets, removed by a butcher, lay in a white enamel dish on the drainer; from these innards, she was supposed to produce gravy. On the kitchen table sat the offending bird in a roasting tin. In spite of repeated basting, it was a bit burnt on the outside, while a skewer used to test the inside continued to produce blood. She had read the book. The theory was twenty minutes per pound, plus twenty minutes added on at the end. 'Joan?' she called in desperation.

Joan Reynolds entered the arena. 'Yes?'

'It won't cook. I've done everything according to the book, but it's raw inside and crisp outside.'

Joan arrived at her friend's side with a cleaver.

'It's already deceased,' Izzy said.

'I'm going to cut it into small pieces and cook it on the hob. Go and sit down, Izzy. I'll deal with this.'

'Why am I such a failure in the kitchen?'

'You can't be good at everything. You stick to acting while I fry chicken.'

Isadora returned to Portia's sitting room. Everyone else could cook. All her daughters were capable of producing meals, but she was an out-and-out failure. She picked up a newspaper and read about Americans and Russians trying to land on the moon within a decade. 'Silly children,' she muttered. 'Why can't they work together and share the technology? And why can't I roast a chicken?'

She put down the paper and wondered how Portia and Theo were faring. They were made for each other – even she knew that, and she was hyper-protective when it came to her girls. Simon seemed to have become fond of Juliet, while Delia had met a possible partner, so all was well. Except for him; except for Richard being here, in Liverpool. 'He'd better stay away from me today,' she breathed. 'Doing battle with a dead bird is enough.' She picked up Tyger. 'Theo will be back, sweetheart, and you shall have some chicken today. If it doesn't kill you, it will be fit for us to eat.'

The phone rang. She put down the kitten and walked across the room. 'Hello? Ah, Juliet . . . what?' She paused while her youngest daughter sobbed the story into her ear. 'When did this happen?' Isadora was suddenly grateful for the chair Portia had parked next to the telephone table.

She sat down, feeling a great deal older than her years. 'Calm down, my love. Concussion? Is he unconscious? Which hospital? Right. Joan and I will be there – I'll phone for a taxi. Where's your father?' Isadora waited again. 'Good. I hope they throw the Bible, the Qur'an and the *News of the World* at him. Walton Hospital. We're on our way. Stay strong, baby.' She replaced the receiver. 'Joan?' she called.

Joan appeared in the doorway, a smudge of flour on her nose. 'What's the matter?'

Isadora took a deep, steadying breath. 'Richard has put Simon Heilberg in hospital. Concussion. He woke up, but Juliet says he's rather confused.'

Joan wiped floury hands on her apron. 'Where's Richard now?'

'On his way to hell, I hope.'

'Seriously, Izzy.'

'In a cell. He'll probably get a suspended sentence at least, because he's already bound over to keep the peace. Or they may lock him up – I don't know. Turn everything off in the kitchen, wash your face and grab your bag while I telephone for a taxi.'

The two women clung to each other in the back of the cab. Both had known Simon Heilberg for many years. He came from a lovely family, his father a GP, his mother a district nurse, his older sister already a consultant paediatrician in London.

Isadora closed her eyes for a few minutes. *Richard didn't like Simon even before the boy reached his teens.*

When Portia and Simon were seeing each other, my husband hit the roof and maintained his position aloft until this very day. Richard is a right-wing freak. We will all be discovered now by the press, and there's nothing I can do about that. O God, please make Simon well.

They reached the hospital and found Juliet waiting for them at the front entrance. While Joan paid the driver, Isadora leapt out and ran to her daughter. 'How is he?' she asked.

Juliet dashed scalding, fresh tears of relief from her cheeks. 'It's going well, Ma. They've done the X-rays. A small hairline fracture. But his brain hit his skull, and he's rather confused, though they think he isn't bleeding. Pa was arrested. Simon's dad's on his way here; somebody is with him to share the driving. Dr Jones will run the practice while Dr Heilberg's away.'

Joan and Isadora followed Juliet to a small room near the double doors to Men's Surgical. The patient in the bed smiled broadly when they entered. A nurse was adjusting his top quilt when the three women arrived at the bedside. She looked up. 'Who's Juliet?' she asked.

'I am.' Juliet took a step forward.

'Good. He may have something to say to you.'

Simon remained silent.

'He just proposed to you. Well, he proposed to me, but he called me Juliet.' She patted his hand. 'Juliet's here now, Doc. I can't marry you because I'm already wed with three children, and my husband's an amateur boxer – he'd put you in a real coma. You'd better ask her instead.' The nurse smiled at everyone on her way out.

Simon frowned. 'Concussion?' he asked.

'Yes.' Juliet sat on the edge of the bed. 'Do you remember what happened?'

'Some of it. We had no lunch.'

Isadora's relief made her sag against Joan, who put an arm round her waist to steady her.

'I want to go home.' Simon tried to sit up.

'You know the drill,' Juliet reminded him gently. 'Twelve hours at least on coma chart. I'll stay with you. I'll even do your stats if they'll allow me. Just rest. It's your turn to do as you're told.' She turned to the other two women. 'Will you bring me some clean underclothes? And toiletries, toothbrush and so forth, because I won't leave him.'

Isadora nodded before addressing Simon. 'You remember me, I hope.'

'Yes,' he sighed as he drifted off to sleep.

'Should he be sleeping?' Joan asked anxiously.

'He'll be watched,' Juliet promised. 'Sleep isn't coma. Thank you for coming, Ma, Joan. He's going to be fine, I think.'

'And your father?' Isadora whispered.

'No idea,' was the response. 'After what he did to Nanny and Simon, I find it difficult to care about him. He isn't a good man.'

Joan, knowing that Juliet, a Christian, must have searched her soul before delivering that statement, hugged the youngest of her charges. 'Life gets hard sometimes, my princess. Your dad is what he is, and it's a little late for change.'

'I can't forgive him for this, Nanny. Always, I tried to look for goodness in him; always, I've made the effort. But I saw the devil in his face when he crossed that room and tried to kill Simon just because he has a Jewish name.'

Isadora changed the subject. 'Would you like one of us to stay with you while the other goes to fetch your things?'

Juliet reassured them that she was fine, that Simon would be well very soon, and apologized for panicking earlier. 'But I must stay with him.'

A thought occurred to Joan. After bidding Juliet goodbye till later, she ushered Isadora into the corridor. 'We're still within visiting hours. Let's find out whether Rosie's mother is here,' she suggested. They enquired at the main desk and were directed to Geriatrics. 'But she's young,' Isadora whispered to her companion. 'Why is she with the elderly?'

Joan tightened her lips and made no reply, though she knew the answer.

As soon as they reached the ward, Joan spotted Sadie. She was still in her twenties, yet she did not look out of place with her lank hair, vacant eyes, colourless complexion and hands plucking at her skirt.

Isadora stopped abruptly. 'She didn't know us before the suicide attempt, so she certainly won't recognize us now.'

But Joan walked on. 'Hello, Mrs Tunstall. We've been taking care of Rosie.' Isadora caught up with her companion.

Sadie stared blankly at the two women. They stood looking at her, and she didn't like that, so she rose to her feet, turned her chair and sat with her back to them. She was waiting for food. All she wanted was food. Eating was her sole pleasure, and they never gave her enough.

Isadora's eyes scanned the ward. Everyone except Sadie seemed to be at death's door – surely this couldn't be the right place for so young a person?

Joan seemed to read her friend's mind. 'It's either this or a psychiatric hospital, Izzy. Who will explain this to Rosie, and who will tell her?'

'Maggie will, Joan. Come along, let's pack a bag for Juliet.'

'I was provoked,' Richard insisted. 'He's with my youngest daughter now, after trying to ruin the life of my eldest.'

Constable Marsden spoke to Sergeant Dunn. 'He was provoked, sarge. Can we spell that?'

'I am a great fan of Laurel and Hardy, officers, but your comedy lacks wit, wisdom and custard pies. Do you know who I am?'

The constable advised the man under caution that he might have been recognized immediately as Richard Bellamy except for the hair. 'So, according to police in Kent, you assaulted a Miss Joan Reynolds in Chaddington Green just a few days ago. Is that the case?'

Richard offered no reply. He had lost everything. None of his daughters wanted to know him, and the future of the Bellamy dynasty was under threat. The Bellamys had never been as successful as Isadora's lot, but they'd been classical actors, dependable, hardworking and worthy. What had Isadora produced? One teacher, one drummer and one nurse.

'Are you with us, Mr Bellamy?' the sergeant asked.

Again, Richard made no effort no reply.

'Well, you'll have a small room here until morning, when you must answer to magistrates. Putting a doctor in a hospital bed was never a good idea.'

The hero of many of Shakespeare's tragedies and histories sat in a holding cell, his prime emotion self-pity. Isadora held the purse strings, and Bartle Hall was falling apart. Prison beckoned. His temper had got the better of him twice in recent days. Didn't people realize what he was going through? Here he was, stuck in the north of England in prison, in despair and in a mess. His reputation had been dragged across acres of newsprint, reporters were dashing about to interview some of his lovers, and there was no hope for him, none at all.

Isadora took Juliet's necessities to the hospital while Joan waved her magic wand over bits of chicken. While she pursued her rescue mission, Joan pondered on the afternoon's events. Simon would probably be fine, but what about poor Sadie Tunstall? No matter what she had been, what she had done, she did not deserve to be in that terrible state. At the age of twenty-five or so, she had been parked like a mouldy old book on a shelf, hidden where few people would see her. It was all the woman's own work, but she had been driven towards suicide because she had lost control over her own life. 'And from such situations children like Rosie emerge,' she whispered to herself.

Isadora returned. 'Sorry I'm late. I sat with Sadie Tunstall for a while. Simon's cracking some embarrassingly feeble jokes, so we needn't worry about him. Sadie's another matter. She can't be left there. According to the ward sister, all she wants is food. When she's finished her own, she wanders about stealing from the older ladies in there. What can be done, Joan?'

Joan had no idea, and she said so.

'Let's eat,' Izzy suggested, 'because sometimes, the ordinary things keep us sane.'

'Jeez,' Theo breathed. There was nothing ordinary about his new beloved's old childhood home. He had already Jeezed his way past cottages, through woods, around ponds and across gardens. He'd met almost tame deer, some noisy geese, a pregnant pony and a mallard with a flotilla of babies. 'Portia? Is this a stately home?'

353

She grinned broadly. 'No, my love. It's a home in a state, a state of advanced decay. It belonged early on in its long life to a Catholic family who hid priests in it. Henry VIII stayed here while on a hunt and well before he decided to fire the pope. Charles II also spent some time upstairs on his way back to reclaim the throne – the family was staunch Catholic. There's a secret chapel where they celebrated Mass, benedictions, baptisms and weddings. It's in the roof, actually. Ma calls it the thinking room, because it's so peaceful.'

They entered the mansion via a door that meant business – solid oak pinned together by huge studs, with a heavy knocker in the shape of a sword through the heart of a dragon, huge, complaining hinges and a letterbox large enough to take the most cumbersome of envelopes. Inside, Theo ground to a halt. 'Holy Moses,' he said.

'No, he never slept here, Teddy.'

He awarded her a dirty look.

Tia grinned at him. She'd known all along that he would fall in love with Bartle Hall.

'But it's a room, not an entrance hall. It's amazing. I was raised in lodgings and trailers about one twentieth of this size.'

She began his education, telling him that the long table under a decorative arch was placed there for visiting dignitaries and for the master. Court sessions were held here, as were meetings regarding tithes, crops and the allocation of cottages and land. He ran his fingers over lathe and lime plaster walls until Tia told him that horse droppings were sometimes in the mix.

Theo looked upward. The black-and-white ornate patterns continued all the way across the ceiling. 'It needs some work,' he said. 'This must be restored and preserved.'

'In houses like this one, the hall was, in effect, a living

354

room,' she told him. 'They would eat in here before sitting round the fire to tell tales or listen to musicians. Those who had over-indulged in mead or barley wine slept where they dropped. Minstrels played for them, and King Henry probably brought his jester.'

Mickle, clearly unimpressed by the monarchy, sat and scratched an ear before following them through living rooms and the great ballroom. By the time they started the exploration of upstairs, the dog had begun to lag behind. Her owners were strange; they wandered about a great deal. Outside was all right, but this place smelled odd.

Theo and Tia sat side by side on Delia's four-poster. 'What the hell are you gonna do with this place?' he asked her. 'Eighteen bedrooms, bits added on at the back downstairs – I'm so glad they left the front alone. But it's too big to be home for one family.'

'I know.'

He studied her face. 'What do you know, Tia? You've a face so honest that it betrays your secrets. Come on, out with it.'

She paused for a few moments. 'OK. Pa owns it and can't afford to keep it. Ma owns the cottages and a lot of the land. She has some sort of plan to buy the hall from Pa and get it repaired before turning it into a home and school for underprivileged and damaged children. Like Rosie. Rosie cut right through Ma's steel armour and reached the twenty-four-carat core. My mother arranged the appointment for Thursday. On Friday, Rosie will be examined for historic physical and psychological damage. Isadora is a woman of principle, and she intends to put her money where her social conscience lies.'

Theo blinked a couple of times. 'It'll cost thousands to get this place into shape,' he said.

'Ma's wealthy, Ted. I think Delia, Juliet and I would

355

prefer her to use her money this way.' She glanced sideways at him. 'My plan goes further. You and I might run it, especially the education side, while Juliet could be Matron. I know she'll marry Simon, so the Heilberg practice would be in charge of any serious medical problems.' She sighed. 'We'd have to leave Liverpool, of course.'

'Not immediately, surely?'

Tia shook her head. 'It will take years to make Bartle Hall habitable and suitable for children. Ma will work on permissions and some government funding, but she won't find it easy. Neither will she fail, because she never does, and she works hard for the NSPCC. It's just an idea she had. I'm embroidering it, so don't make me lose my thread again.'

He stretched out on the bed. The estate was beautiful. Cleaned up and restored, it would make an enchanting haven in which to grow up. 'What about Thursday?' he asked.

'I'll let you know, Sir. Come along, and I'll show you the long gallery. Any valuable items have been removed by Ma, but it still manages to be spectacular. A great space for children to play marbles.'

They walked hand in hand along a stretch of corridor made just to show off paintings. 'Families who lived in the hall hung their portraits here. Look at the ceiling. All those beams will look lovely once restored, as long as someone manages to kill the woodworm. This house must be used, Teddy. That's why I wanted you to see it. Shortly, we'll go to the kitchen and steal food. Mrs Melia will be staying in her cottage while the hall is empty.' She paused. 'Let's hope it stays empty; if Pa arrives, I might just find my gun and deal with him.'

Theo chuckled. 'You wouldn't!'

'I know. But I can dream, can't I?' She stared hard at him. 'Yes, we'll keep that appointment with officialdom on Thursday; it will be the first step towards Rosie's safety. Let's sit here on the windowsill for a little while.' She clung to his hand when they were seated. 'There's something you should know, Mr Teddy Bear. Don't get upset now.'

'Why the hell would I get—'

'Shush.' She placed her free hand on his lips. 'Listen to me, beautiful boy. We can't count on Sadie or Maggie.'

He frowned.

'Teddy, Maggie is dying. The only people who know are Maggie, myself, my mother and Joan – and now you. That's why our friends are in Broadstairs, because I wanted Rosie to have wonderful memories of her nana. Tom and Nancy have no idea, but they'll notice and summon help if Maggie gets worse. She has months at best. Don't cry, Teddy; don't set me off.'

'Dying?'

'Yes. They're making progress with the treatment of leukaemia, but there's little they can do for Maggie. All she wants is to be with Rosie until – well, for as long as possible.' She wiped his tears with her hand. 'Maggie signed herself out of hospital care before you collected her, sweetheart. She didn't need to sit or lie there like a specimen while they studied her death.'

Theo turned his head and looked out on a world distorted by tears and by imperfections in leaded glass. When he spoke, the words were fractured. 'Poor little Rosie. Poor Maggie.'

'Yes.'

He looked at her. 'How do you manage to be so strong?'

'It's not strength; it's loyalty. Remember my namesake in *The Merchant of Venice*? She was honourable rather than strong, and I try hard to deserve her title. I was given two tasks. The first was to tell you about Maggie's condition when the time seemed right, and the second is to do my best for Rosie. My mother will help with Rosie. She could charm the devil, let alone the welfare people, if she put her mind to it. So yes, Thursday's event will happen, because it's our first step. Wear a suit and a smile, as we shall be meeting strangers. Come on, let's find the dog.' She whistled and Mickle arrived within seconds.

Daphne Melia was in the kitchen, an area big enough to cater for dozens. 'I'm making you a casserole and a fruit cake,' she told them after her introduction to Theo. 'I've had no calls from Broadstairs either here or in Lilac Cottage. But Mrs Bellamy contacted me. Your father's been arrested for hitting someone, so you should be left in peace while you're here.'

'Arrested?' Tia's eyebrows moved north.

The cook/housekeeper nodded. 'The magistrates may pass him on to Crown Court because he's done this twice. That's what your mother said, anyway. She told me you were at Rose Cottage and asked me to look after you.' She frowned. 'I'm due to retire, and I'd like to know you're all safe and settled before I do. But your father seems to have lost the plot.'

Tia sat at the vast, scrubbed table. 'I'll visit you when I can, Mrs Melia.'

'And my sister will be living with me – our Ethel. You know Ethel, because she used to have the post office near the green. But I'll miss this daft house.'

Theo smiled. 'It must be difficult to clean.'

'It is, Mr Quinn. I had help from the village, of course. Are you American?'

'I sure am,' he said, smiling at the large, sweet woman.

'They were here in the war. I remember dances in the ballroom. They brought us stockings and chocolate and tinned fruit. Cheerful, they were. Tia, Delia and Juliet used to run up and down the stairs just to look at the Americans and talk to them.'

'We got bubble gum,' Tia said. 'And they gave us sweets. My father didn't approve of foreigners, but he said little because they were huge men and they were helping win our war for us. Pa wasn't allowed to serve abroad because of his eyesight, and he was probably too old. He did a desk job in London, so we got some peace during the war. That sounds odd, doesn't it?'

The dog wandered in. She'd had enough of the dusty, sneeze-making atmosphere and was glad to find the bright, clean kitchen. Wearing the expression of deep sadness common to most large breeds, she sighed heavily and glanced at Mrs Melia. Mrs Melia, for whom this was love at first sight, found the 'good doggie' a nice slice of tongue and some chicken breast.

'Right,' Theo said, 'time to go before she eats everything you have, Mrs Melia.' They left, followed by a reluctant Mickle, who seemed to have resolved to take a degree in begging for food.

With three whole days to enjoy each other's company, Theo and Tia returned to play house in Rose Cottage. Like a pair of teenagers, they larked about in fields and forests, made love, cleaned their kitchen, made love, drove through one of the most beautiful counties in England, made love, and got ready for Thursday, when the first steps towards a decent future for Rosie would be taken.

Every day, food was brought to the cottage by Mrs Melia, a soul of discretion who entered and left by the kitchen door. She never forgot to bring titbits for Mickle, who came to expect treats every evening. They were a happy family, man, woman and dog, content in their precious cottage. But all too soon it was Wednesday evening, and the pretend honeymoon was over.

They sat on the small sofa with Mickle stretched out at their feet. Reality peeped over the horizon. Theo, in an effort to find a diversion, flicked through a magazine. 'It says here that Faversham was once the explosive capital of Kent, because six factories produced gunpowder. So it wasn't all hop fields and oast houses.' He glanced at his companion. 'Portia?'

She sighed. 'Poor Maggie. Poor Rosie.'

'Baby, we can only do what we can do.'

'I feel useless,' she said.

'Isadora would never produce a useless daughter.'

'Teddy, what chance do we have of saving Rosie from being sent away?'

'We have your mother. Your mother is big guns.'

Tia managed a weak smile. 'You're my big gun.'

He chuckled. 'Flattery will get you everywhere, swee-tie. Let's go to bed.'

Joan was cleaning Theo's flat when the doorbell sounded. She put down the duster, patted her hair, removed her apron and answered the door. 'Yes? May I help you?' A very well-groomed young woman lingered under the porch.

Emily Garner blinked. 'Is Mr Quinn available?'

'Er . . . no. He's still away.'

Emily introduced herself and told Joan that she was really looking for Mrs Margaret Stone.

'She's away, too. She's taken Rosie to the seaside for a few days.'

'And Miss Bellamy?'

'She went with them.'

Several seconds passed while the intruder pursed her

lips as if deep in thought. 'Is Mr Quinn with them?' she asked eventually.

'I have no idea, Miss Garner. Miss Bellamy's mother and sister have decided to join them, so there's no one here except me and the cat. I understand that Mr Quinn's family is in America, so he may have gone there. Mrs Stone, Rosie and Miss Bellamy were touring in Kent, I believe.'

The visitor went on to explain that she was concerned about Rosie, as her grandmother was not in the best of health, while the child's mother seemed to have sustained irreversible brain damage after her suicide attempt.

Joan opened the door fully. 'Come in, please.' She led the elegant female into Theo's living room. 'It's been a dreadful time,' Joan commented. 'That murder, Sadie's terrible condition, Maggie's anaemia.'

Emily agreed. 'The police seem to have abandoned the search for the murderer.' She paused. 'Miss Bellamy's mother is *the* Isadora Bellamy, I understand. Richard Bellamy's behaviour has been widely reported. When he's released, this house will not be a safe place for little Rosie. She may have to go into the care of the local authority.'

Joan sat on her anger and on an easy chair, motioning with a hand until the interloper sat opposite her. 'Maggie can take Rosie back to her own house.'

'Is Mrs Stone well enough for that?'

'Yes,' Joan lied. 'She has medication.'

'Do you have a contact number, please?'

'No.' For a reason she could not discover, Joan didn't like this young woman, and untruths came easily. 'They're moving about all the time. Miss Bellamy has a vehicle, so—'

'That sports car?'

'A large van,' Joan answered almost snappily.

'I see.' Emily Garner rose gracefully. 'Are you the cleaner?'

'No. I was nanny to Portia, Cordelia and Juliet Bellamy. I am now companion and dresser to Isadora.' *It's Thursday, Joan. It's ten o'clock. By half past eleven, the first step will have been taken. Please, God, make it work. Rosie must not fall into the hands of people like this creature,* 'If you'll excuse me, I must get on, Miss Garner.'

'Of course. Thank you for your time.'

Alone once more, Joan Reynolds picked up Tyger. There was something comforting about the warmth and playfulness of a young animal. She remembered holding 'her' girls as newborns, as toddlers, as teenagers with all the accompanying angst and enthusiasms. 'Because of you, I couldn't be with my family today, Tyger.' Juliet had travelled with her mother, and Joan missed their chatter. 'But I don't mind, puss-cat. Someone must look after you.'

She cleaned, had a cup of coffee, cleaned again, made a pot of tea and some toast. Every second seemed as long as a minute; every minute was an hour. Portia would be with her mother and her sisters now. Simon Heilberg had stayed in Liverpool, as had his father, though Simon was now almost fully recovered. 'We are always parents, no matter how old our children,' she told the purring feline. 'Even parents by proxy feel the pain and the joy.'

It would be happening soon. She stroked the kitten. 'Please, God,' she breathed yet again. 'Let the plan work for all of them, but especially for Rosie.'

A single tear made its way down a careworn cheek. She suddenly felt homesick for that draughty old house and for the fields and villages of Kent. A clock struck the hour. 'Now,' she whispered. 'It's happening now, little kitty.'

*

In a waiting room within the impressive civic complex of Canterbury, Maggie sat reading Rosie's holiday diary. The little girl had cut pictures out of her 'bro-chewers', and one of them showed Canterbury Cathedral. Having viewed it at closer quarters this morning, Maggie had to admit that she had never seen a building so impressive.

The diary was an interesting mess, because Rosie had been generous with glue, and some pages clung together like lovers. 'You're going to be special, Rosie,' Maggie whispered to the sticky item. She looked up and saw Tom and Nancy at the other end of the room. They were gazing through windows at the splendid city. They'd been for a walk and had returned completely bewitched by medieval lanes so narrow that people in opposing doorways could almost shake hands.

'Nancy found a smashing wool shop,' Tom had said.

Nancy You're-Right Atherton's answer? 'You're right, love. I've spent all my wool money, but I got a lovely four-ply in mauve.'

Maggie smiled to herself. Rosie, Izzy, Tia, Delia and Juliet were getting ready in the Pack Horse Inn. Everyone had to be smart today. Theo was already here. He'd gone into the inner chamber to await the arrival of the rest of the party and to meet officials in charge of this morning's business.

Struggling with her granddaughter's innovative spelling, Maggie read reports on the Kentish seaside. The motto of Broadstairs meant Star of the Sea. Punch and Judy were funny, but Punch hit everyone with a stick, and there was a real dog in the story and sausages, too. The sand was too hot to stand in without shoes. Running a hotel wasn't easy – too much adding up and were there enough potatoes and how many towels had been stolen this month? Then there was all that carpet, loads of sweeping and bed-making and sand everywhere. Rosie Stone was going to be a doctor with a car and a nice house.

Deal made Maggie grin. She whispered the text in an effort to help decipher it. 'We seen France across the water and another castle put in Deal by that fat bad king who cut heads off called Henry. There were lots of people and the water was clean with loads of fishing boats and a man mending nets with a bald head,' she read aloud while trying not to giggle. Spelling and so forth would come later, she supposed. All Margate got was a reference to a 'bewtifull' clock tower and a real windmill. Ramsgate fared better with very blue water, hundreds more boats, lovely churches and a shop where Rosie had acquired a straw hat.

The latest page was wonderful. *I met a Jerman lady and a Jerman man. They was dead nice and very sorry about the boms and intrestin cos their langwij is a relashun of Englich they told me and got me ice cream.* Maggie smiled again. Rosie loved ice cream, so the spelling of it was perfect. *Keep her safe, Lord. Sadie's brain is wrecked, so what we're doing here has to work.*

She squeezed Rosie's diary into her new handbag. 'Come on, Tom, Nancy. They've given us padded chairs through there.'

They entered the larger room where Theo was talking to two officials at a large table.

Tom stared at Maggie. 'Is this what it looks like? Is this a—'

Maggie nodded. 'Keep quiet,' she said.

'She's right,' Nancy whispered. 'If it's a meeting about Rosie, we'd best shut up.' Without her knitting, she was bereft, so she fiddled with a string of glass beads at her throat. Would mauve suit Maggie? Should she have chosen the beige? What sort of questions were these Canterbury folk going to ask about Rosie and her terrible life in the house next door to hers and Tom's?

The door opened. Portia Bellamy, radiant in ivory silk and carrying cream roses, walked in with her mother, who wore blue. The two sisters followed; even Delia had been forced to wear a skirt. Between them skipped little Rosie in a pink organza dress, pink shoes, pink gloves and carrying a pink bag. She grinned at her nana. 'It was a secret,' she announced audibly. 'We didn't know till today. I'm the bridesmaid and the rings are in my hand-bag. I'm in charge.' She waved at her small audience. From her wrist dangled a ribbon holding pink rosebuds arranged in the shape of a small sphere.

Nancy finally realized what was happening and burst into tears. She had nothing to mop her face with, not even a bit of knitting. Tom thrust a handkerchief at her. 'Don't start,' he whispered. 'You'll have us swimming out of here, love.'

Tom, Nancy and Maggie walked behind the party and sat near the front of the register office. Little Rosie was in her element, in her favourite colour from head to foot, and guardian of wedding rings. Even her socks were pink. This was the biggest and bestest part of her whole holi-day, and she would write it in her holiday book later. Oh, and she must ask the bride how to un-stick stuck pages.

Theo watched as his girl walked towards him. She was so elegant, so poised, so . . . so top-drawer English. The fight was over, and she had won, of course. On the eve of their wedding, she had instigated a ritual in which he had been forced to partake. He now knew that the smell of burning French letters was not pleasant. She would have his children, and to hell with what anyone thought or said.

He couldn't take his eyes off her. The dress had no

adornments and needed none, as its simplicity celebrated her figure, her taste and her very essence. That wonderful hair was up and woven in swathes around ivory ribbon. Perfect skin, perfect face, her mother's perfect pearls at her throat.

He swallowed nervously. Did he deserve this beautiful creature? Then he saw her beaming smile and knew that he did, because she had agreed gladly to marry him. Perhaps the wedding might not have happened just yet, but the ill-fated Maggie was going to join Isadora in the battle for the Quinns to become foster parents for Rosie. Sense did not preclude love; nor did love stand at a distance from sense.

'Hi,' the bride mouthed at him. 'You look wonderful.'

He saw the child in pink, noticed Delia, rather angular but smart in light grey, Juliet with a white Juliet cap and in a pale yellow dress, his stunning soon-to-be mother-in-law beautiful in blue. Smiling back at Portia, Theo spoke loudly enough for all to hear. 'And you *are* wonderful,' he said.

This was the point at which Tom's handkerchief went into overdrive. Nancy mopped up the flood and, right on cue, Isadora wept quietly into a lace-edged square after handing her precious daughter to Theo.

Rosie tutted softly. Why were they crying? They had nothing at all to cry about; they should try being responsible for two solid gold rings in a small handbag. She sighed and concentrated on the proceedings. Many people were silly, and most of the daftest were grown-ups. The world was strange sometimes, and she should have used less glue.

Sixteen

Maggie and Tom signed as witnesses to the marriage. Nancy was in too soggy a state to act as signatory; her writing might have been rather shaky and tear-stained, and she had no knitting to calm her nerves. The glass necklace had been twisted towards every point on the compass, and she had bitten one thumbnail almost to its quick. Tom's handkerchief was in knots, as was Nancy's poor stomach. In a strange place with no wool, no needles, and with no opportunity to tell people they were right, she was as lost as the Babes in the Wood. 'Lovely couple,' she muttered repeatedly while rocking to and fro.

Tom tried but failed to calm his wife; her nerves were getting on his nerves.

While Maggie carefully penned her name on the licence, bride and groom glanced at each other, both pairs of eyes glistening with unshed tears. There was a sad side to this happy day. It felt as if Maggie were bequeathing Rosie to them, even though they and she knew that there would be many miles of red tape to disentangle in the future. But there was one huge certainty: everyone in this wedding party loved the child.

However, there would be confusion at school, because a Mrs Quinn was going to teach reception class, while the Miss Bellamy who had been appointed to the post no longer existed. Theo and Tia had discussed the situation in depth, but they had always reached the same conclusion. Both were good teachers; both adhered to the principle that a happy child learned quickly and usually managed to extend to his full potential. Together, they might just be a force for the good, so she would not move to a different school, and the staff at Myrtle Street must get used to their hasty marriage.

Rosie was skipping about the register office like the Queen of the May, though this was July, and she wore no crown. She looked at portraits of dead dignitaries, mayors and aldermen, most with facial hair. She didn't like beards and moustaches, so she went to examine the marriage certificate instead. 'What's a spinister?' she asked Theo.

'Spinster,' he answered. 'A woman who has never been married.'

Rosie looked at Tia. 'But you are married. You just married Mr Quinn. I know, because I was the bridesmaid and that man there told us that you are husband and wife. And thank you for my outfit – it's lovely.'

Tia laughed. 'But I was a spinster when I came in.'

'Oh. Was Mr Quinn a spinster?'

'A bachelor.'

Rosie chewed her lip. 'Did you spin, Miss ... Mrs Quinn?' She giggled. 'That was like a little poem.'

Tia beamed at her. 'No, but that's where the word began, clever girl. Unmarried women stayed at home and spun wool or cotton, you see. Thank you for looking after the rings. You are a wonderful bridesmaid. Now, we're going home to celebrate and eat.'

The child raised her eyebrows. 'Liverpool home?'

Tia placed a hand on Rosie's shining brown curls. 'Kent home, sweetie. My home.'

'Priest holes?'

'Yes, if you can find them.'

Rosie swallowed. 'Dark? Like coal sheds?'

'No coal. And you don't need to shut yourself in.' The bride squatted down. 'If priest holes frighten you, we won't do the hide-and-seek game. Oh, and you and Nana will sleep in a real four-poster bed, but don't play with the drapes, because they're old and falling to bits. Tom and Nancy will borrow Lilac Cottage while Mrs Melia – she's our cook – stays with you in the big house, and my mother will sleep at Bartle Hall, too, as will my sisters, though Delia will have to get back to London soon. It will be fun, I promise. Don't be afraid.' Surely the child would be safe from now on? Teddy would house Maggie and Rosie at Crompton Villa or at another of his houses in Wavertree or Belle Vale, so—

Theo interrupted Tia's thoughts. 'May I borrow my wife, Rosie? We have to go.' He led the party out, noticing that Nancy made a beeline for the van and her knitting. It was as if she had spent her life making security blankets in many different colours, because knitting was her prop. He smiled. *Thank God for women like Nancy, since they redress the balance somewhat. Here comes my bride. She's lively and probably can't knit or be shy. There's going to be fun, and I am one lucky son of a gun.*

At the pavement's edge, a decorated Rolls-Royce awaited the newly-weds. Everyone else would be driven to Chaddington Green by Delia, for whom the converted ambulance was a dream compared to the skiffle van. 'Does it have luxuries like a second gear?' she asked her new brother-in-law. 'And brakes?'

'Yes, it does.'

'Don't all vehicles have second gear?' Tia asked.

'Apparently not. Enjoy the drive,' Theo said.

'Oh, I shall.' Delia clapped. 'I'm sick of double-declutching down to first in Ariadne. We need a new van. One of these days, she's going to die in the middle of a traffic jam. She overheats, too. Probably menopausal.'

Theo chuckled. 'Stop moaning and I'll think about giving you this one. Her name's Lily-Mae, and yes, she was an ambulance in her previous life. So she's built to last.'

Delia's face lit up like Christmas, and she jumped up and down in the manner of an overgrown version of Rosie. 'You're a prince, Theo,' she exclaimed before kissing his cheek. She climbed into the vehicle. 'Wagons roll,' she shouted before closing the door.

Theo held his wife's hand. 'Delia's lovely when she smiles, isn't she?'

Tia paused on her way to the car. 'She has a fabulous brain, too, starts at Imperial College London in October. Chemistry, I believe, but she won't give up the drums. At the age of ninety, she'll probably still be clattering about on her instruments even if she's in a wheelchair.'

Delia blew him a kiss and waved a cheeky hand.

Theo shook his head. Would he ever get used to this multi-faceted family? A family. At last, he had a whole new nest of strong women, a sturdy structure into which he could lean for support. They all knew his history – well, most did. Richard Bellamy, who knew little or nothing, was currently on bail and living where the police and magistrates had parked him pending his appearance in Crown Court. When he finally found out that Portia had married a man of mixed race . . . The groom put a stop to that train of thought and helped his wife into the Rolls. He picked up the hem of her long skirt and swept it away from the door. 'You look terrific,' he told her.

'Thank you, headmaster.'

Shaking his head, he climbed into the Rolls.

They sat side by side. 'Married,' he murmured. 'Mr and Mrs Quinn.'

'Two chiefs and no Indians,' was her typically smart reply.

'Don't count on it, baby. I own you now.'

She grinned broadly. 'Oh, yeah? Wanna bet?'

Theo shook his head. 'Are you American?' he asked.

'Only half and only by marriage.' She kissed him hard.

For almost the whole journey, Tia wore an enigmatic smile.

Theo studied her. *She is up to something. She wore that look the day she built the dolls' house extension and when she made that low table for Harry the Scoot. Oh, and when she beat me soundly at archery class. My beautiful Portia has a secret. When we go to bed, I'll tickle it out of her. My wife . . . oh, she is gorgeous, hates to be tickled, says it's a form of torture. Silence me with kisses, eh? Wait till I get you back to Rose Cottage, you besom.*

'Are you happy?' she asked, the voice calmer than a sleeping baby.

'Yes, very happy, but you're keeping something from me. I can tell by your quiet voice that something's going down.'

'Would I do that to you? You really think I'd keep a secret from the man I love?' She tutted sadly. 'Oh, ye of little faith,' she whispered. 'Don't you trust me, Teddy?'

He raised an eyebrow and asked the driver not to be startled. 'I'm going to tickle her now till she crumbles. I have a situation that requires immediate attention. Things may get noisy back here.'

The uniformed man spoke. 'OK, sir.'

'Not in my wedding dress,' Tia said haughtily.

'Take it off.'

'No.'

'This is day one, and your refusal to cooperate is noted.'

Tia sniffed and poked out her tongue.

Her husband patted his pockets. 'I've an envelope and

a stamp here somewhere. I'll find a use for that tongue, Mrs Quinn.'

She grabbed his arm. 'I'll tell you this much, old man. There is a surprise, and you are going to love every minute of it, so hush. I can say no more, because I have no details. Ma hadn't enough time to make thorough arrangements.'

'Oh?'

'Hush.'

'Make me hush.'

She kissed him again. It was the only way to stop him talking.

It was an amazing sight. The main street of Chaddington Green was lined with people. There were farmhands in smocks and battered hats, men in Tudor clothing that included tights and breeches, children in Victorian costume with the compulsory cover-all aprons on girls, the knee-length trousers on boys. But the most stunning were women in Tudor dresses hired by the bride's mother. This was a Bartle Hall wedding of the eldest child, and historical pageantry must endure. 'Ma's been working hard on the phone,' Tia said.

Theo closed his gaping mouth. 'These chaps in frocks,' he began.

'Smocks, Teddy.'

'What are they throwing under our wheels?'

'Ah, that's corn almost ready for harvesting. Had we married during a different season of the year, they would have thrown seeds. It's to wish us fruitful so that the manor house will have an heir. From today, no matter where we live, Bartle Hall will be our official address.'

He grinned. 'It's wonderful. Americans would pay a few bucks to see this. We should have sold tickets, could have made a fortune.'

Tia laughed. 'Yes, it's fun.'

'You're right, as usual.'

Tia's smile mirrored his. 'This is only the beginning, my darling. Ma didn't get too much time while we made up our minds, but she will have pulled out many of the stops. I wonder what Rosie thinks of these crazy carryings-on?'

'She'll love the madness of it,' he replied. 'And so do I. But I love you more.'

'Same to you, Teddy.' She turned. 'They're doing the walk now. Even the grand ballroom will be packed. See? They're following us. Just be grateful that they're not leading goats and cows like they did in bygone days.'

When they reached the manor house and entered the large hallway, a boy dressed as a page handed Theo a pewter mug, while a man in blue and gold livery presented him with a sword in a decorative scabbard. 'Guard thy house,' the man ordered before relieving the groom of this heavy burden.

Theo blinked a couple of times and watched his wife. She was crowned with a coronet of flowers, and a piece of material was placed in her hands. 'What's that?' he whispered, looking at the cloth.

'It's a placket.'

'A what-et?'

'To be let into my gown when I am large with child. Don't drink that water yet – there's an order of . . . well, there are rules.'

Isadora dashed in. She kissed her daughter and son-in-law before explaining that their thrones were in storage with the rest of the valuable furniture. 'We got you a couple of carvers from the Punch Bowl. Follow me into the ballroom and sit down while the girls do the dance.'

In the huge ballroom, the man who had presented the

sword nodded at some small children. They gathered in a circle, all standing stiffly and with upper limbs rigid by their sides. Blue Regalia, who was clearly master of ceremonies, spoke. 'Take up the hands of friendship and love. We pay tribute to all who died of the Black Death plague and pray God it shall never again blight our cities.'

The little ones joined hands and performed Ring-a-Roses.

'Why?' Theo whispered.

'Because they sneezed and dropped dead. The song is about the plague.'

'Cheerful for a wedding,' he complained.

'Shut up, or I'll gag you with my placket, Teddy.' She would tell him later about Elizabeth I, a great monarch who had decreed that green land must be preserved around cities to separate them from villages, thereby saving farming communities from pestilence. She would give him the history of a master of Bartle Hall who, unwilling to bring disease home to Chaddington, had died of the plague in London. For now, she whispered, 'Children dancing and singing tell the Black Death to bugger off. We can't celebrate unless we follow the rules.'

'I'd better shut my mouth, then, but I will get you later.'

Things cheered up after the Ring-a-Roses dance was over. Blue Regalia ordered the groom to allow his wife the first taste of Chaddington Green well water from the tankard. After fulfilling that task, Theo was allowed to taste it himself. The pair were then handed a lovers' plate whose shape imitated a number eight. From this article, each fed the other salmon with salad while Morris dancers arranged themselves in the middle of the floor.

Theo stared at the men who jingled when they moved. An elderly chap played an accordion badly while eight fully grown males in abbreviated trousers and with bells on their stockings leapt about with sticks. A ninth man, clearly the village idiot, jumped in and out of the set trying to avoid the clashing weapons. 'They'll kill him, Portia.'

Tia shook her head. 'They're skilled in the art of lunacy. When they're not busy, we use them as scarecrows.' She winked. 'Joke,' she said. 'Two are lawyers, one's an accountant, and the lunatic is our vicar.'

'Is anyone here normal, Portia?'

'No. We don't do normal; normal is boring.'

The newly-weds spotted Nancy. Reunited with her knitting, she sat happily in a corner with Maggie and Tom. There was no sign of Rosie. She should have been easy to spot in all that pink, but she seemed to have disappeared. Ah, there she was. The pink had been abandoned, and she wore a bonnet, a floor-length black dress, and a white, cover-all apron over the sombre garment. She was Victorian, and she was playing with two older girls in costumes that celebrated the turn of the eighteenth into the nineteenth century, very high-waisted and Jane Austen-esque. 'Isn't she beautiful?' Tia sighed.

'And brainy,' Theo answered. 'Emily Garner can go to hell.'

Blue Regalia approached the couple once the Morris dancers had finished larking about. Theo stared hard at him; he had never seen anyone dressed like this except, perhaps, in some very bad film about olde England.

'The Charges,' Tia whispered. 'At each pause, say aye.'

'I?'

'A-Y-E. And don't make me laugh.'

'OK.'

The room was suddenly silent.

'Wilt thou hear the Charges?' Blue Regalia asked.

'Aye.'

'Wilt thou honour this woman?'

'Aye.'

'Wilt thou guard her and lay down thy life to save hers?'

'Aye!'

'Wilt thou cleave to her and only to her?'

'Aye!' From the corner of his mouth, Theo whispered to his beloved. 'There's a lot of wilting. What if I wilt?'

Tia exploded with laughter, and covered her mouth with the placket.

Even Blue Regalia showed signs of mirth. 'Wilt thou mind her health and sustain her with food and drink?'

'Aye!'

'Wilt thou guard and shelter thine issue, feed and clothe them well?'

'Aye, I wilt!'

Blue Regalia chuckled quietly. 'Then unto thee we give this maiden, daughter of the house of Bartholomew. Go now to the feast prepared by wenches of this parish.' He bowed, backed off, then turned to walk away. Shaking shoulders betrayed him – he was laughing hard.

'Who the hell's Bartholomew?' Theo asked.

'The original owner. He got cut down to Bart, and there was no anaesthetic back then; it must have been traumatic. He was king of all he surveyed, yet he worked the land. Come, I'll show you.'

'Are we allowed to move?'

'Of course. Protocol ended with the Charges.' She led him through to her father's study. On a wall hung a framed item, a page covered in scrawl and blots of ink. 'See?' she said. 'Bart's work. The house took his name and added a couple of letters – hence Bartle.'

Theo stared at it. *I did plant too many feedf in the rowef and my crop did not thrive.* 'So the F is S?' he asked.

'Fometimef,' was her reply. 'Look at this line here.'

He stared closely. *I did buy for mine wyffe a placket.* 'So she was pregnant?'

'Permanently.'

'Bugger.'

'Yes, that too. They had to get their fun wherever they could back then.'

'Lock up your daughters?'

'And your animals, Teddy.'

'No,' he exclaimed.

Tia giggled. This was unusual, as she seldom giggled. Her laughter was loud and unrestrained, yet here she was, almost behaving herself.

She looked him up and down. 'You have a terrible mind. There were rustlers, just as there were in the wild west of America. If you stole a man's horse, you'd get into more trouble than if you made off with his wife or his daughter. They had their priorities right. Now, we eat.'

'Good. I'm ready to expire.'

Tia narrowed her eyes. 'Don't you dare die on me. Not yet, anyway. You just agreed in the Charges to lay down your life for me, and I'll tell you when I've had enough of you.'

She isn't going to improve, is she, Theo? And underneath all the banter, she's a loving girl, all bark and no bite. Would I prefer a gentler, quieter wife? No. I haven't felt so alive in years. And I will deal with her later, because that's part of my job. She's staring at me. 'What?' he asked.

'I just noticed – you're very handsome.'

'You're right. You'll have to work hard to deserve me.'

She pushed him towards the door. 'Eat,' she commanded.

Trestle tables were being set up in the ballroom. Because Isadora had shifted most valuables, the hall suffered from a serious deficiency in the furniture department, so the local school and inn had been raided.

'Oh, look,' Tia declared. 'We have a three-piece suite. It should be four, but Mr Blake's missing. Ah, here he comes. We're having chamber music. He'll be on the spinet. Gloria Marchant is violin, Sam Sparrow plays the viola, and Judith Collins drapes herself over a cello.'

Enough food to nourish a small African nation was carried in by 'wenches', of which number Rosie was one. To the strains of 'Greensleeves', platters, tureens and a wedding cake were placed on tables. Mrs Melia arrived with Mickle, who ran to greet her master before embarking on a good old skulk beneath laden boards. Lurking was one of her skills, and she knew that the two-legged often dropped tasty morsels, especially when faced with the tragic eyes of a hound. The place was noisy, but she would cope with that as long as she got food.

'My dog is a thief,' Theo complained.

'She's just being a dog,' his wife advised him.

Rosie was having a great time. She had to say everything twice, but she didn't mind, because the reverse was also true, since her companions owned an accent. She noticed that Delia and Juliet were surrounded by chattering people and that Mr and Mrs Quinn went everywhere hand in hand, wandering from group to group. There was so much joy that even a room as large as this could scarcely contain it. She sat down to watch.

Over in the same corner as before, Nancy was making progress with her knitting, while Tom lingered near a door talking to a group of men in smocks and daft hats. Nana was grinning at small playing children, and Mrs Melia was handing something in a bottle to Nana. Everyone was smiling. It was a huge room and it overflowed with happiness.

Rosie crawled under a long tablecloth and lay down, with Mickle acting as her pillow. *So this is rich. It's the same kind of rich as the hotel in Broadstairs, all sweeping and dusting and such a long way to bedrooms. My kind of rich might be a flat like Mr Quinn's and a car and gardens and a dog like Mickle.*

Mam isn't going to get better. Nana told me on Tuesday while I was making sandcastles with my bucket and spade. Mam is like a little girl or even a baby again. She's gone backwards and needs looking after. They done tests on her and said she's not a grown-up no more. There's a bit of sadness in Nana's eyes, even when she smiles or laughs, and I think it's because of Mam. Sometimes, she seems far away, as if she's talking about one thing and thinking about something else, something not nice.

If Mr Quinn and Miss Bellamy – I mean Mrs Quinn – decide to stay here and I go back to Liverpool with Nana, we will have to live in Nana's house. Nana's is better than ours was, but there's still no garden and no cat and no dog. But I mustn't be greedy, cos I've been lucky with this holiday and everything.

A lot has happened today. We got picked up at the hotel and taken to another hotel in Canterbury. I didn't know I was a bridesmaid until they had me all dressed up in pink and told me to mind the rings. They bought my frock at a shop, but it fitted all right.

Tom and Nancy didn't know, either, but Nana did. We all got ready in a room at the new hotel. When we got to the office place, Nancy started crying. They should have let her bring her knitting. She's happy as long as she's knitting. Nana says Nancy's knitting would probably stretch all round the fattest part of the world if somebody stuck all the knitting together.

Juliet joined Rosie and the dog under the table. 'Are you tired?' she asked.

Rosie nodded.

'It is an exhausting business, being a bridesmaid. You did very well, though, like a professional. Have you done it before?'

'No. I never had nice clothes.'

'You looked beautiful.'

'So did you. You look like Miss Bellamy, but smaller. She's Mrs Quinn now.' A short pause followed. 'Juliet, will they live here?'

'No.' Juliet watched as relief flooded the little girl's face. 'But Tia owns Rose Cottage, so I expect they'll come during holidays.'

Rosie beamed. She told Juliet about Harry the Scoot and Martha, his sister, before recounting the tale of her life so far. 'Uncle Miles was murdered and my mam couldn't get gin in hospital or prison, so she tried to go to Jesus. We'll have to look after her, cos she can't look after herself no more.'

The bride's youngest sister took hold of Rosie's hand. 'Did you like Canterbury?'

'Yes, it was pretty.'

'Will you come with me to Canterbury tomorrow? Tia and Mr Quinn will come, too.'

'They're not getting married again, are they?'

Juliet laughed. 'No, but they may have a church blessing while they're here in Chaddington Green. Dr Heilberg's father's partner and I have arranged to get you examined to see if Uncle Miles hurt you. There will be special photographs that show your bones.'

Rosie pondered. 'Why? He's dead, so he can't get in trouble for hurting me now, can he?'

The youngest daughter of the household bit her lip. This child was so precious, so knowing, yet innocent. 'We just want to make sure you're well, Rosie. Afterwards, we'll go and have afternoon tea at the Pack Horse where we got dressed this morning. The owners moved here from Devon, and they do cream teas. You'll love it.'

'All right. Shall I wear my best dress?'

'Not the bridesmaid one.'

'No, I have a red check with matching bag and shoes.'

'That will do nicely, Miss Stone.'

They both giggled.

'Will you marry Dr Heilberg, Juliet?'

'Probably.'

'Is that probably nearly yes?'

Juliet nodded. 'Our secret, yes?'

'Assolutely.'

'Oh, Rosie, I love you.'

On the evening following his wedding, Theodore Patrick Quinn realized that he had learned several things. English eccentricity could be extreme and charming; Queen Elizabeth I had ordered the creation of green, clean areas around cities in order to stop the spread of plague; an owner of Bartle Hall, once Bart's Manor, had died of said plague in order to save his community; Kent, once known to Theo as Hellfire Corner, was a beautiful place; lovemaking without any barrier was bliss.

He stared into a pair of impossibly violet eyes. 'So we begin,' he said, running a finger down the side of her face. 'Because you are a determined madam, and because I love you to the point of insanity, we have opened the baby-making factory. And I wilt keep thine issue fed and watered—'

'You didn't wilt.'

'I'm sorry I laughed – couldn't help it. If he'd said "wilt" once more, I would have slid off my chair.'

'It was a pity that the Tudor thrones were in storage – they're all hand-carved and special. But it was a fun wedding, wasn't it?'

'Will it be fun if we have a coloured child?'

'I don't know. I don't know whether having a child is fun or agony. But I do prefer dark-haired people, because their faces have a frame. Blonde hair blends with fair skin, so it's a bit bland, no punctuation.'

'Maybe we'll get a dark-skinned blonde?'

She agreed that such a person might have an interesting appearance. 'As long as any child of ours doesn't get your father's red hair.'

'Don't discriminate,' he whispered.

'Don't wilt.'

'OK.'

A group of anxious people sat in welcome shade outside the Pack Horse Inn, which was well placed in the centre of a truly magnificent city. They sipped on chilled fruit juices and waited. Waiting wasn't easy. Theo and Tia clutched at each other's hands while Delia tried hard to ignore her watch. 'Juliet may be talking to Matron about doing midwifery in Liverpool,' she said eventually.

Isadora agreed, as did Nancy. 'You're right, love. She'll have loads of mates down here, too, won't she? This is where she done all her learning until now. I hope Maggie likes this colour. I'll keep it meself if she doesn't.' She touched her husband's arm. 'I'm right, aren't I, love? About Juliet seeing all her friends, like?'

'Course you're right, Nancy.' He sighed heavily. 'And to think we were at a wedding round the corner just over twenty-four hours since.' He ran a hand through what was left of his hair. He and Nancy had heard most of Rosie's pain. Closing his eyes, he confronted the sound of Rosie crying, of the shed door banging shut, of his wife weeping while she made jam butties or banana butties or a pan of chips for that poor kiddy.

Isadora studied him. 'Don't, Tom,' she whispered. 'We can't mend Rosie's past, but we sure as hell can make her a suit of armour for the future.'

Nancy changed needles. 'You're right, Izzy,' she pronounced.

'Maggie will be nervous.' Tia leaned her head against her man's shoulder.

'We couldn't all go to the hospital,' Theo said. 'It would have been like an invasion. Juliet knows what she's doing, and all the docs know her. They'll be doing a thorough job, that's all.'

Theo got busy writing I LOVE YOU on Tia's palm.

She responded by outlining WILT NOT on his.

Nancy surprised the whole company by putting down her knitting and standing up. 'I won't be long,' she said.

'Where are you going?' Tom asked his wife.

'Shop next door to the wool shop, love. Toys. They have nice paintboxes and big books with blank pages. And they had a skipping rope with ball bearings in the handles, so it'll turn smooth. I'll ask if they sell glue not as runny as that stuff she uses now. I'd be frightened of putting my knitting down when she's cutting and sticking.'

Tom blinked and his jaw dropped. His wife had delivered a speech. 'Shopping in Canterbury? On your own?'

'That's right. I'm going all by myself.' She walked away.

'Well,' Tom folded his arms, 'there's a first time for everything, I suppose. It took months to make her go round the corner without me.' He paused. 'She was left locked in the house when she was a child. Her mother had to go to work, see. I think that's why Nancy felt so bad for Rosie when she got shut in with the coal.' He smiled. 'Look at my Nancy now, crossing a main road without me. It's a bloody miracle.'

'You love the bones of her,' Theo said.

'Don't Liverpool sayings sound odd with an American accent?' Tia asked.

Isadora laughed. 'Your husband has a lovely accent, Portia.'

Delia agreed. 'And a fabulous ambulance.'

'Don't start,' Theo warned. 'It has to get us home first.'

'I'll drive you home.'

'Cordelia?' Isadora's tone was quiet but firm. 'Behave yourself. If Theo wants to make a gift of the van, let him do it in his own good time.'

Theo shrugged. 'It's not a problem, Ma.'

Isadora grinned. 'Ma! I have a son. At last, I have a son.'

'And me. You've got me.' Rosie was prancing about on the pavement. 'They made a hole in me and pinched my blood. Loads and loads and loads. They put a sticky plaster on it, but it's coming off. I must be nearly empty. Nana says I can have pineapple juice. I have to get re-hided.'

'Rehydrated,' Juliet explained. 'Not because of blood loss, but the weather's hot. She didn't like hospital orange juice and she took just a sip of water.'

Juliet and Maggie stood behind the bouncing child. Both were smiling.

'She did very well,' Maggie told them. 'Never cried when the needle went in, and she told him he was taking too much. He said he needed a bucketful, and young miss here just laughed at him.'

Rosie motored on. 'The doctor with joined-up eyebrows said I was healthy, and if everyone was as healthy as me, he'd have no job. I've got chips on a clavicule . . . something like that.'

'Clavicle,' Juliet told them.

'And my broke ribs mended theirselves. Me hair's frackshered.'

'Hairline skull fracture,' Nurse Juliet said, shaking her head. 'Proof of historic damage.' She gave Rosie a shilling. 'Go to the bar and ask for iced pineapple, there's a good girl.'

When the child had disappeared, Maggie spoke again. 'The blood tests will take a few days, but the upshot is that even if Sadie does get better, it's unlikely she'll be having Rosie back. The poor baby probably slept for days after her skull got fractured. The doctor said she might well have had concussion. She's lucky to be alive.'

Delia's face was brightened by anger. 'It's a good thing that Tunstall's dead, or I'd be in jail for rearranging his future. Whoever killed him deserves a knighthood. As for the child's mother . . .' She stopped. 'Sorry, Maggie.'

Maggie nodded. 'You're not in the wrong, love, so don't be worrying. Sadie was out of control on gin, and she's lost control altogether now because of it. My daughter never put Rosie first. Trouble was, I always put my daughter first, and she turned into a–' She spotted Rosie on her way back. 'Well, we all know what she turned into.' She eyed her granddaughter. 'That's not pineapple juice.'

'No, it's tomato, Nana.'

'Oh?'

'Well, they stuck a needle in the bend in me arm and pinched thousands of blood. Millyuns. This is nearly the same colour, so I can get re-hided.' She took a sip. 'I don't like it, but it's red.' She shrugged. 'I shown him at the bar the needle hole. He said I'll have a big bruise tomorrow and I can charge people a penny for a look at it. See, Nana? They're just the same as Liverpool people except for talking funny.'

The whole company dissolved into laughter. Rosie held her nose and swallowed the rest of the red stuff before placing Juliet's shilling on the table. 'I got it free cos I'm beautiful. Well, that's what he said, but he wears glasses.'

'You are beautiful,' Isadora insisted.

'It's cos I got nice clothes.' She grinned at Tia.

Nancy returned bearing gifts. Within minutes, a sup-posedly bloodless child was leaping about with a special skipping rope, one with ball bearings in the handles.

'Psychologist?' Theo asked quietly.

'There's evidence of some damage,' was Juliet's reply. 'But she's immensely clever and good-natured. She spent ten minutes making him laugh about some poor woman so fat that she looks like Woolworth's with a hairnet. Rosie's afraid of the dark and of closed doors – understandably so.'

'Gasworks with the same hairnet,' Maggie explained. 'She means poor Nella from Ivy Lane. She has to go sideways into Povey's shop when she wants a loaf. You could hide a whole school of children behind her. Lovely woman – it's a damned shame.'

The group sat and smiled while Rosie tried to master double-unders.

Isadora rose to her feet. 'Come along, everyone. Let's go inside for our cream tea.' *We have the beginnings of a battle plan. Letters from the hospital will win us support from the NSPCC. Rosie will be fostered by Portia and Theo, or I'll die trying. The child's looking well, some flesh on her bones, confidence in her voice. Oh yes, we shall overcome.*

Rosie, undiminished by her ordeal by medics, interviewed the waiter on the subject of clotted cream. Neither he nor she had the slightest idea about making clots in cream, but her thirst for information brightened her eyes, just as it always did. She ate two scones, an enormous amount of strawberry jam and more than her fair share of cream. She finished with two cups of milky tea and a hand on her full stomach. 'Perhaps they have special cows and it comes out clotted. What do you think, Nana?'

Maggie smiled and sighed simultaneously; she felt a bit better after taking Daphne Melia's blood tonic . . .

The weekend was spent in happy chaos at Bartle Hall. Managing to forget all about her close and miserable relationship with coal, Rosie Stone leapt head first into the

386

priest hole game. She found six and, with a little help from Juliet, managed to work out the mechanisms that would gain her admission to the dusty spaces behind the panelling. In every hole, there was a present for her. She found books, a spinning top, clothes, ribbons, a pink necklace, and a large pencil case full of crayons and pencils and pens.

'You're nearly there,' Juliet informed the excited child. 'Just one more to go. There are seven altogether, and the last is the most interesting.'

Rosie wiped her forehead. 'Can we have a rest? Can we visit Mr and Mrs Quinn? We haven't seen them since hospital day.'

Juliet explained gently that Theo and Tia were on their honeymoon. 'It isn't that they don't care about us, but this is their alone time before they have to get back to normal.' She stroked Rosie's hair. 'They love you. We all love you.' She lowered her voice to a whisper. 'You and I will be sleeping in the gypsy caravan tonight; it's in the garden behind Rose Cottage. We can lie there and tell stories and jokes. See? Another adventure for you. But now I'm going to show you Bartle Hall's biggest secret. It's the seventh hole, and it's a big one. We call it Seventh Heaven, because it's up in the eaves and nearer to God, and it's a holy place.'

'A holy hole?'

Juliet laughed. 'It's rather larger than the rest, sweetie.'

They ascended a narrow, tortuous stairway that reminded Rosie of a corkscrew. Eventually, they emerged on a landing that opened out into the roof space where rejected items were stored. Juliet switched on a torch. 'The floor remains solid enough for people of our size. Follow me.'

They reached a wall. 'Now.' Juliet placed the torch on a scarred table. 'Can you see where it is?'

Rosie shook her head. 'It's just a wood wall like you have downstairs.'

'A flap in the bottom lifts just enough for a man to

crawl through. Inside, it has bolts so that the priest was truly hidden and safe. This was his last chance to avoid being murdered.' She knelt after picking up her torch. 'Follow me.' Lifting a section of the wall, she crawled through with Rosie hot on her heels. They both stood in total blackness until Juliet swept light across the area.

The little girl gasped. 'But this is a church, a teeny-tiny church.'

There were just two short pews facing the altar. A white altar cloth was falling to bits, though the central tabernacle seemed to have survived. 'Why did it happen?' Rosie asked.

'Hatred. Christians killing Christians. They couldn't accept each other's differences. This is a Catholic chapel. But the Catholics did their unfair share of torture and killings, too. It's stupidity. Never imagine that grown-ups know everything, because they don't.' She picked up an item from the pew to her right. 'This seemed suitable as a gift from Seventh Heaven. It's a Bible with coloured pictures in it.'

'Thank you. Are you a Christian, Juliet? Miss Bellam– I mean Mrs Quinn says you are.'

'I am. But I allow myself to worship just about anywhere, Methodist chapels, Catholic churches, Church of England – I'm not proud. It's one God and one Jesus. The rest is unimportant to me. But you'll find your own way, Rosie.'

Rosie pondered for a few moments. 'What about people who don't believe in Jesus? You know, in jungles and all that. They don't know about Jesus.'

'They have their own chosen faiths which must be honoured. As long as they do good in their lives, they're on the same journey, but they take a different road. It's a case of doing your best.'

'Like Nana?'

'Exactly like Nana. Now, let's grab some lunch. I heard a rumour about apple pie with pink custard.'

'My favourite colour.'

'Exactly. But you must eat your sandwich first.'

They descended the corkscrew staircase.

'Juliet?'

'Yes?'

'Do you think you might stay in Liverpool with Dr Heilberg?'

'It's all under discussion.'

Rosie swallowed hard. 'I don't want to lose you.'

At the bottom of the staircase to Seventh Heaven, Juliet hugged the little girl. 'You won't lose me, baby. Wherever I am, you'll always be in my heart.'

'Thank you, Juliet. I love all of you, too.'

'We know that, sweetheart. Come on – pink custard. Apple pie made from our own home-grown fruit. Scrummy.'

As they walked towards lunch, Juliet held on to her young charge. *I want a daughter just like this one, pretty and strong almost to the point of unbreakability. We have to save her. If necessary, I'll smuggle her out of the bloody country. But first, pink custard.*

While Rosie was interviewing Mrs Melia on the subject of how to make custard pink instead of yellow, Theo and Tia were considering getting out of bed. Lying stark naked on top of the covers, they were still roasting. Theo made a unilateral decision. Water from the previous evening would still be tepid, so they could share a bath.

As he walked towards the door, Tia looked at his scars again. She wasn't allowed to pity him, but the marks on his back made her angry. Angry wasn't good, since it made her even warmer, so she forced herself out of bed to open the window fully. Lighting a fire every evening wasn't a good idea, but it was the only way to get hot water. 'I'll buy one of those immersion things,' she said. She heard him cursing; the hot tap was spitting water and air; the whole place needed newer plumbing.

He stood in the doorway. 'Get in the bathroom,' he ordered, amazed when she blinked just once before showing signs of doing as she was told. *Am I taming her? Do I want to tame her?* 'We have to share,' he said. 'I'll take the end near the taps.' *What's the matter with her?* 'What's the matter with you? You're quiet.' He followed her to the bathroom.

She climbed into the bath and awarded him one of the more brilliant of her collection of smiles. 'I just thought I'd never love so quickly and so hard. I love you more than I did on our wedding day.'

'Three days ago, Portia.'

She nodded. 'I feel very ... fortunate, but that's an inadequate word. Join me – the water's lovely.'

They sat opposite each other, chins resting on knees.

'You make me happy, Teddy Bear. I feel as if the glass slipper fitted and I got the prince.'

'No. I won first prize, baby. Come on; we re-join the rest of the world today.' *My heart's dancing like those loonies with bells on their socks. Or maybe I'm the village idiot, risking pain by allowing myself to love this wonderful woman. We have given ourselves to each other so quickly, yet I feel I couldn't live without her, and she says she feels the same.*

'Do you know where we're taking them?'

He grinned. 'Just onward, baby. I have the map.'

'Leeds Castle?' she asked. 'And hop fields?'

'Yes to the first, and the second will prove unavoidable. But without you, I'd have no map. You're my way home, baby. Let's clean up the act and go.'

*

390

Four people spilled out of the van and stared at the most beautiful castle in England. Tia, Theo, Juliet and Rosie had left the others behind. Nancy was knitting in the garden of Lilac Cottage, Tom was engrossed in *A Tale of Two Cities*, Maggie was chatting in the kitchen with Mrs Melia, while Izzy had gone to take Sunday afternoon tea with friends in Chaddington Green. Delia, who had been extra nice to Theo, had returned to London on the train and was doubtless telling her bandmates that there was a chance of a better van.

Theo recognized the building immediately from the film *Kind Hearts and Coronets*. 'This is Leeds Castle, Rosie. Nine centuries old, but it's been changed and extended many times since the eleventh century. If the owner hadn't placed himself on the side of the Parliamentarians, it might have been destroyed.'

Inevitably, Rosie filed a questionnaire at this point, thereby causing an American citizen to fill in the gaps about monarchists and republicans and Oliver Cromwell with his 'warts and all'. He explained the moat. 'It's there to stop people getting into the castle. What? Oh, they used drawbridges to get out and to let in people they wanted to see.'

Rosie pondered. 'Captain Webb on the matchboxes could have swum it. He went from England to France.'

Theo sighed. She had an answer for everything, and she put him in mind – just slightly in mind – of Colin Duckworth. 'Yes, Matthew Webb probably could have done it, but he didn't.'

'Are you mad at me?' she asked.

'Never, Rosie,' he said. 'You're a breath of fresh air in a very hot world.'

Because of the heat, they spent the rest of the day wandering through villages, eating ice cream, sitting under canopies provided by trees, drinking cold fruit juices, paddling in streams and lying in fallow fields.

'I like Kent,' Rosie said sleepily.

'So do I,' the sisters chimed in unison.

Theo chuckled. 'I'm just glad the RAF didn't send any German wreckage down on Leeds Castle or on any of the wonderful Tudor houses we've seen today. We could have turned this into a real hellish corner.'

'It's hot,' Tia complained.

He chuckled. 'Hot? You should try America, my love. Step outside in summer and, in some states, it feels as if someone has thrown a boiling hot blanket over you. Breathing is an effort. We prayed for rain. My dad used to talk at length about Ireland and its many shades of green. He said summer was a time for considering building an ark, but it was too wet to go out and find the wood.'

'Did he get used to the heat?' Juliet asked.

'No. He's fair-skinned with sandy hair and very red skin in the sun.'

They all looked at Rosie, who was snoring softly. 'Bless her,' Juliet mumbled. 'What will become of her?'

Portia smiled. 'She'll be Izzy-ed. You know about the camel and the needle in the Bible? Ma would have got the animal through the hole.'

Theo drifted towards sleep. He was glad he'd left the dog with Maggie and Mrs Melia, as she would have been panting and weary. Feeling safe and happy, he joined Rosie in the land of Nod.

'No stamina,' Tia whispered.

'You've worn him out,' Juliet giggled.

'Don't be vulgar, Jules. He's amazing and a good cook.'

'You're happy.'

'Happier than I ever felt I deserved. Let's sleep.'

1968

Seventeen

Having enjoyed six idyllic weeks away celebrating their tenth anniversary, Tia and Theo Quinn descended the aeroplane steps following a bump-free landing at Manchester's Ringway Airport. Trident had given them the smoothest, quietest and easiest flight from Paris, and they'd enjoyed a blissful second honeymoon, but they were oh-so-glad to be back.

Manchester's cloud cover was dark grey and heavily pregnant with rain, specks of which were leaking out as harbingers of imminent delivery on a grand scale. But this was England, and England was home. Their small country was green because of her unpredictable weather, and she was a truly beautiful old lady with a history that was often mind-blowing. 'Home, sweet home,' Theo said on his way down the steps. 'Oh yes, the rain's giving us a welcome, baby.'

They reached the tarmac, both grateful for terra firma. 'Thank you for a lovely time, Teddy.' Tia gripped his hand. 'Thank you for New York, for Georgia, for Washington and Niagara and Pennsylvania and Boston and Chicago and—'

'And you're breaking my fingers, Portia.'

'Sorry.' She swallowed, her throat suddenly dry. She had stood at his mother's grave and on the very spot where the poor woman had died. 'Most of all, thank you for marrying me, for introducing me to your family, for taking me to President Kennedy's grave, and for France. Just think, we were in Paris a couple of hours ago. Thank you, Teddy Bear.'

He gazed into her magnificent eyes. 'You're welcome, ma'am,' he drawled. 'Thank you for tolerating me for a whole decade.'

'I love you,' she whispered.

Theo shrugged. 'What's not to love? I'm handsome, rich, famous, generous, amusing, and I wilt not wilt – not yet, anyway. Let's go find your mom and our sproglets. I missed the boys and Rosie. And it's so much easier to breathe here, isn't it? Summer across the Atlantic can be very trying.'

They recovered their luggage, wheeled it through NOTHING TO DECLARE, and almost ran like a pair of smugglers towards the public area. Manchester had begun to do its thing of trying to commit suicide by drowning, but no one noticed the rain battering the windows because Mum and Dad were home. Rosie waved and pushed her foster-brothers forward. 'Here they come, boys. Don't they look wonderful?'

David, aged eight, and Michael, who was five, hurled themselves at their parents. Many hugs and kisses were shared while the two boys expressed their delight. Behind them stood a truly beautiful Rosie, now fifteen, tall and slender, dark-haired, clear-eyed and determined not to allow happiness to spill down her cheeks. 'Oh, I'm so glad to see you safely home. We watched you coming in to land. That's the most beautiful plane I ever saw.'

Theo grinned. 'Better than a Spitfire – I got to sit down and read.'

'Where's Ma?' Tia asked after managing to extricate herself from her older son's crushing embrace.

'There wouldn't have been enough room on the way

back in the taxi, so I'm in charge.' Rosie kissed the two people who had been her unofficial foster-parents for years. 'Nana's tired; Izzy-gran stayed with her, and Joan will be attached to an upstairs window waiting for you.'

Theo frowned. 'Is Maggie still refusing to see doctors?'

'Yes. She says if she'd kept appointments, she would have been dead years ago because she'd have been used as a guinea pig. But she was running out of blood tonic since Mrs Melia died. Anyway, a huge bottle of it arrived last week, left for Nana in Mrs Melia's will. The recipe came with it. I hid that bit of paper under books in the cabinet in Nana's room, because we need to talk about it. But just now, this is about welcoming you home. We missed you. And you look very well and sun-tanned – I'm madly jealous, though the weather's been quite good here.'

When the suitcases were safely stored in the taxi's boot, the family of five squashed bodies into seats and headed for Liverpool.

Portia studied her handsome, sturdy sons. In just six weeks, the boys had changed. Their brown hair owned streaks of summer blond, they were taller and slightly broader, and both were sun-blessed by freckles. They probably needed new shoes again; their feet seemed to grow faster than weeds, and many pairs of good footwear had been sent to the poor via their local church.

She closed travel-wearied eyes. *This is the first time we haven't spent the summer at the cottage. I still miss Chaddington Green, but we're not ready to leave Liverpool yet. Rosie and our sons must complete their education here, and Michael won't be ready until 1980 at the earliest, by which time darling Teddy will be sixty. But with Myrtle Street thriving so well, Teddy and I seem to be firmly entrenched for the time being. Oh, it's good to be back where we belong, with our children.* 'Is a certain person ready to receive a parcel in our garage, Rosie?' she managed sleepily.

'All present and correct, Mum,' was the answer.

Tia placed her head on her husband's shoulder. *I'm so relieved to know that Bartle Hall is up and running at last after all those long years of struggle. Jules and Simon run the health side of things, and Ma imported good kitchen staff from London. She's magic. Oh, I suddenly feel so desperately tired. Aeroplanes exhaust me.*

The head of Bartle School's a wonderful lunatic and, like my Teddy, he doesn't believe in corporal punishment and deals very well with thirty neglected and surplus-to-require-ments children. Why do people have children if they can't be bothered to love them and care for them?

She held Theo's hand and floated towards sleep while her boys and Rosie chattered. Drifting in her dream in the direction of Kent and back through dimension four, she heard her husband speaking into a phone . . . He was talking to his friend Jack Peake, caretaker of Myrtle Street School . . .

. . . 'Yes, Jack, we were married on Thursday. Nancy had no knitting, so we were nearly waterlogged.' He chuckled. 'Have you any money? Good. We'll be back soon. What? Oh, yes, I want it published in the *Post* and *Echo*. Married in Canterbury last Thursday. Yes. Just our names and the date. Theodore Quinn and Portia Bellamy. No need to mention parents, just the bare bones will do, and I'll pay you when we get back.

'Mickle? No, she wasn't a bridesmaid, but Rosie was. Yes. Yes, we do have photos. Oh, it was great. Morris dancers, people in historic costume, a bit of medieval chicanery, all thou and wilt and cleaving. What? Of course she looked beautiful; my Portia always does.

'Right. Don't forget to paint the blackboards, Jack. Oh, the petty cash is in the middle drawer. Do you have the key with you? Good. Open the drawer now and take some money for the *Echo*. I'll top it up next week. And thanks, matey. When school opens, they'll all know we're married.

'Maybe you're right; maybe it is the coward's way out, but I'd rather Miss Cosgrove and Miss Garner got used to the idea before term starts. I can't help being such a catch, can I?' He laughed. 'Nail on the head, Jack. If you have the time, visit Miss Reynolds. She's kitty-sitting while Izzy and her daughters are down here. See you soon, my friend, and look after yourself.'

He replaced the receiver, turned and saw the eavesdropper. She was wearing a peasant-style blouse and a very full skirt. 'Get upstairs,' he commanded. 'Let's do a bit of cleaving.'

Tia woke when the taxi bounced in and out of dips caused by the mining of coal miles beneath the road. 'Did you know, boys, that roughly twenty per cent of all fresh running water in the world tumbles over Niagara Falls?'

David and Theo exchanged a glance. 'Mum, do you always have to be a teacher, even during school holidays?'

Rosie's smile broadened. There was clearly no cure for the disease known as teaching. She spoke to him. 'Teachers are born, not made, David. I may take it up myself.'

'Go back to sleep, Portia,' Theo advised, poker-faced. 'She gets tired and emotional, kids – too many drinks on the plane,' he whispered.

'I heard that,' Tia said sleepily.

'See?' Theo shrugged. 'Even when dozing, she has me shackled.'

Rosie grinned again. This was a perfect marriage, a perfect family. Yes, they had their differences and arguments, but they were best friends and close companions. *I am a truly fortunate girl. I wonder who killed Tunstall? If he'd lived, what would have become of me?*

She thought briefly about her birth mother, Sadie, who had been cared for in a private rest home. She had choked on food regurgitated from an over-full stomach. It had happened in her sleep, and people had muttered about its being 'for the best'. It probably had been for the best, since Sadie Tunstall's quality of life had been terribly poor. Even so, Rosie had grieved.

The fifteen-year-old stared out at houses along the East Lancashire Road. Mam had gained so much weight that she'd needed a reinforced chair and a special bed. *I will do something with my life, first of all for my own sake, but also for Theo and Tia, who have been Mum and Dad for me. Isadora and Joan, too, and my lovely Nana and Tom and Nancy who kept me alive during the dark times. Don't look back, Rosie; be like Theo-dad and march on.*

Joan stood at a window of the flat that had once been Portia's. This was now her permanent residence; it was also a northern base for Isadora, whose film company was enjoying a meteoric success. Izzy had starred in six of the Ealing comedies, and was now using local-to-Liverpool writers, actors and crew to adapt Tom Quirke's books for the big screen under the banner *Isadora Films*.

Joan's husband joined her at the window. 'Still no sign of them, eh?'

'The rain we had earlier will have reached Manchester by now. I think the Pennines burst the clouds and poor old Manchester gets the result. Izzy's downstairs with Maggie, and we should join them. Let's all be in the same place when the taxi arrives.'

He laughed. 'You know, I've never had this much fun since Colin Duckworth brought that dog to school. You've changed my life, Joan. It's like living in a completely different story. And to think I only came to keep you company while you were Tyger-sitting.'

She smiled fondly at him. 'And Tyger's still going strong. Poor Mickle, though. Theo was heartbroken last year, wasn't he? Still, she's buried in the woods in Chaddington. She loved the woods.'

Jack returned the smile. 'For a large dog, she lived a long life, Joan.' Now retired from caretaking, he still did his fair share of looking after both flats, sitting with Maggie, who was increasingly frail, helping in the Quinn household just across the road, sorting out the gardens and lending a hand with Isadora's schedule. 'Yes, let's go down and enjoy the welcome-home party. I think we deserve a treat after minding David and Michael for six weeks.'

Joan didn't trouble to remind her spouse that the Quinn boys were quite well behaved if somewhat boisterous at times. Boys played. Boys needed to play, and the loss of a few panes in the greenhouse was a small matter, surely? And they'd been replaced. 'Straighten your tie, dear.'

Jack wasn't used to ties, but he did as Joan asked. She was a quiet woman, yet the gentleness was plastered over an intelligent and knowledgeable soul. Like many of her gender, she didn't know weed from flower, wrench from spanner, screwdriver from bottle opener, but she knew people, and therein lay her strength. The marriage had been a shock to both of them, but they were happy. It was based in the need for companionship rather than in passion. Jack's health had improved, though he still needed to pace himself, while Joan was simply happy in his presence, because he made her laugh and made her feel safe.

'What did you say I was instead of a caretaker?' Jack asked.

'A concierge.'

'Eh?'

'Concierge. It's French for caretaker or janitor.'

'I'm English.'

'I know.'

'We call a spade a bloody shovel round here.'

Joan shrugged. 'Are your hands clean?'

'Yes, Mother.'

'Shoes?'

'Two – one for each foot.'

'Polished?'

'Yes, ma'am.'

'Are you making fun of me, Mr Peake?'

'Definitely.'

She chuckled. 'Walk on, then.'

When they left the flat, they were laughing, as usual.

Like just about any other incomer, Isadora had been absorbed into the mix offered by the open arms and hearts of Liverpudlians. Yes, there'd been an influx of autograph hunters in the early days, but after ten years of comings and goings she was finally one of theirs. Sometimes she was here, sometimes she was elsewhere, yet Allerton, Liverpool, was her bolt-hole and the place from which she ran her company.

She was currently sitting with Maggie Stone, who had lived over nine years longer than predicted by medics. Depending solely on a home brew concocted by Daphne Melia, she had enjoyed a remission which might have happened anyway, although Maggie's distrust of doctors forced her to say repeatedly, 'They would have killed me,' a comment that became her mantra.

'Will Tia and Theo be here soon?' Maggie asked now.

'They will.' Izzy paused for a few seconds. 'How do you feel today?'

Maggie offered a weak smile. 'Tired. It's nearly my time, Izzy. Daphne told me that the blood medicine wouldn't work forever, but she gave me a good few extra years, bless her. Rosie can please herself now, at fifteen. She's got her place across the road with her foster-mam, dad and brothers, and she's got Joan and Jack upstairs here. And you, of course.'

'Shush. Don't exhaust yourself. Save some energy for the party, and trust us to do our best for your sweet granddaughter when the time comes. I promise you we'll—'

The doorbell sounded. Izzy went to admit Joan and Jack. 'Not well,' she whispered in the hallway. 'I think we're losing her.'

'Shall I get a doctor?' Joan mouthed.

Izzy shook her head. 'Maggie wouldn't want that. Come in,' she said, pitching her voice back to normal. 'The caterers have left food in the kitchen. Help me carry it through, Joan.'

Jack sat with Maggie. 'Hello, me other girlfriend. It's all right; Joan says we can hold hands, like, but no kissing.'

'Like a dinner with no pudding, eh, lad?'

'She's a bit jealous, Mags.'

'I don't blame her. You make her very happy.'

He jumped up. 'They're here,' he called. 'The driver and Theo are taking the luggage into their house.' Izzy and Joan dashed in with platters, placing them on the dining table alongside fruit punch and the welcome-home cake. Izzy ran to the window. 'Portia's as brown as a berry, and Theo's a beautiful colour. The boys are bouncing about like beach balls.' She swallowed hard. 'Isn't Rosie a stunner?'

403

'She always was,' Jack replied. 'Even in the infants department, she stood out like a jewel: beauty, brains and as much cheek as a cow's backside.'

Maggie smiled. Her precious girl had won a scholarship to one of Liverpool's top-of-the-list grammar schools. She was aiming for a degree in English Literature and French and would teach in a school similar to the one she currently attended. *I'll be with our Sadie soon. I hope there's no gin in the next life – and no food. If there's food, they'll have to reinforce the floor joists . . .*

Portia entered the flat that had once been her Teddy's home. She kissed her mother, Joan and Jack before making a beeline for Maggie. In six weeks, Rosie's nana seemed to have lost as much weight as David and Michael had gained. 'Maggie?' Tia knelt and put her arms round the skeletal frame of a wonderful woman.

'Rosie knows I'm going, babe. We've talked about it. She'll be all right; she has you two and the pair upstairs here, then Izzy comes home when she can. I got nearly ten years, Tia. Thanks to Daphne Melia, I saw my Rosie grow up.'

Tia gulped audibly. She couldn't, wouldn't cry. 'Oh, Maggie, we love you. You're one of the wisest people I've met.' She stood and turned to greet her husband, her daughter and her sons. Frowning at the shocked expression on Teddy's face, she shook her head almost imperceptibly. He had seen Maggie, and he hadn't liked what he'd seen. But they both needed to stay strong. 'Food's here,' she said, her voice slightly shaky. 'Don't worry, Ma didn't prepare any of it, I'm told, so we should survive.'

Theo gave his attention to Jack. 'You seem happy.'

Jack laughed. 'Joan's a good cook. Six years we've been wed now. It was worth the sacrifice just for her gravy.' He lowered his tone. 'Actually, Isadora made the cake and iced it. Between filming sessions at Ealing, she took lessons off a corded blue something or other.'

'Cordon Bleu? My mother-in-law?'

Jack nodded. 'Don't tell anybody until they've sampled the cake. Especially Tia, because she thinks her ma's in the same league as Lucrezia Borgia. We've had a few set-backs in the past six weeks, because she still can't do good scrambled eggs, but she's open to learning. Fingers crossed, eh?'

Tasked with the job of doling out presents from foreign shores, David and Michael were harvesting gifts from a deep rucksack. There were silk scarves for Maggie, Joan and Nancy, who had not yet arrived. For Tom, a peace pipe rested in a box on top of a more conventional one, while Jack was delighted with a Polaroid camera from the USA.

Rosie was in happy receipt of her first ever makeup bag from Paris. She found three lipsticks in varying shades of pink, an eyebrow pencil, mascara and a pretty compact of powder.

'You need no more than that,' Tia advised her. 'Don't start blocking your pores with that foundation gunk, or you'll get spots. And the perfume's French, made especially for younger girls. Wait until you're twenty-odd for Chanel No. Five – it's too seductive for a teenager.'

Rosie grinned. Several boys were on her tail, but she was concentrating on her books. Except for . . . except for one boy, who was almost a man.

'And don't wear it at school,' Theo advised.

'I won't. Thank you so much. The makeup's great, but the bag's splendiferous.' The item dangled from golden chains, and its body was covered on one side in sequins laid in the pattern of the French tricolour, while the other side was completely gold. 'Gorgeous,' she breathed. 'Look, Nana. There are even spare sequins in a little packet in case I lose some.'

'It's lovely,' Maggie said.

Isadora tapped her toe as if she were impatient. 'What about poor little me?' she asked, the tone plaintive.

Theo clapped a hand against his face. 'How could you, Portia? How could you forget your mother? After all she's gone through with architects and mains drainage and classrooms and dormitories and the shifting of septic tanks.'

Portia dropped into a chair. 'David, Michael, please go across to our garage and see if anything in there will do.' She looked at Izzy. 'Sorry, Ma.'

'You are up to something, Portia Quinn.'

'Am I?'

'You look as innocent as did Judas after he took the thirty pieces of blood money.'

'Ah yes, I forgot you were at the Last Supper. Exactly how old are you, Ma?'

'I am old enough to know when my daughters are up to mischief.'

A man with his head in a brown paper bag was led in by Tia's giggling boys. 'This was all we could find, Mum. Apart from Mum's woodwork tools, two old bikes and some worn-out skates, there wasn't anything left.' David shrugged nonchalantly. 'It will just have to do.'

The man with the invisible head was carrying a parcel. Michael relieved him of it and thrust it at Izzy. 'There you go, Gran. David and I are off to play softball or kick that American football about. We'll be back for cake.' The boys left.

Isadora knew who the man was, but she went along with the joke. When her parcel was opened, she shrieked with joy. It was a capacious leather bag with MADE IN TEXAS on the label. 'Thank you so much,' she cried. 'It will hold a dozen scripts and all my personal bits and pieces.' She grinned. 'Take the article off your head,

Richard. You're not quite ugly enough to need it.'

Richard Bellamy revealed himself. 'Thank goodness,' he said. 'It's too hot for brown paper bags.'

Ex-husband-and-wife kissed. 'How are you?' Izzy asked.

'Fine, thanks. Though I do hope you'll let me have Lilac Cottage now that poor Mrs Melia and her sister no longer need it. Daphne didn't last long after Ethel died, did she? I want to continue as caretaker, of course.'

'Yes, dear. I don't know how we'd manage without you, frankly.'

Jack smiled to himself. The Shakespearean actor had survived a suspended sentence, the hatred of an unforgiving press, divorce, periods of ill-health, and the sale to Izzy of Bartle Hall. He now occupied a position well known to Jack, though to be fair, Richard did teach English literature part-time to Bartle Hall pupils.

Isadora was busy counting compartments in her American bag. She had no regrets about the divorce, because she had achieved so much as a single woman, while Richard seemed to have finally matured. He had married the mother of one of his sons, and they currently lived in a flat in Bartle Hall where Catherine Bellamy, Richard's other half, taught secretarial skills to older pupils. 'How are Cath and Giles?' Izzy asked.

'Fine, thank you. Juliet and Simon send love, as do Cordelia and Elaine. If you have gifts for them, Portia, I'll take them with me when I leave. Cordelia will be in Kent for a day or two to help supervise while the school's closed for summer. She and Elaine are taking the children hiking.' He shook his head. 'Hiking? Even the devil himself would have trouble coping with temperatures in Kent. Still, school opens again in a few days.'

Isadora smiled to herself, remembering Richard's prejudice against Simon because of a Jewish father, his reluctance to visit Portia, who had married a man who was part coloured. As for Cordelia – well, lesbianism hadn't suited Richard, either.

Richard shook Theo's hand. 'You've made a good job of taming my eldest daughter. Well done. Will somebody feed me, please? Hanging around in a garage waiting for my grandsons to rescue me is hungry work.'

'Help yourselves.' After issuing the invitation, Tia watched her parents, now the best of friends, as they piled food onto plates. They were chattering and laughing and helping each other to bits and pieces from the buffet. Joan was busy choosing food for the boys, who would probably eat outside while playing with their new American toys. Maggie had her eyes pinned to Rosie, her raison d'être, her pride and joy.

Tom and Nancy arrived. 'Sorry we're late,' Tom said, 'but madam here couldn't find her new pair of number nines – knitting needles, not shoes.'

'That's right, love. Still, we got here in the end. Maggie? You all right, girl? Welcome home, happy wanderers.' She had gained in confidence since beginning to travel on a regular basis between Liverpool and Kent. A voluntary assistant at Izzy's school, she taught knitting, crochet and sewing to any child who was keen to learn.

Maggie, whose appetite was seriously depleted of late, sat propped up by cushions on a comfortable chair with her feet resting on a padded stool. This was her place, and these people were her family. She had been a lucky woman, because these wonderful characters had chosen her and Rosie. Isadora had forced the welfare officers to bugger off, so Maggie had gained a daughter and a son in Tia and Theo, older sisters in Izzy and Joan, and a sort of brother-in-law named Jack Peake. She had lived in relative luxury with her beloved granddaughter, and all had been well.

Maggie turned her head and gazed through the window at a turquoise sky with little puffs of cotton wool clouds hanging around like wallflowers at a dance. After this morning's rain, everything looked washed clean and new.

Well, I was never a wallflower, and my Rosie won't be short of dance partners, either. She'll be a lady in nice clothes in a job where she can dress up and be beautiful. And she's a good girl who visits Harry the Scoot and Martha every week. She's never forgot nobody who helped her. She goes to see Nancy and Tom regular, too.

The pain's back. It's like the monthly pain I used to get before the change, but this swine has teeth. I asked Daphne how the end would be, and she was honest about the pain. I've got the powders she sent. They're in that little drawer next to my bed. I don't want these good people to see my pain, and I don't want any bloody doctors going on about how I should have kept appointments and all that doo-dah. Suicide. Well, I've left letters for everybody so they'll know why. I think I'm bleeding to death inside, but I'm not sure. It feels like I'm bleeding to death, anyway.

I'll try and manage a bit of that cake. If Izzy made it, I might not need the flaming powders. See, I'm still me; I can still laugh at the idea of Izzy mucking about with flour and eggs and sugar. She made me an omelette a few weeks back, and I could have soled shoes with it, honest. Rosie laughed till she cried, said her cutlery had bent and could she have another fork?

Look at her now, my little granddaughter. Little? She's five foot six and thrilled to pieces with that fancy bag from Paris. I wish I could hang on for a bit longer, see her through university and all that, but I mustn't be greedy. God sent Daphne Melia to me – well, He sent me to her, really.

She moved her head and stared again at a sky whose brilliance was amazing. The pain was settling down – perhaps the enemy was soaking his false teeth in Steradent. *I feel as if I'm floating up to sit on one of them wallflower clouds. So bright up there today, brighter with*

every tick of the clock. The sun is coming down to meet me.
White, so white, so beautiful. I can't turn my head; I can't
look at her one last time. And there are things hidden here
in this flat – where did I put them? I wrapped the main one
in greaseproof. Please God, take good care of my baby, my
precious Rosie, my . . . my everything . . .

Rosie brought a plate of food for Nana. Nana didn't eat
enough, and– The teenager stopped in her tracks. 'Izzy-
gran?' she called.

'Yes, darling?'

Rosie swallowed hard; Nana had prepared her well for
this moment. 'She said she'd still be here when Mum and
Dad got back from America, and she was. Her eyes are
open as if she's looking through the window, but . . .'

Isadora grabbed Theo's arm. 'Go out and play with the
boys, and don't let them in here. Rosie, sit with your
mummy on the sofa. Portia, keep hold of her – she's shi-
vering. Richard, carry Maggie into her room – it's through
there. Joan, ring for an ambulance, then make hot, sweet
tea for Rosie. Tom, take Nancy home – get a taxi. Jack,
help Richard.' She directed traffic like a policeman on
duty at a busy crossroads.

Tia rocked her foster-daughter. 'We love you, baby.
You've got us, and we'll always be here for you.'

'There is no always,' Rosie whispered.

Tia blinked back a torrent of emotion.

Rosie continued. 'She wants to be buried in her dark
blue suit and white blouse. And I think she should have
the silk scarf you brought back for her. She said she'd like
"Onward Christian Soldiers", and "All Things Bright and
Beautiful" because I used to sing that to her when I was
little. It's all written down. Oh, and Izzy-gran has to read
"Death", by John Donne. I'm going to read something
Nana dictated to me when she told me she was ready to
go. I've put a bit in from me, too.'

'Oh, Rosie.'

'I know, Mum, I know. Oh, we have to wear bright colours – that's written down, too. Nana wants a party, not a funeral. She was lovely, wasn't she?'

'She was one of the best, Rosie. There was a quality in her that's lacking in so many of us – staying power. I'm just so glad that we were in a position to give her a pretty place to live in. She loved this flat.'

They sat, each with arms wrapped around the other, each staring at the empty chair opposite the sofa. 'Remember your wedding day, Mum?'

'Oh, yes.'

'And she never warned Tom and Nancy that they were at a wedding. She had a wicked sense of humour. I was so happy in my pink frock, and I couldn't understand why Nancy was crying. But I understand now, because I know there's no forever, no always. Poets write about that, the transient nature of life. Nana said we just have to get on with it because we're no more than a blink of God's eye. She was clever.'

Tia's control slipped, and she cried like a baby. Rosie kept her company, finally allowing herself to weep for the woman who had saved her life, a real life away from institutions for unwanted or orphaned children. Most of all, she wept for Nana as a person, a good, kind, funny lady who had been her sole living blood relative. 'Thank you, Mum,' she sobbed.

'For what?'

'For loving me and Nana.'

Tia drew in a deep, shuddering breath. 'You're easy to love, as was Maggie. But you still have a mum and a dad and two brothers.'

Rosie almost laughed. 'Can I live in the attic at Brooklands? They're always throwing things.'

'Of course you may. In fact, I'll probably move up there with you.'

They both giggled hysterically.

Isadora, listening from Maggie's room, nodded sagely. They had wept, they had giggled, and bereavement could now commence. The ambulance was here. There would be an autopsy, as Maggie had seen no doctor for years, and a post mortem examination would involve a coroner. Rosie had shown Izzy the recipe . . .

'What do you need?' Richard asked, concern in his tone. 'Shall I stay another night?'

'No, you get back home, but thank you.'

He kissed her forehead. 'Tell Portia and family goodbye for me, Isadora.'

'I shall.'

There now remained in Flat One, Crompton Villa, just Portia, Rosie, Isadora and the frail shell that had contained the soul of Margaret Stone. Joan and Jack had been sent upstairs to Flat Two, and Theo was playing outside with his two sons.

Ambulance men entered the bedroom. Izzy bent and placed a kiss on a cooling forehead before leaving the men to deal with the body. 'Goodbye, my sweet friend,' she said when she reached the door. Then she went to join her daughter and Rosie in the living room. She placed herself in Maggie's chair, laying her head in a hollow in the cushion where Maggie's head had rested. *She was years younger than I am. I may be a famous star, but Rosie's nana was greater than any of us.*

Rosie and Portia seem calmer now. We have each other. Between us, we can carry Rosie through this, though I suspect that she may be the one who carries us . . .

*

Isadora was ready for them. Standing at the window, she watched as they climbed out of the car and slammed both doors behind them before walking up the path that led to Crompton Villa. She had ordered Portia and Theo to stay away; they, too, were probably watching from Brooklands, their house across the way.

Izzy's eyes followed the movements of two detectives, both in ill-fitting suits and shiny shoes. One suit was blue, the other brown. Although their car was unmarked, they were unmistakably policemen. Well, she was fired up for this confrontation. Throwing open the door before hearing a knock or a bell, she faced them. 'Gentlemen, good morning. Please come in.' She stepped aside and awarded them a huge smile, glancing fleetingly at their warrant cards.

They entered the flat, clearly uncomfortable in the presence of Isadora, star of the big screen and famous enough to need no surname. She sat at the dining table and indicated with a nod that they, too, should sit. They sat.

'Right,' she began, 'when will we be able to give Mrs Stone the burial she wanted and deserves? She has a granddaughter who needs to move on with her life, while you keep putting full stops on the page.'

They glanced at each other, and the older man cleared his dry, nervous throat. 'Mrs . . . er,' he began haltingly.

'Just Isadora, thank you.'

'Well, the decision to release the deceased will be made by the coroner, ma'am. The case must be heard in Coroner's Court, I'm afraid. Mrs Stone was poisoned, and it's believed that she had been consuming a restricted substance for some time, probably for years.'

She nodded. 'I suppose that may be a possibility, yes.'

Both men blinked as if surprised by the ready admission.

Their hostess motored on. 'I have letters from a Mrs Daphne Melia to Mrs Stone. I also have a recipe in the same handwriting for the blood tonic given by Mrs Melia to the deceased over a period of at least nine years. Maggie Stone had leukaemia and, a decade ago, was given months to live. The tonic kept her alive.'

The second visitor spoke. 'And you knew she was taking poison?'

'I found out on the day she died.' Rosie had guided her, but she left Rosie out of the tale; the poor girl had enough to cope with. 'I discovered the formula in her bedside cabinet while searching for a necklace she always loved – she will wear that necklace in her coffin if you ever allow us to have the funeral.'

Both men were astonished. 'But you said nothing.'

Izzy raised her eyebrows. 'When questioned by another of your number, I did say something. I informed the other . . . gentleman that Maggie refused to see doctors and that she had survived on a blood tonic provided by a lady who had been my cook and housekeeper for many years. Frankly, Mrs Melia's spelling was poor, and I thought I had, perhaps, been too quick to identify the ingredients. Even had I trusted her spelling, the post mortem would have happened, so what was the point?'

Confusion reigned; confusion owned very poor dress sense. Each man glanced several times at his partner.

With great patience, Isadora explained the situation as she saw it. 'I have done some research via my son-in-law, who is a doctor. Here.' She placed on the table a letter from Simon.

The younger man scanned the page. 'Chemical therapy?' he asked quietly.

Izzy nodded. 'The infamous substance found in Maggie's body has been tested on sufferers of leukaemia for some time – with varying results.'

'But this Melia woman isn't a doctor.'

'No, she isn't. Mrs Stone had a phobia where the medical profession is concerned. She trusted only Daphne Melia.'

'But—'

'But, officers, Mrs Melia probably knew that the noxious ingredient would slow the cancer before killing Maggie. Country folk are notorious for dabbling in cures. And it did give Maggie years of respite. As the months and years passed, the amount of poison was possibly increased, though no one can be sure. Oh, I have a flagon of the mix. It was sent up from Kent quite recently. You may take it and have it analysed.'

An awkward silence ensued. 'Mrs Melia will be arrested,' whispered the detective in the terrible brown suit. 'Is she still in Kent?'

'Yes, she is.'

'The coroner may decide that it was murder or manslaughter, ma'am.'

'He may, indeed. Oh, I shall give you all the correspondence. If you need help with Mrs Melia's scribble, I'll make myself available.'

Brown Suit shook his head sadly. 'Kent police will have to arrest her. Is she still at the same address?'

Izzy shook her head. 'She moved.'

'Do you have her new address?'

She nodded. 'Chaddington Green Cemetery, otherwise known as St Faith's churchyard. She's the one under a newly planted lilac tree, as she spent most of her life at Lilac Cottage. Daphne Melia was one of the most wonderful people I ever met. Maggie Stone was another such. Tell the Kent police to take a spade if they want to talk to Daphne Melia. Follow me to get the flagon.'

She left the room with Blue Suit and Brown Suit in her wake. It was clear that neither knew what to do or say.

Maggie, you would have enjoyed that, though I think I may have been cruel to these poor creatures. Say hello to Daphne for me. The coroner may decide on misadventure or open verdict, and the underlying cause will inevitably be leukaemia. Whatever, you'll have your navy suit, white blouse, the necklace Rosie bought you and the scarf from America. Sleep well, my friend.

The detectives drove away with the huge bottle of blood tonic, notes sent from Kent to Liverpool and the letter from Dr Simon Heilberg.

I must warn Chaddington Green, because someone local may have furnished Daphne Melia with a touch of that lethal element, a substance not easy to come by. Oh, life is such a complicated business, and I was expected ten minutes ago at the rehearsal rooms in Hope Street.

She dashed across to tell Portia and Theo about the meeting before heading off in a taxi towards central Liverpool. There was going to be a read-through of Theo's – well, Tom Quirke's – *An Eye for an Eye*. Isadora's wealthy son-in-law was going to be even richer. She chuckled. He'd been talking about buying a pig farm in Derbyshire, and Portia had battered him with a cushion. They were so happy . . .

In death, Margaret Stone was finally famous. National presses had picked up the story, and there were film as well as still cameras lining the route to the church. She had proved the medical profession wrong by outliving doctors' estimated span, and the method she had used was unusual. The primitive form of chemotherapy she had employed had been brewed by a working class countrywoman who could scarcely read.

The church was packed, mostly by people from the Lady Streets. One of the coffin bearers was a tall young man of eighteen, his hair calmer and darker these days. Colin Duckworth, preparing to read law at Oxford, was proud to carry a woman who had fought the good fight for Rosie Stone, who had helped look after Mickle, whose granddaughter was the best-looking girl in Liverpool.

Maggie's hymns were sung, and the congregation was glad of the interruption, because the vicar had the sort of voice that might have been better employed by a hypnotist. Isadora read John Donne, before Rosie stood and walked to her nana's coffin when the last line of Donne's defiant and uplifting piece had been delivered.

Dressed in red and navy, Rosie read her tribute to Maggie. 'Nana taught me to read, write and count; she said I should always carry a handkerchief and she made sure that my shoes were polished. "That way," she said, "you'll always shine at one end if not at the other." Not a single day passed when she didn't make me laugh, and she convinced me to believe in myself.

'After my foster-parents had left for their second honeymoon in America and Europe, my grandmother spent hours with me, explaining that her treatment was no longer effective. With her usual love and kindness, she began to lead me along the route to this special day. Warning me that the provider of her blood tonic might be criticized to the point of damnation, Nana asked me to be her voice and to say the following.'

Rosie cleared her throat of emotion. 'Nana said, "Tia, Theo, Isadora, Joan, Jack, Nancy and Tom, Harry and Martha, thank you for your friendship and hospitality. You nourished my Rosie, and I know you will keep her safe now that I have gone.

'"I grow weaker every day, yet life still makes me smile. I am smiling now, because Rosie is changing my words and making me seem posh when she reads this back to me. Every colour is brighter these days, every sound clearer, every scent more beautiful. The little food I manage to eat is more tasty, and I feel that all my faculties (Rosie's word) are enhanced (there she goes again with her fancy talk) as I near my end. My sheets are so smooth, and Rosie's skin feels like velvet, while her hair is silk.

'"Don't grieve too long for me, but heed my advice. Make your own decisions in this life, but seek information first. Don't be a piece in a game of chess, because hands that move those pieces often make mistakes. Choose the people who will help you. Don't let a national institution of lawyers or doctors decide your fate. Trust in your friends and in yourself. The educated may be of use to you, and if that is the case, trust in them, too. Remember, choice is yours – it's your right.

'"The woman who extended the length of my life is now dead and beyond the reach of those who would punish her. Leave her to rest, and carry me now to my last little patch of England. God bless you all. With love, Margaret Rose Stone."'

Rosie folded the sheet of paper and smiled through unshed tears at a very colourful congregation. After a few seconds of silent hesitation, the people stood and clapped. While such behaviour was unusual at a funeral, it seemed right. Maggie Stone had wanted a party rather than a wake, and her audience applauded her. All that remained now was the task of placing her in the ground from which mankind had risen.

As chief mourner, Rosie led the people out behind the coffin. Outside, the streets were wet from a sudden shower, and the sun was shining fiercely to dry the earth. A huge arc of colour stretched over Liverpool, all seven colours clear and bright. 'That's Nana,' Rosie said to her foster-mother. 'She always had to have the last word.'

Eighteen

In the middle of September, Isadora moved into Flat One, the ground-floor apartment that had been Theo's home before becoming shelter for Maggie and Rosie Stone. Rosie had removed the memorabilia she wanted to keep, though the suicide letters had already been incinerated as soon as the funeral was over. After opening the envelope addressed to herself, Izzy had decided to dispose of all these unnecessary messages. Powders labelled *Gentul Piosin* (Daphne Melia's version of gentle poison) had been removed, too, so no one needed to know that Maggie had been in pain great enough to merit the planning of self-harm.

Izzy remembered her cook/housekeeper fondly. As her position dictated, she had been addressed as Mrs Melia, though she had never married. How had she read cookery books? Perhaps she hadn't needed to; perhaps she'd been a natural cook, or one who had learned skills at her mother's side. 'Unlike me,' Izzy grumbled aloud. 'I'm hopeless. Cordon Bleu? Cordon Failed would be nearer the mark.'

The upper storey of the villa was now the private residence of Mr and Mrs Peake, though Tyger continued to visit both flats in order to plead starvation and gain extra food. Even with a feline intruder, Joan and Jack now had the privacy they needed and deserved, while Isadora had gained the freedom to work whenever she pleased without disturbing others.

In the room that had once been Theo's body parts sanctuary, Izzy found an envelope containing some photographs that must have belonged to Maggie; Rosie seemed to have overlooked them in her search a few days after the funeral. Isadora discovered Maggie captured as a beautiful young bride linking arms with a handsome, moustachioed husband. She then picked up Sadie, a very pretty girl with dark, curly hair and a mischievous smile that displayed wonderful teeth. Oh, here was baby Rosie, so cuddly, so happy, with no idea of the grim future she would be forced to share with Sadie and company.

Izzy dropped into Theo's old writing chair. She felt rather like a Peeping Tom, an intruder. She now knew that one of the items had been hidden rather than stored. It had been separated from the rest and placed nearer to the bottom of Theo's stack of blank paper. 'If I hadn't moved that decaying pile, I would never have found these. Oh, Maggie.' She now knew why Maggie had attempted to hide the last of the photographs. She held up the picture that had been concealed and wrapped separately in greaseproof paper; it showed an image of a young fellow with a grinning Sadie by his side. There was something familiar about the man's face . . .

She turned the item over. On it was written in pencil and in Maggie's hand, *Frank Turner, Rosie's dad?* 'Oh, my God.' *Breathe, Isadora, breathe. Take your time, think about this and discuss it with Portia and Theo before reacting. Rosie's had enough shocks in her life without discovering a father who might be dead or in prison or . . . Stop this now. You'll make yourself ill, and nothing good will come of that. Think, think.*

Turner is not an uncommon name. There could be thou-

420

sands in Liverpool, hundreds in the telephone directory. Might a private detective find this man? Rosie is fifteen, so her father should be in his mid to late thirties, early forties at the oldest. Sadie would be thirty-five or six now, had she lived. But look at his forehead, his cheekbones, his chin. Maggie always said she had no idea about Rosie's father, yet the photo proves that she nursed her suspicions. This is Rosie's father; I'd bet my last farthing on it. I believe she even has his eyes. Oh, Lord help us.

Some people watched birds in the wild, while others waited for trains and scribbled numbers in little books. The Flying Scotsman had attracted thousands of devoted men, but Theodore Quinn's favourite pastime was watching his wife at work, and he wasn't one in a huge crowd looking at a steam engine. Would he ever tire of this wonderful woman? She was an amazing teacher.

Her rules were few, but clear. A chart on the wall was filled in daily; when a child had three ticks on the chart, he or she could choose a play activity in a previously disused area leading off the classroom. Once a place where coats were hung, it was now devoid of hooks and shoe shelves, and Tia had filled it with games, a small water trough, a sand pit, a Wendy house, a 'shop', dressing-up clothes and a painting corner. In order to achieve the freedom offered by the play area, pupils worked hard to get the three ticks that would release them.

The playroom was where they began to learn how to tell the time. There was a large clock on a wall and, as they were allowed thirty minutes only, they stayed until the long hand was in a position opposite to the original. When the half hour was up, it was a quick wash, a removal of dads' shirts, which were adapted and worn back-to-front as aprons, then back to quiet reading or story time in the classroom.

Tia had positioned her desk so that she might oversee both rooms, though her charges were so well behaved and keen to please her that very few needed admonishment. Theo grinned. Sometimes in the afternoon, if reading, writing and so forth were out of the way, Tia got herself made up by little girls in the Wendy house. She often arrived home with huge circles of red on her cheeks, very strange lips, massive eyebrows and hair that needed logarithms to work out the tangles. She was theirs, and they matured greatly after that year of carefully planned fun mixed with education. 'I'm a bridge,' she had been heard to opine. 'I'm the span between parents and academia.'

There was a second chart. Each of Tia's charges was listed under days of the week. Theo had been seated at the back of the classroom when his then new wife had explained the first copy of the list ten years earlier. 'Children, sit down, please.' When all were quiet and seated, she had explained, her face deadpan except for a wink in her husband's direction, 'The truth is, this room is too small for us. We must take turns to laugh, because the noise is terrible sometimes. You are each in a group that has a laughing day. When it's your turn, you may laugh; when it isn't your turn, don't even giggle. This way, we may get some actual work done at last.'

Ten years later, Theo sat at the back and watched her again. He called in at all classrooms, always unexpectedly, thus keeping teachers on their toes by offering comment and suggestion regarding principles and practice of education, also teaching methods. His wife had never needed help except when wheedling extras out of him when it came to yearly requisitions, because she was born for this. She was also a natural wheedler, almost a blackmailer . . .

The ridiculous laughter chart guaranteed that each child would laugh every day. Her other subtle methods involved double takes, where she would look at a child, look away, then glance back very quickly, thereby making the room a comedy show; furthermore, she would occasionally yell 'Stop!' apropos of nothing at all, before declaring that she felt a song or a poem coming on. The kids adored her, as did he. She had even set up a home book system so that she and parents might communicate regarding the welfare and progress of a pupil.

She was reading to them. 'Worzel,' she whined, her accent stationed somewhere in a Somerset orchard. Earthy Mangold was calling Worzel, but Worzel had forgotten to don his thinking head, and all he wanted was a cup of tea and a slice of cake. Tia brought to life everything she read, and her class hung on each word she delivered. This was Portia Bellamy, who might have become a household name, and she had become just that, but only in a small part of Liverpool.

Theo crept out and returned to his office, reluctant to sound the end-of-day bell. Portia's children would be left hanging and wondering where the scarecrow had left his thinking head. 'I know I'm biased,' he said aloud, 'but she is darned brilliant.' Although the Worzel Gummidge books were aimed at older children, Mrs Quinn believed in talking up as opposed to talking down to children when it came to literature. He sat at his desk and waited for her, because he had some disturbing news to impart.

She followed her man when school had been dismissed for the day. 'What's wrong?' she asked. 'I can see something in your expression, so out with it. You're up to no good, Teddy Quinn.'

I can't hide anything at all from her; she's looking inside my head. Again. I must go through my thoughts later to check whether anything's missing. 'Ma phoned me. She found a photograph in the body parts room.'

'And?'

'On the reverse, Maggie had labelled it Frank Turner, Rosie's dad, followed by a question mark.'

Tia dropped into a chair. 'But . . . but she always insisted that she had no idea about Rosie's father.'

Theo nodded. 'Exactly. Whoever or whatever the man is, Maggie wanted better for Rosie. And Portia, Ma said she can see the likeness.'

She sighed heavily and stayed silent for a few seconds. 'Had Rosie's father been decent and findable, Maggie would have gone out of her way to contact him.'

He drummed fingers on his desk. 'Then why didn't she destroy the photograph, Tia?'

'I have absolutely no bloody idea.' A few beats of time passed. 'But what if . . .' She stopped while processing her thoughts. 'What if he knew about Rosie? What if he murdered Tunstall?'

Theo absorbed the words his wife had just delivered. The man would have been forced to lie low if he'd killed the dragon to save the princess, but where had he been for the first five years of Rosie's life? 'Where was Sadie educated?' he asked finally.

'Here and Ivy Lane, Maggie told me.' Tia pursed her lips and concentrated. 'You think she may have known him at school?'

'I can look in the annals, or I can get Mrs Moyles to do it.' Mrs Moyles was a school secretary who shared her time between Myrtle Street and Ivy Lane schools. 'Meanwhile, we say nothing. Rosie's had enough to cope with, and she's never known her father. She's settling well in our attic, working hard for her exams next year.'

'And if he simply turns up at our door?'

'We cope.'

'And poor Rosie?'

'Look, nothing's changed, Portia. That photograph has existed for years. Let it ride for now, baby.'

She shrugged. 'We need to have a meeting with Ma. And yes, get Mrs Moyles to look for a Frank Turner – say he has an old friend trying to contact him, and the friend thinks that Frank may have been in school with Sadie Stone. We can calculate the years she would have been at Ivy Lane or here.'

Theo grinned and aimed for a less weighty subject. 'Just one question, my dear.'

'Oh?'

'Does Worzel find his thinking head?'

She stood up. 'Yes, and you'd better find yours,' she snapped before leaving the room.

In spite of the potential seriousness of the situation, Theo chuckled. Tia was the same girl he'd met just over a decade ago. There had been no discernible improvement whatsoever, and he was delighted.

That same evening, they invited Isadora for a meal. David was at football practice, Michael had a music lesson, while Rosie was visiting a school friend.

Theo glanced at the clock. 'We don't have long. Let's see this chap, Ma.'

The Quinns studied the monochrome picture. 'Rosie has her mother's hair,' Tia said. 'But yes, there is a resemblance.'

Her husband agreed. 'So why didn't Maggie tell us, then?'

Isadora thought about that. 'She did become slightly confused towards the end, Theo. It's possible that she may have had several hiding places for this. Perhaps she moved it from time to time and couldn't remember where she'd left it. The question remains; what must we do?'

'Eat and think,' Theo suggested.

They ate and thought.

'Rosie still takes most meals with you, doesn't she?' Izzy asked.

'Oh yes,' Theo reassured her. 'She has her own little apartment because she can listen to her music and do her school work without being interrupted by low-flying objects. Our sons are lively.'

'I know,' Izzy replied tartly. 'Joan, Jack and I looked after them for six weeks. I came close to putting them up for adoption.'

Tia chewed and swallowed. 'Could he lay claim to her?'

'She's not left luggage,' Theo said. 'She's our daughter. Because of her age, adoption should be a breeze as long as she wants us as official adoptive parents. There's nothing about a father on her birth certificate. I'll ask her.'

'Turner will still be out there somewhere.' Tia waved a hand towards the window. 'And another point, Teddy – she has the right to know him.'

Isadora squared her shoulders. 'Very well, let's find him. Get your search done at school, Theo. But remember that Sadie was twenty when she had Rosie, so Frank Turner might well be someone she met after leaving school.' She pondered for a few moments. 'The elderly in the Lady Streets may prove helpful. And I'll search my flat again, because there could be more information hidden by poor Maggie.' She looked up at the ceiling. 'Oh, Maggie, why didn't you tell us?'

They all knew the answer to that one. A line used frequently by Maggie was 'If it's not broke, don't mend it'. She had wanted the best for her granddaughter and, in

Maggie's book, the Quinns were the best. 'I'd bet a dollar to a dime that Maggie found him. If the man wasn't good enough in Maggie's opinion . . .' Theo's voice was suddenly strangled.

'Don't cry, sweetheart!' Tia grabbed his hand.

'We can't lose her,' he managed. 'And I'm not crying. Well, not really.'

'OK, so stop not-really-ing. You've dripped on your shirt.'

'That's water, Portia.'

'Of course it is. You're a drip.'

He wiped his face with a table napkin.

Michael entered with his guitar and a grim expression. 'I need longer fingers,' he grumbled before making his way towards the hall. 'I'll put this away,' he announced. 'I'm not going to guitar classes any more; I want to learn the trumpet.'

'God help us,' Theo muttered. 'We'll need to be soundproofed.'

Tia went to fetch her younger son's meal. 'Wash your hands,' she yelled.

David fell in through the door. 'Ten-nil, ten-nil, ten-nil, ten-nil,' he sang tunelessly.

After placing Michael's food on the table, Tia glared at her older son. 'Why are you wearing a field?' she asked. 'And is that a bird's nest or your hair?'

'There was that thunderstorm while we were at school. The playing field was a bit flooded,' was his reply.

Tia pointed to the hall. 'Get in the bath,' she ordered, 'and this time, use soap, sponge and loofah.' She followed him into the hallway. 'Neck and ears,' she called, 'and find the nail brush. I don't want to see black under your nails.' She turned. Her husband and her mother were sniggering at her. 'What?' she growled.

'You're beautiful when you're angry – isn't she, Ma?'

'She arrived angry, Theo. She screamed for eighteen months, and her first word was NO! It arrived fully furnished in capital letters with an exclamation mark. But she was precious and interesting and wilful. Adorable.'

'She's still all of those, plus stubborn as a mule.'

Tia sat. 'Shut up,' she ordered, 'and stop talking as if I'm not here. Ma, pick up the photograph. Theo, you must have wiped up some blue chalk with that handkerchief – it's all over your face. I'm going to check on the hellion.' She left the room.

Izzy and Theo listened while she dealt with David. 'That's a mud bath,' she shouted. 'Get out and start again. How do you expect me to get your kit clean? As for the boots in the porch – deal with them yourself.'

Theo raised his shoulders. He could cope with hundreds of children, but Isadora's daughter was beyond repair, thank goodness. 'I love that woman,' he mouthed at his mother-in-law.

'I know you do, Theo. And she loves you.'

'But of course she does.' He grinned. 'I'm very lovable.'

Michael was shovelling food as if he hadn't been fed for months. 'Slow down,' Izzy said. 'What's the hurry?'

'I've got a book about dinosaurs. Did you know that birds are their nearest relatives?'

'You'll ruin your digestive system,' Theo admonished.

The boy paused for a few seconds. 'You'd think it would be alligators and crocodiles, but it's birds. They must have come from pterodactyls. They could fly. I wonder if they had feathers.'

'Good question,' Theo replied. 'Some say yes, some say no. They were reptiles that glided from one place to another. Look it up in your encyclopedia.'

'May I leave the table, Dad?'

'Oh, go on, before you get to elephants and the like.'

Michael fled while the going was good. This was a

toss-up between shepherd's pie and tyrannosaurus rex. It was no contest.

Isadora crossed the road between Brooklands and Crompton Villa. The lights were on upstairs, because days were becoming shorter, and the tang of autumn hung in the air. 'They're at home. No time like the present,' she mumbled under her breath before walking up the side of the house to ring the bell.

Jack answered. 'Hello, Izzy. Come in; we were just choosing wallpaper for the sitting room. Joan's making a brew, so you can have a cuppa with us.' He followed her up the stairs.

Over the cup that cheers, the married couple forgot wallpaper and listened while Isadora outlined the story. She begged Jack to talk to elderly people in the Lady Streets.

'They don't need to be elderly,' was his response. 'Though I admit the over-sixties remember best. But Rosie's only fifteen.' He pondered. 'Sadie left the area when Rosie was born. She came back with Rosie and Tunstall, and . . . well, we all know what went on after that. Turner,' he said almost under his breath. 'The only Turner I heard of painted pictures of ships. I'll put the word out, Izzy.'

He sat back and rooted about in his memory. *No, Jack. You do remember, you do, and it's nothing to do with a painter. I wish these two would shut up for a few minutes while I get me head straight. Shoplifters. Pickpockets. It was a number twenty-seven on the door, but which bloody street? They all look the same, them streets, if I remember right. There was an Alec with buck teeth; he was better natured than the rest. Was there a Frank? There were five or six of them. No girls. Their mam was a barmaid at night*

429

and a waitress during the day. I never saw the dad. He was supposed to have been lost at sea, but weren't there rumours about him knocking about with an usherette from the Odeon in town? Didn't they move to Gateacre? Was there a Frank? Think, man, think!

Joan's skin, always pale, turned ashen. 'Could he take her away from us? She's happy here; she has parents, brothers, us. Three households look out for her and keep her safe, Izzy. Leave it alone, please.'

Izzy tried to reassure her friend. 'She's fifteen, Joan. No court would attempt to force her to do anything.'

'But she doesn't need the disturbance it would bring,' Joan insisted.

Her husband jumped to his feet so suddenly that his chair fell over backwards. 'Jesus Christ,' he whispered, his eyes fixed to the photograph on the table.

'What?' the two women asked simultaneously.

'I can't tell you yet,' he replied. 'But I'm going for Theo. I may be wrong, so I'm saying nothing.' He grabbed his jacket and left.

Izzy and Joan stared at each other. 'What happened there?' Izzy asked. 'He seems to have upstaged both of us.'

'No idea,' was the reply. 'We're supposed to be unpredictable because we're women, but Jack's like a flea on a dog sometimes, leaping about without warning. I think he just had what people call an epiphany. With angina, epiphanies are not necessarily a good thing.'

'So an idea dropped into his mind without warning?'

Joan nodded. 'Don't worry, there's plenty of space for it in his head.'

They laughed, though the sound arrived strained.

'I couldn't bear to lose him,' Joan admitted.

'He'll be fine; he has you to live for.'

They heard Theo's car starting up. The beloved MGs were still parked in a large garage behind the house, though the Quinns frequently used a family car since the children had arrived. Izzy dashed to the window. 'Jack's with Theo. Ah, they're gone. Shall we ask Portia what's afoot? Oh, hang on; here comes Rosie, so we must stay where we are.'

They had to wait. Izzy, who had practised calming through yoga in many dressing rooms, sat down and managed to contain herself. Joan began to pace about. 'Oh, God,' she muttered at least five times.

'Joan?'

'Yes?'

'Go and wash dishes, clean the oven, paint a ceiling or whatever.'

'Sorry.'

'Forgiven. But go away.'

Joan went away.

Alone, Izzy closed her eyes and aimed for calm, but she never quite got there. Frank Turner. Who and where the hell was he?

'Where are we going?' Theo asked. 'Tia believes I've left home.'

'I'm thinking,' was Jack's reply. 'We'll kick off down the Dingle. I'll find out whether they've moved.' *I need to remember. Come on, Jack Peake, wake up. Was I courting a girl in the Dingle? What was her name?*

Theo applied the brakes. 'I know you have your thinking head on, but I must ask you this – whether who's moved? What the hell in a wagon is going on?'

Jack shook his head. 'Look, it's just a thought and I could be wrong. The photo made me wonder, that's all. I don't want to say anything in case I'm at the mucky end of the stick. Just drive while I try to remember stuff.'

'What stuff?'

'Stuff I'll remember better if you shut up. I had enough in the flat with Joan and Izzy nattering on like bloody market traders. That's it. One of them had a stall on Paddy's Market when he grew up.'

'One of which or what or whom?'

'Button it, Mr Quinn. I'm sixty-five and I'm looking for number twenty-seven with no idea of the street. Just drop me when I say, then come back in an hour.'

'But—'

'Please don't talk.'

'OK, keep your hair on. You can't afford to lose any more.'

Jack sat back and stared through the windscreen, hoping against hope that something would catch his eye – a clue, a hint, a– 'Stop,' he yelled.

The car squealed to a halt. 'Jeez,' Theo breathed. 'You made me jump, and you're doing no good for my tyres.'

'Come back for me in an hour,' Jack begged. 'I'm going to find some Turners. Go into the flat and make sure my Joanie's all right. She frets.'

'Turners?' Theo raised a quizzical eyebrow.

'They may be the wrong ones.'

'Right.'

'No, wrong ones.'

Theo groaned. 'Jack?'

'What?'

'Get lost; I'll see you later.'

When Theo had driven away, Jack got busy wandering up and down streets that all looked the same, one door, one window, another door, another window, the smell of rancid fat emanating from the chip shop on the corner. It was the shop that had given him a clue, because its door cut across the corner of the terrace. But he discovered that several of the streets had a shop with a similar entrance, so . . .

He pulled himself together and knocked on a door that was not twenty-seven; it was twenty-four. In his experience of terraced-house living, neighbours across the way often knew more about those living opposite than they did about adjacent families.

An old woman with a splendid moustache answered. 'What do you want? I'm listening to me programme.' She fiddled with her hearing aid.

'Do you know any Turners?'

'What? Speak up, me battery's playing the fool again, bloody rubbish.'

'Do you know any Turners?' He separated every syllable.

'Turners?'

He nodded.

'Him at number eighteen works a lathe. He's a turner, goes across on the ferry every day, ironworks in Birkenhead.' She closed the door.

Jack covered four streets. His feet ached, his head ached, and most parts between these extremes were unhappy. Theo would be back soon.

On street five, he hit what Theo would call pay dirt, gold among dry earth and rocks. There was something here, on this spot, a memory, a picture of two boys running from police and into a house, into this house. He recalled sending the cops in the wrong direction, thereby letting the lads get away with whatever they'd done, because they were poor. Yet the place looked the same as all the others, so why did he recognize it?

'Here goes,' he muttered. For a reason he still didn't fully understand, Jack knocked at the door. It was number twenty-seven in a warren of streets he hadn't visited since God alone knew when.

A man opened the door. He was in his mid to late thirties, dressed in brown corduroy trousers and a blue shirt. 'Can I help you?' he asked.

Jack cleared his throat. 'I'm looking for the Turner family,' he said.

'I'm a Turner,' the man said, stepping aside. 'Who are you?'

'Jack Peake.'

Mr Turner smiled. 'I remember you. You never grassed on us when the coppers were on our tail years back. You were going out with that Lucas girl – what was her name? Eileen. Eileen Lucas. Come in.'

Jack swallowed hard and went into the house. No longer dirty and smelly, the place was cheerful, clean and decently furnished. He perched on the edge of a small armchair. 'Have you always lived here?' There was a whiff of new paint in the air, so the house had been decorated recently.

'No, I moved to Seaforth and came back here just about a month ago. It's nearer to the station, you see. I'm a fireman.'

Hoping that Theo would wait for him, Jack began to ask his questions.

Theo and Tia joined Joan and Isadora in the first-floor apartment. Rosie had been appointed to cope with the boys' bedtime, as she was well capable of dealing with her younger brothers.

'So you just left Jack there?' Joan's tone was almost accusatory.

Theo shrugged. 'He practically told me to bugger off, so off I buggered.'

'Is it safe?' Izzy asked.

'You should have parked and waited,' was Tia's contribution.

The other two nodded in agreement.

'It's safe enough. I saw no Comanche, no Sioux or

434

Apache,' Theo told them. 'Jack needed to be alone to think. Every time I asked him what was going on, he ordered me to shut up. He's not a child, ladies, though I must admit that he made little sense. Anyway, stop apportioning blame. One of my closest friends asked me to come home, and I did just that.' *Ah, here they go with the tea ceremony. Three of them in the kitchen just to make one pot of tea. Tea is always the panacea on these small islands.*

What the hell are you up to, Jack? I've three distressed females here, and a fourth across the street who may well become distressed very soon. I'm her father, Tia's her mother, Izzy-gran is Izzy-gran, and Joan and you are aunt and uncle. She has another aunt and uncle in Juliet and Simon, and two further aunts are Delia and Elaine. No one can take her away from us after all this time. She's inherited my Portia's stubborn streak, because nurture won over nature, and she's a brilliant student because of us. No matter what, she'll stay here. Don't find him, Jack.

We taught her at Myrtle Street, though we sent the boys to a different school, because they never lived in the Lady Streets. Ashburner School is almost as good as mine, and we fill in any minor gaps at home. Just a few minutes to wait now, and I can go fetch him. And I'm drinking no more tea in case I drown in the stuff.

The women returned with tea and biscuits.

'He's thinking,' Tia announced. 'The frown gives him away every time.'

Theo scowled at his wife.

'Well,' she said, 'you're always talking about me as if I'm elsewhere.'

'That's because although you're with us in body, your mind has a habit of wandering off.' He jumped up. 'No more tea for me. If I drink any more, I'll start to look Chinese or Indian.'

Tia grinned. 'What about your octoroonship?'

'That ship has sailed,' he answered tersely.

'Our children are sixteeneroons,' she answered smartly.

He nodded. 'Sometimes, I manage to see that there is a strong case for the application of corporal punishment.'

Tia folded her arms. 'Oh yeah? Try it, mister.'

He startled her by crossing the room and planting a sloppy kiss on her forehead. 'I'm going for Jack.'

'Good.'

Theo left.

Joan heaved a sigh. 'Do they have a disease, I wonder? Some kind of genetic flaw that makes them talk rubbish and wander off like lost dogs?'

Tia burst out laughing. 'You don't sound in the least like my Nanny Reynolds. If you mean men, yes. It's testosterone. They start off in their teens with a surfeit of it that drives them demented and, as they get slightly older, it starts to come and go without warning. So you're living with a cross between a sex-crazed lunatic and a moonbeam who starts criticizing your sewing.'

Joan's cheeks coloured slightly while Izzy howled with laughter. 'When does the wandering start?' Joan asked.

'When they crawl,' was Tia's quick answer. 'And you know they're completely past it when they get attached to slippers and one chair. No one else must sit in that chair. Thus far, my Teddy is retarded – still a teenager. I have to wear running shoes when the children are out. But I'm lucky, I suppose.'

Izzy shook her head. 'You're still a naughty girl, Portia.'

'Good. Ah, we have a visitor. I'll get the door, Ma. I hope it's not Rosie!'

'Don't worry, Joan,' Izzy advised quietly. 'He'll be back.'

Tia returned looking upset. 'It's Martha Foster,' she said, dashing away a tear that meandered down her cheek. She turned and pulled the door wide. 'Come in, Martha.'

Martha crept into the living room. 'Rosie said you were all here. I didn't tell her anything; Harry wanted Theo to tell her.' She held up an envelope. 'Where is Theo?'

'We don't know. He's gone to pick Jack up, and we don't know where he is, either, so we—' Joan cut herself off. 'Tia, grab her; she's going to faint!'

Tia caught Martha and placed her on the sofa.

'Has she fainted?' Izzy asked.

'No,' Martha replied feebly. 'I wouldn't mind some sweet tea, though. I can't eat. I haven't eaten since yesterday. He was dead when I went to wake him this morning.'

The other three women were now suddenly seated. 'Harry?' Izzy's voice broke on the second syllable.

Martha nodded. 'In his sleep. I boiled his egg and made toast, but he was cold when I went to give him his breakfast.'

Joan pulled herself up and went to make yet more tea. *How many sugars do I use for shock? And how many things can go wrong in one day? We don't know where Jack is, we don't know where Theo went, Rosie may have acquired a father, and now poor Harry and poor, poor Martha. He was her life, bless her. They were devoted to each other. Izzy will think of something; Izzy and Portia usually think of something. Martha loves Rosie, and Rosie has always adored her and Harry. This is a terrible day.*

'What next?' she muttered as she spooned sugar into the mug. 'Come home, Jack, I need you here.'

Martha's hands trembled as she accepted the tea. 'He beat me twice at dominoes last night. Some lads from the *Echo* were talking about taking him on a trip in a boat; they were going fishing, and he was so excited. People went out of their way to buy their newspapers from him,

437

and it wasn't pity – it was because he was always joking, saying things like he couldn't get legless on a Saturday night and how he'd been stopped for speeding on his trolley in a built-up area. He was the best.'

Tia swallowed hard. 'Rosie will miss him. We all will. We bought our newspapers from him, too, when we were in town.'

The visitor sipped at her tea, wondering what she was going to do without Harry. She had a part-time job in a shop, but he had been her reason for living. She looked at Izzy. 'Would you mind if I stopped here tonight? I know I'll have to learn to be in the flat on my own, but his breakfast's still there. I think the dominoes are in the box on that table you made for him, Tia. All his clothes, his special gloves, the trolley . . .' A long, shuddering sigh made its way out of her lungs. 'My brother's being cut open down the hospital. They think he had a heart attack, but they have to be sure. It's the law, you see.'

Izzy told Martha that she could stay for as long as she liked. 'Post mortem is compulsory, Martha, if the cause of death isn't evident. Rosie had to go through the waiting when Maggie died. And I think Harry was a kind of grandfather to Rosie. So she's lost two important people in a matter of weeks.'

'He loved her. I love her.' Martha dried her eyes before adding, 'Will you make me a bit of toast, Joan? I feel a bit better in normal company away from ambulance men and doctors fussing about.'

'Of course. Marmalade or jam?'

'Just butter, please.'

Half an hour later, Martha was tucked up and asleep in one of the spare rooms. That letter from Harry for Theo was propped up behind the mantel clock in the sitting room. The three remaining women were silent, though Tia's brain was going like a bat out of hell. *Rosie,*

438

my Rosie, you've lost your nana, your chosen grandfather, and you may have gained a biological father. Maggie was not a dishonest person, and she must have had her reasons for being confused by and afraid of that photograph. Teddy, where are you? We need you; we need you now. Jack, come home; your wife was in a state of worry about you an hour ago, and she's plucking at her skirt now, so her nerves are raw. We have to tell Rosie about Harry . . .

Izzy watched Joan, who was, indeed, picking invisible lint from her skirt. She turned her head away from Joan and glanced at her eldest daughter, who was clearly deep in thought. There were teacups everywhere, and side plates covered in crumbs and half-eaten biscuits. Theo and Jack were taking their time, and Martha had entered the sleep of the truly exhausted. Izzy wouldn't clear the crockery, since she wanted the silence to endure for a while, because Martha Foster deserved and needed peace.

Tia's chair was nearest to the window. When the nose of the family car entered the avenue, she jumped up. She kept her voice low. 'Whatever they know or don't know about Frank Foster will have to keep. Tonight belongs to Harry.' She dashed downstairs.

'Where the hell have you two been?' she demanded when the car stopped on the driveway to Brooklands.

Theo alighted from the driver's seat. 'Don't ask.'

'So don't tell,' she snapped. 'Harry the Scoot died last night in his sleep. Martha's upstairs in the flat, in bed. Harry left a letter for you, Teddy. Your name's on the envelope with IN THE EVENT OF MY DEATH underneath in capital letters. Martha says she wants you to tell Rosie.'

Theo closed his eyes.

'So wherever you've been is in second place for now, Teddy. First, we have to break our daughter's heart. I'll be at your side when you tell her, darling.'

439

'Sweet Jesus,' Jack said softly.

Theo walked round the car and grabbed his friend's hands. 'We need to keep quiet, mate. There's enough going on without heaping this on the heads of others. Let's deal with it another time, huh?'

Jack nodded. 'I need to sort my head out anyway. I feel like me brain's tied in knots after what's happened tonight.' He spoke to Tia. 'Sorry we were gone so long, love, only we've had a shock – I can tell you that for no money. But you're dead right as per usual. Harry comes first, God rest him.'

They crossed the avenue until they reached the gate of Crompton Villa. 'Don't let slip anything about what you found out, boys,' Tia begged. 'Martha needs rest, so we do what must be done, no more than that.'

They walked up the side to the door that had once been Tia's. 'Deep breaths now. In we go,' she ordered. 'You've a letter to read, Mr Quinn.'

Theo emerged from the used-to-be-body-parts room, left the lower apartment by the front door and stood in the garden. He remembered that evening when Tia had come to look at the first-floor accommodation; he remembered falling in love with a face and a BBC-here-is-the-news voice and hair that tumbled when she crawled under the table to meet Tyger-One. He looked back at his fear of producing a dark-skinned child, recalled Tia explaining that he was thinking like a racist and that they would have children.

He'd needed to be truly alone while reading Harry's letter, but he now had to return to all who waited upstairs. He was weeping, and he didn't care about how he looked. Still unable to recover from the evening's earlier discovery, he found himself having to absorb a

440

second trauma. On leaden legs, he returned to the first floor.

Tia's heart seemed to swell when she looked at him. Her Teddy had a tendency to become emotional, because he was filled with love for humankind in spite of the species' foibles and the torture he had endured when young. She crossed the room and wiped his face. 'I'm here, beautiful boy. We're all here for you and for Harry.'

Theo sniffed. 'Izzy?'

'Yes, darling?'

'Have you any plans for my body parts room?'

Izzy pondered. 'Not really. I was just beginning to tidy it, and I intended to use it for storage. I don't need it. Why?'

Theo inhaled deeply. 'Martha may need a bolt-hole.' There was no other way, so he cut to the core of the matter. 'Harry killed Miles Tunstall.'

Silence reigned. The tick of the mantel clock seemed to grow louder by the second. It announced the half-hour in soft Westminster chimes. Theo continued. 'That room is off to one side, so you'll still have your privacy when she stays with you.'

'To hell with my privacy,' Izzy snapped. 'She's family. They dined with us at least once every month for ten years.'

Practical as ever, Tia wanted to know how Harry had managed to kill a grown man.

'He doesn't give full details, Portia – not to me, anyway, but he prepared me in his way.'

'How?' Tia asked.

'He used to say that his trolley could knock down a grown man and that his own upper body was strong enough to inflict damage.'

No one spoke, so Theo continued. 'There's a second letter inside mine. The envelope is sealed, and it's addressed to the Chief Constable, Liverpool police. We are charged by Harry with the task of minding Martha. She's an accessory before and after the fact.'

'Bugger,' Tia muttered. 'She's frail, Teddy. She will crack if questioned.'

'Right.' Theo straightened his spine. 'Tomorrow, don't allow her to be alone. I'll give the official letter in at a police station once Martha has been indoctrinated. We must make sure she pleads ignorance. We have an actress and two teachers among our number. Between us, we can make sure that she honours her brother's request.'

For the first time ever, Nanny Reynolds, now Mrs Peake, swore. 'He killed that bloody bastard. St Peter will let him in.'

A door opened quietly. 'It's all right.'

They turned as one person and stared at Martha Foster, who was wearing a robe belonging to Joan. 'I've already been trained, so don't worry. I made a promise to my brother, and I know nothing. Me and Harry never let each other down, and I've no intention of going back on my word. Is there any brandy?'

Nineteen

For Rosie, it was like Nana dying all over again. Still in mourning for Maggie, she took the news of Harry's sudden death like a kick in the gut. Winded, she sank to the floor, a heap of limbs and clothes topped by a magnificent head of long, dark hair. She finally managed a few words. 'He can't be dead – he's going sea-fishing next week with his *Post* and *Echo* friends.'

Theo picked her up and placed her on the sofa in the drawing room of Brooklands, their treasured family home. Tia hovered, feeling helpless and useless and untypically lost for words. She wrapped her arms round her upper body as if protecting or hugging herself. After a few seconds, she managed to retrieve a level of control. 'He went quickly, darling, and in his sleep. Doctors said he wouldn't have suffered.'

'He was my adopted granddad.'

'We know, honey.' Theo stroked his daughter's arm.

'Where's Martha?' Rosie asked.

'She's staying with Jack and Joan, then Isadora's going to give her the body parts room, and she can come and go as she pleases, baby. After the funeral, we may send her with Nancy and Tom to stay in Rose Cottage for a few weeks, or for as long as they wish. If they agree to go, we'll have their luggage sent down a couple of days before. Nancy and Tom are too old to carry cases.'

'They'll be next,' Rosie murmured.

The two adults stared at each other. There was more to tell, as Harry had left the letter . . . With no need for words, the couple asked each other the question, both nodding almost imperceptibly in reply. It had to be done. The message for the police needed to be delivered, and presses would release their hounds as soon as the news broke.

Tia decided to relieve her man of the biggest burden. 'Rosie?' she whispered, tears held in check. 'Harry saved your life.'

Rosie lifted her head. 'Yes, he taught me to cross roads in town when I was five. And he listened when I told him about . . . about things at home.'

Tia and Theo knelt side by side next to the sofa. 'He killed Miles Tunstall,' Tia whispered.

The fifteen-year-old blinked as if stupefied. 'But . . . no, he couldn't have done that. Harry wouldn't hurt a fly, and he had no legs – they stopped at his knees, Mum.'

'Where there's a will, there's a way, my love. He left a written confession for the police, plus a letter for Teddy. You have to know, because we don't want you to learn it by reading it in the papers. We can probably keep your name out of it because of your age, and we'll try to keep Sadie and Maggie out of it, too, although–'

'No,' Rosie replied breathlessly as she sat up. 'No,' she repeated quietly. 'My teachers know, my friends know and the Lady Streets know.' She hugged her parents. 'I want to be by myself, please.' She paused for a few beats of time. 'Murder is wrong, but if someone hadn't removed Tunstall, he might have removed me. Now, I'm removing myself, but only as far as the attic. I need . . . I need to think about things and just to be quiet for a while.'

After a minute or two, Tia and Theo crept up the stairs

and stood at the bottom of the flight to the attic. They heard her sobs, but remained where they were. Rosie Stone was possessed of a level of dignity that was unusual in one so young. 'Remember the glue?' Tia whispered. 'And her lying under the table at our reception with Mickle as her pillow?'

He nodded. 'And her love for all things pink or red. She still has the red shoes Simon bought for her, Tia, and the red clutch purse you gave her. She keeps them wrapped in tissue paper inside shoe boxes. They're her treasures.'

Tia wanted to ask about Frank Turner, though she didn't. Both she and Joan had agreed not to pester their husbands on the subject of their disappearance into the bowels of the city. Harry took priority, as did his sister.

Theo sat on the top stair of the lower flight. 'I read her work,' he murmured like a man making a confession. 'She wrote an essay entitled *Meet Me at the Pier Head*, and the whole story of her young life was there. I never told anyone I'd read it, because I felt like a spy, an intruder. I bet she got good marks for the piece – it was so vivid. It was also heartrending.'

Tia joined him on the step. 'She's a brave young woman. I hope she manages to cope with Harry's funeral.'

He grimaced. 'Knowing her, I guess she'll organize the whole thing. Like my wife, she's a bossy besom. God, don't her tears break your soul into a thousand pieces?'

The crying had slowed, so they went back downstairs.

Like Maggie Stone, Harry Foster became famous in death. His demise made front-page news in most nationals, while newspapers local to Liverpool were filled with praise for the deceased. Readers sent in scores of letters referring to his heroism, and Rosie was interviewed about the man who had beaten her and locked her in a coal shed, and about a mother who had been addicted first to gin, later to food. Although she took care not to condone the act of murder, Rosie expressed her heartfelt gratitude to Harry, who had saved her.

The fifteen-year-old comported herself admirably. After a few days of sporadic weeping, she answered questions concisely and truthfully, because life had equipped her with backbone, while her foster-parents had taught her good manners. Photographs of her with Harry, Martha and Maggie appeared everywhere in magazines; when paid for her time, she donated the money to Bartle Hall, which now enjoyed both the status of a registered charity, and the support of many stars of stage and screen.

Harry's funeral was huge. The self-confessed murderer was celebrated as if he had eliminated a disease from the streets of the city. People spilled into aisles, while many had to stand outside, as the church was so packed that its occupants felt they needed to take turns to breathe. In spite of the lack of oxygen, Rosie did her bit, singing *a cappella* 'The White Cliffs of Dover', just as she had all those years ago to the accompaniment of Harry's mouth organ. She delivered every note clearly and accurately while the congregation wept. Dry-eyed at the end of her song, she rebuked her audience gently. 'Listen to me, please,' she begged. 'Harry doesn't want you to cry.'

And she read her piece entitled 'Harry the Scoot'.

'I asked him where his legs were, because I was only just five years of age, and he didn't look right to me, perched as he was on that famous trolley. He said the Krauts had blasted his legs off. It was a while before I realized that he was referring to Germans, and I eventually stopped looking under my bed for hideous little gremlins that came along in the night and stole pieces of people.

'He gave me the confidence to sing and dance at the Pier Head while he played the harmonica. My pennies were saved for me by Harry and his sister, Martha, both of whom have been greatly loved and appreciated by me and my family.'

Tia squeezed her husband's hand. Rosie knew her whom from her who, and she also knew her real, true family.

'My nana died, and Harry has followed soon afterwards. But this is what happens to all of us, and let there be no doubt that Harry has taken his place with my nana at the right hand of God, because he knew no other way of saving me. There is medical proof of my injuries, and Harry put a stop to the abuse. I take this opportunity to thank the Liverpool police, especially PC Mary Twist, who was so kind to me when the news of what Harry had done for me finally broke.

'Do not pity me, as I have a mum, a dad, two brothers, and a family that extends to the other end of this country. But pray for Harry and raise a glass in his memory, and please contribute to the NSPCC.

'I apologize to Shakespeare, whose work I now misquote. "The evil that men do lives after them; the good is oft interred with their bones. So let it *not* be with Harry the Scoot Foster." Remember the fun of him, his music, his good nature, his very individual call, "E-e-echo", when he sold his newspapers. Thank you for coming to say goodbye.'

After the burial, key mourners returned to Brooklands for drinks and a buffet. For most, there existed a sense of closure after the waiting for post mortem results about Harry's coronary occlusion. But for Theo and Jack, there was little respite, since they still had a message to deliver to a select few, and Rosie would be left out of the mix, as would Martha, sister to the deceased.

Joan and Portia, wives of the two men involved, had asked no questions while funeral preparations were being made. Each man watched the other's unease, and Theo and Jack spent time together in order to discuss what they had discovered in the Dingle while Martha had waited to give them the news of her brother's death. She had stayed every night since with Isadora at Crompton Villa. Theo and Tia had gone to Martha's flat and shifted Harry's breakfast, his trolley and his clothes, thus saving Martha from a task she had dreaded.

'She's known no other life beyond a few hours in a shop and looking after her brother,' Izzy had said before sending her daughter and Theo to the flat. 'She needs us now. Oh, save his last pair of shoes. He hung on to them for years.'

Tom and Nancy Atherton had been given the task of escorting Martha to Chaddington Green for a holiday at Rose Cottage. Their luggage had been sent on before them, and they would travel tomorrow, the day after Harry's funeral.

Another item was on the agenda, as Theo and Jack had news to impart. Only Isadora, Portia and Joan would hear full the truth. Yes, the time had come. Tomorrow, the tale would be told.

After the compulsory making and drinking of tea, Isadora and Joan seated themselves on the sofa in the ground-floor flat, while Tia occupied an armchair that faced them.

'I wonder what they're going to tell us?' Izzy mused, almost to herself.

Tia, believing that she had worked out the answer, decided to offer no opinion in the matter. She might be wrong, and not for the first time. Frank Turner was

Rosie's father, and he was either dead or in jail. If he was alive, Rosie should probably be told. *Let him be dead, God. We can't lose her now, and she can't lose us because she's already lost more than enough. Is it wrong to wish an unknown person dead? And for her sake, let her not be disturbed by any more unwelcome news.*

Jack and Theo arrived, and the latter acted as main spokesman. He stood in front of the fireplace. 'You've waited long enough. We don't want you to worry any longer, so there'll be no rigmarole and I'll cut to the end, the last line on the page. Harry killed Miles Tunstall. Miles Tunstall was Rosie's father.'

Even Tia hadn't expected this. 'Are you sure he was her father?' she asked eventually, a hand held to her throat.

'Oh, yes. Sadie was wild, but not as bad as people seemed to think.' Theo swallowed. 'According to Tunstall's brother, Rosie is a child born of rape. Frank's five brothers turned on him and beat the shit out of him when they found her half dressed and in tears, so he left the neighbourhood and changed his name by deed poll as soon as he came of age.' He shook his head sadly.

'Andy Turner is a decent fellow, a fireman. They were all troublemakers in their youth, shoplifting, stealing and fighting. They were fatherless. Mr Turner left the family, and Mrs Turner worked two jobs to keep the wolf from the door. But the real wolf was at the wrong side of that door. He was a resident in the house.'

Jack butted in. 'He turned Sadie Stone into a prostitute by getting her hooked on drink. Andy didn't even go to his brother's funeral; none of the family did. The police spoke to the Turner men after Tunstall's death, as they were aware of the name change, but the Turners knew nothing about the murder, though they weren't surprised by it. Andy had no idea where Frank – or Miles – was.

449

Andy and his wife moved back to the Dingle just weeks ago to be nearer to his work, and he happens to rent the family's old house. That was where I found him.'

A short silence followed. Then Tia asked, 'Did Maggie know about the change of name?'

'I imagine so,' was Theo's ready answer. 'The police questioned her, because Sadie was drunk then brain-damaged, so Maggie had to speak for her.'

'So Maggie probably knew that Tunstall was Rosie's father?' Izzy asked.

Theo nodded.

'More than likely,' Jack said.

'But he isn't on the birth certificate,' Joan stated, her voice shrill. 'He was trying to adopt her. I'm glad PC Twist didn't tell Rosie the truth. That's one good woman.'

Jack intervened again. 'Sadie got away from him towards the end of her pregnancy, because she was always covered in cuts, bumps and bruises. When she registered Rosie, she said the father was unknown. But Tunstall, when he found Sadie, would see the child as his property to do with as he wished. Our Rosie's real father locked her up and knocked her about. So we can't tell her. She's never asked about a father, and she wouldn't recognize him from that photograph, because he put on a lot of weight.'

'She might recognize the resemblance to herself,' Tia whispered.

'The photo should be destroyed,' Izzy pronounced. 'Rosie is a bright girl with a good imagination. Why should she be tainted? Why should she worry about having Tunstall's bad blood?'

Theo sighed. 'The brothers agree – the Turner men. They will forgo the pleasure of meeting their niece. That's for Rosie's own sake. Good men, they are. There's a fire-man, a market trader, a motor mechanic and two who've opened a pet shop over the water – Wallasey, I think. They're ashamed of Frank.'

Tia's head was in her hands. *If she must find out, Lord, let it happen when she's older with her character and her career fully developed.* She raised her face. 'Nothing's changed,' she said. 'He was always her father, and Maggie probably knew it. Her decision not to tell Rosie is completely understandable. We must carry on regardless. Come along, Teddy, we have young to feed.'

While she cooked the meal, Tia thought about her own father, a man with values that had been somewhat Victorian. Like many heads of families during those sixty glorious years, Richard Bellamy had played away from home while trying to keep a stranglehold on his daughters. He had changed eventually, and was now a sweeter man who enjoyed his duties at Bartle Hall.

Might Tunstall have changed had he lived? No, she decided. *He would have looked at Rosie now and might have put her to work. She's so beautiful, perfect skin, that wonderful fall of long, dark brown hair, less curly now since the length and weight caused it to be smooth and lustrous. She might have made his fortune. Then why am I smiling? Yes, because I'm sure she would have given him advice on urination and travel. And I dare say Maggie might have done what poor Harry was moved to do. I wonder how he did it? The police will have those details.*

She jumped when a pair of arms crept round her waist.

'It's only me,' Theo said.

'Good. I thought it might be the milkman again.'

'Ah, the milkman. I thought the mailman was the problem.'

'It's both.'

'I see. Well, I can't say I blame them.'

451

She turned in his embrace. 'You don't care who handles me, do you?'

'Oh, Portia,' he whispered before kissing her hard. They regained their composure, and he continued. 'You're not just my ball and chain, honey, you're my safe haven, my heart's home.'

She smiled. Underneath it all, Teddy was an incurable romantic.

POST SCRIPTUM

Christmas 1968, Kent, England

Nancy, Tom and Martha had remained in the south since September. The Athertons' old bones were treated with better respect by the warmer winter, and they had settled nicely in Rose Cottage, moving into Lilac Cottage only when Richard, his wife and their son left to spend Christmas in London with friends.

Theo had expressed the opinion that Martha would probably remain in Kent for the rest of her life, as she spent most of her time in Bartle Hall with the children. She was a born carer, and she had found people who appreciated her. A natural listener, too, she drew the children out and got them to talk to her.

The rest of the clan were to travel down in Theo's Bedford Dormobile, a vehicle into which they could all fit with room to spare, as there were relatively few of them. David had to sit near a window. Michael had to sit near a window because David would be sitting near a window. Rosie didn't care where she sat as long as it wasn't anywhere near either of her brothers. She loved them, but preferred to love them from a safe distance. Michael had no idea when it came to sitting still, while David had a tendency to chatter before becoming travel sick, so most people avoided close contact with him during a journey of any length.

This time, there were just six travellers, as Joan and Jack had chosen to stay at home and have a quiet Christmas with Tyger as their only visitor. So David and Michael got their windows, Rosie sat at the rear of the van away from her brothers, and Izzy placed herself behind Tia, who would share the driving with Theo.

Theo climbed into the driver's seat. 'Does David have a bucket?'

'Yes,' Tia replied, managing to endow the single syllable with patience, impatience and do-you-think-I-came-down-the-Mersey-in-a-tin-bath-yesterday?

Rosie addressed her parents and Izzy-gran. 'We could put the bucket on Michael's head until David feels sick. That way, we won't have to sit through a running commentary about how many animals he sees between here and Kent.'

Both boys ran to the back of the vehicle and threw themselves at the girl who would soon be their real adopted sister. She screamed and brushed them off, threatening dire punishment including Chinese burns to their arms, a clout round their ear 'oles and no help with their holiday homework.

Tia and Theo exchanged grins. It was all so normal, wasn't it? Their young sons depended on this grown-up sister, loved her, disliked her, and admired her even though she was 'only a girl'.

Izzy took charge. 'Rosie, ignore them. If you fight back, they'll hang around like a bad smell on the landing. Michael, sit. David, get back to your seat and try not to kick the bucket.' She tried not to grin while delivering the deliberate double entendre. His bucket was metal, and he often attempted to get a tune out of it before needing it for its true purpose.

Again, Theo and Tia Quinn exchanged smiles. They were the perfect imperfect family whose offspring fought, laughed with, cried with and helped each other. Rosie had even assisted Mum and Izzy at Michael's birth, as he had arrived early, quickly and screaming like a banshee. Five years later, there was little improvement, as he was always too early, especially when mealtimes came round, and he continued to be loud.

'Have you left your keys with Joan?' Izzy asked.

'Yes, Ma.'

'Did you turn everything off, Portia?'

'Yes, Ma.'

'Is the MG garage locked?'

Tia glared at her mother. 'Yes, Ma.'

David turned his bucket upside down and stood on it. 'Let's see how far we get before I fall off.'

Izzy raised her eyes upward as if begging for heaven's help. 'Do you plan to spend Christmas in hospital, David?' she asked.

'I know how to fall, Gran.'

'I'm not thinking about a fall,' she answered. 'I'm talking about grievous bodily harm inflicted by me.'

He jumped down, righted the bucket, folded his arms, sat down and glowered. Fun was off the menu. 'He's breathing,' he announced.

'Good,' Izzy said. 'Let's hope we're all taking in oxygen.'

'He's breathing on the window and drawing pictures in his breath. Dad said we aren't meant to do that.'

Rosie sang, 'Tell-tale tit, his mother had a fit, gave him a clout, locked him out, tell-tale tit.'

It was Michael's turn to sulk. His brother had grassed on him just for drawing a snowman.

With exaggerated patience, Theo turned and gazed at his children. 'We haven't left home yet, and you're fighting. Your mother and I have to go, because we're covering for staff who went home for Christmas. I'm sure Joan and Jack won't mind babysitting while we're away.'

'No!' the boys shouted in unison.

Theo started the engine and reversed into the road. It was seven in the morning, and it was going to be a long journey with stops for food and drink, for David's car-sickness and for the relief of Michael's small bladder. He spoke to his wife. 'Shall we take them or leave them?' he asked.

'Take them,' she replied, 'because it's the Christian thing to do. We shouldn't inflict them on anyone, especially on Joan and Jack. They deserve some peace.'

Two personae non gratae bowed their heads in pretended shame.

'That's better,' Izzy said.

Rosie chuckled softly. The quiet would last for five minutes at best, though Izzy-gran was currently riveting them to their seats with very cold eyes. Rosie put cotton wool in her ears, donned earmuffs and carried on reading *Silas Marner*. Silas had just found Eppie, and the little orphan would probably improve his life beyond measure, for such was the purpose of orphans. Wasn't it?

It was nearing pitch black by the time they reached Chaddington Green. Rosie ran off towards Lilac Cottage to visit Martha, Nancy and Tom. Theo gripped his two sons by the scruffs of their necks to prevent them from following her. 'Bed,' he growled.

'Why can she do what she wants and we can't?' Michael whined.

'Because she's three times your age, and almost twice your brother's age.'

David worked that out. 'Dad's right,' he said. 'She's three times five and nearly two times eight.'

Tia had had enough. 'Get in the house,' she snapped. Children were great in large numbers, though they weren't really suitable for domestic situations. As for shopping . . . oh, she couldn't bear to think about it. 'Do as your father says, but clean your teeth and wash your hands and faces before going to bed. Baths will have to wait until tomorrow.'

'He smells of sick,' Michael complained.

'Do you want a birthday party?' Theo asked his younger boy.

'Yes, when I'm six.'

'And you want to live until you're six? Get him up the stairs now, David.'

Both boys fled. From tomorrow night, they would sleep in a dormitory in the hall, and their parents would occupy a teacher's flat. Isadora might help at the school, visit friends in the village, or spend time with Nancy, Tom and Martha. More importantly, she would have Rose Cottage, her bolt-hole for many years, all to herself.

The three adults flopped onto the cottage suite. Theo was the first to find words. 'Why is it that I can manage a school, but my own boys are impossible?'

'Different hat, different costume,' Izzy answered. 'At home, you're a daddy; at school you're Blackbird. It's all a play, as Shakespeare said. We have our work selves and our home selves. Simple. Each and every one of us is an actor. And it's a well-circulated rumour that teachers and nurses make the worst parents. Doctors are in a similar league, but it's probably nonsense.'

Tia expressed the opinion that Dr Simon Heilberg was an excellent father, as was Nurse Juliet, his wife.

'It must be just teachers, then.' Izzy yawned behind a hand. 'I'm going to wedge myself into that cupboard of a third bedroom.'

'Just for one night, Ma.'

'I know.' She smiled at them. 'You are excellent parents,

and you know it. Goodnight, sweet prince and princess. I'd do a grand exit, but my legs are aching.'

They stared at healthy flames born of a fire set earlier in the evening by Martha or Nancy or Tom. Cuddling up to each other, they dozed. Tia had a nightmare about trying to buy shoes for Michael, who hated the process; Theo dreamt of a summer's day in the back garden at home, a picnic with his children, Tia, Izzy, Joan and Jack. Tia had made ice-cold lemonade, the real deal brewed from fruit and sugar with slices of lemon floating about in it.

They endured a rude awakening by Rosie accompanied by a gust of cool air that was a pale imitation of weather further north, though it wore the scent of a December night. 'Mum?' she called. 'Oh, sorry. I didn't know you were asleep.'

The couple could see that she was bursting with news. 'Out with it,' Theo said sleepily.

'Martha's going on a course if the board agrees. The headmaster's thinking of taking in a couple of handicapped boys if you and Izzy-gran'll allow it. Martha would be a great help, and she's happy to study for her certificate.'

'Interesting idea,' Theo mumbled. 'Trust Pete Wray to come up with it. I sometimes think our headmaster is on a mission to save the world.'

'A bit like you, then,' was Rosie's pert answer. 'And there's something else – well, somebody else *and* something else. He's a surprise.'

'Wheel him in,' Tia ordered.

And in he came, all six feet of him, a grand-looking young man with brownish-reddish hair, twinkling eyes and decent clothes.

Theo blinked. 'Colin?'

The visitor grinned. 'Was you in the war, Sir? Did you come over before all the other Yanks, like? Did you kill Germans?'

Tiredness forgotten, Theo leapt up and hugged one of his star pupils. 'How's life?' he asked.

Colin Duckworth shrugged. 'It's OK as long as I ignore the public school lunatics. They're not right, you know, not right in the head. I'm managing to keep up with them well enough, and they find my accent charming. I wish they didn't. Sometimes, I feel like a pet animal or some rare exhibit in a museum – caveman, Neolithic man, then Scouser.'

'I'm sure you manage to confound them.'

The younger man laughed. 'Well, I've won two debates on the nature of socialism and one on the rehabilitation of recidivists.'

'How did you find us?' Tia asked.

Rosie blushed. 'We write to each other,' she admitted.

Both parents remained stock still and silent for several seconds. 'So you're penfriends?' Tia asked at last.

Rosie stared down at the floor. 'We like each other.' The chin rose not in defiance, but in respect for her parents. 'A lot. We like each other a lot.'

Colin took Rosie's hand. 'Don't worry, Mr and Mrs Quinn. I know she's only fifteen, so nothing untoward will happen.'

Theo grinned. 'This isn't the football all over again, is it, Colin? Sleepwalking, tearing the downspout off a prefab and telling me a load of hogwash?'

'No, Sir.'

'And where are you staying?'

'With Mam and Dad at the Punch Bowl. Everybody else is at Auntie Bertha's. It's terrible at Auntie Bertha's. I think she peels her sprouts in September and boils them for a couple of months. But Mam, Dad and I have read so much about what you've achieved here that we decided to see for ourselves.'

Rosie chipped in. 'Is it OK if they come to Christmas lunch at Bartle Hall, Dad?'

'Fine,' Theo replied. 'They're great people.'

'It's all right,' Colin advised them, 'I've taught them knives and forks and spoons, and they're nearly up to toothpicks and finger bowls. They're past the chip butty stage, and Dad doesn't wipe his mouth on the tablecloth any more. He even goes to the bathroom to break wind these days – limbering up to come here, you see.'

Rosie dug him in the ribs. 'Go and get it.'

'No, you go and get it before it gets too cold.'

'It's your present as well, so you fetch it, Col.'

'Bossy boots,' he muttered before leaving the house.

Tia took the chance to grab her daughter's hand. 'Don't get serious, sweetie. Be young. It's too early for steady boyfriends. Grab your youth and enjoy it.'

'We're not steady. We just like each other and we both love writing letters about how silly and sad life is.'

Colin returned with a basket. 'We decided – Mam, Dad, Rosie and I – that it was about time to get you one of these. She's eight weeks old, and her ears haven't decided what to do with themselves yet, but she's a little cracker and her mother was best of breed at that Crufts dog show.'

Theo raised the lid and lifted out the baby Alsatian. 'Welcome back, Mickle,' he said, his voice unsteady. 'Welcome home.' And for some reason he couldn't explain even to himself, he suddenly knew that Rosie was safe with Colin.

It was chaos. Worse still, it was chaos in a very small house.

Izzy had stalked off in the direction of Lilac Cottage after declaring her intention to take a bath among civilized people. Theo was cleaning up puppy mess, Tia was

462

battling with her hair, muttering darkly about having it cut short, Rosie was playing with Harriet, whose name she had chosen in honour of Harry, while the boys were at war in the bath.

Theo waved a mop in his wife's direction. 'Do not cut off your hair without a papal dispensation from me. I'd have nothing to wipe my nose on in bed, and I don't want to be forced to soil the sheets. Harriet is leaving enough deposits to open a savings account, and that bath will come through the ceiling if those two don't stop fighting.'

Tia walked to the foot of the stairs. 'I want the pair of you dry, dressed and down here in ten minutes, or you'll have to sleep in the flat with me and Dad tonight.' She turned her attention on Rosie. 'Get yourself dressed, missy, and put away the folding bed.'

'At least I won't have to sleep in the same room as those two tonight,' Rosie said. 'David talks even in his sleep, and Michael snores.'

Tia sighed. 'He'll be better once his tonsils and adenoids are gone, but there's nothing we can do about David, I'm afraid. Give Harriet to me, please.'

Introduced to Tia's mane of hair, the pup started to chew it. Rosie's footfalls echoed from the stairwell, the boys were running about in the second bedroom, and Theo washed his hands in preparation for making breakfast. 'Glad we have a big house?' he called.

She placed the puppy in her basket and walked through the kitchen and into the dining area. 'Sometimes, I think this must have been a quieter place when the pigs lived here.'

'I agree,' he said.

'And pigs are cleaner than boys.'

Theo took the hairbrush and pins from the pocket of his wife's robe. Like a true expert, he shaped her hair into a chignon. 'You'll do,' he pronounced. 'Go sort out our litter of piglets while I cook the eggs.'

A lecture was delivered by Dad at the breakfast table. 'This is a dog, not a toy. You may stroke her and help train her on a leash, but do not fight over her, do not chase her while she's a pup, and do not stand on her or slap her. She is a sentient creature, so she feels pain and reacts to it. Michael, put the salt down – there is enough salt in the food on your plate, and too much salt can kill.'

The parents shared a glance that teetered on the brink of despair.

'She's young,' Theo continued, 'and she needs a lot of sleep, just like a human baby. If you are rough with her, she may grow up nasty, because this breed is endowed with huge intelligence and Alsatians will deal with you the way you deal with them. She will learn from us. Listen to me, Michael!'

The younger boy switched on his I-am-attentive expression.

'If humanity hurts her, she will hurt humanity and the police will have her put down. Bad dogs are not born bad; they are made bad by bad people. We are good people. Finish your breakfast, then go play somewhere. Preferably outside and beyond earshot.'

The boys bolted their food and left.

'We shouldn't have bought her,' Rosie said sadly. 'I forgot about the daft duo.'

But Theo's thinking in the matter was miles away from Rosie's. 'The pup will make them grow up, you'll see. They have a little, four-legged and furry baby sister. Remember Mickle and how you became responsible for her? Take Harriet outside and stay with her until she performs.'

'Thanks, Dad.' She went into the back garden with the puppy in her arms.

Both parents slumped into a relaxed state once all the young ones were out of the house. They drank more coffee and sat in welcome peace for a few precious minutes. Sometimes, however rarely the chance arrived, it felt good to be child-free and carefree lovers.

Tia broke the spell. 'I wonder what they're up to out there?'

Theo walked to the window. 'Perhaps they're playing with razor blades on the railway lines.' He paused. 'Come look,' he said after a moment or two.

And there they were, all three of them with their new puppy. Rosie was teaching them how to stroke the little dog, showing them how Harriet's ears would look when she was older, how to praise good behaviour. 'I've never seen Michael so still,' Tia said. 'Even asleep, he wriggles like a fish on a hook.'

'We must enjoy them, Portia. They will grow and go, because that's how it works. Come on. We are going to be late for school.'

The residential school was beautiful, since much thought and a great deal of money had gone into its creation. Attics had been reinforced to contain two dormitories, plus accommodation for some staff and four fire exits which, though hardly things of beauty, ran down the sides and the back of the building.

The first floor was mainly for residential staff, and two student flats had been created, one at each end of the level. Older pupils could win a place in a flat, thus gaining the ability to live in a smaller commune where social and life skills might improve of their own accord. It didn't always work out, though Pete Wray had taught staff and students to be forever hopeful.

The ground floor boasted a music room, a science lab,

a domestic science kitchen, a library and a large art department. Small study rooms were used for individual tutorials for older children. Wood- and metalwork classes took place in large sheds at the back of the house, and Portia indulged her love for carpentry every time she visited.

Within days of opening, the place was full. Until further notice, only thirty places existed at Bartle Hall, though that number would probably increase in time. There were just three home rooms, as the classrooms had been named. Since there were just thirty children, the homes were labelled Infant, Junior and Senior. Each home room held roughly ten pupils, so individual attention was easier for every home-based teacher, and all three were residential with staggered weekends off.

There were day staff who came in to teach their specialist subjects for a few hours, but the three deputies had been chosen by Theo Quinn and Pete Wray, a rotund, excitable little man with a positive attitude and a great sense of humour. Homers, as Pete named them, had to be a near-impossible cross between parent and educator.

He hugged every member of the Quinn family, Theo included. 'You're looking so well, all of you. Isadora's upstairs wearing a curtain as a cloak and giving a lesson in acting. I left her to it – she can be quite fierce with adults.'

'We know,' chimed the Quinn parents.

'And with kids,' Michael muttered. 'She was going to do grieving bodily harm on David because he stood on his bucket.'

Tia looked at the ceiling. 'Pete, don't ask.'

He didn't ask. 'I've given you Tommy Gallagher's flat. He's gone home to Ireland to do war with a cousin about a racehorse. As you just said, don't ask.'

466

'OK. What about Rosie?'

'She can have the guest room next door to Tommy's flat.'

He led them to the grand ballroom, which was partitioned into three home rooms for much of the time. Now, the partitions had been drawn back, and a fire blazed in each of the two fireplaces. Magnificent Christmas trees covered in decorations stood a few paces away from each of the log fires.

'Wonderful,' Tia said, remembering her own Christmases in this massive room. She 'saw' Ma dressed as Fairy Clodhopper in a beautiful dress, all floaty and graceful, a sparkling tiara in her hair, twinkling wings on her back and black Wellington boots on her feet. 'I fell out of my tree,' she had moaned, throwing glitter dust over her girls.

Pa had been Santa with a cushion stuck under his clothes, while Portia and her sisters were often elves. This was a house for magic, and Tia hoped with all her heart that the residents would enjoy it.

'You heard about the idea for a couple of disabled students?' Pete asked.

'Yes. Once certificated, Martha Foster would be a boon. Are the disabled kids affected only physically?'

'Indeed they are. One has an IQ at genius level. They need some help; they also need a future. Their families abandoned them.'

Theo nodded. 'Go ahead. There will be no discrimination in Isadora's school. And remember, we must all remain colour blind. By the way, the basket Rosie is carrying contains a very young and totally incontinent puppy.'

Pete took it all in his stride. 'Our boys and girls will help clean up after it.' He smiled broadly, causing his eyes to disappear in his round, plump face. 'Very little fazes pupils here, since they've been through so much before they came to us. Go and sort out your accommodation while I find a couple of dozen children. They're out walking with Miss Stephenson; botany's her speciality.'

And so Christmas at Bartle Hall was about to begin.

By Christmas Eve, when all the children were in bed, though not necessarily asleep, the ballroom looked like fairyland. The vast ceiling was covered in floating strings of silver, some long, some short, and a few that stretched for yards. A huge table that was really several pushed together was dressed in red cloth with silver runners down the centre. There were crackers and napkins and place names; a bran tub sat next to each tree, while balloons filled with fairy dust hovered in the air. Tomorrow, after the meal, Theo would burst them all with a long stick, and the children would be covered in fairy dust.

A few of the older pupils joined in with preparations. Too mature to believe in Santa, they were happy to create the illusion for younger residents. Among these helpers, Rosie found her niche. Because she was of their peer group, they talked to her after she spoke about her life as a small child. She was one of them, and this was where she would work. 'I'll stick with my chosen subjects,' she told her mother, 'but I'd like to be a homer here.'

Tia said nothing; Rosie was at the age where ambitions changed as often as the British weather. Instead, she begged a favour. 'Rosie, we've put you next to a girl called Eileen. She hasn't said much yet, but her infancy reads like a horror story. Eileen's very thin, and she often refuses food. She was poisoned after scavenging from dustbins. Look after her, darling.'

'Of course.'

A baby Alsatian tumbled past them; she was covered

in shreds of silver known as lametta, to which she'd accidentally become attached while investigating Christmas decoration boxes. Rosie grinned. 'Don't say it, Mum. I'll take her outside.'

The boys had joined in the search for holly – bushes at Holly Cottage would be denuded by now. Tia sat down suddenly. Cottages. What about deprived children who still had one loving parent? What about a mother trying to protect her children from an abusive father? There would be fathers whose wives had died, good dads who could no longer work because of their children. She wrote a note in her head. Prefabricated cottages? There was enough land, for heaven's sake. Like Topsy, this place would grow and grow ... But would the rejected be upset by some day pupils having a home and a parent?

Ma was up to something. She'd been buzzing about all day, and a piano had been moved into the ballroom. Hmm. What was Isadora planning? Music hall, probably. She'd do the one about a boy in the gallery, then the woman chasing through London with a caged bird as she tried to catch up with the removals van, Tipperary, knees up, plus a few she'd invented herself. Pete Wray would play the piano, Rosie would probably sing, too ...

Tom, Nancy and Martha were happily busy with place settings. Martha looked years younger, slimmer, fitter and almost confident. Nancy was without her knitting bag – things were looking up.

This evening, Jules and Simon would arrive with Abigail and Stephen, their delightful offspring. Delia and Elaine, too, were on their way. Family. It was about family. And now, all these extra children were members of the clan.

A hand touched her shoulder. 'Portia?'

'Yes, Theodore?' She noticed that he was carrying the pup's basket.

'Get upstairs,' he ordered. 'There's cleaving to be done.'

They're drifting past, coming, going,
Hurrying, thinking, talking, walking,
Frowning, blinking, finding, seeking
The start of their Liverpool day.
Perhaps one will see me, free me.
My city, where's Pity? Is she here?
So pretty, so knowing, cheeks glowing
With anger boiling, soiling the air.
She stood tall in the hall for me, just for me,
While I hid in the back, concealed but not free
Cos they're coming for the Brat, little cat.
(Marks on his face from brawling before crawling
Home, where I waited, agitated. The man who can
Beat me, defeat me, destroy me, annoy me
By being alive).

Just a girl. Curl into myself on a shelf in my head
Waiting. Will she buy me, untie me, put me to bed
In a new place? Shelter. Helter-skelter, I return to the rails
Might she come? The hum of traffic behind me. Please
*   find me.*
Portia. Her name, a game played by her father, who
*   would rather*
Pick heroes from Shakespeare, a writer long dead. She
*   said,*
'I'll be there half past eight, you must wait and bring
*   nothing.'*
So I've No Thing from then, though now hasn't started.
Are we parted already? Liver's time, tick tock, ten o'clock.
'Pier Head,' she said. Led me back to my chair, touched
*   my hair*
'Sit there.' I sat and was proud, my heart in my ears
The fears will go. That's what she told me.
Last thing she said? 'Go to the Pier Head.'

'A fighter, little blighter, an urchin, needs birching,'
He said, waving his jerry can. The American
Didn't speak, stared at the freak, then at me
Grabbed my hand, made me stand near his door
Where I lingered, light-fingered. 'She steals!'
Yes, I did, needed meals.
Then the man from New York brought a fork
And his dinner. 'You're thinner,' he said.
Sad eyes, deep frown, black gown, Headmaster
Striding faster
Crossed the floor, closed his door and swore.

He swore, and the word rhymes with luck.
Please don't tell. I'm eating his tuck.
I await my fate, half past eight
Long gone. Will she come?
Angry river makes me shiver
Dread and tears mingle
Fingers tingle.
Is this a cruel game?
Did somebody shout my name?